For Sandra:
    Without whose assistance this book could not have been published.
        C. D.

Crisis in the Heavenly Capital

Chinese Materials Center Publications
Asian Library Series No. 35

CRISIS IN THE HEAVENLY CAPITAL

by
Li Ch'ing

Translated by
Djang Chu

CHINESE MATERIALS CENTER PUBLICATIONS

1987

Printed in the Republic of China

"When the river darkens, the rain will soon arrive; as the wind starts to blow, the waves turn white."

Ho Hsün in "Bidding Farewell"

"The whistling wind creates mysterious sounds; sailing clouds display themselves in wonderous colors."

Chiang Yen in "Song of Departure"

TRANSLATOR'S INTRODUCTION

In the middle of the nineteenth century, after the humiliating defeat in the Opium War, there occurred in China a
stupendous revolution, known as the T'ai-p'ing Rebellion,
which shook the very foundation of the Manchu government.
Traditional Chinese historians, emphasizing the T'ai-p'ing
leaders' total disregard for the Confucian tradition and their
wanton destruction of property and indiscriminate killing,
condemned them as bloodthirsty mobsters and called them
"Longhaired Bandits," because they refused to shave their
foreheads and wear queues as the Manchus dictated. One
century after their dramatic rise and sudden downfall, however, they were heralded by Marxist writers as the forerunners
of the so-called scientific socialism and were accorded with
many patriotic and revolutionary virtues. The controversy over
whether they should be properly labelled "revolutionaries"

or "rebels" and "heroes" or "hooligans" has never ceased. It flared up again during the time of the Cultural Revolution.

The T'ai-p'ing Rebellion of 1850-1865, a gigantic convulsion in which thirty million people perished, spread with incredible speed. In 1851, its leader, Hung Hsiu-ch'üan (1814-64), with a scanty and perverted knowledge of Christianity, proclaimed himself the Heavenly King, the Son of God, and the Junior Brother of Jesus Christ. Within three years, his army ravaged seven southeastern provinces, culminating in the capture of Nanking in the spring of 1853. An expeditionary force he sent north crossed several metropolitan provinces within four months, only to meet total eradication within 120 miles of its target, Peking itself. The T'ai-p'ing movement's sudden collapse was as dramatic as its rapid rise, mainly due to the internecine struggle between its leaders which broke out shortly after the establishment of the Heavenly Capital in Nanking.

This novel is a chronicle of the internal strife among the leaders. The story starts with a T'ai-p'ing spy in Nanking before its capture, who was enamored of a courtesan. After the establishment of the Heavenly Capital, she fell into the hands of one of the T'ai-p'ing leaders, the Northern King. His powerful rival, the Eastern King, coveting the renowned beauty, acquired her from his comrade by force, thus creating animosity between the two. When the Eastern King entertained the idea of appropriating the throne for himself, the Heavenly King conspired with the Northern King to have the potential usurper murdered. But the Northern King, now conscious of his power and favored position, became as ambitious as his one-time rival. He created havoc in the capital by indiscriminate slaughter and wanton destruction as a means to consolidate his power. The Heavenly King was obliged to order another leader of the movement, the Assistant King, to have him removed. Shortly afterwards, under the suspicion that he might follow the footsteps of his predecessors, the Assistant King was forced to leave the capital with his troops to seek his fortune elsewhere, thus hastening the collapse of the Heavenly Kingdom.

The novel, with the exception of a few romantic subplots thrown in, is based on historical facts. The names, places, events, dates, and documents are taken from the historical records recently discovered and research work done by modern scholars. The novel is presented in the grand tradition of the *Romance of Three Kingdoms* in ten action-packed chapters. Each chapter has its structural design to hold the interest of the reader. Its style is coventional and its language lucid.

It is perhaps relevant here to give a brief summation of the historical events leading to the calamitous struggle and wanton massacre to help the reader better understand the plots in the novel. The spiritual leader of the T'ai-p'ing movement, Hung Hsiu-ch'üan, started as a frustrated student who had failed the state examination several times before he stumbled into a few Christian tracts which he picked up on his way home. He became ill for forty days, and in his delirious fits he claimed that he met God, the Heavenly Father, and Jesus Christ, his Heavenly Brother. He described God vividly as an old man with a golden beard who gave him a "demon-slaying sword" with which to exterminate all those who worshipped idols, including Confucius, and all demons whom he identified as the Manchus and their cohorts.

In order to carry out his mission of establishing God's Kingdom on earth, Hung and a close friend, Feng Yün-shan (1822-52), established the God Worshippers Society. They adopted a few rudimentary religious practices of Christianity without having a real grasp of its theological meaning. From the traditional Chinese secret societies, they borrowed the concept that all men were brothers of equal standing, a sense of loyalty that bonded the members together into a close-knit society, the practice of sharing a common commissary for daily necessities, as well as the reality of the existence of a hierarchy of leaders who were more equal than others and could enforce absolute authority and discipline over their followers. The religious rites and magic together with the claim of a supernatural mandate attracted thousands of desperate and dispossessed peasants. The insurrection began to spread like wildfire, radiating outward from the rough countryside of Kwangsi.

At the outset, the leadership consisted of a few of Hung's sworn brothers, all from Kwangtung and Kwangsi. Among them Feng Yün-shan was a farsighted organizer and strategist who had become a believer and preacher of Hung's new religion. Unfortunately Feng died in June 1852 in an ill-fated campaign against the government troops at the Fisherman's Raincoat Ferry, near Ch'üan-chou, Hunan. Another leader was Hsiao Ch'ao-kuei (d. 1852), a valiant fighter who was married to Hung's sister, Hung Hsüan-chiao. Hsiao claimed that he possessed the divine power while having seizures to communicate with Jesus Christ who spoke to the converts through him. In a fierce battle over Changsha, the capital of Hunan, Hsiao suffered a gun wound and died in October 1852.

The most shrewd and ambitious among the leaders was Yang Hsiu-ch'ing (1824-56), a charcoal kiln laborer by profession, who joined the God Worshippers Society with a group of his fellow workers. Emulating Hung's claim of being the son of God, Yang also claimed that he was often possessed by the Holy Ghost, the Heavenly Father, who spoke through him during his sporadic delirious trances. On such occasions, he possessed an even higher authority than Hung himself. Hung accepted this because it proved to work wonders among his fanatic religious followers. The T'ai-p'ing leaders recognized Yang's performances as genuine manifestations of God's will and termed such occasions as "The Heavenly Father's Descent to Earth." Detailed descriptions of such comical performances were duly chronicled and distributed as official documents. Gradually, by hoaxes and manipulations, Yang succeeded in assembling all military and political powers in his hands. Nevertheless, Yang was a superb strategist and an astute general under whose direction the T'ai-p'ing army marched from Kwangsi to Nanking almost unchallenged within a short span of three years. By claiming that he could speak for the

Heavenly Father, his actions were supposedly sanctioned by the divine will. He used this power to humiliate Hung and to degrade his comrades, and his arrogance finally triggered the eruption of the merciless power struggle that ended not only his career, but also his life.

Another of the original founders of the movement, Wei Ch'ang-hui (d. 1856), came from a wealthy family and was fairly well-educated. He purchased a literary degree entitling him to be a student of the imperial academy, which he never attended. In a lawsuit with his neighbor on a trumped-up charge, he lost the litigation. Out of spite, he joined the God Worshippers Society with his whole family and contributed his entire family fortune to the common treasury. Since he was the only one among the rebels who originally belonged to a gentry family, he naturally looked down upon all others as the riffraff of society. After the T'ai-p'ings settled down in Nanking, Wei became the chief rival of Yang Hsiu-ch'ing. When the latter entertained the idea of usurping the throne, Hung ordered Wei to have Yang assassinated. In the wake of the power struggle, Wei massacred thousands of Yang's relatives and adherents. In turn, Wei became arrogant and cast a coveting eye on the throne himself. He attempted to murder the only remaining sworn brother, Shih Ta-k'ai (1831-63), who narrowly escaped by lowering himself over the city wall. Finally, Wei was murdered by his own bodyguard.

Shih Ta-k'ai was perhaps the best educated and most respected among the T'ai-p'ing leaders. He was a born military leader who treated his soldiers well. He was also known as a man of high literary talent, capable of composing elegant poems and imposing essays. Many early proclamations of the T'ai-p'ings were said to have been written by him. However, modern researchers have found that several collections of poems and essays, and, even the diary attributed to him, were forgeries. Stories about him became folklore. Shih joined the T'ai-p'ing movement while he was only nineteen years old. Under his command, his troops fought well and won many important victories over the imperial army. While the Heavenly Capital was drenched in blood in a fratricidal massacre, Shih was fighting seesaw battles with Tseng Kuo-fan (1811-72), the leader of the Hunan Army, a formidable foe of the T'ai-p'ings. Shih was then recalled to the Heavenly Capital to take charge of the government. But the Heavenly King, wary of fraternal struggles, could not trust him, and entrusted political and military powers to his own brothers and a few sycophants. Apprehensive about his own safety, Shih left the capital in May 1857 with two hundred thousand of his followers to seek a new start in Szechwan. Not unlike the Long March undertaken by the Communists eighty years later, Shih led his soldiers in a roundabout way, through Anhwei, Kiangsi, Chekiang, Fukien, Kwangtung, Hunan, Kweichow, and Yunnan, fighting all the way until he finally reached the promised land of Szechwan. But by then his men were exhausted and they were ambushed by the imperial army at a ferry in May 1863. In an effort to spare the lives of his followers, Shih agreed to surrender on such terms. Nevertheless, Shih and many of his men were summarily executed in Chengtu, the capital of Szechwan, in 1863.

These six leaders were the founders of the T'ai-p'ing movement. True to the tradition of Chinese secret societies, they treated each other as sworn brothers and promised to share bad and good times together. At the beginning of the movement they formed a solid nucleus which provided effective leadership for the organization. On January 11, 1851, which happened to be Hung Hsiu-ch'üan's thirty-eighth birthday, they proclaimed the establishment of a new dynasty, the Heavenly Kingdom of Great Peace, at Chin-t'ien village, near Thistle Mountain, the base of their operations. Hung was inaugurated as the Heavenly King. In order to solidify the spirit of brotherhood among the leaders, the other five co-revolutionaries were also given the title of kings. Thus Yang Hsiu-ch'ing was made the Eastern King, Hsiao Ch'ao-kuei the Western King, Feng Yün-shan the Southern King, Wei Ch'ang-hui the Northern King, and Shih Ta-k'ai the Assistant King. Perhaps it was intended that after the final victory each would be awarded a feudal domain corresponding to the four cardinal directions. Later, Hung ordered that he be addressed as the "Lord of Ten Thousand Years," a salutation traditionally reserved for the emperor. In an magnanimous mood he designated similar salutations for his sworn brothers: Yang the "Lord of Nine thousand Years," Hsiao the "Lord of Eight Thousand Years," Feng the "Lord of Seven Thousand Years," Wei the "Lord of Six Thousand Years" and Shih the "Lord of Five Thousand Years." However ludicrous they might sound, they were in complete conformity with the traditional mentality of the Chinese secret societies. Between the leaders themselves, Hung allowed the members of the elite to address him as the "Second Brother," Jesus Christ being the elder brother, and Yang the "Fourth Brother," and so forth. Hung, in turn, addressed Yang Hsiu-ch'ing as "Brother Ch'ing," Wei Ch'ang-hui as "Brother Ch'ang" and Shih Ta-k'ai as "Brother Ta." Sworn brotherhood among members of secret societies has a long tradition in China, popularized by such famous novels as the *Romance of Three Kingdoms* and the *Water Margin*. Within the small circle, members share their lives and possessions together; outside the small circle, everything is legitimate loot.

The T'ai-p'ing ideology was a hodgepodge of distorted Christian theology, ancient Chinese tradition, and convenient Confucian dogmas, mingled with esoteric secret society practices. The small band of leaders took care of their own interests first, last, and always. By the time they reached Nanking, the revolutionary fervor had already been spent. The leaders began to enjoy luxurious lives and acquired large harems for themselves, while abstinence and frugality were demanded of their followers; even the second or third echelon officials were not exempt. Most critics have opined that the T'ai-p'ing movement was not a true peasant revolution aiming at a more equitable distribution of land. However noble their original intentions of overthrowing the Manchus and equalizing people's wealth were, they were forgotten the minute the leadership succumbed to greed and concentrated on ac- .

cumulating the accoutrements of the good life on this earth for themselves and their descendants, while making dubious promises of happiness and glory in heaven after death to their followers.

At the outset, Hung not only assumed the role of a political and military leader, he was also the religious head of a church. In his essays, poems, and edicts, which were numerous, such Christian notions as salvation, the creation of the world, the original sin, and the Sermon on the Mount were all there, however distorted, but he had somehow missed the real spirit of Christianity. He used military power to enforce his newly instituted religion. Under the T'ai-p'ing rule, everyone was supposed to attend church service every week. T'ai-p'ing officials served both as preachers and administrators. Hung's writings were usually used as the text of sermons. However, Hung himself often quoted sections of Confucian literature, such as the passage on Grand Unity to illustrate his point (see p. 29), although the books of Confucius and Mencius were declared heretical publications and anyone found possessing, reading, or buying them was punishable by law. Although Hung seemed to be a true believer of the religious dogmas of his own creation, it is questionable how much the other leaders believed in the T'ai-p'ing ideology.

The T'ai-p'ing organization was supposedly based on the *chou-li* system, a utopian conception attributed to the Duke of Chou, the founder of the Chou dynasty. It attempted to make all farmers into soldiers in time of war, turning them back into farmers in time of peace. Local administrative units were structured on a military basis and local officials were commissioned officers of the army. Men and women were organized into separate units, stationed in separate camps. No sexual relations between male and female were permitted. Even married couples were borbidden to have sexual contacts under the pain of death. The smallest unit was a squad, composed of twenty-five men, or women, in the women's corps, headed by a sergeant (*liang-ssu-ma*) who also served as pastor, teacher, and judge. Five squads were combined into one

battalion under a lieutenant, five battalions into one brigade
under a captain, five brigades into one division under a colo-
nel, and five divisions into an army corps under a corps commander, which was the largest army unit composed of 13,156
men or women and officers. This was the organizational
scheme on paper which did not achieve universal application
or uniformity. Above the corps commander, there was a hierarchy of top metropolitan officials, regular and honorary,
such as military supervisor, army controllor, general, marshall,
chancellor, and state minister. Military and metropolitan
officials with merits were invested with titles of nobility, and
marquises and kings were created abundantly in later years.
All titles of nobility could be inherited by the holders' descendants.

The T'ai-p'ing regime at its early stages was handicapped
by the lack of literate aides, since all those who joined or
volunteered were desperadoes and fortune seekers. The rank
and file were mainly composed of peasants who sought opportunities to escape from their physical plights. After the
establishment of the capital at Nanking, following the prec-
edents of previous dynasties, metropolitan examinations
were given to recruit talents for the administrative service.
The titles given to successful candidates were the same as
those given by the Ch'ing; the one at the head of the list was
designated *chuang-yüan*. So far as modern scholarship has been
able to ascertain, there were examinations also for female
candidates. A talented woman, Fu Shan-hsiang, had the unique
honor of being the first female *chuang-yüan* in an examination
given in 1853.

After the T'ai-p'ings settled down in Nanking in the spring
of 1853, the character of the revolutionary movement changed
from a mobile force to a stationary entity. Had they continued
their rapid thrust as an invincible army onward to Peking, the
T'ai-p'ings could have easily thrown out the Manchus within
a short period of time. But the luxury and comfort of Nanking
were too much of an attraction to the leaders, and only a
small contingent was dispatched north to undertake the

gigantic task, which failed miserably. Indeed there had been hot debates among the leaders whether they should continue their march northward or settle down in Nanking to consolidate their conquests. The crucial decision of establishing the capital at Nanking proved to be one of the contributing factors to their ultimate failure.

Among the social and political changes the T'ai-p'ings tried to implement, the proclamation of a new calendar, mainly for superstitious reasons, was utterly meaningless and futile. A year was divided into 12 months and 366 days. The odd months had 31 days each and the even ones had 30 days. Every fortieth year, there would be only 336 days, giving each month 28 days. The calendar first came in force in 1851 and lasted only twelve years until 1862 when it was abolished. The year of the twenty-eight-day month never had a chance to see the light of the day.

The T'ai-p'ing movement attracted attention from foreigners in China at its very inception. An English newspaper, the *North China Herald*, in its September 14, 1850 issue, first mentioned the "Kwangsi Rebels" that had devastated much of that southern province. Foreign merchants and Protestant missionaries were sympathetic toward the rebels at their early stages, because the rebels professed to be believers of Christianity. Foreign traders were pleased with the prospect of enjoying better trading relations with the rebels, but were worried about their prohibition of opium which was the most lucrative commodity. Missionaries were happy to find so many new converts to the faith of Jesus Christ, but were offended by the erratic theology, as improvised by Hung, bordering on blasphemy. The British government dispatched its plenipotentiary, Sir George Bonham, and his interpreter, Thomas T. Meadows, to Nanking to gather first-hand information. They arrived at Nanking in April 1853 on board H.M.S. *Hermes* (see page 82). They were received by the Northern King and the Assistant King, but failed to meet with the Eastern King, much less the Heavenly King. Here the story in the novel deviates from the facts as recorded by Thomas T. Meadows in his

The Chinese and Their Rebellions (London, 1856). Bonham left a letter spelling out the British rights and privileges under the existing treaties and proclaimed the British position of neutrality. Much to his surprise, the Heavenly King's reply stated that he was glad that the people of a "dependency" had come to pay tribute and graciously permitted the British the privilege to trade. Accompanying the letter were a few T'ai-p'ing tracts to enable the British to percieve the truth of Christianity.

The government troops—the Green Standard Army and the Manchu bannermen—were no match for the well-organized and zealous rebels, starting out with a messianic mission from Kwangsi. A Chinese general, Hsiang Jung (d. August 1856), was ordered in July 1850 to suppress the insurgents. Being a cowardly man, Hsiang trailed the T'ai-p'ings all the way from Kwangsi to Hupeh without fighting a decisive battle. Only in Wuchang did he put up the semblance of a dogged resistance. Nevertheless, the capital city fell into the rebel hands on January 12, 1853. Hsiang was appointed imperial commissioner to save the situation. The T'ai-p'ings took Nanking on March 19, 1853. Ten days later, Hsiang reached the outskirts of that city with his troops. His battered forces were stationed at Hsiao-ling-wei, a suburban town, and his camp came to be known as the Great Camp of Chiangnan, or the South Camp. A Manchu general Ch'i Shan (d. August 1854), a veteran of the Opium War, was appointed imperial commissioner to head the camp at Yangchow, known as the Great Camp of Chiangpei, or the North Camp. The two camps were poised on both sides of the Great River, waiting to pounce on Nanking. But unfortunately, due to lack of cooperation of these two camps and the low morale of the government troops, both were utterly annihilated by the T'ai-p'ings in surprise attacks carried out in April 1856 under the direction of Yang Hsiu-ch'ing. Hsiang Jung committed suicide soon afterwards, while Ch'i Shan had died earlier. The T'ai-p'ing celebration dinner of their victories led to a series of events which prompted the crisis that shook the foundation of the

T'ai-p'ing regime.

Flushed with success and proud of his part in the victory, Yang Hsiu-ch'ing decided that it was about time for him to take over the throne from Hung. Earlier in 1853 he had used his trance to humiliate Hung by impersonating the Heavenly Father to interfere in Hung's personal life and to deprive him of the power of inflicting capital punishment (see pp. 197ff). Since then the visitations from the Heavenly Father became more frequent. During one such visitation the Heavenly King was coerced to abdicate in Yang's favor and to concede him the salutation of the "Lord of Ten Thousand Years," a designation heretofore reserved for Hung alone. What followed was the story of the implacable fratricidal struggles vividly portrayed in the novel, a story as ancient as the struggle between Cain and Abel.

The author of the novel is a historian who specializes in the history of the T'ai-p'ing movement. Relevant historical anecdotes are sprinkled liberally in the pages of the novel. Although these anecdotes are familiar to Chinese readers who learn them through reading popular novels and attending theatrical performances or storytelling sessions, they would be unintelligible to Western readers without explanations. For example, during the victory celebration dinner when the Heavenly King and Eastern King exchanged diatribes (see pp. 166ff), the names of Liu Pang and Hsiang Yü were mentioned. The contest between the two for the control of Ch'in's territory happened in the third century B.C. Liu Pang started out as a lowly village headman, while Hsiang Yü could boast of his illustrious lineage. The battle for the throne dragged on for five years. At first Hsiang was in ascendancy, but his propensity for arson and butchery alienated him from the populace. On one occasion Hsiang could have Liu killed in a meeting at Hung-men, but out of generosity he had Liu's life spared. One of Liu's bodyguards, Fan Kuei, originally a dogcatcher, was capable and brave. He helped Liu in a campaign to have Hsiang's forces hemmed in at a place called Kai-hsia. At night Hsiang heard the besiegers all around him singing the song of his native place. "Liu must have already conquered my native place, or else why are there so many of my native fellows in his army?" Hsiang asked in dismay. Keeping his company were two of his favorites—Consort Yü, his concubine, and his war steed called *Chui*. That night he drank to his capacity. To solace him, Consort Yü performed a sword dance while he accompanied her with the heart-rending stanza:

> My strength can uproot mountains,
> My spirit fills the gap of the universe.
> When bad times strike me, my horse, *Chui*,
>   can't gallop,
> What are you going to do, Consort Yü?

At the end of the song and dance, Consort Yü cut her own throat with the sword.

By dawn, Hsiang broke through the enemy lines, intending to return to Ch'u, his native place, followed by only a few dozen horsemen. But he lost his way and asked an old man in the field for directions. The old man deceived him deliberately by pointing to the wrong direction. Hsiang found himself literally stranded at a ferry along the River Wu. A lone ferryboat was moored at the landing. The boatman urged him to cross quickly, before the pursuers arrived. Hsiang replied with a laugh, saying, "Heaven has deserted me! I once crossed the river with eight thousand young men and now I have come back alone. How am I going to face the elders back home?" With a slash of his sword, he cut his throat. The story of Hsiang Yü and Consort Yü has been canonized in numerous plays, novels, poems, and operas and has become the perennial favorite of Chinese theatre goers (see pp. 175ff).

The story of Ts'ao Ts'ao and Chu-ke Liang was alluded to by the author in the novel on several occasions (see pp. 234ff). Both historical figures were immortalized by the famous novel *Romance of Three Kingdoms*. From 220 to 280 A.D. the empire was divided into three kingdoms. Ts'ao

Ts'ao, a powerful and evil minister, put an end to the Han Dynasty and became the founder of the Kingdom of Wei. Chu-ke Liang was a strategist and loyal minister to his master, Liu Pei, the emperor of the Kingdom of Shu. Chu-ke Liang was remembered as a genius who often matched wits with his opponents and won. One of his famous ruses was in connection with a certain city that he found he was unable to defend. He therefore opened the gate, had a few soldiers sweep the street, and sat himself on the top of the city wall playing a lute. His enemies came, had a quick look and retreated, for fear of an ambush. But all along Chu-ke knew that the Kingdom of Shu was doomed. In spite of the precarious situation, he still devoted his energy to its defense, because he considered himself a loyal friend of his master. On the Chinese stage, Ts'ao Ts'ao was often portrayed as a villain, while Chu-ke Liang was a hero. In this novel, Shih Ta-k'ai was uncertain whether he should emulate Ts'ao Ts'ao or Chu-ke Liang and whether the popular verdicts of these two historical figures were correct. So in the end he forsook the Heavenly King to seek his fortune elsewhere. Shih Ta-k'ai has since become a legendary figure because of the many stories of heroism and wisdom attributed to him. He was known as a refined poet and essayist, but it has been found that at least some of the writings attributed to him were faked by later writers who admired his character as an upright person and pitied him for his ill fortune. The poems attributed to him toward the end of the novel are cases in point. History, indeed, is nothing but a fable agreed upon, so declared Napoleon. Who is going to challenge that statement?

The author, Li Ch'ing, is a historian and novelist. During the Cultural Revolution period, he was attacked as a rightist for his articles in defense of the Loyal King, Li Hsiu-ch'eng, a capable T'ai-p'ing general, who was active at a later stage. Somehow these articles offended the sensibility of Ch'i Pen-yü, a cultural czar under the protection of Chiang Ch'ing. Li Ch'ing was imprisoned for several years, including periods of reform through labor. When the turmoil was over, he was rehabilitated by order of Teng Hsiao-p'ing. Much of the plots and the ways of presentation of this novel were formulated while he was in confinement. Lacking stationery and time in prison, he was unable to put the words down on paper. The novel was written after his release and was published in 1981 in Canton in *Hua-ch'eng Monthly,* a popular literary magazine. Li Ch'ing is now working on a full-length novel in five parts, encompassing the entire history of the T'ai-p'ing movement. The first volume has been published in Szechwan. Novelists create fictional characters out of historical figures and pick up the threads of their successes or undoings to fabricate an interesting tale. These writers who do not profess to be historians cannot be held responsible for lack of authenticity in their stories. By the same token, it would be a futile attempt if the reader tries to link the past with the present.

The translator wishes to take this opportunity to express his gratitude to Robert L. Irick for expressing an interest in the manuscript, editing it, and undertaking its publication. I would like also to thank my student at St. John's University, Ellen Klempner, who brought this book to my attention and my friend, John Watt, who encouraged me to undertake its translation. Both have read the manuscript and offered editorial suggestions. Sandra Esposito typed the manuscript professionally despite my almost illegible handwriting. My wife, Jane, offered research and editorial assistance that should have warranted her the title of a cotranslator, but out of modesty she declined the title.

CHARACTERS

Hung Hsiu-ch'üan, *the Heavenly King*

Yang Hsiu-ch'ing, *the Eastern King, Commander-in-chief of the Army*

Wei Ch'ang-hui, *the Northern King*

Shih Ta-k'ai, *the Assistant King*

Feng Yün-shan, *the Southern King (died early)*

Hsiao Ch'ao-kuei, *the Western King (died early)*

Hung Hsüan-chiao, *sister of the Heavenly King and widow of the Western King*

Hou Ch'ien-fang, *alias Fang Ch'ien-hou, a spy and official*

Hou Hui-fang, *Hou's sister*

Red Phoenix, *a courtesan*

Chang Ping-huan, *aliases Yeh Chih-fa and Chang "the Seventh," an instigator*

Hu I-kuang, *the King of Yü*

Ch'in Jih-kang, *the King of Yen*

Fu Shan-hsiang, *the female* chuang-yüan

Ho Chen-ch'uan, *the Court Recorder*

Meng Teh-en, *a sycophantic official*

Yang Wen-fu, *a blind musician*

Yang Ch'ang-mei, *the blind man's elder daughter*

Yang Shui-chiao, *the blind man's younger daughter*

Hu Yüan-wei, *a defected Ch'ing official*

Hsiang Jung, *a Ch'ing Imperial Commissioner*

Consort Hsieh, *the Heavenly King's concubine*

Consort Fang, *the Heavenly King's concubine*

ONE

It was the fifteenth day of the twelfth month of the second year in the reign of Hsien-feng (January 23, 1853). Snow flakes as large as goose feathers danced through the air at dusk, silently falling on the city wall of Nanking. But the hustle and bustle on the Ch'in-huai River went on as usual. One pleasure boat after another, gaily decorated with red gauze palace lanterns and filled with the sound of soft music and incessant laughter, glided effortlessly, leaving countless golden shimmering ripples on the surface of the dark green water. Illuminated by the brilliant light of countless candles, the buildings on both sides of the river, with carved railings, decorated casements, and painted windows hung with pearly curtains, cast their reflections in the water. At a distance, the delightful sound of stringed musical instruments and bamboo flutes played by the singsong girls of the "old establishments" entertaining their clients could be sporadically heard.

A more pedestrain scene presented itself in the vicinity of the Confucius Temple and the Shrine of the God of Literature. The evening shows in the taverns and restaurants were in full swing. Story-telling, drum-playing, folk-song singing, monkey and magic acts, and a variety of other forms of entertainment commanded the attention of droves of carefree patrons. Food vendors with their portable stoves, selling meat-dumplings, *wontons,* five-flavored eggs, candied-fruits, and sticky-rice pastries cheerfully hawked their wares at the top of their voices on the streets, despite the heavy snow. Others beat on sheep-skin drums, brass gongs, or hallowed bamboo rattles to peddle their goods. Displayed on the counters of taverns and small eateries were such delicacies as fried shrimp-cakes and baked crab-meat, together with rice-flour pudding, boiled water-chesnuts, and candied sweet potatoes. On the pot-bellied wine urns were signs printed on scarlet-red paper advertising their contents—"Fermented *Chin-ling* Wine" or "Aged *Hua-tiao* Liquor."

Among the noisy, boisterous night-market revelers, three particular figures could be seen walking side by side on the snow-covered cobblestone road—a two-stringed fiddle player, grey-haired and blind, supported by a young girl on each side. The blind musician played his instrument while slowly pacing the street. Slim and tall in build and slightly hunchbacked, the old man had a pair of whitish-grey pupils in his sunken eyes which nearly matched the color of his frosted temples. The two girls were also slim and pale, with the same look of despair in their large eyes. Both bound their thick braids with red yarn ribbons, and were attired in deep-blue homespun printed cotton blouses. One could tell at a glance that they were sisters. The older girl could not have been older than eighteen or nineteen, while the younger one was only sixteen or seventeen. Half supporting and half dragging their father on the snow-blown road, the exhausted girls stared blankly at the busy activities of the night market. Snow flakes had accumulated on their emaciated shoulders, but they made no attempt to brush them off, for the snow had already frozen into a sheet of thin ice, which stuck tenaciously to their clothes.

The music produced by the old man on the fiddle was tender, sad, and melancholy, depicting the mental state of the blind player. As his music built up into a sobbing crescendo, the old man stopped abruptly and sighed: "Come, Ch'ang-mei and Shui-chiao! It's time for dinner. The new year is approaching. We can go to restaurants and taverns to earn a few coppers after dinner."

The two girls, Ch'ang-mei and Shui-chiao, helped their father to sit down under the eaves of a building near a meat-dumpling vendor's portable stove. The delectable aroma of the dumplings and the hot steam emerging from the boiling pot instilled a bit of warmth into their exhausted bodies. A dash of color appeared on the girls' pale faces.

After eating a few meat dumplings, the three of them went to the Six Dynasties Retreat, a restaurant well-known in the area. The falling snow increased in intensity. Red and orange lights emanating from the buildings on the river banks and the moving pleasure boats mingled together with the reflections of the crystal white snow on the ground to form a gay pattern covering the whole river area. The sound of moving oars, the music of distant flutes, the colorful illumination and reflection of the snow brought forth an atmosphere commensurate with the vibrant nocturnal life of the Ch'in-huai River. Who could have imagined that the city of Nanking with such a pulsating night life would soon be besieged and surrounded by merciless enemies?

Just as the father and two daughters stepped into the front door of the Six Dynasties Retreat, a pleasure boat anchored at its back door landing. Soft, feminine laughter rang out from the cabin of the boat. On the front deck stood two well-appointed and lavishly attired young dandies, each with an open painted umbrella in hand, vying with each other to escort a beautiful girl emerging from the cabin. Under the red light of the lanterns, the smiling girl, clad in

a silver fox cape, spoke in an effeminate Soochow dialect:
"Young Masters Lu and Fang! Please go on ahead. I don't
need your help."

Young Master Lu was a dark, swarthy young man
in his later teens. Short in stature and uncouth in action, he
had a broad chin, big ears, protruding eyes, heavy eyebrows,
a square mouth, and a level jaw. The other, Young Master
Fang, was a little older than his friend. He was endowed
with a handsome figure, a delicate fair complexion, a pair
of seductive eyes, as well as a cultivated comportment. Young
Master Fang turned his head and told the maidservant who
stood behind the girl to go home, saying: "You go back by
boat. Red Phoenix and I will enjoy the snow and a few drinks
with Young Master Lu, so we'll be late tonight. Please tell
her mama to send two sedan chairs by twelve o'clock to the
Six Dynasties Retreat."

The maidservant responded smilingly and retreated into
the cabin. As Fang, Lu, and Red Phoenix stepped onto the
stone steps leading to the restaurant's waterfront pavilion,
the boat disappeared into the mingled reflections of snow
and light, accompanied by the splashing sound of oars striking
the water.

The two dandies and Red Phoenix entered the door of
the pavilion. After displaying perfunctory courtesy, Fang let
Lu ascend the stairs first and then followed immediately with
Red Phonix hanging on his arm. Red Phoenix, a famous
Nanking courtesan, frequented these public places often and
was known to the waiters who greeted the three young people
with enthusiasm. Although she was only in her late teens, all
her clients were either high officials, rich merchants, or their
scions. She had arrived at Nanking from Soochow, her native
place, three years ago and immediately became a much coveted
"virgin entertainer." It was a rare treat to enjoy a cup of
tea in her boudoir and even a rarer one to have her sing and
entertain at dinner parties. Ordinary clients could not buy
a simple smile from her with even a hundred taels of silver.
Young Master Lu, whose full name was Lu P'an-lung, was the

son of the Imperial Commissioner and Viceroy of Chiangnan and Kiangsi provinces, Lu Chien-ying. Young Lu had only a scanty knowledge of the classics, but was well-versed in the art of "raging with the winds and sporting with the moon-beams." He had spent no less than a thousand taels of silver on Red Phoenix, but had not received so much as a kindly glance from the girl in return. Several months ago, his father had received an imperial order to station troops in the upper reaches of the Yangtze River to guard against the invasion of the "long-haired bandits." Young Lu, therefore, free from restraints, spent all his time in brothels. Two months earlier, he came to know Fang Ch'ien-hou, who claimed to be a student and the son of a fabulously rich merchant from Kwangtung. The two had become fast friends and took up residence in a brothal in Rouge Well Lane, called the "House of Pear Fragrance," to which Red Phoenix belonged. Unex-pectedly, in less than two months, this young and handsome student from the south had become the focus of Red Phoenix's love. An arrangement was made with the House for Fang to "pick the cherry" of Red Phoenix in exchange for an offering of fifteen hundred taels of silver. The news that a certain young student had "changed the hair style" of the popular courtesan became a hot item of gossip in all the taverns and restaurants in the Ch'in-huai district. Although young Lu was livid with jealousy, he was helpless in this matter, knowing full well that he was far inferior to Fang in the art of carousing and love-making. Besides, Fang was chivalrous as well as generous with his purse—the money he spent flowed like water. In two months' time, Lu accompanied Fang every-where—to brothels, theatres, taverns, and restaurants—for it was Fang who always paid the bills.

The trio sat down near the window in the waterfront pavilion. The waiter presented the menu and stood beside the table waiting attentively. With a simple gesture, Fang ordered the usual fare. The waiter responded quickly and disappeared downstairs.

The night scene along the Ch'in-huai River was brightly

illuminated by lights from buildings and boats. Snowflakes flew like catkins drifting in a dreamland. Countless pleasure-boats laden with fun-seeking men and women crowded the waterway and the sound of muscial instruments could be heard here and there without interruption. Indeed, this had been a pleasure-hunting ground since the Six Dynasties, an exciting and enchanting haunt of the wealthy and the blessed.

In a little while, delectable dishes with ingredients from the mountains and seas were spread all over the table. Red Phoenix sat between the two young masters and urged them to drink cup after cup of wine.

"Honestly, Elder Brother Lu!" Fang said smilingly, raising a cup full of wine to toast his friend, "Though my humble family cannot be compared with yours in wealth and prestige, we've always managed to support ourselves comfortably. Unfortunately, since the long-haired bandits brought havoc to the South two years ago, I was forced to leave my modest home to spend my time wandering about the countryside. I heard that the bandits have occupied Wuchang in Hopeh province and that their advance toward the east is inexorable, 'like the splitting of bamboo timbers.' Your honorable father, the imperial commissioner, who is stationed in the front, must have a strategic plan to defeat the invaders."

"Brother Fang!" replied Lu with an affected smile. "Since we are intimate friends, I need not hide anything from you. My father is only an old scholar who had spent ten years with his nose in the books before becoming a government official. He obtained the position of commander of a whole region by luck, but knows next to nothing about military and strategic matters. The long-haired bandits started the rebellion and the government ordered him to fight, that's all. In other words, when the master orders his servant to die, the servant has no other alternative but to obey."

Fang was surprised, yet he tried his best to disguise his feelings. "The city of Nanking is a strategic place," he said, "with topographical features similar in form to a crouching tiger and a coiled dragon, making it difficult to capture. The Ch'ing court must have built strong fortifications and sent heavy reinforcements, so there is no cause for worry."

"Aiya, Brother Fang!" Lu clapped his hands in amazement. "You too are a full-blown bookworm. My father's army, twenty thousand strong, is now stationed in the upper reaches of the Yangtze. In Nanking itself there are only three thousand Machu braves of the Green Garrison who are more expert in the handling of opium pipes than in guns and rifles."

Fang was completely astonished at the naïveté of his friend, but managed to say, "I've heard that when the long-haired bandits occupied Yüeh-chou, they commandeered all civilian boats and floating timbers, which shows that they are aiming at attacking Nanking. Should they come by way of the Yangtze, your honorable father's forces are no match because of the enemy's huge numbers. If this happens, won't Nanking be in jeopardy?"

"What am I supposed to say?" Lu sighed lightly. Then, lowering his voice, he continued, "Brother Fang, this is just between us. About a month ago, my father ordered our family stewards to pack all our valuables and have them shipped back to our hometown. It is inevitable, in my mind, that this pleasure land of the Six Dynasties will one day be a scene of fierce combat. Brother Fang, you remember the poem that says, 'How long can a good time last in one's life? Never let your golden cup go empty when you have the moon as your companion.' Look, so long as we have fine wine and the company of a beautiful woman, who cares whether the bandits arc long-haired or short-haired? Drink!"

The two friends drank several cups in succession. Their conversation became more and more animated. Red Phoenix, pouring wine for her clients, was carried away by what she had heard and could not refrain from asking: "Young Master Fang, you've just arrived from Hunan. They say that long-haired bandits have all the southern provinces under their control. Have you ever really seen one of them?"

"I haven't seen any, but I've heard many stories about

them," Fang replied with a smile.

"What do the long-haired bandits look like?" she asked. "I've heard that they all have red beards and green eyes, and that when they see women they grab them and make them their tent-wives, and that when they get hold of babies, they tear them apart and eat them alive, bones and all."

Hearing this, Red Phoenix's two companions burst into hearty laughter. Lu then lowered his voice and implored, "Elder Brother, would you tell us a story or two about the long-haired bandits?"

"During the fourth month, this humble brother of yours was in Changsha," Fang proceeded with his tale. "It was said that the long-haired bandits' main forces had been ambushed at Fisherman's Raincoat Ferry in Ch'üan-chou. It was also rumored that they had been badly defeated and that a ring leader, the so-called 'Southern King,' was killed. Commander Hsiang Yung of the imperial army reported to the throne that the Kwangsi rebels had been completely exterminated, thus ensuring peace. Unexpectedly, the long-haired bandits regrouped their forces only two days later, and attacked and took Tao-chou in Hunan in the course of one night. The people of Tao-chou were astounded and thought that the bandits had somehow descended from heaven. You know how government troops plunder and rob everything in their path after a defeat. The local people figured that since the long-haired bandits were newly defeated, they would surely drench the city with blood. As if rudely awakened from a dream, the whole population fled the city in such a hurry that some women left their children behind. Contrary to popular expect-ations, the long-haired bandits didn't take so much as a single straw from the people after they entered the city. Not even the dogs and chickens were disturbed. After hiding in the mountains for one or two days, the people screwed up their courage and went back to have a look. They found that the long-haired bandits had already departed."

"What happened to the children?" Red Phoenix inquired with real concern.

"They found some of the children sitting in bed and others playing on the floor. Each one had a ring hanging around his or her neck."

Lu, too, was amazed at this cryptic tale and asked, "Why did they hang rings around the children's necks?"

"The rings were made of baked dough!" Fang said matter-of-factly. "Not a single child left behind starved to death. The people were so grateful that they burned incense and kowtowed toward the north, unmindful of the dire consequences of reprisals from the government troops."

Red Phoenix was quite moved and made an effort to suppress her tears. Lu muttered meekly, "That shows that even the long-haired bandits are not entirely devoid of compassion."

"That will depend upon whom they are dealing with," Fang said emphatically. "Sometimes they are very unpredictable. After the long-haired bandits conquered Tao-chou, the people of Changsha were sitting on pins and needles; rumors were thick as flies. Within two days, posters proclaiming the impending attack on Changsha were pasted on walls in tea-houses, taverns, main thoroughfares, and small alleys. Hunan's governor, Chang Liang-chi, ordered a thorough search. Who would have imagined that instead of unearthing culprits, the search would have resulted in a proliferation of posters which invaded even the yamen compound? Posters appeared in the main hall, the guest hall, the kitchen and the lavatories. A few pieces even found their way under the pillow of the governor's eighth concubine!"

"How terrible!" Lu exclaimed in dismay.

"The city wall was still intact. How did the posters get in?" Red Phoenix asked innocently.

"I'm not so sure what happened," Fang grinned amiably. "Someone said that the agents of the long-haired bandits are all acrobats who can walk on the eaves of buildings and jump over high walls with ease. Others say that the long-haired bandits have planted their spies among people in all walks of life. But as to who slipped the posters under the pillow of the governor's eighth concubine, I'm at a complete loss. Only Heaven knows!"

"I've got it!" Lu said smilingly after a pause. "As a rule, nine out of ten concubines of high dignataries and officials have lovers. Maybe the lover of the governor's eighth concubine is a spy for the long-haired bandits."

"Dear Brother Lu, your quick thinking is laudable," Fang complimented his friend. "Your guess is as reasonable as it is plausible. In my humble opinion, that is exactly what happened."

Seized with a sudden feeling of panic, Red Phoenix asked, "In case the long-haired bandits come into the city, what will they do with girls like me?"

Lu loved to tease the girl. "I've heard that there are women soldiers among the long-haired bandit troops," he said, "commanded by big-footed, uncouth country women from Kwangsi. When they come into the city, you can enroll in the women's battalion."

Fang seemed to be amused by the conversation and said jestingly, "You're such a beautiful girl. Maybe one of the bandit kings or generals will take a fancy to you and make you his tent-wife. You can never tell."

Red Phoenix laughed and mockingly spat in her friend's direction. They continued to drink.

After a little while, they heard the sound of a noisy argument emanating from downstairs; the level of noise increased quickly. As Lu and Fang sought information from the waiters, two retainers of the Lu family came running upstairs and reported to their young master breathlessly.

"A blind musician and his two daughters were performing downstairs just now. A gentleman ordered them to sing a few songs and refused to pay, on the grounds that their singing was poor. In addition, the gentleman made a lewd remark to the younger girl. The blind man was furious and created a scene in front of all the customers and waiters. Would the master tell us what to do? Shall we chase the blind man and his daughters out, or . . . ?" One of the retainers stepped forward and whispered to Lu, "Your humble servant knows who that gentleman is. He's Chang Ping-huan, a stipend licentiate from the county of Shang-yüan and a relative of the provincial judge, Ch'i Su-tsao."

Hearing that there were two singsong girls downstairs, Lu's interest was aroused. He told Red Phoenix to wait there for a little while and dragged Fang downstairs to investigate. All the customers were standing around the protagonists to see what would happen. The grey-haired blind musician was in an uncontrollable rage. Stabbing a finger in the direction of a thirty-odd-year-old man dressed in a scholar's robe, the musician rebuked him loudly.

"If you're a student of the local academy, you should be aware of the teachings of Confucius. Whose backing are you counting on anyway? Not only haven't you paid for the singing, but you have insulted my daughter with your indecent remarks as well. Come, gentlemen of the audience, please decide whether his behavior has been reasonable or not."

A murmur of indignation rose from the spectators, but not a single person stepped out to mediate or interfere in any way. The two sisters, both in tears, tugged their father by the sleeves and implored, "Daddy, please! Let's get out of here fast!"

The blind musician was still in a fury and continued his uproar: "Some stipend licentiate! Some disciple of the Confucian school! I may have never obtained any degree, but I'm aware of Confucius' teaching against making improper remarks and taking improper actions. I don't know what you've done with your Confucian teachings. Have you thrown them into the cesspool?"

The spectators responded with a burst of laughter. The accused stipend licentiate, flushed with anger, pointed at the blind musician with one hand, while banging a wine pot repeatedly on the table with the other. At the top of his lungs, he roared, "You deserve death! Do you think you can intimidate me like this? I have plenty of money, but

I'll not pay a penny for a poor performance. If you continue to make a fuss, I'll send you to the governor's yamen and have you thoroughly lashed."

A waiter went over to snatch the wine pot from his hand and said smilingly, "Honorable stipend licentiate, you can send him to the yamen to have him lashed, but please don't break our wine pot!"

Another round of laughter rose from the audience. The stipend licentiate's cheeks twitched with fury, and a wave of purple flooded his face. The scholar was at a loss as to what to do next.

Several spectators shouted, "Master musician, we don't have much money, but we're willing to help. Young lady, bring out your tambourine!"

Holding her tambourine upside down before her, the elder girl walked around the hall. All the spectators threw coins into the tambourine. Coppers flew like butterflies, clanking against each other as they fell.

Just then, Lu and Fang came downstairs. All the waiters knew who they were and made way for them.

Lu saluted the stipend licentiate and said with a smile, "Brother Ping-huan, how are you? It is an auspicious occasion that we meet here." When Chang Ping-huan saw that he was being greeted by the son of the viceroy, his embarrassment became all the more pronounced. He stammered, "Young Master Lu, it is indeed a real pleasure to meet you. I was just having a little drink here today when this old goat started a rumpus . . ."

"My honored brother," Lu interrupted. "You are a man of high social status. Why should you argue with such riffraff?" As he finished speaking, Lu ordered a retainer to hand him a large piece of silver and threw it into the tambourine. His eyes remained fixed on the two singsong girls as they hurriedly departed with their father.

Then he introduced Chang to his friend Fang: "This is brother Chang Ping-huan, a stipend licentiate from Shang-yüan county and a relative of the provincial judge Ch'i Su-tsao. This gentleman here is Fang Ch'ien-hou, an intimate friend of mine. If it pleases you, Brother Chang, let the three of us go upstairs and drink a few more cups together."

Raising their clasped hands, Chang and Fang saluted each other. Chang was a swarthy man of medium stature in his early thirties. His manners and actions were rather unpolished. A black mole with a few hairs protruding from it stood out prominently near his mouth. A smile revealed two full rows of yellow teeth. Fang instinctively felt repelled by this person and refrained from further conversation.

Lu ordered his retainers to remain below and invited his friends to mount the stairs. Fang tried to locate his servant but failed to find him. As he was puzzling this over, he spotted the servant walking into the restaurant from the front door, winking at him discreetly. The three went upstairs and started to drink again. Red Phoenix dutifully poured wine for Chang. An insipid conversation ensued and everyone felt constrained.

They had just finished the first cup when a commotion started again downstairs, the noise mingled with the sound of people running. All the customers in the restaurant were quite upset. The two Lu family retainers and Fang's servant came upstairs in a hurry.

"Now what happened this time?" Lu shouted.

A retainer answered breathlessly: "Reporting to the young master, there is nothing special. . . . Only someone downstairs said that he saw a proclamation posted on the door of the Six Dynasties Retreat."

"A proclamation! What's so special about a proclamation? Why the commotion?" Lu retorted.

Lowering his vioce, the retainer muttered, "It's a proclamation of the long-haired bandits!"

Getting up abruptly, Chang saluted Lu and Fang and suggested, "Why don't we go down and have a look?"

Red Phoenix protested in mock annoyance. "We're supposed to be enjoying the snow and having a drinking party. This is all quite unsettling. Young Master Fang, I'm going home. How could the entire Ch'in-huai district have turned into such a topsy-turvey mess in just three days? The long-haired bandits might as well come in right now!"

"Red Phoenix is upset. I'll stay to keep her company," Fang volunteered.

"Then I'll remain, too," Lu rejoined.

"Please wait here for a little while. I'll take a quick look and be right back," Chang said, hurriedly departing.

All the customers downstairs seemed to have disappeared. A few waiters were gathering up utensils while talking to each other in hushed tones.

"No mistake at all. It's a proclamation of the long-haired bandits, red characters on yellow paper, with the imprint of a vermilion seal!"

"What does the proclamation say?"

"Go and read it yourself. It's pasted on the front door."

Unable to suppress the palpitations of his heart, Chang ran out as fast as his legs would carry him. A huge crowd had already gathered in front of the door of the Six Dynasties Retreat. A bespectacled, grey-haired old man was reading aloud the proclamation of the long-haired bandits.

Teacher of the Ignorant, Redeemer of Afflictions, Commander-in-chief of the Left Regular Army Yang, the Eastern King of the mandated Kingdom of Heavenly Peace, hereby solumnly proclaims that people of all walks of life shall pursue their livelihood as usual and in peace. Whereas the will of Heaven has manifested itself, the people must comply religiously. . . . Ever since the savage barbarians occupied the land of China, they have slaughtered our brethern and maltreated all living beings. Their greed for money is unrivaled and our people are sorely oppressed. Farmers and laborers are subject to their exploitation and merchants and tradesmen are mercilessly taxed. People within the four seas are grieved; the populace of the central plain is incensed. I, the Commander-in-chief of the Army, cannot bear to witness the sufferings of the people. We have raised the flag of righteousness in our quest to exterminate the savage barbarians and have sent our invincible army to attack the heinous devils. In every department and county that we have reached, the people welcome us as rainfall in time of drought. Our flags are pointing toward salvation and relief. . . . Since the revolution started in Kwangsi, all those who fought against us have relinquished their arms. The instant they see that we possess the mandate of Heaven, the demons are struck with fear. . . . We are building a new government and, therefore, proclaim to the multitude as follows: all students should continue with their studies; all farmers must continue tilling their land; all laborers must keep working in their shops, and all traders must keep their business running. After the posting of this proclamation, everyone must remain in his native district and carry on his usual trade. The sacred army will not disturb your lives, and the masses have no reason to be afraid. When the market is not disturbed, then peace can be restored. . . . Hear ye! Hear ye! Let no one violate this command!

The old man read the moving passages with passion, skipping over other passages that sounded seditious. His voice trembled and his eyes were full of tears. The spectators who stood on the snow-covered ground listened in silence. After the reading was over, a number of people squeezed to the front to have a closer look and touch the proclamation with their own hands. They saw that it had been written in red ink on yellow paper, with the imprint of a vermillion seal. The paste all around it was still wet. Clearly the proclamation had not been there long. As the spectators debated among themselves, they heard a loud shout behind them.

Ha! What are you doing assembling here? Disperse immediately! This poster is the work of lawless, godless, antigovernment, antiscoial rebels. It should be torn down and reported to the authorities. Who asked you to read it aloud? Anyone who reads it again will be considered an accomplice of the long-haired bandits. Disperse now!

Looking back, the spectators saw that the man who had

interrupted them was none other than the stipend licentiate who had refused to pay the old musician. They knew that he was not someone to contend with and so dispersed as he had ordered. Chang stepped forward to have a closer look. He bristled with rage as soon as he saw the words "the mandated Kingdom of Heavenly Peace." Looking around, he did not detect the presence of any suspicious persons, so he began to tear the proclamation off with the intention of bringing it to the viceroy's yamen for a reward. Before he could finish, someone else emerged from the Six Dynasties Retreat. Placing his hand over the poster, he said: "Hey, brother, who told you to tear this off? I've already sent people to the viceroy's yamen to report the incident. If you remove it, I'll have no evidence. Unless you are. . . .?"

"My friend," Chang replied defensively, "please don't misunderstand me. If you have already reported to the viceroy's yamen, there will be no need for me to do anything." Chang saluted him with a bow and returned to the restaurant.

A new group of customers had gathered in the downstairs hall, animatedly discussing the proclamation. Chang went upstairs and told Lu and Fang about the incident.

"What did I say?" Fang said triumphantly. "Now do you believe what I told you before? It is evident that the long-haired bandits have spies within the city of Nanking." As he heard these words, Lu suddenly turned pale. He stood up and insisted on leaving.

Red Phoenix also declared her intention of leaving. "First there was a rumpus. Then the proclamation of the long-haired bandits. How can we continue to drink and enjoy the snow? Young Master Fang, let's go home!" she pleaded.

"I also feel that tonight's events have not been auspicious. It is almost midnight now. The sedan chairs we sent for should be here," Fang said.

As they were ready to leave, yet another uproar started downstairs. This time the hubbub was muffled and they could hear every word clearly.

"Oh mercy! The long-haired bandits have entered the city! The long-haired bandits . . . have entered the city!"

The customers in the upstair's room rose from their tables almost simultaneously and dashed toward the stairs where they ran head on into a waiter carrying a tray full of food and drink. Dishes and bottles fell to the floor with a great clatter. Ignoring Red Phoenix and the others, Lu rushed to the head of the stairs and leaped down in a thoughtless plunge. Holding fast to Fang's hand, Red Phoenix trembled like an aspen leaf in the wind. Only Fang appeared calm. He whispered into Red Phoenix's ear, "Don't be afraid! The long-haired bandits are still far away!"

Chang Ping-huan also rushed toward the head of the stairs in an attempt to escape, narrowly avoiding a head-on collision with the man who had previously stopped him from tearing down the proclamation. Holding Chang by the collar, the man roared: "I've caught the long-haired bandits' spy! I've caught him! He's the one who posted the proclamation!"

In the uproar that ensued Chang had no chance to argue. With a jerk, he freed himself from his captor's grip and lurched down the stairs through the panicking crowd. Lu P'an-lung, the son of the viceroy, was lying motionless, stiff and silent on the ground, his face white as a sheet. Lu's two retainers crouched besides him, crying, "Young Master! Young Master!" Chang presumed that the young man had already given up the ghost and, without so much as a lingering look, he fled the restaurant as fast as he could.

When the uproar subsided somewhat, a young gentleman accompanied by a well dressed young woman stepped out of the restaurant and mounted their waiting sedan chairs. Following behind on foot was the young gentleman's servant— the man who had seized Chang and accused him of being a spy.

R ouge Well Lane was an ordinary Nanking alley—yet it was also extraordinary at the same time. It was ordinary in that all the lanes and alleys of Nanking had the same appearance—narrow and secluded, flanked by high walls on either side with a stone paved path in the middle. Green moss blanketed the base of the walls almost all year round. The tops of the walls were sprinkled with petals of fallen flowers in the spring, followed by dry, red leaves in the autumn. In the morning and at dusk, anyone who walked in the alley would hear the echo of his own footsteps. It was extraordinary in that romantic tales of history had played themselves out here; dramas of love and hate, of trickery and sacrifice were constantly unfolding before the observer's eyes. On the banks of the Ch'in-huai River, singsong houses, brothels, taverns, and restaurants crowded together, competing for business from all those who sought entertainment and pleasure. A few high class brothels catered only to the rich and powerful and their scions. At a distance, such a brothel might take on the appearance of a secluded red pavilion hidden amidst tall trees. Upon closer inspection, one might find a building with a pair of brass rings on its door and the draperies on its windows tightly drawn. Stepping inside, one would find a house of exquisite construction and decor, and a garden full of flowers. If one were permitted to enter the hall, one might be surprised by the sound of a parrot calling "Tea for the guest!" followed by a polite reception by the madame of the house. The whole atmosphere was quiet, elegant, and peaceful—part of a cherished tradition handed down through centuries since the hedonist days of the Six Dynasties. Truly, it was a land of enchantment for rakes and dandies in silken breeches and embroidered sleeves.

Red Phoenix had first arrived a little over three years ago at the House of Pear Fragrance in Rouge Well Lane, a peasant girl of sixteen from a village near Soochow. That had been in the summer of the twenty-ninth year in the reign of Tao-kuang (1849), when the provinces of Kiangsu and Chekiang suffered a devastating flood, the worst one in several hundred years. After Red Phoenix's parents had perished in the flood, her younger brother managed to eke out a living by working as a cowherd in a rich neighbor's family. She herself had fallen into the hands of a slave trafficker, and after a few transactions, had been sold to the brothel in Nanking.

Thus Red Phoenix had been transplanted from one world to another. The first world was a simple one; its life was fraught with hunger, hardship, and sorrow. But to her, a bowl of thin gruel was tasty and a bed of straw was a land of sweet dreams. Her present world was a multifaceted and multicolored kaleidoscope. But no matter how she turned it, the picture inside was the same—the face of a wolf, with a pair of fierce fangs and two greedy, green eyes. . . .

As time went on, all the faces she saw were still wolfish, only now their greed was vaguely concealed with cunning smiles. For instance, to her, the madame was a she-wolf, and in the first year, her mouth seemed equipped with a pair of fangs half-a-foot long, dripping with saliva. In the second year, the fangs receded considerably, and in the third year, her snout-like mouth was often wreathed with an affected smile. In the short span of three years, the innocent peasant girl had learned, under the madame's prodding and instruction, how to earn money with licentious and enticing smiles.

Spring breezes and autumn moons followed each other in quick succession for three years and the body of the peasant girl had attractively filled out. But her soul, once pure and clean, had shrivelled within its beautiful shell. She had forgotten the tragic death of her parents. She had forgotten her younger brother, emaciated and thin, earning a meager living as a farm hand. She had also forgotten herself—the innocent, simple farm girl. Her dark, rough complexion had become soft and white; her hollow, colorless cheeks were now plump and sported two dimples. Her lifeless, bitter smile had turned into ringing laughter, teasingly intriguing, designed to tickle the hearts of the innocent. She had learned how to employ a timely frown or a pleased smile in order to extract silver from the pockets of her clients. She had learned, too, the art of teasing, browbeating, and cajoling her patrons, as well as the technique of annoying, cheating, and pestering her madame. But in the end she realized that the one who was being cheated, defrauded, and insulted was none other than herself. She decided to retaliate with the only weapons that were available to her—her charm and beauty. Only on rare occasions, deep in the night, when she was alone, would she bury her face in her pillows and weep long and hard, washing away all her anger, grief, and sorrow.

Her experience of the past three years had told her that every client was either a smiling wolf or an unsmiling one. Her conviction, however, had been challenged this autumn when she met the son of a rich merchant from southern Kwangtung. The self-proclaimed student did not, however, possess the usual attitudes peculiar to scholars. Nor did this supposedly rich merchant's son have the rakish ways typical of his station. He was a spendthrift, and would throw away a thousand taels of silver without a second thought. In this fashion he had conquered the greedy heart of the madame and had made the House of Pear Fragrance his private villa with Red Phoenix as its only courtesan. All in all, Fang Ch'ien-hou was different from the other patrons who were obsessed only with carnal pleasure. Fang left early in the morning and came back late in the evening every day, spending his time visiting scenic spots—the sprawling hills and meandering rivers inside and outside the city of Nanking. He travelled alone, accompanied only by a servant of similar age. His "servant," however, did not act like a bodyguard or a retainer, but behaved more like a business partner. Fang lived in the House of Pear Fragrance, while the servant stayed in an inn. Fang had a wide circle of acquaintances including private secretaries in charge of taxes and correspondence of the various yamen and the patrol leaders, company chiefs, battalion heads, and regional commanders of the garrison forces. He entertained his friends in taverns and restaurants frequently and lavishly. Hence, Red Phoenix privately entertained doubts about his claims to be a student and a rich merchant's son. Although as to his manhood, she did not detect that Fang was any different from other men. Still, she did not understand why, as a client, he did not treat her as a prostitute—to him she was just a simple woman. In addition to their conjugal relations, they often carried on intimate conversations in which Fang expressed deep sympathy for her sufferings. But he had never uttered a word about his own past history or future aspirations.

Perhaps this sympathy of his had struck a chord in the numbed heart of the young courtesan who in the past had experienced nothing but rejection and indifference. Her role in her relations with Fang Ch'ien-hou, part prostitute and part wife, pleased her. As they lay side-by-side, she had quietly confessed to Fang her desire to marry him, a desire so strong that it mattered little to her whether she would be a concubine or kept woman. Fang only replied with a smile, "Let's talk about it later!"

The Six Dynasties Retreat incident only strengthened Red Phoenix's resolution to marry him. In such a topsyturvy world what could a young prostitute expect in the end?

Her life experience of nineteen years had proved to her that there was really nothing except bitterness and sorrow in the reality of human existence. She detested the way society was run and hoped that someday it would improve. But what kind of society could she aspire to live in? In what kind of a world would a girl like her not be insulted, maltreated, or abused? She had no clear conception at all, and only hoped that the god of fortune would someday smile on her and guide her to a better life. She had made offerings and burned incense before the golden statue of the Goddess of Mercy and contributed money to the Temple of the King of Hades. Would these pious acts redeem the "sins" she felt she had committed? She wasn't sure.

Early the next morning when Red Phoenix was still only half-awake, she found that Fang had already gotten out of bed.

The pavilion's window curtain had just been drawn and the morning breeze brought a little chill into the room. Tree-tops and surrounding roofs were still covered with a thin layer of snow; icicles clinging to the eaves had not yet melted.

Hungry sparrows made a riotous noise on the snow-covered ground. Wrapped in a sable coat, Fang Ch'ien-hou stood on the veranda enjoying the snow scene. A faint smile came to his face as he recalled the comical episode in the restaurant the night before.

From a hook by the window he took down a bird cage made of split purple bamboo. He removed its black cotton cover, revealing a white parrot inside.

"It's snowing!" exclaimed the parrot gaily.

Fang placed more grain and water into the receptacles in the cage and fed the bird with a piece of layer cake. Red Phoenix was doing her toilet in front of a mirror, combing her long hair which almost touched the floor. She wore a morning robe and a pair of embroidered slippers. The white parrot jumped up and down in his cage. Suddenly, it chirped "Little Orchid is here."

A flower vendor, a girl of sixteen or seventeen, carrying a bamboo basket full of plum flowers, was approaching along the stone path outside the high wall. She hawked her wares in her usual melodious tone: "Plum flowers for sale! Welcome the spring plum! Green calyx plum!"

The vermilion door of the House of Pear Fragrance opened with a creaking sound. The madame called out, "You're early today, Little Orchid!"

Smiling, the flower girl asked, "How about something for the flower vase in Red Phoenix's room?" She held up two sprigs of green calyx plum from her basket.

The madame took the flowers and went upstairs. Meeting Fang on the veranda, she said, grinning amiably, "You rise so early, Young Master Fang. It's a cold morning. Why don't you stay in bed a little longer?"

Without waiting for a reply, she proceeded to speak to Red Phoenix through the window. "Ah! Phoenix, my child. The Shih family's Little Orchid has just been here. Look! Here are the green calyx plum flowers you like best. They look as if they've just been picked this morning."

Red Phoenix put down her comb and took the flowers

Red Phoenix heard the parrot call him "the long-haired official."

through the window, then happily arranged them into a vase. The madame turned around and said to Fang, "I'll bring your breakfast and pay my respects to you presently."

The parrot hopped joyfully and mimicked the madame's words: "Young Master Fang, pay respects to you presently."

Fang tapped the cage gently and coaxed the bird in a low voice: "Why don't you say pay respects to the long-haired official?"

The parrot rolled his eyes obliquely in Fang's direction. "Pay respects to the long-haired official!" he cried.

Fang roared with laughter and tossed a piece of layer cake to the bird as a reward. Encouraged, the parrot continued chattering enthusiastically, "Pay respects to the long-haired official! The long-haired bandits are here!"

"Where did the bird learn that last sentence?" Fang wondered. Then he remembered that he had talked with Red Phoenix the night before about the incident in the restaurant. The bird was a fast learner and had repeated the sentence automatically.

Feeling a little chill, Fang went back into the room. Red Phoenix had finished her toilet. Apparently she had overheard the conversation between Fang and the parrot. Pretending not to have noticed anything, she continued to adjust the flowers in her hair.

"I am going to Wuchang in a day or two," Fang said casually.

Red Phoenix was startled and couldn't believe what she heard. She asked anxiously, "Wuchang! Hasn't it been . . . occupied by the long-haired bandits?"

"Indeed, it has!" Fang commented with a smile. "Other people can't go there, but I can."

In a flash, Red Phoenix grasped Fang by his sleeves and knelt before him. "Young Master Fang, tell me who you really are!"

"Did you hear my conversation with the parrot?"

"Yes, I did."

"Fine! I had to let you know sooner or later anyway."

Red Phoenix's eyes were brimming with tears now. She pleaded, "The long-haired bandits are rebels. When they're caught by the imperial army, they'll be exiled, decapitated, or exterminated along with their nine clans."

"The T'ai-p'ing army has been engaged in rebellion for three years now," Fang spoke calmly. "They have attacked cities, occupied territory, and killed numerous generals and governors. Imperial commissioners and viceroys have fled even before the start of military confrontations. Within half-a-year the Heavenly Army will occupy Nanking. From here they'll march to Peking. Soon the Heavenly King will sit on the imperial throne."

Overwhelmed by feelings of both fear and hope, Red Phoenix held Fang's hand tightly and pleaded, "Young Master Fang! Who are you? If you trust me, please tell me the truth. . . ." Without finishing her sentence, she began crying uncontrollably.

"Have you ever heard of the invincible and ever-victorious T'ai-p'ing army general called the Eastern King? This son of a rich merchant and student who now stands before you is *Hou Ch'ien-fang,* military supervisor of the T'ai-p'ing army, in the service of the Eastern King. Fang Ch'ien-hou is not my real name."

"Your Excellency!" Red Phoenix fell to her knees again, tears rolling down her cheeks. "I've heard that the long-haired army doesn't permit people to marry. Even husbands and wives are subject to the death penalty if they meet privately. Besides, when the Heavenly Army reaches Nanking, you'll have forgotten that your poor Red Phoenix ever existed."

Hou Ch'ien-fang said, "The Heavenly King has decreed that as soon as we occupy Nanking, the 'lesser paradise,' everybody will be permitted to marry. I swear I'll marry you when the Heavenly Army marches into the city, and we'll live a happy life as man and wife forever!"

"Then, this down-on-her-luck girl will be the wife of the military supervisor of the T'ai-p'ing army!"

"A military supervisor is nothing! I'm aspiring to be

controller, general, commander, general supervisor, and even state minister!" Hou was full of self-confidence. "However, you must not receive any more clients or marry another man. You must wait for me faithfully! There's a note for eight hundred taels of silver in my box here. That should last you for half-a-year. Be careful, Red Phoenix! If you should have another client or marry another man, I'll cut you in half when I return!"

"I'll cut you in half!" clearly repeated the parrot in the corridor.

Still kneeling, Red Phoenix cried her heart out, her head in her hands.

The next morning, Hou Ch'ien-fang and his mysterious "servant" disappeared from the city of Nanking without a trace.

A multitude of people, all bubbling over with excitement, were assembled on the vast military exercise ground of Wuchang where they had gathered before dawn. Everyone was following an oral order of the Eastern King transmitted by T'ai-p'ing army officers who had made the announcement in the streets, sounding gongs as they walked, the day before. The people had learned a new term—"Delivering semons." A few seemingly knowledgeable people became a target of great admiration when they proudly and elatedly explained the meaning of this strange T'ai-p'ing ceremony. The kings, marquises, commanders, and state ministers were going to come here to personally explain to the assembled masses the mysterious story of the creation of the world, its rivers and mountains; to announce the truth that the emperors of the Ch'ing dynasty, to whom their ancestors had owed allegiance and paid respect for successive generations, were nothing more than "monsters and demons"; to reveal the fact that "God, the Heavenly Father" together with the "Heavenly Mother" had sent their eldest son Jesus to the world to save the people, and that after the brutal crucifixion of the latter, had then sent their second son, armed with a "demon-slaying sword," to descend to earth in order to carry on the work of salvation; to elucidate the theory that all human beings under heaven were the children of God, the Heavenly Father; and to propagate the new and hitherto unheard-of theory that "All men under Heaven are brothers and belong to the same great family."

The high platform constructed with fir timbers only the day before was decorated with apricot-yellow draperies. Red banners fluttered in the wind and the gleaming weapons displayed on the platform dazzled the eys of the spectators. On the platform's flying eaves were hung vermilion gauze lanterns. A square table placed in the center was covered with gold-embroidered cloth. The aura of pomp and celebration deeply impressed the spectators. Despite the bitter cold breeze coming from the upper reaches of the Yangtze which had frozen their noses and numbed their toes, wave after wave of latercomers continued to arrive, swelling the crowd. Many of the spectators were middle-aged and young women— women who normally had little occasion to even step out their front doors. Light-hearted, carefree, and proud of their new freedom, they greeted their neightbors and acquaintances with a cheerful, "You're early today," at the same time shushing and pacifying their restless children. In short, they acted just as if they were attending a noisy, local temple fair or a riotous holiday celebration.

As the light of the rising sun pierced through the dark clouds, spreading its rosy radiance over the meeting ground, a group of riders in silken hats and embroidered robes galloped down the main thoroughfare along the river bank. Straining to catch a glimpse of the arriving dignitaries, the spectators found their view obscured by the rising cloud of dust kicked up by the hooves of the galloping horses. But this temporary frustration only heightened their sense of excited expectation.

The riders were now approaching the meeting ground. The clatter of their horses' hooves could be heard clearly.

The crowd assembled in front of the platform voluntarily parted to make way for the mysterious visitors. A spontaneous gasp of admiration went up from among the audience, as the riders became visible. Dismounting, the strangers ascended the platform in single file, under the gaping stares of the gathered multitude.

Dressed in a yellow robe, with a golden crown on his head, the Heavenly King, Hung Hsiu-ch'üan, strode slowly to the front of the platform, his countenance solemn. Flanking him around the table stood his comrades-in-arms in a neat lineup: the Commander-in-Chief of the Left Army and Chief of Staff, the Eastern King, Yang Hsiu-ch'ing; the Commander of the Right Army, the Northern King, Wei Ch'ang-hui; the Commander of the Rear Army, the Assistant King, Shih Ta-k'ai; the Commander of the Women's Army, Chief-of-Staff, and Consort of the deceased Western King, Hung Hsüan-chiao; Regular State Minister Ch'in Jih-kang; Regular State Minister Hu Yi-huang; Vice State Minister Lin Feng-hsiang; Regular State Minister Li K'ai-fang; General Supervisor of the Imperial Guard Huang Yü-k'un; General Supervisor of the Imperial Guard, Second Class, Ch'en Ch'eng-yung, etc. All were attired in military uniform.

As the audience began to quiet down, the Heavenly King started to preach. His voice was so low that even people standing in front near the platform could not hear him clearly. But this did not in anyway dampen the enthusiasm of the audience, numbering no less than ten thousand. For nothing really mattered other than catching a glimpse of the Heavenly King—the Son of God the Heavenly Father, and his subordinates. They wanted to know how this unsuccessful candidate for the *hsiu-ts'ai* degree could have raised the flag of rebellion, assembled an army of several hundred-thousand strong and occupied an area of several thousand square *li* in the short span of three years. What kind of person was he really, they wondered. Did he possess the "dragon countenance" of a "genuine Son of Heaven"? Did he have the bearing and demeanor of an empire builder? What kind of clothes did he wear? What did his famous "demon-slaying sword" look like?

Now that the people had seen him in the flesh, the first impression they had received was that of a man with a swarthy complexion, sunken eyes, high cheek bones, and thick lips. However, his tall stature, broad shoulders, heavy black eyebrows, piercing gaze, and deep voice which seemed to come from deep within his chest convinced his observers that the King was a solemn and obstinate, yet trustworthy man. The young people in the crowd began to feel affection for him. But the older folks felt disappointed—they had envisioned a god with golden rays emanating from his entire body. But "God" had turned out to be a mere mortal, and a very common one at that!

When the Heavenly King discovered that the multitude was little interested in his tale of the creation of the universe, he quickly changed the focus of his subject from heaven to earth. He declared:

> God, the Heavenly Father, is the Father of all the people. The mountains, rivers, and all living creatures in the world are the common property of the people, to be shared by all. All men are brothers and all women are sisters. God, the Heavenly Father, does not permit the ownership of private property; even coveting another's property is forbidden. Therefore, K'ung Ch'iu once said, "When the Great Way was practiced, the world was shared by all alike. The worthy and able were promoted to office and men practiced good faith and lived in affection. Therefore, they did not regard as parents only their own parents, or as sons only their own sons. The aged found a fitting close to their lives, the robust their proper employment; the young were provided with an upbringing and widows, widowers, the orphaned, and the sick, with proper care. Men had their tasks and women their hearths. They hated to see goods lying about in waste, yet they did not

hoard them for themselves; they disliked the thought that their energies were not fully used, yet they used them not for private ends. Therefore, all evil plotting was prevented and thieves and rebels did not arise. People could leave their outer gates unbolted. This was the age of Grand Unity." The Ch'ing demons, contrary to God's will, have occupied our land and murdered our people. They are not children of God, but "Yama devils" and "snake demons!" Two hundred years have passed since the Ch'ing demons came to occupy China. Our people have nothing to live on—their spirit is nearly broken. The demons have turned the blessed land of China into a hell on earth. However, it is Heaven's way that peace follows strife and light follows darkness. The sun has now risen after a long night of despair. It is our hope that our brothers and sisters shake off the devils' shackles and follow the way of God. Let us together destroy the living hell with the help of the Heavenly Army and build a paradise on earth!

After the Heavenly King finished his sermon, the assembled multitude still felt unsatisfied. They wanted to be told how the Second Son of God could so unequivocally call the emperors of the Great Ch'ing Dynasty "Yama devils" and "snake demons"; how he could so explicitly refer to all people as brothers and sisters; how he could so manifestly declare his plans to establish a "Heavenly Kingdom" on earth in which all people would love each other. A group of older men who had studied the *Four Books* and *Five Classics* nodded their heads in approval. To them the Heavenly King had expressed a simple truth: the "Heavenly Kingdom" of God was none other than the "World of Grand Unity" of Confucius. Still, the Heavenly King was a little too boorish, too ostentatious. How dared he call the "Supreme Sage and Ultimate Teacher" by his name—K'ung Ch'iu? But, of course! He was the Heavenly King, the genuine ruler. Hadn't Confucius been given the title "King of Cultural Accomplishment" by a later emperor? So why couldn't the Heavenly King call the Master by his name? Since he was bold and forthright enough to express himself in this fashion, it was evident he was the genuine Son of Heaven. . . .

A joyous ovation, loud and prolonged, came from the audience. The Heavenly King and his subordinates descended from the platform to greet the masses. Spectators standing in front automatically stepped aside to let them pass, while older people lowered their heads and stood attentively in accordance with the traditional etiquette. Others contemplated kneeling, but after glancing furtively at their neighbors, remained standing for fear of violating the customs of the T'ai-p'ing Army. Younger people in the crowd, unaware of traditional etiquette, stood there unabashedly. A few women even smiled openly, revealing their white teeth.

The Heavenly King and his subordinates squeezed through the human sea. Another round of shouting began and the phrase "May he live ten thousand years!" could be clearly discerned.

Suddenly, the leaders of the T'ai-p'ing Kingdom stopped amidst a group of old men and young women who were now able to have a closer view of the Heavenly King. Perhaps attracted by the King's fatherly smile, a young two-year-old boy with only a tuft of hair growing on his shaven head thrusted himself forward, laughing gleefully, from his young mother's arms, his two plump 'hands outstretched. The terrified young mother was at a total loss as to what to do. The Heavenly King took her child into his hands and raised him high. The child laughed audibly. With tears in her eyes, the mother first stared at the face of her son and then, daringly, at the face of the Son of God. She saw the glow of the wintry morning sun on both faces and their equally warm smiles.

A white-bearded old man—perhaps the child's grandfather—went forward and knelt before the Heavenly King. In a trembling voice, he said: "Heaven perceives all! A genuine Son of Heaven has arrived to save the common people."

Then he turned to the child held by the Heavenly King, "This is the savior of the people, child!"

The Heavenly King handed the boy back to his mother and helped the old man to his feet with both hands. "It is the will of God," he said, "that when the Heavenly Army enters Nanking, the 'lesser paradise,' the people will till the land together and be fed and clothed on an equal basis and enjoy the blessings of the Heavenly Father and Heavenly Brother!"

By now the sun had risen high in the sky. The Heavenly King and his subordinates mounted their tall horses and vanished into the brilliang light of the morning sun, as the people stood there, wiping their tears with the backs of their hands.

The riders dismounted when they reached the bank of the Yangtze River. Morning clouds cast a sheet of red over the water, already rippled with dazzling reflections from the breaking waves, as the great river rolled forever eastward.

Along the river bank were countless warships with masts like trees in a forest and sails like layers of accumulated snow. A clamor arose from the horses and armed men on the shore where the celestial soldiers were busy loading spears, guns, provisions, and military gear onto the anchored vessels. On the floating bridge the T'ai-p'ings had built from Ching-ch'uan Pavilion in Han-yang to Han-yang Gate in Wuchang, the crowd moved about like a swarm of ants, their activities diverse yet orderly.

Pointing toward the lower reaches of the Yangtze with his whip, the Heavenly King queried his comrade-in-arms, the Eastern King:

"Brother Ch'ing, do you know how long it will take to reach Nanking from Wuchang, following the current?"

"Second Brother," replied the Eastern King with a smile of confidence. "From Wuchang to Nanking it is 1,200 *li* by land and a little longer by water. Lower Nest Lake and Rat Gorge, south of Wu-hsüeh, are guarded by the Ch'ing devil, the so-called Viceroy of Chiangnan and Kiangsi, Lu Chien-ying, and his army from Kiangsu, Anhwei, and Kiangsi.

The little boy held up high by the Heavenly King smiles at his mother and grandfather.

The enemy has no less than twenty thousand men in these two strategic places. But their soldiers are a mixed lot. When our naval flotilla sails down the river, these twenty thousand devils will melt away like a wisp of smoke."

"Good! We'll give the order to advance," said the Heavenly King enthusiastically.

"Everything is in order except for one factor," the Eastern King whispered.

"What do you mean?" asked the Heavenly King.

"'If thou knowest thyself as well as thy enemy, one hundred battles will result in one hundred victories,'" answered the Eastern King. "Nanking is an important strategic town in the Southeast and the center for the collection of the region's tribute rice. The Ch'ing demons will not give it up without a struggle. Before we took Changsha three weeks ago, I sent a couple of capable officers to Nanking to spy on the Ch'ing demons' defense force, its capabilities and fortifications. They were supposed to have completed their assignment within three months and meet us in Wuchang. Now that the three-month period has ended our men should be here presently." As he spoke, the Eastern King trained his lone hawk-like eye toward the north bank of the river.

At almost high noon a rolling cloud of dust could be seen on the official highway on the north bank. Two riders galloped toward the entrance of the pontoon bridge. Cantering across in a few minutes, they reached the south bank with an easy leap from the bridge.

"They've come back!" exulted the Eastern King.

Before he could finish his sentence, two spirited horses, perspiring and whinnying, came to a stop straight in front of the Eastern King. Hou Ch'ien-fang and his "servant" dismounted quickly and knelt before him.

"Your Highness, Lord of Nine Thousand Years! Your subordinate, Hou Ch'ien-fang, has returned to report on the execution of your Highness's order."

"Well done, my brothers!" the Eastern King said gladly, helping them to their feet.

Hou Ch'ien-fang pulled out from his pocket a diagram on Nanking's fortification plans and respectfully presented it to the Eastern King with both hands. Without so much as a glance, the Eastern King presented the diagram to the Heavnely King.

"My good brothers, you have displayed persistence as well as forbear∴nce. Our Heavenly Father and Heavenly Brother will bless you!" said the Heavenly King, truly moved.

"Your Majesty, Lord of Ten Thousand Years! We, your subordinates, are willing to die a thousand deaths for the glory of the Heavenly Father, the Heavenly Brother, and you, the Heavenly King!" said Hou.

The Eastern King gave a command to a mounted officer behind him:

"Order the look-out pavilion on Yellow Crane Hill to raise the flags and beat the drums; the army is to march on at once."

Soon, one could see flags being hoisted and hear tattoos on drums from the pavilion. Thousands of vessels began to sail down the river. On the north bank, the sound of men shouting and horses neighing filled the air. The noise of clattering horses' hooves reverberated on the floating bridge.

It was the seventh day of the first month of the third year, *Kuei-hao,* of the T'ai-p'ing calendar. With flags fluttering in the roaring north wind, the half-million-strong army of the Heavenly King, Hung Hsiu-ch'üan, embarked from Wuchang on its eastward expedition.

TWO

Orioles could be heard warbling for hundreds of *li* around Nanking late that spring. The vast river was enveloped in mist and swallows flitted to and fro amidst the profusely blooming trees. Everything was verdant green—Bell Mountain and Rain-flower Terrace as well as the Ch'in-huai River itself. Small flecks of vermilion speckled the verdure—flecks that were not, however, blossoming azaleas, as one might expect, but the gold-embroidered red tunics of the court officials and military officers of the T'ai-p'ing government.

A column of women cavalry soldiers rode proudly on the flagstone highway on a patrol around the city. At its head was Hung Hsüan-chiao, sister of the Heavenly King and consort of the deceased Western King. About twenty-three or twenty-four years of age, the slender Hsüan-chiao was blessed with fine brows and large eyes. Her gleaming black hair was coiled into a bun high up on top of her head. Due perhaps to the hot sun of the rural south, or if not that, to long years of military campaigning and hardship, her complexion was somewhat swarthy. Yet a compelling aura of heroism revealed itself on the lovely, delicate oval face. She wore a round-collared short mandarin coat of marten fur over a gold-embroidered red satin padded jacket, and a pair of lavender embroidered wide-legged silk pants. On her feet were red-tasselled felt boots. With one hand resting on the sword by her side, the other grasping the reins, she sat leaning slightly backwards on her tall, glistening snow-white mount. Her head almost reached the eaves of the nearby buildings. Riding close behind Hsüan-chiao were her two closest followers—Ah-hsiao, a tall girl with delicate white skin, high arching eyebrows, and expressive, liquid eyes; the other, Ah-li was short, stocky and dark with thick eyebrows and large eyes, and above her slightly protruding lips was a broad, stubby "lion" nose. Ah-li had come from the same village as had the widow of the Western King. Both girls wore identical red padded jackets under their yellow silk military tunics and blue silk pants. As if to provide a contrast with their commander's white steed, the two young girls were mounted on deep-chestnut-colored horses.

Whirling their whips in the air, the hundred-odd mounted women soldiers calmly cantered on.

Heading straight their way was Hou Ch'ien-fang, also mounted on a horse, wearing a plain red court gown under a jacket decorated with the double-coiled dragon insignia of a T'ai-p'ing civilian commander. For some unexplicable reason, the presence of Hung Hsüan-chiao, the younger sister of the Heavenly King, always made Hou feel apprehensive, restrained, and a bit fearful. With a short tug on the reins, he quickly made his mount turn off into an alley. Then, smacking his whip smartly on the horse's flanks, Hou quickly disappeared from view.

The T'ai-p'ing army had occupied Nanking for an entire month now. Everyone in the city, of all ages and either sex, had become quite accustomed to the sight of these girlish calvary-soldiers who, led by their young commander, made a tour of the city every few days. Somehow people had learned from sources unknown that the younger sister of the Heavenly King had once been merely a common country girl. She had cultivated the fields, fed pigs, transplanted rice seedlings, and harvested grain—in short, she was proficient in any kind of farm work. Later, she had led soldiers in battle, charging and shattering enemy lines with incomparable courage. Unfortunately, her husband had perished in the attack on the city of Changsha, leaving her alone with just a five-year-old son. Yet she was unwilling to retire to the royal residence where she could have lived peacefully and comfortably. Instead, she insisted on remaining in the women's camp and continued to take part in the military patrols and inspections necessary in the defense of the city. In addition, she also was responsible for the managing of the women's quarters. As a result, she was extremely mobile and could be found everywhere within the city or without, visiting sentry posts and women's quarters in places both remote and near.

Oddly enough, although the residents of Nanking were so accustomed to seeing the Heavenly King's younger sister, no one had caught even a glimpse of the Heavenly King himself. It was said that ten days after the fall of Nanking, a yellow felt-covered sedan chair, flanked by guards in armor with gleaming weapons in hand, followed by scores of gorgeous veiled women on horseback, had been seen being carried through the Western Water Gate. After the sedan chair had disappeared into the *yamen* of the viceroy of Liangchiang, it had not been seen again. When the viceroy's *yamen* had been transformed into the royal palace, people said that the person riding in the yellow felt sedan chair had been none other than the Heavenly King himself. Others rumored that the Heavenly King had long since "returned to Heaven" on the battlefield and that the "King" riding in the sedan chair was, in fact, nothing more than a wooden spirit tablet made in his memory.

Of course, the officials and officers of the Heavenly Kingdom dismissed such foolish talk with a smile. Before taking Nanking, everyone of them, including the lowliest "sacred soldier," had almost without exception seen the Heavenly King either in battle or on the march. As far as they were concerned he was not only the Son of God, the Heavenly Father, but the leader of the God Worshippers Society as well. Besides, the Heavenly King had received the same cotton clothes and straw sandals from the Sacred Commissary as had everyone else, and had eaten on the march the same food from the same pot as had the common soldiers. However, this particular image had gradually receded from their minds since the taking of Nanking. The Heavenly King had retreated into the secluded inner palace chambers with his harem where he had exchanged his soldier's uniform for a golden crown and a yellow royal robe; the music of bells and gongs had replaced the sound of cannon fire, while the delicate scent of orchid and musk had taken the place of the stench of blood and dirt. The various officials and generals had radically different views regarding the change in the Heavenly King. A minority worried that the King had already betrayed the righteousness and moral fervor of the early days of the T'ai-p'ing military camp. Peking had not yet been taken, nor had the Ch'ing demons been destroyed, yet the Heavenly King was indulging himself in pleasure. If this continues, they thought, the consequences would be disastrous.

The majority however felt that the change had been natural and inevitable. Born of a peasant family in a mountainous rural region and having failed to pass the examination to become a *hsiu-ts'ai*, the Heavenly King had fought tooth and nail with the Ch'ing demons to reach his present status. What had he been fighting for if not for this? If, after moving into Nanking, the magnificient, luxurious capital of the Heavenly Kingdom, the Heavenly King continued to wear an ordinary soldier's uniform and peasant sandals, and slept on the same pile of straw together with all the others, it would have been downright outrageous!

Hou Ch'ien-fang belonged to the latter faction. He had been wandering throughout the country since leaving home as a boy, and had become quite quick-witted as well as experienced. Hou had never read any books on history and was totally unfamiliar with the tales of the vigorous efforts of Emperor T'ai-tsung of the T'ang dynasty to make the country prosper; nor had he heard of the unremitting work performed by the Sung emperor T'ai-tsu in building the nation. He had read, however, in works of popular fiction and historical anecdotes, descriptions of the state of affairs that supposedly would follow the establishment of a new dynasty in which "All enemies having surrendered, peace had been restored throughout the country; there were so few problems that the emperor did not have to convene the court, and could therefore rule by doing nothing." Hou thought this was an apt description of the Heavenly King's present situation—he was simply "ruling the country by doing nothing."

There was one thing he just could not understand, however. Back at Yung-an-chou where the T'ai-p'ing system had been established, Hou had heard the Eastern King orally transmit a decree of the Heavenly King, promising that after the country had been won and Nanking, the "lesser paradise," had been taken, everyone could be reunited with his own family; and that, more important to Hou, single soldiers would be permitted to marry and have children. Much of the country had now been conquered and the "lesser paradise" had been taken for one entire month. But while the Heavenly King and the Eastern and Northern kings were acquiring more and more consorts and concubines, the other brothers, including the six state ministers and ten regular and alternate generals, still lived as bachelors, and could only visit in secret their mothers, wives, and daughters in the women's quarters, at the risk of public beheading for violating the Heavenly law!

Due to his meritorious service in gathering military intelligence concerning the Ch'ing demons, Hou had been promoted, after the taking of Nanking, to the rank of civilian marshall with the duty of transmitting decrees of the Heavenly Court, skipping over the intermediate ranks of army controller and army general. But other than acquiring a house to use as an office and a few improvements in his food and clothing, nothing had really changed. According to the Kingdom's regulations Hou no longer wore an animal mask motif helmet decorated with a single tiger and a hundred bat design. He had exchanged that for a helmet decorated with a pair of dragons, a single lion, a single phoenix, and numerous butterflies, and his yellow jacket, instead of being embroidered with peonies, now was lavishly decorated with a double coiled dragon design. The words "honorary marshall" were embroidered on his plain red gown. Mindful of the old saying, "A real man should return home wearing the silk garment of an official," Hou was obsessed with the desire of fetching Red Phoenix after his promotion. But during the sack of Nanking, the Eastern King had ordered Hou to remain in the camp for the time being to see to military affairs. Hou had wanted to rush to Rouge Well Lane right after the capture of the city, but his immediate superior, the Eastern King, had just issued an order announcing, "Anyone taking so much as one step into a citizen's home will have his offending foot cut off!" That very day, the Eastern King promptly ordered the arrest of several "sacred soldiers" (all new brothers who had joined the army in Hunan or Hupeh), who had entered civilian homes. They were bound with heavy rope and had had either their feet or heads cut off. The "new brothers" no longer had any reason not to believe that the spirit of the Heavenly Father had entered the body of the Eastern King, thus enabling him to be aware of all that happened without even leaving his palace. Therefore, they submitted docilely to their punishment. Although Hou Ch'ien-fang frequently had the opportunity to visit the area around Rouge Well Lane and the Ch'in-huai district on the pretext of attending to official business, he had not once caught a glimpse of

Red Phoenix.

Today he had been given an official mission which would allow him to ride through the city. For the past month, the cobblestone streets of Nanking had become cleaner, and there were fewer loiterers or idle pedestrians who had nothing to attend to in particular. All the shops selling "sundry products from both North and South" had ceased doing business and were replaced by new market places selling daily necessities. The taverns and tea houses had all been closed as well, so the city seemed particularly quiet and peaceful.

Hou Ch'ien-fang followed the road leading to the river bank. The green waters looked the same as ever, but the houses along the shore were quiet, showing little sign of activity, and the pleasure boats had disappeared. Gone too was the sound of refined singing and dance music that had filled the gilded halls only a few months before. Nor could the raucous shouts and laughter of guests playing drinking games be heard. Having reached the Six Dynasties Retreat, Hou saw a big red official seal of closure on the locked front gate. A white wooden sign hung from the side door. Inscribed on it were the words, "Official Beancurd Manufactory." T'ai-p'ing camp brothers and short-jacketed or bare-backed men busily carried in large quantities of soybeans; others left laden with full baskets of beancurd and bean residue. The beancurd was steaming, fresh from the pot. Although the men carrying the bean products were busy, they labored with joy and the sound of their shouts filled the air. Even their bodies seemed to emanate the fragrant odor of soybean milk. Hou stared at them blankly for a while, then with a crack of his whip, headed off towards Rouge Well Lane.

Galloping through streets and alleys, Hou reached the entrance to Rouge Well Lane. Relaxing his grip on the reins, he allowed his grey horse to clip-clop through the alleyway at its own speed. Hou gazed up at the high walls on both sides of the lane. All the windows and shutters were tightly shut—not a sound could be heard. The sounds of lovely music, soft words, and coy laughter of a few months prior had vanished along with the people who had produced them. Lost in thought, Hou arrived at the front gate of the House of Pear Fragrance where he leaped lightly from the saddle. The vermillion gate was half open, and the gold-fleck plum-red paper sign printed with the huge character, *"shun"* [meaning "submit"], on one corner of the door had not yet faded. Hou glanced at the entrance to the lane and, realizing no one was in sight, plucked up his courage and entered with a light push on the door.

The courtyard was strewn with fallen flowers; the steps were overgrown with grass—clearly no one had lived here for sometime. The grey horse sniffed wildly at everything. Then after chewing on a few blades of grass, raised his head and let out a loud whinny. Afraid of being seen by a comrade, Hou quickly latched the gate, muzzled the horse and tied him to the peach tree. Not until then did he notice that the tree was laden with blossoms as pink as the rosy evening clouds. The grey horse lightly rubbed against the tree trunk, and peach blossoms tumbled down like a crimson rain. "Is anyone upstairs?" Hou softly called. Failing to elicit an answer, he slowly mounted the stairs. Just as he reached the second floor balcony, he suddenly heard the sound of a coquettish voice: "Young master is here! Mama, bring tea!"

This gave the totally unprepared Hou a start. Composing himself, he saw that it had been only Red Phoenix's white parrot calling from the cage in the window of her room. Hou had long since forgotten the little bird, but now his eyes brimmed with tears at memories of things past. Overwhelmed for an instant by emotion, Hou turned to the parrot and asked, "Is the mistress at home?" The bird responded irrelevantly, repeating the same words, "Young master is here! Mama, bring tea!"

Hou tapped the purple bamboo cage with his forefinger. "I'm asking about your mistress!" The parrot blinked his eyes and hesitated as if thinking to himself. "The mistress? The mistress?" he asked.

Hou Ch'ien-fang smiled wryly. Just as he was about to

enter, he heard a quavering voice behind him, "Master Fang, Your Excellency! You've come back!"

It was the madame. Rushing forward, she knelt at Hou's feet.

"Your Excellency! You've come back! My Phoenix will be saved!"

Hou felt his heart leap. "How is she?" he asked.

"When the Heavenly soldiers first entered the city, she waited and waited. . . . But there was no sign of you, sir!" sobbed the madame. "About half a month ago, several female officials on horseback came. They rounded up all the women in Rouge Well Lane together and sent them off to the women's quarters. 'Men belong with men, and women with women,' they said. Poor little Phoenix and I were separated and sent to different quarters. Aiya! That female sergeant of ours is so tough! She's a big-footed savage from Kwangsi!" Stealing a glance at Hou, the madame quickly modified her previous remark. "I mean a big-footed woman official, that is. She makes us whittle bamboo spikes. Each of us has to make three hundred of them each day. And the last ten days, they sent us outside the city to dig trenches. I said to her, "Honorable sergeant, you have big natural feet. Digging ditches is no problem for you. But with these three-inch golden lily bound-feet of mine, how am I going to muck around in the mud?' That savage—I mean woman official—gave me a crack on the head with her horse whip and said, 'You mean it's okay for you to debase young girls but not okay for you to dig trenches? If you keep yapping, I'll 'light your heavenly lamp!' Aiya! How mean she is!"

Losing his patience, Hou pressed her. "So where is Red Phoenix?" he asked.

"I don't know! We were separated the day we were sent to the women's quarters. . . . Someone said she was in the Wuyi Lane women's quarters. Red Phoenix is young and pretty. If a search is made for beautiful girls and she's there, she might marry a king or a state minister. . . ." Sensing that she had gone too far, the madame quickly corrected herself. "I mean she might marry someone like you, sir, and she'll be set up for life! There's no way she'll end up like me—an ugly woman over fifty, digging trenches everyday, stuck up to her knees in water. My poor feet hurt me so much and I can barely stand it!"

Unwilling to listen any longer, Hou turned to go down the stairs. The madame took the cage down from the window and handed it to Hou, saying, "Your Excellency, why don't you take the parrot with you? If he stays here, he'll starve to death. I go out of the city everyday to dig trenches. Sometimes I have to wait two or three days before I can sneak back and give him a little grain and clean water. He was Red Phoenix's darling!"

After Hou had gone down and tied the cage to his horse, the madame rushed to his side. She spoke with great urgency. "Your Excellency, when you find my poor Red Phoenix, marry her, but then *please* don't forget, whatever you do, to get me out of the women's quarters! If you don't, I'll die in the city moat for sure!"

Hou left the House of Pear Fragrance with feelings of loathing and disappointment. Seeing that it was nearly noon, he urged his horse forward and headed toward Wuyi Lane. When he found the women's quarters, Hou presented his credentials, inventing a story about having been sent by the Eastern King to investigate the status of a certain woman there. Not daring to disobey, the sergeant offered Hou a plaque listing all the twenty-five residents of Wuyi women's quarters. Hou was perplexed to see that Red Phoenix's name was not on it. Unable to make up his mind, Hou had no choice but to directly inquire about her. The sergeant responded with a grunt of recognition. "Oh yes!" she said. "When we first set up the women's quarters, we didn't have a name plaque yet, but I do remember there was a young woman named Red Phoenix. They said she had been a Rouge Well Lane courtesan. She was really pretty—tall, slender, with big eyes and fine eyebrows. She hadn't been here for more than three days when the Northern King, Lord of Six Thousand

Years, arrived with a whole retinue to pick women to be his consorts. He chose Red Phoenix just like that!"

Hou felt as if he had been doused with cold water from head to toe. After a long moment of stunned silence, he asked: "Did she ever come back after moving into the Northern King's palace?"

"Now, what would she want to do that for?" answered the sergeant, clapping her hands in amazement. "As consort of the Northern King, she can dress and eat like a queen, and live a life of peace, wealth, and honor. Isn't that a lot better than staying here whittling bamboo spikes and lugging sacks of rice around?"

With an angry crack of his whip, Hou spun around on his heel, his teeth grinding audibly.

In accordance with the wishes of the Heavenly King, the first formal court of the new dynasty was convened in Golden Dragon Hall of the royal palace a month or so after the taking of Nanking for the purpose of proclaming the city as the new "Heavenly Capital."

After entering "lesser paradise," a great many changes had occurred in the life style of the Heavenly King, Hung Hsiuch'üan, that not even he had anticipated. The sound of cannon fire had disappeared along with the smell of gunpowder. The noisy din of signal drums, war conches, and gongs had been replaced by an absolute silence and the viceroy's *yamen* had been reconstructed into a palace for the Heavenly King. At first the emerald green tiles, upward arching eaves, and elaborately decorated pillars and beams made the Heavenly King feel insignificant and lonely. Every time he spoke with his consorts or female officials, the deep echoes of their voices resonating in the vast, empty palatial chambers aroused in him an inexplicable feeling of terror. It was spring, the weather outside was glorious, yet not a sparrow was in sight. Nor could the golden rays of the sun penetrate the inner recesses of the palace. An atmosphere of gloom and darkness pervaded the palace, accompanying the empty echoes. The halls and chambers were pregnant with the smell of sandalwood incense mixed with a dank, almost moldy odor of moss. The yellow and white flowers in porcelain pots on the veranda had already quietly begun to lose their petals. In dark corners of the palace, young concubines and maids so recently selected glided seriously and quietly by like fish in water, their fine skirts making a soft swishing sound.

But after little more than a month's time, the Heavenly King had completely adapted to his new life. The halls and courts that had once seemed so cavernous and lonely now appeared quite ordinary, if not a bit narrow to him. He no longer felt insignificant surrounded by high-flying eaves and huge red-lacquered pillars; to the contrary, the Heavenly King now felt himself acquiring a majestic awe-inspring air. All he had to do was cough once, and all the giggling teenage southern beauties fell immediately silent. With one fleeting frown, he could cause all his female officials to drop to their knees in their silks and brocades and begin to kowtow, pounding their heads on the floor at a fast and furious speed. He felt omnipresent and boundlessly omnipotent, and no longer doubted the veracity of his self-imposed sacred title of the "Second Son of God." Increasingly, he believed that every whim and vague thought that popped into his mind must certainly be the holy will of God the Father, revealed only to him; that all the rhymed semipoetic utterances that occasionally fell from his lips had to be holy prophecies from God. He frequently enjoyed the pleasure of listening to the sound of his own resonant, golden voice echoing in the palace's vast halls. Watching his concubines and female attendants as they devoutly and reverently hung on to his every word with expressions of fear and trepidation written on their faces, he deliberately raised his eyes still higher and cast a sweeping glance across the tops of their heads in order to give his face an even more sacred and exalted appearance.

As early as the Chin-t'ien Camp days, T'ai-p'ing leaders

had raised a military slogan that everyone could understand: "First take Nanking, then take Peking; the Ch'ing dynasty is finished and their army will be annihilated." No one was sure exactly who had invented the slogan, but it had truly captured the spirit of the goals of the Heavenly King and his comrades-in-arms at the time. Seeing that many T'ai-p'ing officials and soldiers felt homesick after the taking of Yung-an-chou, the Heavenly King and the Eastern King raised the second slogan of "Take Nanking and enjoy celestial blessings" to boost military morale. It was precisely at this time that Lo Ta-kang, Second Commander-in-chief of the Left Army, proposed his two alternate schemes for "attacking the north and stabilizing the south" to the Assistant King, Shih Ta-k'ai. The general idea behind these two strategies which had won the approval of the Assistant King consisted of either going on immediately after the taking of Nanking to attack Honan and the north all the way to Peking, thus destroying the Ch'ing forces and conquering all China; or establishing a capital at Nanking, then sending the army to consolidate the nine southern provinces to stabilize the rear, followed by a division of the army into east and west wings to take first Hsien-yang, Anhwei, Honan, Hsüchow, and Yangchow and then a regrouping of forces to attack Peking. The Heavenly King was deeply impressed by the two alternate strategies which he had received in the form of a written memorial from the Assistant King. The Eastern King also felt that Commander Lo's plans made a good deal of sense, but due to his prejudice against men such as Lo who had secret society backgrounds—in Lo's case the Heaven-and-Earth or Triad Society—the plans were shelved. The Eastern King had always felt that Triad men were an undertalented, overambitious lot of braggarts, and so suggested to the Heavenly King that discussion be postponed on the matter until after the capture of Nanking.

But since Nanking had been taken with barely a shot, the Heavenly King had entered "lesser paradise" where he now sat on the throne deep inside the palace wall well ahead of schedule. It was here that he received the Assistant King's memorial expressing his approval and support of the "two strategies" submitted by the newly promoted Commander of the Imperial Guards, Lo Ta-kang, who had drawn them up while stationed in Chinkiang only several days after entering "lesser paradise." The text went as follows:

Your humble servant has heard that Honan province is the heart of the empire, a point that can be reached from all four directions. If we are to conquer the entire country, Honan must first be taken; if Your Majesty's presence in Honan is made to be felt, our army could then cross the river and attack Peking. The Ch'ing demons will certainly crumble without a fight and the kingdom will be ours. This is my preferred plan. My alternate plan is to first consolidate the nine provinces of the south in order to stabilize the rear, and then divide the army into three sections, one attacking Han-chung, then rapidly advancing on Hsien-yang; the second section is to attack Hunan, Anhwei, and Honan; the third is to attack Hsüchow and sweep on to Yangchow and occupy all territories east of the T'ai-hang Mountains. Once Hsien-yang has been captured, the three armies are to regroup and start from the west of the T'ai-hang Mountains to take Peking. Even a Chu-ke Liang could not resist us.

Over a month had passed since the memorial had reached the Heavenly King, but no reply was forthcoming.

After much dawdling and delay the Ch'ing imperial commander, Hsiang Jung, who had been trailing the T'ai-p'ings on their march, finally arrived with his troops outside Nanking more than ten days after his opponents had captured the city. There he set up camp at Hsiao-ling-wei, south of Nanking—this was referred to as the Great Chiangnan Camp or the South Camp. Half a month later, another high Ch'ing official, Imperial Commissioner Ch'i Shan, arrived at Yang-chow with a combined infantry and cavalry force numbering in the tens of thousands representing the entire regional armies of Chilin, Heilungchiang, and other northern areas. This second force stationed itself at Yangchow, north of Nan-king, and was called the Great Chiangpei or the North Camp. The two great Ch'ing army encampments faced the Heavenly Capital like a pair of monstrous, living pincers, glaring greedily at their prey. Confronted with this precarious situation, the Heavenly King was forced to come to terms with the possibility that Lo's "two strategies" might be the correct choice after all. But after living for more than a month in "lesser paradise," the celestial monarch had come to regard the bloody, dank stench of battlefield life as quite tiresome indeed. Besides, he had already promised to allow his subordinates to reunite with their families and enjoy a life of blessed leisure after the capture of "lesser paradise." Since every utterance of the Heavenly King revealed the will of God, how could he now eat his words?

The memorial sat on the desk of the Heavenly King's study for over a month, yet he vacillated still.

Finally, the time had come to hold his first imperial court. The Heavenly King thought to himself: There will certainly be much discussion among the officials and officers concerning the sacred army's future moves after I announce at court the selection of Nanking as our capital. Let's see what benefit I can reap from it.

A hubbub of voices could be heard just before noon outside the gate of the Heavenly Palace where T'ai-p'ing civilian and military officials had long since been waiting for court to begin. The construction of the palace had not yet been completed and normally the area would have been buzzing with the sound of masons and carpenters at work amidst piles of bricks and stone. In order to hold court, work had been suspended for half a day, and all workmen had returned to their barracks.

The Heavenly King wore on his head a crown decorated with a double dragon and phoenix insignia. Dressed in a yellow satin robe embroidered with nine dragons, the Heavenly King emerged from the inner palace surrounded by a group of female officials, and walked towards Golden Dragon Hall. As he mounted the throne, women accompanying him arranged themselves on either side. Two rows of freshly-planted snow-pine trees lined both sides of the newly paved white marble path. From Golden Dragon Hall to the palace gate these trees cast a mottled pattern of light and shadow onto the waiting soldiers revealing glistening weapons and shining armor.

At either side of the palace gates stood official door-keepers dressed in civilian attire. Within stood twenty-four imperial guards, their tunics decorated with insignia representing the twelve horary characters. Another forty-eight imperial guards, armed to the teeth, each with an insignia representing the twenty-four solar terms on their tunics, were positioned just in front of the armored soldiers. At both ends of the corridor three hundred court musicians stood at reverent attention waiting for the signal to lift their woodwind and stringed instruments. On either side of the steps leading to the throne stood a scribe with an assistant, waiting behind a small table on which had been placed a brush-pen, an ink stick and slab, and paper.

The hands of the great clock in Golden Dragon Hall pointed at exactly twelve noon; a full artillery salute began outside the gates. Just at this moment Yang Hsiu-ch'ing, the Eastern King, Wei Ch'ang-hui, the Northern King, and Shih Ta-k'ai, the Assistant King, galloped in, each accompanied by a mounted honor guard. Arriving at the bridge over the imperial moat, the three kings straightened their clothing and crossed on horseback, leaving the guards behind. As they approached the "dismount" tablet all three men leaped simultaneously from the saddle.

The palace gates were now open wide. The civilian and military officials who had been standing on both sides of the court eagerly rushed forward to meet them. The military

was represented by State Ministers Ch'in Jih-kang and Hu
I-kuang; following them were: Hung Hsüan-chiao, widow
of the Western King and Commander-in-chief of the women's
army; Vice State Minister Lin Feng-hsiang, who had just
returned from the frontlines at Yangchow; State Minister
Li K'ai-fang, Commander of the Naval Forces; and Civilian
State Minister T'ang Cheng-ts'ai, and others. The civilian
admistration was led by Vice Minister Ch'en Ch'eng-jung and
State Minister Huang Yü-k'un, followed by Vice Minister
Lai Han-ying, brother-in-law of the Heavenly King, and the
Heavenly King's two elder brothers, Hung Jen-fa and Hung
Jen-ta, and others. All in all, over three hundred civilian and
military officials were present. The remaining generals were
still with their troops inside and outside the capital.

As the Eastern King led the Northern King and the
Assistant King, escorted by their assistants, toward the gates
of the palace, the ceremonial marshall proclaimed in a loud
voice, "The Heavenly King has decreed: 'Let the Eastern,
Northern, and Assistant kings enter in that order.'"

The three kings strode through the palace gates. The
marshall again raised his voice in command: "Kneel!"

The three kings fell to their knees at once. Straightening
their robes, all other officials present followed suit at the
same time and knelt on all fours, lowering their heads to
the ground.

A second ceremonial marshall took the place of the
first and loudly proclaimed: "The Heavenly King has decreed,
'Let all officials enter in single file and stand respectfully in
proper formation!' Unnecessary noise while kneeling and
rising is forbidden. After shouting 'Long live the King' three
times, you will listen to the imperial proclamation. After
the royal audience comes to an end, you will remain standing
on either side of the hall!"

"Long live the Heavenly King, may he live ten thousand
years! One hundred million years!" cried the three kings
together with the assembled officials in one voice.

The three leaders rose to their feet cremoniously and

approached the table in front of the Heavenly King in Golden Dragon Hall. Outside the gates, the assembled officials rose together and enterd the hall single file, arranged according to rank. Once inside, they separated into military and civilian sections and stopped somewhat behind the three kings.

This was the first formal audience since the founding of the new state; its mood was one of dignity and solemnity. The Heavenly King felt joy and excitement to see the affectionate, devoted faces of his comrades from whom he had been separated for over a month. His tightly knitted brows slowly but surely relaxed.

Just at that moment a female court official standing respectfully to one side of the hall, dressed in full court regalia, began to solemnly read the proclamation announcing the establishment of the Heavenly Capital in Nanking:

By the grace of the Heavenly Father, we shall rule over the empire in perpetuity. Our invincible army, having raised the flag of righteousness at Chin-t'ien, is now laying the foundation of the Empire in the city of Nanking, which is now to be called the Heavenly Capital in conformity with the mandate of Heaven. The dynasty is to be named "Heavenly Peace" and will be administered in accordance with the will of God. The Heavenly Capital is centrally located, surrounded by three rivers and five lakes, and blessed with strategic configurations resembling coiled dragons and crouching tigers. Its surrounding area includes the ancient states of Wu and Yüeh where the land is fertile and the people prosperous. Henceforth, we shall rest our soldiers and horses and bask ourselves in the radiance of Heavenly grace. We shall retire our military units and engage in cultural activities, so that we may enjoy the blessing of the Heavenly Father. It is so ordered!

Listening with his eyes half shut to the rhythmic cadence of the reader's voice, the Heavenly King felt an intoxicating sense of satisfaction. However, when he heard the last few lines of the proclamation, a frown suddenly appeared on his face. Without turning his head, the Heavenly King spoke as if conversing with himself to a young female official at his side, "Who wrote the proclamation?"

"Begging to inform Your Majesty," began the young woman, not sure of what was to follow, disaster or good fortune, her voice trembling slightly. "I heard it was the Court Historian Ho Chen-ch'uan who wrote it."

The Heavenly King nodded his head slightly in acknowledgement.

The proclamation came to an end. The crystal clear voice of the reader seemed to reverberate back and forth in the spacious, open hall. The court was filled with a great silence as the Heavenly King waited for its reaction.

The stillness of Golden Dragon Hall was in marked contrast to the unrest felt by the gathered officials. The Northern King, Wei Ch'ang-hui, cast a glance at the Eastern King, Yang Hsiu-ch'ing. Yang seemed not to have noticed and stood there gazing in an upward direction, apparently smiling to himself. State Minister Hu I-kuang stole a look at Shih Ta-k'ai, the twenty-two-year-old Assistant King for whom Hu had always felt so much respect. Shih's broad chin trembled violently.

As Hu had expected, Shih Ta-k'ai strode forward and began to speak, his voice trembling with emotion:

"Second Brother!"

"Brother Ta!" The Heavenly King sensing that Shih was about to present a portentous report, appeared unexpectedly calm. "Is there something you would like to say?" he asked.

The Assistant King made an effort to control himself. "Second Brother!" he said. "The Ch'ing demons have not yet been entirely destroyed, and the situation still isn't settled. The chief demon Hsien-feng is casting his greedy eyes on us from Peking; his generals Hsiang Jung and Ch'i Shan can't wait to get their hands on our Heavenly Capital. The Heavenly Kingdom has only won half the country. I fear that . . . that this is hardly the time to rest our soldiers and horses and retire the military to engage in cultural activities!"

Silence filled the great hall. The assembled officials, both military and civilian, followed the unfolding drama with bated breath. The Assistant King continued:

One month ago, General Supervisor, Brother Lo Ta-kang, submitted his two strategies to me, which I then presented to you, Second Brother, in a memorial. I would like to take this opportunity to elaborate further on them. The heart of military strategy is clearly the same today as it was in ancient times: attack at the first drum roll while morale is high. If you delay once, weakness sets in; if a third time is required, military collapse is imminent. Ever since the Chin-t'ien uprising, our army has always pressed forward without let-up. In less than three years' time we have captured I-yang, Yüeh-chou, Wuhan, and Nanking, now the Heavenly Capital. The Ch'ing demons have lost their nerve and the entire country has turned toward us. Nanking is the richest city under heaven and is well supplied with grain. Almost totally surrounded by barriers of mountain and water, the city is completely protected from the east and south. With a base of such material abundance, we can surely destroy the Ch'ing demons and unite the country so long as we press immediately on to Peking. If we continue to live spartanly and strongly press our offensive we will surely get twice the result with half the effort. This would be the preferred strategy. Now that we've decided to set up our capital at Nanking, we will have to first consolidate our victories in the nine southern provinces, then send the army to attack in four different directions before regrouping for the final assault on Peking if we succeed. If we fail, we will have to settle for half of the country and wait for future opportunities. However, we will have delayed too long. The men will be worn out and our supplies exhausted. We will have to double our efforts to reach the same goal. This would give the Ch'ing demons a chance to recoup their losses and begin to attack and harass us from every direction. We will have to be constantly on the move just to keep them from our throats. Therefore, I consider this strategy to be only second best. If, however, we choose to cling to this little corner, satisfy ourselves with only the conquest of the southern half of the country and fail to continue our offensive, it will give the Ch'ing demons enough breathing space to save themselves from destruction and to roll back everything we have gained. Settling on such a policy would be courting disaster; no man of vision would possibly choose it!

A low murmur arose among the gathered military officers. Their hushed whispers stirred the congregation like a gentle breeze sweeping through an empty hall.

"Brother Ch'ing," said the Heavenly King, his forehead bathed with perspiration as he turned toward the Eastern King. "What is your opinion?"

"To attack Peking right away with our victorious army, of course, would be a correct policy," replied the Eastern King, stepping forward with a cynical smile. "But we must be aware of the fact that after more than two years of bloody fighting, our soldiers are exhausted. As we have just entered 'lesser paradise,' their morale will be dampened if they are ordered to embark on a northern expedition."

"Brother Ch'ang," the Heavenly King turned to the Northern King while wiping his forehead with one hand. "What do you think?"

"May I report to Second Brother," Wei Ch'ang-hui replied

with a smile. "The ancient military strategists have taught us that swiftness is the first principle of any military campaign and that we must attack at the first drum roll. However . . ." Wei gave a quick glance at the Assistant King before continuing. "When we captured Wuchang, our Second Brother proclaimed that after we entered 'lesser paradise' the brothers would be permitted to reunite with their families and that single men and women could marry. The family is the foundation of the state. Without it the state cannot survive. Furthermore, the head of state must rule with credibility as well as righteousness. As our Second Brother speaks on behalf of the Heavenly Father and Heavenly Brother, he can't disregard his own words. Yet I must admit I'm rather ignorant. If I've said anything absurd," he paused to cast a glance at the Heavenly King and the Eastern King, "our Second Brother and Fourth Brother will correct me." Having finished, he returned to his original position.

"That's right!" cried Hung Jen-fa, elder brother of the Heavenly King. "You are the Heavenly King. You can't go back on your own words! Now that we've established the capital, you've moved into the imperial palace. But what about our brothers who have shed their own blood fighting the enemy? Each of them should be entitled to an official residence and a few beautiful women, at least. Now that you have all the glory and pleasures of an emperor, shouldn't they, as the pillars of the state, be entitled to something too? Take Brother Ch'in Jih-kang as an example—he is well over thirty and still a bachelor! I think he should be given a wife!" Hung spoke with his usual heavy Kueichow accent. He loved to poke fun at Ch'in Jih-kang.

The sound of laughter reverberated throughout the hall. "You can speak for yourself for all I care," Ch'in retorted quietly, "but don't make fun of me!" Although Ch'in had spoken in hushed tones, everyone had clearly heard what he had said. Another round of laughter ensued.

Attempting to put a stop to this unceremonious levity, the Heavenly King quickly cast a disdainful look at his brother.

Quietness and solemnity returned to the hall.

"Your Majesty, Lord of Ten Thousand Years!" State Minister Hu I-kuang spoke up solemnly and evenly. "Your servant remembers that when the Heavenly Army occupied Yung-an-chou the year before last, some brothers didn't feel like venturing outside their hometown and wanted to stay on in that little, isolated city. Luckily, Your Majesty and the Eastern King displayed clear vision and led the army northward. Soon we conquered Yüeh-chou and Wuchang. Your Majesty and the Eastern King were always in complete command of the situation and the Heavenly Army advanced with lightning speed to defeat the Ch'ing demons. In your servant's estimation, the situation today is comparable to that at Yung-an-chou. Although the Heavenly Capital is rich in resources, your servant wishes Your Majesty will consider seriously an old adage, 'A boat floats on water, but can also topple over and sink under water.'"

"The words of the Assistant King and State Minister Hu are as precious as gold and pearls," declared Hung Hsüan-chiao, widow of the Western King, in a clear voice. "The Heavenly Army has disrupted the military plans of the Ch'ing demons. If we don't embark on a northern expedition right now and, instead, stay on in this isolated city, we will lose a golden opportunity. It will be regrettable indeed!"

"Second Brother!" the Assistant King Shih Ta-k'ai walked toward the imperial table and addressed the Heavenly King in deep and solemn tones. "Though I am untalented, I am willing to lead my army of fifty thousand to play the part of vanguard in the northern expedition. Fourth Brother will command the main army to attack the central region and cross the Yellow River in support. State Minister Hu I-kuang should be appointed to guard the Heavenly Capital and take care of logistics. Second Brother could then make his imperial appearance known in Honan. When the imperial regalia moves toward the north, people will know that our intention is not limited to the occupation of the southeast corner of the country alone. Our army must be always on the move."

"No one could fill the job of vanguard commander better than the Assistant King!" Hu I-kuang expressed his support.

"No one could fill the job of vanguard commander better than the Assistant King!" echoed others in the hall.

"Your Majesty!" A man approximately forty years old, with a light complexion and sparse beard, detached himself from the assembled line of military officials. "Your servant would like to put in a few words, but doubts if they are appropriate," he said respectfully.

"You may have. your say," commanded the Heavenly King. He appeared to relax as he saw that the new speaker was T'ang Cheng-ts'ai, Civilian State Minister and Commander of the Naval Forces. "Years ago when your servant was a timber trader, he visited Honan. Although the province is part of the central region, it suffers from frequent severe droughts. The land is infertile and the people are poor. Even when there is a good harvest, people still eat coarse buns. At times of famine, all they eat are elm tree bark and the droppings of passing wild geese. When the Heavenly Army, half-a-million strong, reaches Honan, what are they going to eat? The Heavenly Capital is well endowed with grain and supplies and fortified by city walls and deep moats, with the Yangtze River providing further protection. It has many advantages for either offense or defense. From time immemorial it has been the seat of government for many empires. In the opinion of your humble servant, it would be better to hold on to the Heavenly Capital and in the meantime build up our military supplies and construct a huge naval fleet. Our navy can put up a strong stand in the upper reaches of the Yangtze and then send our well-recuperated and trained army on a northern expedition. It is unnecessary for Your Majesty to lead the army personally on an expedition now!"

T'ang Cheng-ts'ai's words coincided perfectly with what the Heavenly King had in mind. T'ang's navy had achieved a great deal during the campaigns in Yüeh-chou and Wuchang; hence his words carried weight. More important, his idea of holding on to the Heavenly Capital and sending refreshed troops to the north at a later date was identical with the un-spoken but cherished idea of the Heavenly King himself.

At this time, a man in his thirties, tall in stature with a round face of light complexion and a cultivated demeanor, stepped forward from the foot of the steps. His name was Ho Chen-ch'uan, a *hsiu-ts'ai* degree holder, who had joined the T'ai-p'ings in Kwangsi in the early days of the uprising. His present position was that of court historian with the responsibility of recording the activities and decrees of the Heavenly King. Carrying a pile of documents in his hands, Ho ascended the steps slowly and presented a report to his sovereign with measured dignity.

Nanking has been the cradle of empires, ancient as well as modern. It is sheltered by the Bell Mountain, surrounded by the Yangtze River, connected with all the main thoroughfares of the realm, and cushioned by the Rear Lake at its back. Its geographical configurations symbolically resemble coiled dragons and crouching tigers and it holds the strategic keys to the adjacent Wu and Ch'u territories, where there are abundant sources of food and numerous men of talent. Indeed Nanking is the place where the foundation of an eternal empire should be laid. Your servant Ho Chen-ch'uan and other civilian officials, forty-one in all, have each respectfully written an essay on the topic "On the Establishment of the Heavenly Capital in Nanking" to celebrate this auspicious occasion. May we present them to our beloved sovereign!

Completing his oral report, Ho presented the documents with both hands. A female official received them and placed them on the imperial table. Ho returned to the place where he had stood.

The light in the Golden Dragon Hall gradually diminished

as the sun sank in the western sky. It seemed that among the military and civilian officials none was ready to advance further ideas.

"The establishment of the Heavenly Capital in Nanking," the Eastern King declared, and with a general sweep of the audience, continued with a deliberate tone, "is based on the will of the Heavenly Father, Heavenly Brother, and Second Brother. No more discussion on the subject is necessary for the time being. Brother Ta-k'ai is truly commendable for having volunteered to lead the army on a northern expedition. However, an old saying tells us that 'those who win the heart of the people win the country.' Second Brother has publicly said that we will rest our soldiers and horses after the taking of Nanking. Such a promise must be kept at all costs. In my humble opinion, as Second Brother is the sovereign of the state, he should not leave the capital; and since Brother Ta-k'ai is a pillar of the nation, a more urgent mission is going to be assigned to him."

"What about the northern expedition?" asked the Heavenly King.

"There are two able generals who can accomplish the northern expedition competently. Vice State Minister Lin Feng-hsiang and State Minister Li K'ai-fang have become seasoned in battles and are still in their prime. These two generals can perform this arduous mission in lieu of the Assistant King. Brother Lo Ta-kang, being intelligent and brave, should remain in Chinkiang to look after military affairs. This arrangement, I believe, will be appropriate."

"We are glad to accept the mission of a northern expedition," declared the two generals, Lin Feng-hsiang and Li K'ai-fang, stepping forward and kneeling before the Heavenly King. "We will not flinch from the task even if it means dashing our brains on the ground or dying a death of ten thousand cuts."

Facing the assembled officials, the Eastern King made an official announcement: "In view of the fact that Anhwei province has just been incorporated into our territory and that the people have not yet been completely pacified, the Assistant King is hereby ordered to rush there with his soldiers to undertake pacification work. Further, an elite corp of ten thousand men selected among the soldiers of the great camp shall be put under the control of Generals Lin and Li to embark on a northern expedition starting from Yangchow."

Silence again prevailed in Golden Dragon Hall. The deep, resolute voice of the Eastern King seemed to reverberate around the rafters and beams. As the Eastern King cast a sharp and meaningful glance at the Heavenly King, the latter felt a sense of relief and satisfaction.

"Since the uprising of our righteous army at Chin-t'ien," the Heavenly King said in a deliberately slow voice to the two kneeling officers, "Vice State Minister Lin Feng-hsiang and State Minister Li K'ai-fang have performed extraordinary, meritorious services. Lin Feng-hsiang is hereby invested as the Marquis of Ching-hu and Li K'ai-fang as the Marquis of Ting-hu. It is hoped that they will march on Peking directly without wasting time in attacking less important cities!"

"We are most grateful," said Lin and Li, respectfully knocking their heads on the ground, "for the grace shown us by the Heavenly Father, Heavenly Brother, and Your Majesty. We'll follow the instructions of Your Majesty and will march on Peking directly and bring the head of the chief demon Hsien-feng back to be offered as a trophy before the throne!"

The Heavenly King's pronouncement astonished several generals and military officers, including Shih Ta-k'ai, Hu I-kuang, and Hung Hsüan-chiao. But by this time, the Eastern King had turned to face his sovereign and all military and civilian officials followed suit, kneeling before the throne to shout "May the lord live ten thousand years!" three times. Thus concluded the first imperial court meeting of the T'ai-p'ing government.

The day after the court meeting, State Minister Hu I-kuang arrived at the residence of the Assistant King to bid farewell on his Anhwei assignment. Generals Lin Feng-hsiang and Li K'ai-fang, who had been appointed to head the northern expedition had also come to ask for advice. Being intimate friends of the Assistant King, the three were invited to the study to have a heart-to-heart talk.

The four men spoke emotionally about what had happened at the court meeting and the discussion concerning the northern expedition. Very much agitated, Shih Ta-k'ai paced the floor back and forth grasping and ungrasping the handle of his sword.

"Lord of Five Thousand Years," said Lin Feng-hsiang. "You know that Brother K'ai-fang and I were blacksmiths by profession. We have never read a book and can recognize only a few characters. And although we've fought a few battles, it was only by the grace of the Heavenly Father and Heavenly Brother and the planning of the Eastern King and you, the Assistant King that we've been able to avoid disaster. But I'm not sure if the chief demon Hsien-feng would willingly offer his head to us this time. My lord, you must give us your advice as you have before!"

Originally a blacksmith from Hsün-chou, Kwangsi province, Lin Feng-hsiang was a swarthy, sparse-bearded man of short stature and thin build. But he had a loud, ringing voice of bell-like clarity. Li K'ai-fang cut a tall and imposing figure. He had sunken eyes and high cheekbones, and seldom laughed or spoke, giving the impression of being constantly immersed in deep thought. In their youth, the two had been apprenticed to a master blacksmith and later partners in a smithy. Together they had joined the God Worshippers Society at Thistle Mountain. Since the time of the Chin-t'ien uprising, they had always fought together as vanguards, attacking cities and battling enemies with exceptional valor. Although neither was any more than twenty-seven or twenty-eight years old, they had fought no less than one hundred successful battles.

Li K'ai-fang remained silent, but his deep-set eyes were fixed unblinkingly on the face of the Assistant King.

"Peking is the lair of the Ch'ing demons," said Shih Ta-k'ai. His voice revealed deep concern, although he appeared to be gazing at something outside the window. "It is well protected and heavily fortified. Furthermore, it is more than a thousand *li* from here, separated from us by rivers and mountains. To venture deep into enemy territory with a small army of ten thousand men is against every principle of sound military strategy."

"I am aware of that," said Lin Feng-hsiang emotionally. "The northern expedition is a difficult task which can be taken up only by able generals like the Eastern King or you, the Assistant King. But the Eastern King is committed to the defense of the Heavenly Capital and you, the Assistant King, to the pacification of Anhwei. Brother K'ai-fang and I have no other choice but to take up this heavy burden ourselves."

"If we fail to obtain the head of the chief demon Hsien-feng," Li broke his silence. "We won't be able to return with impunity."

"Comrades!" Shih Ta-k'ai said. "I don't doubt for a minute your talents and loyalty. What worries me is the idea of your small army penetrating deep into enemy territory. If I were to remain in the capital, I could constantly remind the Heavenly King to send more supplies and reinforcements. But I've been assigned the thankless job of pacification in Anhwei." Turning to face Hu I-kuang, he continued, "I-kuang, the task of sending reinforcements to the northern expedition army and other matters in the court will squarely rest on your shoulders!"

"Lord of Five Thousand Years!" Hu cried, his voice breaking. "Please rest assured that as long as I remain in the court, I'll do my duty to assist in state affairs." Hu then turned to face the two generals. "After the army embarks on the expedition, I'll report to the Eastern King to send supplies and reinforcements."

"From the very beginning you must march day and night

without rest," Shih advised. "It is imperative to exterminate the Ch'ing demons with lightning speed. Fight only when you are sure to win. Otherwise, leave the enemy alone. You have to reach Peking as fast as you can. The heavenly soldiers coming from Kwangtung, Kwangsi, Hunan, and Hupeh are not accustomed to the climate and diet of the north. Therefore, a fast advance will be to our advantage and delay may very well spell defeat. As for military strategy and tactics, they should be flexible and adjusted to the circumstances. No established rules should be followed."

The two generals listened with rapture, stood up and saluted, bowing deeply. "Lord of Five Thousand Years! We'll remember your advice!"

"Are there any further instructions regarding the affairs of the court?" Hu inquired.

"As far as that goes, we can only wait and see!" replied Shih resignedly with a deep sigh. "There are plenty of relevant historical examples. Huang Ch'ao in ancient times and Li Ch'uang in the recent past both made the same mistake. As soon as they captured the capital, they built palaces, appropriated beautiful women, hid themselves in the deep recesses of their palaces, and forgot all about the destiny of the empire and the sufferings of the people. I'm not afraid of the scourge of war, but of success eluding us at the last minute!"

The three listeners were deeply moved and remained silent for a long while. "I'll remember the farsighted words of my Lord of Five Thousand Years!" Hu finally broke the awkward silence in the room. "We who are in the service of the sovereign can only do our utmost until we die. I, Hu I-kuang, hereby respectfully bid my lords farewell and wish you success in your ventures!"

n mid-August of that year (1853, the third year, *Kuei-hao*, of the T'ai-p'ing calendar) there was an atmosphere of great festivity in the official residence of the Eastern King. The presidents of the six boards, regular and assistant secretaries and retainers, both male and female, busily worked to prepare for the celebration of the birthday of the Eastern King, his first since entering the Heavenly Capital.

On the day of his birthday, the red main gate of the Eastern King's official residence, freshly decorated with yellow satin panels on which dragon and phoenix designs had been painted, was wide open. From the gate to the main hall, a row of red palace lanterns hung high overhead. Soft music was played by musicians in both corridors while gatekeepers in official attire stood at attention. Eight ushers deployed themselves on both sides of the hall, receiving well-wishers—military and civilian officials and comrades old and new. Presidents and vice-presidents of the six boards—personnel, finance, rites, military affairs, punishments, and works—were assigned the duty of receiving important guests and their gifts. Female officials of the Eastern King's establishment, attired in gold-embroidered red robes and round gauze hats with the centers hollowed to free their lofty coiffures, strolled aimlessly back and forth to display their fineries. Concubines and maids, also in high spirits, paraded their charms.

Since early morning, military and civilian officials had been arriving in droves at the official residence of the Eastern King. Each bore gifts and was followed by attendants. They filed through the gate according to rank to offer their congratulations. Among the well-wishers were men who had worked in the fields or in the charcoal kilns together with the Eastern King on Thistle Mountain and old comrades who had joined his army in Chin-t'ien. Although still low in rank, these men had pooled their resources in order to buy him a few gifts. The Eastern King had ordered the gatekeepers and the presidents and vice-presidents of the six boards to receive all guests politely regardless of social station. Some guests were even granted private audiences with the Eastern King to reminisce about old times. As the sun gradually sank below the western horizon and the flow of guests slackened, the Eastern King felt a little fatigued. He retreated from the main hall to his Purple Cloud Enclosure in the rear garden for a rest.

The Eastern King's official residence had originally been the home of the Ch'ing Commissioner of Salt Transport of Shantung province. There was a garden in the rear which had been repaired and the flowerbeds had been replanted with a large number of peonies and hibiscus. Fresh lotus blossoms and green leaves filled an artificial pond. A riot of dark red and light purple graced the water and the flowerbeds. On a previous occasion when the court historian, Ho Chen-ch'uan, paid a visit to the garden, the Eastern King, in a pleasant mood, had ordered Ho to give a name to his pleasure ground. Without hesitation, Ho wrote on a piece of paper three big characters— "Purple Cloud Enclosure"—which were later carved on a horizontal placard and hung in the entrance hall. Later, the Eastern King ordered two pavilions built besides the lotus pond. One was called "Cloud Gazing Tower" and was used as his study; the other was named "Rarity Depository Tower" and was filled with antiques, treasures, paintings and calligraphy— gifts from officials and generals under his control.

As the Eastern King mounted Cloud Gazing Tower, he could see beautifully attired concubines, maids, and female officials rushing to and fro among the artificial rockeries and footpaths. All of them were in a joyful mood, giggling and chattering incessantly. Some of the girls carried fruit baskets and pastry containers; others held teapots and cups, spittoons, and featherdusters. Still others attended to incense burners or were simply there to clean the windows. The fragrant smell of lotus blossoms and leaves and the soft music of strings and pipes floated in the air, following the gentle breeze.

A young official, led by two female officials, walked on a flower-strewn path towards Cloud Gazing Tower. On his head was a hat decorated with the design of a double dragon, a single phoenix, and a hundred butterflies, and was embroidered with his official title "Honorary State Minister." The young man's yellow robe and jacket of dragon design also displayed the embroidered title. In one hand, he carried an object in the shape of a lantern covered with a red satin hood. As they stopped in front of the tower, a female official went upstairs to report his presence. Soon she descended and announced pleasantly, "His lordship of Nine Thousand Years welcomes your honor."

As the official reached the top floor, he saw the Eastern King attired in leisure dress gazing at the evening clouds by a golden painted railing. As he dared not disturb the Eastern King, the young man held his breath and waited patiently. The Eastern King was looking at a red-walled, green-tiled palace in the distance. The white marble steps in front of the main hall could be counted in the reflection of the setting sun. Painted pillars and flying eaves added majesty to the building's appearance. The sound of bells and drums from within the red walls could be heard from time to time. This was the palace of the Heavenly King.

After a long silence, the Eastern King turned to face his visitor.

"Ch'ien-fang, my younger brother!" he said. "Why are you so late? There may not be any more longevity noodles left for you!"

Putting down the lantern-shaped object on the floor, Hou Ch'ien-fang knelt before the Eastern King in greeting.

"Your servant is late," Hou said smilingly, "and dares not ask for any longevity noodles! Please, your lordship, pardon me for old time's sake. May your lordship live nine thousand years!"

A female official brought in tea, placed it on the table and retreated.

"Now that you're an honorary state minister," declared the Eastern King with a broad grin, "you've learned to talk mandarin like the others—'your servant,' 'beg your pardon,' and so on. I don't care for such expressions!"

"By the grace of your lordship," Hou said, "your servant was promoted to the rank of honorary state minister a month ago. Your servant had long intended to come to express his deep gratitude. But much time was spent on finding a suitable present for your lordship. Your servant was aware that there would be a crowd here today, so he purposely came late."

"My brother! Such thoughtfulness is rather unnecessary," said the Eastern King. "What's hidden there?" The Eastern King liked to hold gab sessions with his comrades from Kwangsi who had shared hard times with him. Such sessions gave him the feeling of putting on slippers after having walked in a pair of heavy boots.

Leisurely, Hou held the object in question high over his shoulders and removed the gold-embroidered red satin cover. Thus revealed a splendid gold-wired bird cage with ivory fittings. A white parrot, newly groomed, hopped up and down in the cage, seemingly dazzled by its new surroundings. The bird tilted its head and stared at Hou with a puzzled look. Coaxed by a low whistle from Hou, the bird responded loudly:

"Wishing the Eastern King happiness! Long live the Eastern King! May he live ten thousand years, ten thousand years!"

"You're wrong!" the Eastern King gave forth a hearty laughter and tapped the cage lightly with his middle finger. "I'm the Lord of Nine Thousand Years, not ten thousand years!"

The white parrot repeated stubbornly, "May the Eastern King live ten thousand years, ten thousand years!"

"Where did you get this queer bird?" inquired the Eastern King.

"Your servant sneaked into Nanking last fall to gather military intelligence by order of your lordship. All the time, he had in mind to find a birthday present for your lordship," answered Hou Ch'ien-fang respectfully.

"You devil!" the Eastern King slapped Hou's back affectionately.

"As birthday gifts always come in pairs," said Hou, "your servant has prepared an even more precious present for your lordship." Lowering his voice, Hou continued, holding one thumb up. "A rare treasure from the south of the Yangtze!"

"What is it?" the Eastern King's interest was aroused.

Hou told his story slowly and deliberately. The Eastern King first expressed astonishment, then frowned slightly, and finally broke out into hysterical laughter, much to the surprise of Hou Ch'ien-fang. Suddenly, the expression on the Eastern King's face turned icy cold.

"What a devil you are!" roared the Eastern King, banging his fist on the table. "I appointed you to gather military intelligence and you spent huge sums of money from the sacred treasury on a prostitute. Your 'retainer' has already reported that to me, but I didn't want to expose you on account of our past relationship. Now that this woman's been snatched by someone else, you're trying to sow discord between the Northern King and me. Ch'ang-hui and I are like brothers and we are both pillars of the state. Would I jeopardize our brotherly relationship just for a woman? I think you've defected and turned into a spy for the demons! Don't think I'll spare your life for that! Where are the attendants?"

Frightened by the loud outburst, the parrot chattered incoherently, excitedly flapping its wings.

Hou Ch'ien-fang fell on his knees and banged his head on the floor until blood appeared on his forehead. "Lord of Nine Thousand Years! Let me finish what I have to say before your lordship puts me to death!"

Two beautifully attired female officials entered the room and stood on one side breathlessly waiting for instructions.

An expression of amiability returned abruptly to the Eastern King's face. Pointing a finger at the bird cage, he commanded, "This is a gift from Honorary State Minister Hou. Take it away and feed it well. Then hang it in my study."

The two female officials looked at each other nonplussed, and went downstairs with the cage.

"You may say what you want. But beware of my sword if you make a mistake!" the Eastern King said gravely.

"Your servant's original intent was to use the brothel as

The parrot is presented to the Eastern King as a birthday present.

a safe place to hide himself," Hou reported, wiping the cold sweat from his forehead. "As soon as the heavenly soldiers entered Nanking, he would have presented Red Phoenix to your lordship." After a short pause, he continued, "Of course, the Northern King had no way of knowing your servant's intentions. Otherwise, he would not have dared take Red Phoenix to his official residence. Your lordship gives first priority to the brotherly relationship between the leaders of the state, an attitude which conforms exactly to the old saying, 'The magnanimity of a prime minister should be as boundless as the ocean.'"

Detecting a softening in the expression on the Eastern King's face, Hou continued. "Several months ago, I had sent for my mother and a younger sister from Kwangsi. Your lordship is over thirty years old. He may need a woman of tender heart to take care of him. If your lordship doesn't mind . . ."

The Eastern King did not stop him, nor did he show indignation. Reassured, Hou made a forthright proposal: his younger sister, Hou Hui-fang, would substitute for Red Phoenix. Although she offered no comparison to Red Phoenix in beauty, she was nonetheless a virgin.

The Eastern King accepted the unusual gift. Several days later, without the knowledge of Hou Ch'ien-fang, the Eastern King dispatched a female aide to the official residence of the Northern King to deliver an oral message: "It is said that the Northern King has taken on a Rouge Well Lane prostitute named Red Phoenix. This prostitute has rendered service to the Heavenly Kingdom by assisting in the collection of military intelligence before the occupation of Nanking. It is the intention of the Eastern King to reward her with an official position." To this oral message, the Northern King gave a straightforward reply: "There is no prostitute in your younger brother's residence, nor any woman answering to the name of Red Phoenix. If Fourth Brother wishes to search for her in the other official residences, I'll be glad to assist."

Upon hearing this response, the Eastern King angrily

smashed a delicately carved red jade lion on the floor in his study. An hour earlier, a tribute vase made in Ching-teh-chen was also smashed in a similar fashion in the study of the Northern King. Of course, the Eastern King could not have heard it.

THREE

Following the taking of Nanking by the T'ai-p'ing army, the Ch'ing court hurriedly dispatched "competent officials" to reinforce the two camps that had been set up to the north and south of the Yangtze River. The commander of the South Camp, Hsiang Jung, had been trailing the T'ai-p'ings all the way from Kwangsi to Chiangnan. Always timid and vacillating, he had never fought a decisive battle. Yet among the Ch'ing generals, it was Hsiang who was most familiar with the real situation in the T'ai-p'ing army. Although fully aware of the general's mediocrity, the emperor Hsien-feng did not want to discard him outright. Instead, he was given the title of Imperial Commissioner and placed on probation in that position on the battlefield of Nanking. The commander of the North Camp, Ch'i Shan, was a capable Manchu general who was regarded with high esteem and great expectations by

74

the emperor.

An array of newly appointed officials had been sent to assist Commander Ch'i Shan in the North Camp. Ch'en Chin-shou and Sheng Pao became his assistants in military affairs. A number of other important government officials were drafted from various provinces to strengthen the leadership of the camp. Since Yangchow, the seat of the North Camp, was on the main thoroughfare connecting Nanking to Peking, its strategic importance was obvious. From the commander down, all generals responsible for military operations were Manchus. In the South Camp, the court appointed one Chiang Chung-yüan to assist the commander. In addition, many other officials were added to the roster of assistants. As a result, the two camps were filled with capable officials and seasoned generals, all the best of the land.

The commander of the South Camp, Hsiang Jung, had received the seal of Imperial Comissioner when he was trailing the T'ai-p'ings en route to Chiukiang. Grateful for the honor yet somewhat perturbed, he was anxious to win a quick victory. Day after day he stood beside the river and gazed at Nanking, quietly formulating his plans. His main army, twenty thousand strong, was stationed in Hsiao-ling-wei, south of Nanking. He had sent small detachments to attack Bell Mountain, Chung-ho Bridge, T'ung-chi Gate, and other localities, defeating in some skirmishes the T'ai-p'ing army. Thus he regularly sent reports of grossly exaggerated victories and impractical military plans to the court to placate the emperor. However, since the Eastern King had adopted an entrenchment policy, Hsiang Jung could do no more than wait outside the city, and certainly was not making any real attempt to attack it. Nanking was bound by the Yangtze in the west, protected by a lake in the north, and surrounded by a chain of hills and rivers to the east and south. The only approach to the city was by way of Purple Gold Mountain and Dragon Neck Trail where heavy fortifications and deep ditches had been constructed by the order of the Eastern King. As part of the T'ai-p'ing's well-conceived defense plan, even inmates of the women's quarters had been ordered to whittle bamboo spikes and plait heavy ropes to be used for defense purposes. Facing such odds, Hsiang Jung was at his wits' end and could do nothing. In addition, after the occupation of Nanking, Honorary State Minister T'ang Cheng-ts'ai, commander of the T'ai-p'ing naval forces, had constructed fleets of fighting frigates and transport boats and had trained naval cadets and sailors. From Wu-hu down to Chinkiang, the Yangtze River had been transformed into the transportation canal of the Heavenly Kingdom. Hence there was an abundance of grain and supplies for the army and both men and horses were well fed, while Hsiang Jung's army was poorly supplied and soldiers were not regularly paid. Being a Han Chinese general, Hsiang Jung was held in contempt by the Board of Finance which openly displayed prejudice against him. The amount of payments in arrears often reached as high as several hundred thousand taels. Further, the corrupt practice of discounting payments and deliberately overrunning expenditures was rampant among the generals. When wages and rations finally trickled down to the common soldier, he was left with next to nothing. Naturally, soldiers couldn't fight on empty stomachs and incidents of rioting and plundering occurred frequently.

As the T'ai-p'ing army embarked on the northern expedition and threatened Honan, Emperor Hsien-feng was alarmed. The commander of the North Camp, Ch'i Shan, sent urgent requests for reinforcements night and day. Since all the available forces of the nation were concentrated in these two camps, the court could do nothing except to order Hsiang Jung to send his men to the North Camp. Thereafter, every time the T'ai-p'ings took action, whether in Kiangsi, Chinkiang, or Yangchow, the court would order Hsiang Jung to contain them, as if the South Camp were a military reserve from which the court could withdraw on demand. In this fashion the scores of generals and the twenty thousand troops and officers of the South Camp were gradually depleted. Once distinguished by its stock of men and equipment, the South Camp had become as hollow as a giant termite-ridden tree.

Waiting anxiously for the news of a victory over the T'ai-p'ings, Emperor Hsien-feng became furious when no such definitive report was forthcoming from Hsiang Jung.

"Your troops have surrounded the city for a long time," wrote the Emperor in vermilion ink to the commander. 'If no other plans are devised to affect a successful attack, the result will be the exhaustion of the troops and the depletion of your supplies." On another occasion he wrote, "How shameless of you to use clever arguments to evade responsibility!" And again: "Since becoming commander, . . . your reports have been full of either excuses for your failure to attack or vague descriptions of future plans. For the past several months not a single report of a solid victory has reached us. . . . It seems that you, the commander, are plagued by your irresponsibility and craftiness, and that you have no intention to make amends. You are thoroughly despicable!"

The reaction of Hsiang Jung to these insults was at first one of trepidation, then nonchalance, and finally indignation. A few grumbling sentences began to appear occasionally in his memorials to the throne. "My troops and generals are reduced daily," complained Hsiang in one report, "because men have been sent to other sections as reinforcements and generals have been ordered to take up defense duties elsewhere." On another occasion he wrote, "My troops are tired of giving support to all quarters!" And again: "The difference between being hungry and having a full stomach and between being exhausted and well recuperated is obvious to all, not necessarily to the wise alone!" Finally in desperation Hsiang had the gumption to state, "To attack on land is impossible, while to attack by water is impractical; we are facing a well-fortified city without viable means of conducting a siege." In addition, Hsiang adopted Ch'i Shan's strategy and requested the transfer of one thousand cavalry troops from the North Camp to reinforce his army. This evoked an angry reply from Hsien-feng in yet another vermilion rescript: "Since you started trailing the bandits from Kwangsi to Chiangnan, you have achieved nothing at all. How dare you ask for troops from the North Camp?This can never be permitted! If you persist in making this request, you might as well send your head to Peking!" Following this merciless scolding, Hsiang was again ordered to attack Nanking immediately.

These heated exchanges of polemics between the emperor and the commander were of course not known to the Eastern King and his generals. But his two year's experience of fighting the Ch'ing soldiers told him that their intermittent gunfire, aimless shooting, and meaningless movements of small detachments of troops were merely necessary actions by which the Ch'ing army could justify its meager allowance of military supplies.

The situation convinced the Eastern King that his policy of entrenchment was entirely correct. The policies of "attacking the north" and "pacifying the south" advocated by Shih Ta-k'ai and Lo Ta-kang had proved to be superfluous. The Eastern King firmly believed that due to the reputation of the T'ai-p'ing army and the fear generated thus far in the hearts of government officials and the populace, the two seasoned generals, Lin and Li, with their ten thousand experienced Kwangtung and Kwangsi soldiers would certainly enter Peking and capture the head demon Hsien-feng alive in a short time. Within the Heavenly Capital, the Eastern King was personally responsible for the city's defense; on the outside, General Lo Ta-kang and others stationed in Chinkiang and elsewhere could respond in case of emergency. The Yangtze River, patrolled by the T'ai-p'ing's well-equipped and well-trained naval forces, provided convenient transportation for supplies. The hinterland of Anhwei and Kiangsi became natural barriers and providers of resources for the regime. The unification of the entire nation under the T'ai-p'ings, in the estimation of the Eastern King, would be realized within two or three years.

As far as the Eastern King Yang Hsiu-ch'ing was concerned, the sporadic sound of gunfire from the Ch'ing camp was nothing to be worried about, because he was convinced that all his plans and actions had been correct. Weren't the numerous victories that the T'ai-p'ing army had won in the past two years proof enough? To him, the final victory and the conquest of all China was a foregone conclusion. From the standpoint of the Heavenly King, Hung Hsiu-ch'üan, the present and future success of the T'ai-p'ing movement was merely the result of his ability "to interpret the Heavenly Mandate." Ten years ago he was only a conscientious and intelligent village teacher who had, with the image of a black-robed, golden-bearded God in his mind, established the God Worshippers Society. Of the past ten years, he had spent the first eight on the battlefield as the leader of the uprising and the commander of the rebel forces. While fighting, he constantly and earnestly tested his strong belief in the religion of his own creation. During the last two years, however, he had retreated gradually to the position of a mere spiritual leader and the head of a religious sect. In the recesses of his palace, he was now waiting, . . . waiting for the grace of the Heavenly Father that would award him peace and glory.

Ever since the demise, or rather the "return to heaven," of the Southern King, Feng Yün-shan, and the Western King, Hsiao Ch'ao-kuei, the year before at Fisherman's Raincoat Ferry and the city of Changsha respectively, all political and military affairs of the Heavenly Kingdom had begun to rest on the shoulders of the Eastern King alone. In generosity and prudence, the Eastern King could not measure up to the Southern King, Feng Yün-shan. Nor could he be compared with the Western King, Hsiao Ch'ao-kuei, in sincerity toward friends and loyalty to the leader. But in making strategic decisions, the Eastern King was versatile and resourceful and on the battlefield his bravery and resolution were legendary. From Yung-an-chou to the Heavenly Capital, every battle he won enchanced his reputation and authority. Furthermore, the frequent mystical trances he experienced in which the Heavenly Father "revealed Himself" via the Eastern King as medium added an aura of divine sanction to his authority. In these trance sessions, important public policies were often devised and difficult decisions made, most of which had later turned out to be correct. The name of the Eastern King, therefore, was respected inside and outside the court, in the barracks as well as in civilian quarters, and there was always a sense of mystery attached to his name. Even the Heavenly King himself, while claiming the ability "to interpret the Heavenly Mandate," sometimes wondered why the Heavenly Father had selected this man to transmit His will. Still, there was no denying that some officials and people had the feeling that the behavior of the Eastern King was a little too arrogant. Sometimes even in the presence of the Heavenly King, he shed all inhibitions. However, since the establishment of the Heavenly Capital, he had managed political and military affairs well. Everything went on without a hitch. The war effort was pursued as planned and the people were contented. The two Ch'ing military camps with their tens of thousands of troops commanded by imperial commissioners and viceroys could not intimidate the Eastern King in any way.

The Eastern King was the Great Wall of the Heavenly Kingdom. With him by his side, the Heavenly King could afford to enjoy a carefree life in his palace. After the conquering of Wuchang and Nanking, General Supervisor of Court Affairs Meng Teh-en, who was in charge of the women's barracks and women's quarters, had selected no less than one hundred young maidens to fill the Heavenly King's harem. All these pretty girls, ranging from sixteen to nineteen in age, came from well-to-do families in Kiangsu, Chekiang, Hunan, and Hupeh. However, despite their infinite charm and alluring figures, they did not make an overwhelming impression on the Heavenly King, a man who had spent half his life in poverty and hardship. To him the presence of these lovely young creatures was not any different from the exotic flowers blooming in the imperial garden.

Among all the women in his harem, the Heavenly King was most attached to his first wife whose maiden name was Lai. She had always shared his fate, sufferings, and crises in life, and was loyally at his side whether he was unsuccessfully taking the civil service examinations or organizing the God Worshippers Society; she was there when he had started the conspiracy at Thistle Mountain and when he began the open rebellion at Chin-t'ien. Throughout these trying times, she had been his wife and companion and was one of the first converts to his religion. In their hometown, they had lived in a dilapidated hut, and sustained themselves on nothing more than congee and potatoes, while working bare-footed in the fields together. Although she had never spent a single day in school, she had learned the traditional morality requir- ed of women and respected her husband. She understood only vaguely the religious doctrines of the God Worshippers Society, but she sincerely believed that what her husband did was right. She was the only woman permitted to remain in camp with her husband during their campaigns. She had to walk, straw sandals on her feet, behind her husband's mount in the daytime. At night, she would prepare his sleeping bag, darn his uniform, and nurse his wounds, even sucking out pus from them when they became infected. Upon the establishment of the Heavenly Capital, she automatically was given the title of Queen, but she did not know how to enjoy the luxurious life appropriate to her station. The Bureau of the Imperial Wardrobe presented to her beautiful satin dresses and pearl-studded shoes, the likes of which she had seen only on the stage when she was a young girl. She kept these treasures in trunks and wore them only on occasions, once a month or so. When the officers of the Bureau of the Imperial Kitchen respectfully inquired what she wished to be served at mealtimes, she asked only for some cabbage and rice which to her were luxuries compared with the fare to which she had been accustomed. The Heavenly King did not feel offended by her excessive modesty, because he understood the tempera- ment of his wife, and knew that it would be better to leave her alone than to force her to live a life of luxury. Each time the Heavenly King returned to the inner quarters after holding court, she would lead a battalion of palace women, most of them of her daughter's age, to welcome him. She always sought to persuade her husband to retire to the quarters of one or another consort and never demanded him for herself. Sometimes she felt apprehensive about the Heavenly King's overindulgence, but knowing his stubbornness and hot temper, she kept her peace. The only pleasure she enjoyed in the palace was conversation with her husband when he was in a good mood. On such occasions, they would reminisce on their sweet memories when they were newlyweds, and the social customs of their native village, exchange interesting battlefield stories, and so on. Sometimes they burst into hearty laughter together. But she now discovered that such occasions had become fewer and far between. The Heavenly King always lowered his voice when he talked about old times or even ordered attending women to leave the room, as if such conversations would diminish the dignity of the monarch. Sensing this change, she would feel overwhelmed by a wave of impotent sadness.

Among all the consorts, two were the Heavenly King's favorites. One was a twenty-odd-year-old girl, Consort Hsieh, from Kuei-p'ing county, Kwangsi province. When the Heavenly and Southern kings preached in Hsün-chou and the vicinity, this barely literate teenage daughter of a poor village teacher came often and listened attentively. Her mother had died young and she had been brought up by her father. Both enlisted when the uprising started and the father was appointed custodian of the Sacred Commissary. The intelligent and good-natured teenager soon caught the fancy of the Heavenly King's wife who took her in as her personal aide. Unable to cope with the hardships of travelling and changing climates, the father soon died of illness while on the march in Hunan. His daughter, however, had blossomed into an attractive young girl despite the arduous camp life. After the T'ai-p'ings captured Yüeh-chou, the Heavenly King's wife, out of pity for the orphaned girl, had made her her husband's first concubine. Although raised in a poor family, Hsieh had acquired some knowledge of the classics and history from her father, but still retained the naiveté of a country girl. Among all the consorts of the Heavenly King, with the possible exception of the Queen, Consort Hsieh understood the temperament and habits of the Heavenly King best, since she had shared the life of her lord during his younger years. The latter's love for her sprung largely from his memories of his struggles in those early days.

Another favorite was a nineteen-year-old girl, Consort Fang, who came from the same province as the Heavenly King. Originally from a merchant family of Hsiang-shan, she had, as a child, accompanied her father abroad on a business trip. When she returned to Kwangtung, she was already a teenager. On their way to Wuchang in the winter of the year after the rebellion started to visit her aunt, they had gotten caught in the fighting between the T'ai-p'ings and the Ch'ing army. Knowing that Wuchang could not be defended, the Ch'ing army plundered and looted before retreating. Many innocent people were killed, the girl's father and aunt among them. She herself was captured by the Ch'ing soldiers, but was later rescued by the men under the command of Meng Teh-en, now General Supervisor of Court Affairs, who was impressed by her past history and experience—she had lived abroad as a child and knew the language of the English barbarians. To avenge the deaths of her father and aunt, the girl resolutely begged the strangely attired "long haired official" to permit her to enlist as a private. Meng Teh-en appreciated a rarity when he saw one. Knowing how to curry favor with his chief, he presented the girl to the Heavenly King. Soon after she became a consort, her talents were discovered. Not only was she well-versed in the Chinese classics and history, but also knew a great deal about the social customs and etiquette of the Western barbarians. A month after the taking of the Heavenly Capital, Sir George Bonham, Plenipotentiary, Superintendant of Trade, and Governor of Hongkong, arrived at Nanking aboard the frigate "Hermes," commanded by Captain Fishbourne and accompanied by T. T. Meadows, an interpreter. The minister secured an audience with the Heavenly King who for the first time as the sovereign of a state received a representative of the "foreign brethren." Consort Fang was ordered to don the court costume of a male official to perform the duties of an adviser and interpreter. The blue-eyed, yellow-bearded foreign diplomats felt that the T'ai-p'ing leaders were forthright and reasonable who had none of the perverted, debased habits characteristic of the Ch'ing mandarins. They were even more impressed by the young official, beautifully attired and admirably mannered, who spoke fluent, flawless English in an effeminate voice.

When the T'ai-p'ing empire was first established, all consorts in the palace were forbidden to participate in state affairs. Female officials, no matter how high their ranks, were only assigned such routine duties as drafting decrees and transmitting orders. The Heavenly King would become extremely angry whenever he found out that any of his consorts had discussed anything concerning state affairs. The punishment could be extremely severe. Only Consorts Hsieh and Fang were exceptions. Not only could they ask the Heavenly King about political and military matters when he was found in a good mood, but he had occasionally explained to them perplexing problems and even solicited their opinions as well. After holding court, the Heavenly King spent most of his time at either the quarters of Consort Hsieh or that of Consort Fang. Being a talented artist, Consort Hsieh could paint beautiful pictures of birds and flowers, and could play Chinese chess expertly. Consort Fang was not only an excellent player of the Chinese musical instrument *p'i-p'a*, but also the organ, euphemistically called the "eight-note box." In his leisure time, the Heavenly King frequently played chess with Consort Hsieh while listening to music performed by Consort Fang. An entire afternoon could be spent pleasantly analyzing historical events and discussing painting and poetry with the two women.

The work of converting the former residence of the Viceroy of Liang-chiang into the Imperial Palace started in the fourth month of the third year, *Kuei-hao*, of the T'ai-p'ing calendar (June 1853). Sacred soldiers of the masons' and carpenters' camps together with thousands of common laborers were mobilized to undertake the project. The Heavenly Front Gate and the Main Dragon Hall were completed in a short time. The inner palace quarters were finished in six months. All timbers and bricks had been taken from the former Ming Palace and several dismantled Buddhist and Taoist temples in the city of Nanking. The buildings looked magnificent after they were completed. By early fall, only the work on the imperial garden remained unfinished.

Prior to the reconstruction of the imperial garden, an elder brother of the Heavenly King, Hung Jen-ta, had volunteered to tour all the gardens in the vicinity of Nanking to gather ideas on garden design. He had pictures of the best gardens painted and presented them to the Heavenly King. Gratified by this effort, the Heavenly King invited his brother to visit the palace and the rear garden. Hung Jen-ta, who had been a field hand all his life until recently, was dazzled by the sight of the green tiles and flying eaves of the main Dragon Hall and the white marble railings and painted beams of the corridors. As they walked to the rear garden which was separated from the inner palace quarters by a wooden picket fence, they saw over a thousand masons, carpenters, and common laborers busy at work, carrying bricks and stones, planting flowers and trees, building artificial rockeries, constructing pavilions, making screen walls, and paving roads. The workers streamed in and out without stop, giving an impression of great urgency. The Heavenly King and his brother halted at a site where an artificial rockery was under construction. "This rockery standing here alone looks like a plain boulder," said Hung Jen-ta. "Even with flowers and grass planted on its surface, it won't have the appearance of a natural hill. Recently, I saw a garden which once belonged to a demon dignitary that had a huge pond with two big artificial rockeries inside. The rockeries were covered with moss and were green all year round. Groves of dwarf bamboos and other trees were growing right in the middle sections of the rockeries. There was a little clay temple with figurines of women and children inside one rockery, while a pavilion with a figurine of a long-robed old man drinking tea had been placed in the other. Viewed from a distance, they looked like the Double-Knot Mountain of Kuei-p'ing county in Kwangsi where we had a hard battle with the demon soldiers. The rockeries sat in a pond with a white sand bottom that had been mixed with red and white pebbles. The water was crystal clear and a swarm of golden carps was swimming in it. It was certainly different from the green muddy water-holes we had back home. However, there were no lotuses or lilies in the demon's pond. I can't understand why the demon dignitary had three words '*Hsiao P'eng Lai*' or 'A Bed for Fairies' carved on a piece of marble right in the middle of one of the rockeries."

The Heavenly King knew that his brother, being almost illiterate, could recognize only a limited number of characters. They must have been "Abode of Fairies." But he just smiled and didn't correct his brother for his misidentification of characters.

"Listen, there were other strange things!" cried Hung Jen-ta. "In that big pond, in addition to the golden carps, there was a tortoise whose back was covered with green moss. When I was there, he was sunning himself at the foot of the rockery. As soon as he saw me approaching, he jumped into the pond with a splash."

The Heavenly King burst out into hearty laughter. He knew too well that his brother had worked in the fields most of his life. Despite the fact that he was only a little over forty, wrinkles lined his face and grey hair covered his head. Though he had contributed little to the war effort, he had suffered much hardship and gone through a great deal of danger just the same. Even though he was now enjoying a comfortable and luxurious life, he was still a country bumpkin in habits and thinking. However, as a brother, he was always solicitous and helpful.

"That's easy," said the Heavenly King. "We'll dig a large lake and build a pavilion in its center, then add a few pleasure boats in the lake. I bet it'll be better than the demon dignitary's "Abode of Fairies."

"If you intend to dig a lake," Hung Jen-ta said, "You'd better start early. The weather in Chiangnan is different from Kwangtung's. There will be frost and snow in winter. We won't be able to do anything then."

Consequently, an order was issued to dig a huge lake in the imperial garden. Experienced shipwrights were recruited to build pleasure boats. Construction work on the rear garden progressed rapidly and soon the inner palace quarters were no longer separated from it. Common workers, therefore, could no longer work there. Meng Teh-en, who had just been promoted to the position of state minister and was always resourceful and anxious to please, offered to select four hundred young girls from the women's quarters to undertake the task. He further selected four girls of seventeen and eighteen years of age to be appointed supervisors.

These Nanking girls coming from social backgrounds quite different from the Kwangtung and Kwangsi girls, had never done a single day's work in manual labor in their lives. They had lived under the rule of the Heavenly Kingdom for six months. Most of them had had their feet unbound after they were moved into the women's quarters. Limping about the garden, digging, and carrying mud was quite painful for them. However, they were young and active, and working in the imperial garden with their peers was better than languishing in the women's quarters. With hoes in hands and carrying-poles on their shoulders, they labored enthusiastically, ignoring their blistering hands and swelling feet. To them it was a novel experience in a new and fascinating environment.

One autumn day, when the crisp breezes began to chase away the summer heat and the chrysanthemums started to bloom, the Heavenly King paid a visit to the rear garden accompanied by the Queen, Consorts Hsieh and Fang, and a few female officials. They came with the intention of resting in a pavilion to enjoy the flowers and view the digging in progress. A big hole around the rockery had already been dug. The four hundred young girls, with their sleeves and trouser legs rolled up, dug and carried mud diligently. Gingerly they walked up and down the planks that had been placed over the mud, laughing and joking innocently. A lively atmosphere filled the air of the otherwise quiet garden.

In a pleasant mood, the Heavently King ordered a female official to summon the four girl supervisors. Having no time to change their clothes, the four girls appeared before the Heavenly King barefooted and with their hair disheveled. They knelt before him in silence.

The Heavenly King asked the first girl to tell him her name, hometown, and the whereabouts of her relatives.

"My name is Yang Ch'ang-mei; I am a native of Nanking," answered the first girl with self-assurance. "My father Yang Wen-fu had studied the classics when he was young, but never succeeded in passing the examination. Later he lost his eyesight. In desperation, he changed his profession and gave his children, my sister and me, singing lessons so that we could earn a meager living by singing in public places in the Ch'in-huai district. My sister is named Yang Shui-chiao. We lost contact with her when the Ch'ing demons fled the city and we are not sure whether she is still alive. But my father was made a chief of a men's quarters in Ch'in-huai district after the heavenly soldiers liberated the city. As he feels much happier than before, his health has improved and thirty or forty percent of his eyesight has been restored with treatment."

"Your father and I have shared the same fate—we both failed in the examinations given by the Ch'ing demons," said the Heavenly King with a benign smile. "Now I've become the Heavenly King and your father the chief of a men's quarters. He has twenty-five men under him and the rank of *liang-ssu-ma*. So both of us have obtained titles."

All the women present, including the female officials, laughed in response to the Heavenly King's light-hearted joke. Turning to the second girl, he asked the same questions.

"My name is Shih Ting-lan. My father was a flower farmer and we made a living by selling dried chrysanthemums and jasmines to herb pharmacists. Occasionally on the first and fifteenth days of a month and on festival days we sold sprigs of fresh flowers in the city. Our earnings were so meager we could only afford to eat congee most of the time; when business was bad, we ate flowers."

"How can flowers be eaten?" inquired Consort Fang innocently.

"Lotus and chrysanthemum petals can be mixed with wheat flour and baked into cakes. Hibiscus can be cooked in rice to make a tasty congee."

The Queen and Consort Hsieh sighed lightly in sympathy with the girl.

"One of you can sing and the other knows how to plant flowers. After the completion of the imperial garden, I'll appoint one of you to head the female musical troupe and the other chief gardener," promised the Heavenly King.

The two girls kowtowed to thank the Heavenly King for his grace. The other two girls were similarly questioned. Both were named Chu Chiu-mei, and were natives of Nanking; one was nineteen and the other seventeen. The seventeen-year-old was so naïve that she giggled constantly and audibly. Instead of feeling offended by the young girl's lack of decorum, the Heavenly King ordered the Bureau of Pastries to reward them with four boxes of Soochow style pastries. The Queen also gave each one of them a silk floss jacket. Finally, the Heavenly King told them that by the grace of the Heavenly Father and Heavenly Brother, the job of digging the artificial lake could proceed at a slower pace and need not be completed in such a hurry.

To their surprise, the four girl supervisors found the Heavenly King, who according to rumor was noted for his quick temper and extreme demands, very kind and accommodating. As his order reached the laboring girls, they felt relieved and gratified. Instead of slackening their pace, however, they redoubled their efforts at the site. But as the project progressed, the work became more difficult. In the beginning, the girls could still wear shoes and socks. After a month, water appeared in the depressed areas. At first, they used buckets to scoop out the accumulated liquid. Later, they had to use irrigation wheels to bail the water out. The work slowed down as the labor was thus divided. The ever-wet mud was difficult to dig and transport. These Chiangnan girls had never experienced such hardship. Their slender fingers became raw and bled, their delicate shoulders swelled, and their faces became haggard with exhaustion. Finally the sound of their ringing laughter gradually dissolved into rhythmic panting.

Time passed quickly. The Heavenly King had not visited the garden site for a while. In the eleventh month of the same year, State Minister Meng Teh-en and the Heavenly King's two brothers presented a joint memorial through the Eastern King, in which, besides the usual compliments, it was stated that the ninth day of the twelfth month of this year would be the imperial birthday and that it would also be the third anniversary of the uprising at Chin-t'ien. The memorial further stated that the petitioners intended to fast and cleanse themselves three days before the imperial birthday and to lead all the government officials to celebrate in the Imperial Palace as a means to solicit Heavenly Grace. Just as the Heavenly King finished reading the memorial, a female official, kneeling before him, reported that the weather had turned colder, and that the water in the digging site had become deeper. Many of the four hundred girl workers had fallen sick and several had "returned to heaven." She further reported that one of the supervisors, Yang Ch'ang-mei, implored that the work be suspended until next spring and that she was waiting for the imperial order at the gate of the garden. Upon hearing this report, the Heavenly King was extremely displeased. He ordered the female official to tell them that the work had to be completed on time and that no delay would be allowed.

A few days later, the Eastern King came to the palace to discuss preparations for the celebration of the imperial birthday. He reported that his subordinates had already drafted a proclamation requiring all court officials and military officers, regardless of rank, and relatives of high dignitaries to celebrate the occasion with appropriate gifts in the imperial garden. A copy of the proclamation was presented to the Heavenly King for his perusal. After reading it the Heavenly King felt delighted and moved. Then the Eastern King asked about the construction of the garden and the lake.

"I haven't been there for quite a while," said the Heaveny King. "Brother Ch'ing, why don't we have a look at the construction site?"

The next day, the Eastern King arrived at the imperial garden, accompanied by a seventeen-year-old trusted female official. The young woman, Yang Shui-chiao, had been presented to the Eastern King as a birthday gift by Meng Teh-en who had selected her from one of the women's quarters. Being clever and literate, she quickly ingratiated herself with her master, and in no time gained his confidence. She was appointed as a transmitter of orders together with three other girls, Hu Chiu-mei, T'an Wan-mei, and Hsieh Wan-mei. Of the four girls Yang Shui-chiao was the youngest, but, being the brightest and most articulate, she became a favorite of the Eastern King. When the Eastern King entered the imperial garden, the Heavenly King was already there waiting for him in a pavilion.

A heavy snow had fallen not long ago; the sky was still heavily laden with dark clouds and a fierce north wind blew angrily. On the garden site, the newly planted trees had shed their leaves. Snow flakes as big as goose feathers had started to come down in earnest, against a background of green tiles and red walls. During the first several months, the working force had been reduced from four hundred to a little over three hundred, due to sickness and death. They could be seen at a distance dressed in tatters, their hair disheveled, burdened with heavy tools, struggling in mud and water. Their groans could be heard distinctly. The Eastern King ordered Shui-chiao to measure the depth of the water in the lake, while enjoying the snow scene with the Heavenly King. Shui-chiao came back in the amount of time it took to cook a pot of rice and reported distressfully:

"Your servant has just measured the depth of the water. It has been found that in some places the water is eight feet and five inches deep while in other places it is approximately four feet. Since the arrival of winter, the soil has been frozen solid. It is necessary to build a fire on top of the ground before digging can proceed. Since a large number of girls have fallen sick or died, the reduced force has encountered some delay."

"Have you asked the supervisors when they expect to finish the job?" asked the Eastern King.

"The project is too big and the workers are too few. It is unlikely that the work can be finished this winter," replied Shui-chiao.

The face of the Heavenly King turned ashen white. He ordered a female official to summon the four girl supervisors immediately.

Yang Ch'ang-mei, Shih Ting-lan, and the other girls arrived presently and knelt outside the pavilion. The Eastern King saw at one glance that the girls' faces were blackened, their eyes sunken, their hair disheveled and their bare feet smeared with blood and dirt. Yang Ch'ang-mei, the only one who still had some color left in her cheeks and a glint of brightness in her eyes, answered the Heavenly King's questions in a trembling voice. Her facial expression had a dreamlike quality as if she was in a trance. Not having paid much attention to their responses, the Eastern King suddenly saw the Heavenly King rush out of the pavilion, raise his right foot, and kick Yang Ch'ang-mei right square in the chest. Uttering a sad cry, Ch'ang-mei covered her heart with both hands and spat out a few mouthfuls of fresh blood, adding several patches of bright red to the snow-covered ground. Terrified, Shih Ting-lan, who was kneeling beside her, banged her head on the ground incessantly, her frightened eyes wide open, but did not dare to look at the countenance of the Heavenly King. Merciless snow flakes hurtled down onto the four kneeling figures, covering them with a layer of white, their clothes froze as the snow accumulated, yet they dared not move. The Eastern King turned his head and looked at Shui-chiao who remained silent, her head lowered and tears hanging on her eyelashes.

"Second Brother," said the Eastern King, "the weather in the north is different from that of Kwangtung and Kwangsi. The ground is frozen in winter and digging is difficult. I think it would be better to start again next spring."

A feeling of compassion swept over the Eastern King which made him forget the obstinate character of his lord, a man who had never changed a decision once it was made. Furthermore, soon all government officials were scheduled to celebrate his birthday in the imperial garden. The Eastern King mistook his silence for acquiescence and spoke to the four kneeling supervisors:

"You may get up! I promise you to suspend work on behalf of the Lord of Ten Thousand Years!"

As if receiving a pardon, the four girls began to kowtow to express their gratitude to the King.

"Wait!" roared the Heavenly King unexpectedly. "Do you listen to the Eastern King or to me? When I issue an order, several hundred thousand heavenly soldiers obey. Not a single person would dare say 'no.' Yet a few of you girls wish to ask for clemency? Get out of my sight; you will each receive forty lashes. Start to dig day and night and finish the job in half a month!"

Having finished issuing this order, the Heavenly King stomped out of the pavilion with a shake of his sleeves; several of his female officials followed him closely. The four supervisors continued to bang their heads on the ground without uttering a sound. Even the Eastern King was briefly dumbfounded. When he realized what had happened, he comforted himself with a cynical grin; the Heavenly King had already returned to his palace.

That afternoon the Eastern King sent a few trusted orderlies to the women's quarters from which Yang Shui-chiao had come to investigate her background. They also found out her father Yang Wen-fu's whereabouts. In the evening, the

Eastern King summoned Yang Shui-chiao to his study, Cloud Gazing Tower. After saluting her master in the customary fashion, she stood to one side, her heart palpitating, uncertain of the fate that would befall her. Her swollen eyes and subdued manner clearly indicated her sadness and trepidation.

"When I came back from the imperial garden this afternoon," the Eastern King said smilingly to the frightened girl, "I fell into a fitful sleep in my study. The Heavenly Father came to me in my dream, saying he had orders for me."

Upon hearing this, Shui-chiao fell on her knees involuntarily, wondering why she had been chosen to share this secret.

"The Heavenly Father has revealed to me the whole story about your sister, Ch'ang-mei, in my dream. I know all about it now," the Eastern King declared expansively. "As the Heavenly Father was about to leave, He said, 'In a few days I'll have instructions for Hsiu-ch'üan, the ungrateful one.' Then I woke up."

Mixed feelings of surprise, joy, and gratitude overwhelmed the girl, who, recalling the unfortunate fate her sister had suffered in the morning, started to cry uncontrollably, even in the presence of the strict disciplinarian, the Eastern King.

"When I was ordered this morning by the Lord of Nine Thousand Years to measure the depth of the water," said Shui-chiao, still sobbing, "I heard someone calling my name. I turned around and saw it was my sister—we haven't seen each other for half a year since our separation. My sister told me that she had been sick and feverish recently, because her work was too heavy, and that if she didn't die of illness, physical exhaustion would certainly claim her life. Today she suffered a kick from the Heavenly King directly in the area of the heart and will have to endure forty lashes as an additional punishment. Most likely she will not live long. I certainly did not expect that the Heavenly Father would reveal himself to you, Lord of Nine Thousand Years, in this regard! My ill-fated sister may be saved after all." After she told her lord the sad story, she broke into a bitter wailing.

"The power of the Heavenly Father is omnipresent," declared the Eastern King. "In recent months, He has not revealed Himself. It must be that He was too busy with celestial affairs. But celestial secrets cannot be revealed. What I told you just now should not be divulged to anyone." Silence ensued.

"I am going to sleep here in Cloud Gazing Tower tonight," continued the Eastern King with a meaningful wink. "You may wait on me."

Possessed by feelings of fear, solace, and resignation, Yang Shui-chiao spent the night in the mist-enshrouded Cloud Gazing Tower.

A few days later, the twentieth day of the eleventh month of the year, *Kuei-hao*, of the T'ai-p'ing calendar (December 12, 1853) was a day of worship. Wei Ch'ang-hui, the Northern King, Ch'in Jih-kang, the newly promoted Marquis of Ting-t'ien, and many principal officials of the court met in the Eastern King's official residence to discuss state affairs. When the meeting was adjourned and the participants were stepping out of the main gate, they heard the sound of rapid firing signal guns coming from the main hall and front gate. All the court officials and military personnel, expecially those from Kwangsi, knew that the sound was a signal for the occasion of the Heavenly Father's "descent to earth." In such an event, all important officials, with the exception of those who had garrison duties, were required to report to the main hall of the Eastern King's residence to receive instructions from the Heavenly Father. Sometimes, the Heavenly Father would choose to descend to one of the official residences of the various kings who would receive instructions while kneeling.

The news of the Heavenly Father's impending "descent to earth" was reported by the gatekeepers of the Imperial Palace to the female officials. The latter went immediately to Consort Hsieh's quarters to inform the Heavenly King who was playing chess there. Upon hearing the news, the Heavenly King stopped the game instantly. With knitted brows and a heavy heart, he ordered the Bureau of the Imperial Carriages to have his sedan chair ready. Consort Hsieh helped him don his court dress. With only a few female officials and body-guards attending him, the Heavenly King hurriedly left the Imperial Palace.

As soon as he was outside the palace gate, he saw in a distance the Northern King walking beside the Eastern King's sedan chair, followed by the latter's female officials, Yang Shui-chiao among them. A group of officials headed by Ch'in Jih-kang were trailing behind. The Heavenly King quickly dismounted and waited respectfully to one side for the approaching procession. At that instant the Eastern King's sedan chair stopped. The Northern King, the Marquis of Ting-t'ien, and several state ministers took the place of the sedan-chair bearers and carried the chair from the front palace gate directly to the Dragon Hall. The Heavenly King followed them into the hall and waited to one side.

As the sedan chair was set down in the middle of the hall, the four female officials helped the Eastern King, who was in a deep trance, to descend from the sedan chair, but the girls were not strong enough to support the heavy weight of the Eastern King. Ch'in Jih-kang stepped forward and bodily carried him to the bejewelled imperial throne. The Eastern King, still in a state of trance, sprawled on the throne, his legs spread-eagled. All present from the Heavenly King down stood at attention on the steps of the Dragon Hall. There was an atmosphere of solemnity and absolute quietness. No one dared make any move to disrupt the silence.

After a few moments which seemed like an eternity, the Eastern King, the host of the Heavenly Father, gradually came to. His eyes stared straight ahead and his face was devoid of any expression.

"Hsiu-ch'üan, the ungrateful one, where are you?" said the Heavenly Father through the mouth of the Eastern King.

"This worthless one has heard that the Heavenly Father

was descending to earth," said the Heavenly King in a deferential tone. "He is waiting here."

"Don't pretend! Do you know your mistake?" The voice of the Heavenly Father became more stern and harsh.

A cold sweat broke out on the Heavenly King's forehead. Although he was unaware of what mistake he had supposedly committed, he had to admit it blindly. "This worthless one knows his mistake," said the Heavenly King, kneeling in front of the throne. "He begs mercy from the Heavenly Father!"

"You do know your mistake. That's fine." The Heavenly Father raised his voice in anger. "Where are the attendants? Give him forty lashes!"

This sacred order came as a surprise, not only to the Heavenly King himself, but also to all officials present, including the Northern King. They all fell on their knees at once. The Northern King banged his head on the ground and implored:

"Heavenly Father, please have mercy on us. All of us are to be blamed. This insignificant one is willing to be punished in place of Second Brother."

The Marquis of Ting-t'ien, Ch'in Jih-kang, State Minister Ch'en Ch'eng-jung, State Minister Huang Yü-k'un, Court Hsitorian Ho Chen-ch'uan, and other officials fell simultaneously on their knees, crying in unison, "We are willing to take the place of our sovereign for punishment!"

Others who stood beneath the steps of the Dragon Hall could not hear the dialogue carried on between the Heavenly Father, the Northern King, and the Marquis of Ting-t'ien; they all kowtowed rapidly, pounding their heads on the white marble pavement, creating dull thudding sounds.

Rising above the sound of pounding heads, roared the voice of the Heavenly Father through the mouth of the Eastern King, still in a trance, "He who errs must be punished! Come, give him the lashes!" The Eastern King's eyes seemed ready to burst out of his head.

Shui-chiao, the leading female official of the Eastern King's establishment, was stunned by what had happened. The mixed feelings of fear, mystery, and gratitude that had overwhelmed her for the past few days returned in full force. The most sacred and powerful Heavenly Father was indeed omnipotent and omnipresent, she thought to herself. Not even the Heavenly King was immune from punishment for having kicked her sister so savagely. When she realized that her sister could be saved from the brink of death, her soul trembled with elation.

"Call for State Minister Huang Yü-k'un," Shui-chiao yelled at the top of her voice, tears moistening her eyelashes.

Huang Yü-k'un, in charge of criminal justice and punishment for the T'ai-p'ing regime, quickly adjusted his court dress, stepped forward, and knelt in front of the throne. "This insignificant one awaits the sacred command," he said fearfully.

"The Heavenly King is the sovereign of the state. No ordinary lictor should inflict punishment on his body," announced Shui-chiao loudly, repeating what she was ordered to say. "Huang Yü-k'un, as the minister of punishments, administer the lashes!"

In the meantime, two female officials of the Eastern King's establishment, T'an and Hsieh, grabbed the golden-painted, tigerheaded whipping stave from a lictor and threw it on the ground where it fell with a clang. Huang Yü-k'un had never personally administered punishment on anyone before; now he had no choice but to pick up the stave. He could not imagine how he could possibly beat the Heavenly King. But from past experience as a witness to the "Heavenly Father's descent to earth" he had learned that the Lord was just as hot tempered as his sons, the Heavenly King and the Eastern King. If he cheated in administering punishment on the Heavenly King, by lightening his blows, he himself would incur the wrath of the Sacred Father.

Huang Yü-k'un then decided to perform the unimaginable. He closed his eyes tight, raised the stave high over his head and brought it down in full force right on the buttocks of the crouching Heavenly King. A deadly silence prevailed in the Dragon Hall.

Soon several officers began weeping furtively in the back of the hall. "Heavenly Father, please have mercy on our sovereign!" they wailed. "We are willing to suffer any punishment in his stead." Their pleas were groaning cries of desperation and hopelessness prompted by their fear of the Almighty God and sympathy for the Heavenly King. Evidently, among the several hundred sons and daughters of the Heavenly Father assembled in the court, only two genuinely enjoyed a sense of satisfaction over the unfolding events.

With each blow, Huang Yü-k'un, his forehead bathed in sweat, lifted the whipping stave high and hit the Heavenly King fair and square. Truly hurt both physically and emotionally, the Heavenly King could stand no more. "Heavenly Father," he pleaded, "this insignificant one now admits his mistake!"

The soft weeping both inside and outside the Dragon Hall now turned into loud wailing.

"In that case, then I won't have to beat you to your senses." The voice of the Heavenly Father was slow and deliberate.

As if he himself had been granted a pardon, Huang Yü-k'un threw down the stave and knelt beside the crouching figure of the Heavenly King. His clothes were soaked with cold sweat. Quiet returned to Dragon Hall.

"The Alimighty Heavenly Father has descended to earth and given us instructions today. We are most grateful," said the Northern King, still kneeling. "All the brothers and sisters enjoy the blessings of eternal joy. Second Brother may have committed a mistake, but that would be also the mistake of us all—his brethren and subordinates. May this humble one implore the Heavenly Father to reveal His sacred wishes."

"Hsiu-ch'üan," the voice of the Heavenly Father addressed the crouching figure of the Heavenly King. "Among your female officials, are there any girls named Yang Ch'ang-mei, Shih Ting-lan, and Chu Chiu-mei?"

Only then did it dawn on the Heavenly King what mistake he had made. Anger and a sense of impotence swept over him. Without considering the adverse consequences, he inquired boldly, "Heavenly Father, do you need these girls to serve you?"

"Listen to me!" berated the Heavenly Father. "Female officials attending court affairs may sometimes show lapses of disclipline. You should give them instructions and overlook their minor mistakes, so that they will not be in a constant state of trepidation. You are as hot tempered as I am, but are lacking in the compassion that I have. Digging an artificial lake is not nearly as urgent as digging trenches in the battlefield. Although the ground was frozen, you ordered the girls to dig despite snow and inclement weather, and then punished them without justifiable reasons. This is not in accordance with the principles of benevolent government."

"This worthless one will carry out the Heavenly Father's order with all respect," spoke the Heavenly King almost inaudibly.

"Yang Ch'ang-mei and Shih Ting-lan should be considered as relatives of high dignitaries. The two Chu Chiu-meis have provided meritorious service in performing an arduous job. They all should be transferred to the official residence of the Eastern King to enjoy a comfortable life. Since this is the season of heavy snow and frozen ground, the digging of the lake in the imperial garden should be postponed till the spring."

"The Heavenly Father's command shall be carried out immediately," mumbled the Heavenly King.

"There are other things which I have instructed your Fourth Brother to tell you later." Having said this, the Heavenly Father announced that he would return to Heaven immediately. All civilian and military officials hailed "Long Live" three times.

The Eastern King "woke up" amidst the cheering. He yawned widely, twisting and stretching his body nervously. Opening his eyes, he found himself sitting on the imperial throne with the Heavenly King kneeling before him. Expressing utter astonishment, he quickly jumped off the throne.

"Where am I?" he asked in bewilderment.

The Northern King stepped forward and related to him briefly the episode of the Heavenly Father's descent to earth. The Eastern King then kowtowed repeatedly toward the north, saying, "Hsiu-ch'ing was unaware of the Heavenly Father's presence. Please pardon him for his negligence."

"Fourth Brother," the Northern King reminded the Eastern King. "Before the Heavenly Father returned to Heaven, He said that He had something for you to tell Second Brother."

Standing in front of everyone in the hall, the Eastern King glanced obliquely at the Heavenly King. "Second Brother," he reported solicitously, "The Heavenly Father has already told you what he wanted you to know. He thinks, Second Brother, that you should be more lenient toward all officials, male or female. If anyone commits a crime, it is my duty to investigate. If there are mitigating circumstances, I'll report to you to have the sentence suspended. If a criminal deserves capital punishment, I'll report to you to have the sentence carried out. It is up to you, Second Brother, to decide if what I have said is correct."

"What you have just said *is* correct." The face of the Heavenly King remained pale as he replied in a trembling voice. "This proves that you are more acquainted with the concept of compassion than we are."

The Eastern King looked less solemn than before. He declared magnanimously, "This incident only illustrates the farsightedness of the Heavenly Father and the amendability of our Second Brother." Turning around, he addressed the assembled officials, "Brothers and sisters, we should all appreciate the Heavenly Father's charity and Second Brother's broad-mindedness!"

Composure returned to the Heavenly King, who now felt compelled to say something to cover up the indignity he had just suffered. "When I visited the Heavenly Father in his palace years ago, His temperament was even more excitable than it was shown today," he said pretentiously. "The Heavenly Father is always compassionate. He did not punish me too severely. I recall that when the demons invaded the

Heavenly Palace, the Heavenly Father told us that we should forgive them if they would admit the error of their ways. I punished the female officials recently for committing a few minor mistakes, which shows I am lacking in generosity."

"Second Brother has inherited the hot temperament of the Heavenly Father," said the Eastern King, realizing that it was unwise to push his opponent too far. "The old saying 'a chip off the old block' applies exactly to Second Brother who is in fact not lacking in generosity. Second Brother, you are tired today. Why don't you take a rest?"

The Northern King then signaled the civilian and military officials to perform the full kowtow ceremony, hailing the Heavenly King three times before retreating from the Dragon Hall. Everyone felt relaxed now. Although all were surprised at what had transpired during the Heavenly Father's descent to earth, they were relieved that they had not suffered punishment themselves.

The Heavenly King returned to his inner palace, pale and shaken, like a man recovering from a bout of chills and fever. There he was met by two maids who reported that two female officials of the Eastern King's establishment had requested the transfer of the four supervisors of the construction crew and the release of the three hundred-odd workers to their respective women's quarters. The Heavenly King silently gestured his acknowledgement by a wave of his hand. Thus the four supervisors, including Yang Ch'ang-mei, Shih Ting-lan, and Chu Chiu-mei, all on the verge of death, were transferred to the Eastern King's establishment, and the three hundred-odd battered and emaciated workers were sent back to their respective women's quarters in a joyful mood.

The Heavenly King sat alone in a reception hall of the inner palace. A few female officials waited on him in trepidation, stealing glances at him from time to time, and they found his mood changing constantly—one moment a sarcastic grin appeared on his face; the next he gave out short sighs and long groans; then in a little while he entered a contemplative mood, followed by impatient pacing. The women remained at a loss as to what to do. After a long while, from the imperial garden came the sound of the nightwatchman's hollowed bamboo clapper, signifying the start of the second watch. The Heavenly King rose, showing his intention to retire, but did not indicate to which apartment he wished to go. The women followed him quietly. Seeing him hesitate before Consort Hsieh's apartment, one of the female officials stepped forward and cried, "Consort Hsieh, receive the imperial presence!" Consort Hsieh who was in her sixth month of pregnancy, had gone to bed early that night. Hearing the call, she hurriedly threw on some clothes and faced her master with disheveled hair and little make-up. Without uttering a word, the Heavenly King raised his right foot and landed a heavy kick right on her abdomen. With a loud cry, the consort fainted.

Some palace maids reported the incident to Consort Fang. Young and agile, she quickly came to Consort Hsieh's apartment with two maids to administer first aid and sent another maid to inform the Queen. By this time, the Heavenly King had retired to the Queen's apartment. Word was sent out to summon the honorary state minister Li Chün-liang who served as the palace physician. Picking up his medicine kit, Li mounted his horse and cantered to the palace, followed by two attendants on foot. As soon as he reached the apartment of Consort Hsieh, he was informed that there had been a miscarriage of a male fetus and that the mother had suffered a severe hemorrhage. There was nothing he could do except perfunctorily take her pulse and retreat to the antechamber to write a prescription. Consort Hsieh remained in a coma for an hour before she was revived, thanks to the attentive nursing administered by Consort Fang.

The Heavenly King spent a sleepless night in the Queen's apartment. He felt a fire burning within him; his body was racked by fever and chills. The Queen had learned of the incident of the Heavenly Father's descent to earth from one of her trusted servants. She was surprised at what had happened, but kept counsel to herself, harboring a sense of guilt for her failure to remind her husband not to punish the female officials too severely. If she had done so, she figured, her husband would not have been punished publicly by the Heavenly Father.

Recollections of past episodes paraded one after another before the Heavenly King's eyes. . . . Five years ago, when one of the leaders of the God Worshippers Society, Feng Yün-shan, was arrested by the Ch'ing demons on Thistle Mountain, he himself had been preaching in Kuei-hsien. Without leadership, the God Worshippers Society was on the verge of collapse. At this critical moment, the Heavenly Father lodged in the body of a charcoal kiln attendant, Yang Hsiu-ch'ing, and performed the miracle of descending to earth. Through his mouth Yang transmitted the will of God, commanding the members to be "resolute and patient, and to work together harmoniously as true believers." Not only did God's words through Yang's mouth make a deep impression on the members, thus ensuring the continued existence of the God Worshippers Society, but through his voluntary contribution of several thousand cash, Yang succeeded in bringing about Feng Yün-shan's release from prison as well. All members of the Society had since become true believers and trusted comrades. From then on, the anniversary of the incident had become a festival day in commemoration of the "Heavenly Father's descent to earth."

Two years ago, a would-be defector, Chou Hsi-neng, conspired with the Ch'ing demons to engineer a coup, with Chou acting as the contact man. This scheme, if successful, could have shaken the very foundation of the T'ai-p'ing movement. Not only were all the leaders, including Feng, Hsiao, Wei, and Shih, unaware of the conspiracy, but even the Heavenly King himself had no inkling of the plot. It was not until the last moment when the Heavenly Father descended to earth once more, again through the mouth of Yang Hsiu-ch'ing, that the conspiracy was exposed. Chou Hsi-neng was arrested and pleaded guilty while Yang was still in a trance.

However, it had never occurred to the Heavenly King that he himself would have incurred the wrath of the Heavenly Father and suffered puishment in front of his subordinates. In the full view of high officials, he had been humiliated not only by being subjected to flogging, but also by being ordered to have the female officials taken away, and work on the imperial garden suspended. From now on, how could he expect his orders to be respected? "Oh, poor Hsiu-ch'üan," he said to himself, "the descent of the Heavenly Father to earth was my ingenious invention, but now it is being usurped by this upstart to his advantage!"

Queen Lai could not sleep either. By the gleam of the crescent moon, she could discern the outline of the Heavenly King with both his hands under his head, lying quietly under the silk quilt that undulated rhythmically with his breathing. Minutes later, she heard him sigh lightly.

The nightwatchman sounded the fourth watch. The moon had moved gradually to the Western horizon. To Queen Lai's surprise, the Heavenly King suddenly jumped up from his bed and took down the "demon-slaying sword" that was hanging on a bedpost. Before the taking of the Heavenly Capital, the sword had never left his side even for a brief moment. Since then, it had been hung in his sleeping quarters. With sword in hand, he walked toward the window, drawing the weapon from its scabbard in a swift movement. Queen Lai scrambled out of bed quickly, and, almost naked, rushed to snatch the sword from his hand. Its gleaming edge produced a deadly, cold reflection in the moonlight. The Queen fell on her knees before her husband, tears running down her cheeks like raindrops. The Heavenly King heaved a long sigh and threw the sword onto the ground. Then falling on the bed, he began to sob. The Queen, not wanting to disturb anyone, put the sword back into its scabbard and waited for dawn.

The next morning at nine o'clock, a female official reported that the Eastern King, the Northern King, and the Marquis of Ting-t'ien were waiting at the front gate of the palace, requesting an audience. Although the Heavenly King had regained some of his composure, he wasn't at all sure what other tricks the Eastern King was going to play. But without an alternative, he had to grant the audience.

As it turned out, they had come to comfort the Heavenly King.

"The descent of the Heavenly Father," began the Eastern King in a benign tone, "was for the purpose of warning all brothers and sisters on earth. It was we, your younger brothers and sisters, who have committed mistakes, so the Heavenly Father punished Second Brother to set an example for all others."

"Second Brother didn't commit any mistake at all," the Northern King quickly added. "If there were mistakes, they were committed by brothers and subordinates like us."

"Brother Ch'ang had it right," the Eastern King continued. "Although our Second Brother is bright and prudent, on occasions he may overlook some minor points. We who are his younger brothers and subordinates have the responsibility to report to him when we see such small transgressions. This is the way to express our loyalty and love for him."

Hearing this, the Heavenly King did not know whether he should laugh or cry. Mumbling with an effort, he answered, "What Brother Ch'ing said was entirely in conformity with the Heavenly Father's and Heavenly Brother's ideas. Brother Ch'ing, you are the very model of a loyal minister, the like of which is celebrated religiously in Chinese history. Brother Ch'ang, although you have great love for me, you are less forthright than Brother Ch'ing who deserves my hearty commendation." The three visitors kowtowed as an expression of their gratitude.

"Now that the Heavenly Father has removed four female officials from the palace," the Eastern King added as if it was an afterthought, "your younger brother has selected four young and attractive girls, one of them named Hou Hui-fang, from the women's quarters to take the place of those who have left. Your younger brother has personally made the selection. Whether the selection is appropriate will have to be decided by the Heavenly King himself." The Heavenly King merely smiled without making any comment, naïvely believing that the incident was over. He was surprised to find out that the Eastern King had ordered the court historians to have the records of the "Heavenly Father's descent to earth" sent to the Bureau of Engraving and Printing to be included in the tome entitled *Proclamations Made of the Heavenly Father During His Descents to Earth*. The book was distributed to all civilian and military officials in the T'ai-p'ing regime. The humiliating record of punishment sustained by the Heavenly King was thus engraved for all posterity in the history of the T'ai-p'ing Kingdom!

FOUR

The tenth day of the twelfth month of the third year, *Kuei-hao* (January 15, 1854) was the Heavenly King's birthday. To the civilian and military officials of the T'ai-p'ing regime, this day was more important than any of the religious holidays. All personnel of the court, army, men's and women's quarters, with the exception of those who were in charge of defense facilities were given a holiday.

From early morning, the clip-clop of horses' hooves could be heard incessantly on all the main thoroughfares. All official residences of high dignitaries from kings on down and headquarters of various handicraft bureaus had their front gates decorated with congratulatory messages written on red paper scrolls, as well as multicolored streamers and lanterns. Ministers and retainers of the various kings' establishments were busy dispatching birthday gifts to the imperial palace. Everyone was in a jovial mood. Common people, who seldom had a chance to take leisurely strolls, were out in force, donned in their Sunday best. Some were mounted, while others were on foot. When acquaintances met by the roadside, they knelt to salute each other and inquired after each other's health. According to regulations, common people were not permitted to wear red or yellow, but today they were allowed to wear red headgear in honor of the Heavenly King's birthday. The usually peaceful and quiescent Heavenly Capital became suddenly transformed into a boisterous and colorful metropolis.

At eight o'clock sharp, the Heavenly King received the congratulations of a group of high officials led by the Eastern and Northern kings in Dragon Hall. Afterwards, he returned to the inner palace for a rest. Another audience had been scheduled at two o'clock to receive the three categories of successful graduates, both male and female, who had passed the "Imperial Examination" which had been held only a few days prior.

When the T'ai-p'ing army took Yung-an-chou, the first examination for the recruitment of talent had been held in the first year, *Hsin-k'ai* (1851). The Heavenly King assumed the role of chief examiner. The roster of successful candidates contained forty-odd graduates, with Feng Yün-shan at the head of the list. After the taking of Wuchang, another examination was given and successful candidates were assigned government posts. In the spring of the current year, at the suggestion of the court historian, Ho Chen-ch'uan, it was decreed that four different examinations were to be held each year on the birthdays of the four kings, designated the "Imperial Examination," "Eastern Examination," "Northern Examination," and "Assistant Examination" respectively. The first one to be given, the "Imperial Examination," was divided into male and female sections and was completed just before the Heavenly King's birthday. Each of the top three graduates of the first category—*chuang-yüan, pang-yen* and *t'an-hua*—was bestowed the title of honorary marshall. Graduates of the second category which had no fixed quota were given the title of honorary general. The third category also had no fixed quota and the graduates received the title of honorary controller. The participants of the Imperial examination totalled no less than several thousand. The male section had twelve hundred graduates. At the top of the list was one Wu Yüan-hsün, over forty years old. The female section had one hundred-odd graduates, headed by one Fu Shan-hsiang, only a teenager. The heads of both lists—the *chuang-yüan*—were natives of Nanking.

At approximately one o'clock that day, the male and female graduates, donned in silken robes and embroidered shoes, arranged themselves in two rows according to their order on the list, and waited outside the main imperial gate. Spectators, including government employees and common people, stood quietly beyond the imperial drawbridge to observe the goings-on—some gazed at the decorations displayed on the imperial gate with great attention, while others animatedly discussed the appearance of the graduates. High on the imperial gate were hung several dozen gold-splashed, red gauze palace lanterns; hundreds of fluttering flags were planted on the walls—truly a dazzling spectacle. Among the graduates were mere teenagers, their faces beautiful and shining, as well as bald-headed, wrinkled oldsters. Some of the successful candidates smiled vaguely and bashfully, while others were personification of contentment, holding their chins high and looking straight ahead. The kaleidoscopic scene was indeed spectacular!

At two o'clock sharp, the palace master of ceremonies shouted, "The time for audience has arrived!" The male and female graduates marched in two files inside the front gate accompanied by the sound of soft music. Standing at attention in the white marbled corridor, they cried "Long live the King" three times before performing the kowtow ceremony. The master of ceremonies then led the six graduates of the "first category" of the male and female sections to Dragon Hall where they stood behind a dozen or so high dignitaries of the court. Thus they paid homage to the Heavenly King and congratulated him on his birthday.

The Heavenly King was in good humor that day. A little while ago, when he watched the thirteen hundred well-groomed graduates kowtow before him in a formation, as neat as a flight of wild geese and as colorful as a mass of gathering butterflies, he was reminded of the famous aphorism of the Emperor T'ai-tsung of T'ang that "all men of destiny in the world have played into my hands." A sense of satisfaction overwhelmed him, and addressing the assembled officials and graduates he said:

> When I was young, I studied the classics for ten years and took the examinations four times. Clad in cotton clothes with straw sandals on my feet, I made several trips to Canton. At that time, corruption was rampant in the examination halls. If you had money to bribe the examiner, no matter what mumbo-jumbo or rubbish you wrote, you were sure to get your name on the list. On the other hand, if you were talented but poor, you were out of luck no matter how well you wrote. I was infuriated by such unfairness and vowed that I would never take part in the examinations again and never wear the demon court dress. I had hoped that someday I would give my own examination to recruit talents. This former unsuccessful *hsiu-ts'si* candidate has become your examiner today. Ha . . . Ha . . . Ha!

These humorous, old ancedotes concerning examinations provoked a ring of laughter among the officials and new graduates. The Eastern King did not quite understand the implications of the joke, but also laughed out of courtesy.

At this juncture, the sound of soft music commenced again. According to the prearranged agenda, this was to be the time for the male and female *chuang-yüan* to present their eulogies to the Heavenly King. The male *chuang-yüan* Wu Yüan-hsün adjusted his court dress and performed the presentation ceremony before he started to intone the following ode in archaic style:

> Great is our sovereign, majestic and profound;
> His benevolence reaches the myriad beings, and
> His rule extends to the Four Seas and beyond.
> On His Birthday, let us wish him longevity and good
>   health.
> From now on, the Heavenly Kingdom will rise.
>   And the Ch'ing demons will go down.
> In this proud land of ours, people will rejoice, and
>   dance around;
> As they enjoy the blessings of Paradise later found.
> Oh! how glorious and magnificient are our days.
>   Peace and prosperity without bound!

After the recital of the ode, the sound of music was heard again.

"I couldn't understand a word he said," said the Eastern King, *sotto voce*, to State Minister Ch'en Ch'eng-jung standing right behind him. "What a *chuang-yüan*! A shrimp of a man with a mouth of a toad!"

"His speech contained nothing but praise for the Heavenly King," whispered Ch'en with a smile.

As the music stopped, Fu Shan-hsiang, the female *chuang-yüan*, stepped gracefully forward and reported in a crystalline voice:

> By the grace of the Heavenly Father and Heavenly Brother and through the kindness of the Heavenly King, your little sister, Fu Shan-hsiang, is able to attend the Heavenly court and to participate in its proceedings. Although uninformed, your younger sister is willing to offer her opinions for consideration. At the present time, the Ch'ing demons have

not been completely eliminated and our revolution is not yet complete. Millions of our brothers and sisters are still suffering in shackles. The Heavenly Capital is surrounded by tens of thousands of demon soldiers, waiting to pounce on us. All people under heaven, craning their necks and standing on their toes, eagerly await the arrival of the Heavenly Army. It is the ardent wish of this little sister that Your Majesty give up the enjoyment of physical pleasures, avoid the flattering words of sycophants, and give the state and people first priority above everything else. There should be judicious selections of officials to improve the administration and thorough training of soldiers and cavalry units for both defense and offense. With the implementation of these measures, the Heavenly Kingdom shall prosper and the people flourish. This is the wish of your younger sister!

All the assembled officials were greatly astonished at her eloquence and courage and expressed their admiration. The male *chuang-yüan* felt ashamed of himself; sweat trickled down from his forehead.

The music began again. The Eastern King stole furtive glances at the Heavenly King, whose face had beamed with pride and contentment until he heard Fu Shan-hsiang's speech. Suddenly, his expression changed from one of total satisfaction to forboding displeasure.

The audience came to an end and the Heavenly King and Queen pinned paper flowers on the male and female *chuang-yüan*. Then the thirteen-hundred-odd male and female graduates paraded in front of the Dragon Hall once before passing through the Heavenly Front Gate onto the street. Although no one was mounted, the parade was in fact a continuation of the old imperial tradition of honoring the new graduates before the populace.

The procession caused a big commotion outside the

Heavenly Front Gate. The spectators were dazzled by the sight of the new degree-winners in their silken gowns and embroidered hats parading before them. Some expressed their admiration, while others silently begrudged the good luck of the graduates. A few volunteered to walk in front of the procession to clear the way, while others squeezed through the crowd to catch a closer look.

Among the spectators, an old man, rather tall and slim, holding a walking staff, tried to get a glimpse of the male and female *chuang-yüan.* His graying temples, flushed cheeks, broad shoulders, and long, slim fingers enabled the old man to present a distinguished appearance amidst the nondescript masses. He had studied classics when he was only eight years old, starting by memorizing the *Trimetrical Classic*—"Men at their birth are by nature radically good"—and the *Millenary Classic*—"The Heavens are sombre; the earth is yellow," etc. He had entered the examination hall on numerous occasions, but never obtained the title of a *hsiu-t'sai.* Grief stricken by the death of his wife at the age of fifty, he gave up all hope of obtaining official appointment by passing the state examinations. Then, deep sorrow and disappointment had led to the loss of his eyesight. Since he had been an amateur musician in his youth, he chose to take up the profession of an itinerant musician and managed to eke out a living. He taught his two teenage daughters a few songs which they sang while he accompanied them on the violin. Thus the trio made a meager living singing on the streets and in other public places.

The old man, Yang Wen-fu by name, happened to be the father of Yang Ch'ang-mei and Yang Shui-chiao. When he and his elder daughter were separated and assigned to the male and female quarters, he had lost track of his younger daughter. Later, when the two sisters were reunited at the imperial garden and became officials in the Eastern King's establishment, they frequently sent messengers to bring food and clothes to the old man. Although originally from a poor family and without an official degree, Yang had a forthright character and was well liked by his neighbors. Hence with the establishment of the Ch'in-huai men's quarters, he was promptly elected chief of the quarters, in charge of twenty-five men. This change of fortune—from a life of misery and a world of indifference to one of decency and warmth—provided him with such a spiritual liberation that his eyesight, after receiving proper care, was partially restored. Whenever an assignment was given him by a superior, whether it was whittling bamboo spikes or sweeping streets, Yang was always at the head of his men. On days of worship, he was the most devoted among the brethren in praising the Heavenly Father. Yang commanded the respect and affection of all his subordinates—men who were also mostly over fifty years of age. Sometimes they teased him a little, calling him a "relative of a high dignitary," but he never took offence. Witnessing the parade of successful graduates, Yang was moved by mixed feelings of both envy and sorrow. That morning he and his men had risen early and walked to the Heavnely Front Gate to watch the important ceremony. Being old and lame, he stood in the back of the crowd. As he watched from a distance, Yang tried to listen to people's comments on the day's events in order to gain a more complete mental impression.

"Look, the two *chuang-yüan* have come out of the Heavenly Front Gate," he heard someone say in a low voice. "The female *chuang-yüan's* face is flushed. She must have drunk the Heavenly King's royal liquor."

"Bah! Nonsense! Drinking is forbidden by law in the Heavenly Kingdom. Don't you know?" rejoined another.

"Yeah! You're right. She must have received the 'joy of rain and dew' from the Heavenly King! Ha, Ha!" said the first one. Both snickered derisively.

"Haven't you heard?" continued the first speaker. "Among the graduates, including the *chuang-yüan*, *pan-yen*, *han-lin*, and *chin-shih*, there are plenty of monks, Taoist priests, fortune-tellers, and the like."

"The male graduates must have come from these professions," said the second man. "No doubt there are quite a few prostitutes and women of pleasure among the female graduates!"

"Ai!" the first speaker heaved a deep sigh. "All the riff-raff from the three religions and nine professions have become graduates. Our three-thousand-year-old cultural heritage has been trampled in the dust. Our teacher of all eternity, Confucius, will surely turn over in his grave."

"You've inspired me to compose a couplet which should be hung on both sides of the Heavenly Front Gate," rejoined the other spectator.

"Let's hear it!" said his companion.

"The whole realm, mountains and rivers included, covers an area no more than seventy-two and a half square miles.

"The civilian and military officials of the imperial court are recruited from the three hundred and sixty different trade guilds."

The two men broke into hearty laughter.

"Haven't we met before?" asked the composer of the couplet. Then, looking more closely, he discovered the identity of the other. "Aren't you my cousin . . .? Why do you look so different?"

"I have also suspected that you are my cousin Wu," the other man said in a low voice. "Let's go somewhere to talk!" Together they left the crowd.

Old man Yang Wen-fu had developed a keen sense of hearing since he had lost his sight a number of years ago. Although he was over fifty years old his memory was still as good as ever. As he listened to the two strangers, he realized that one of the voices sounded quite familiar. After concentrating further on their hushed conversation, he felt positive that one of them was the very same gentleman who had refused to pay for entertainment, and had made advances to his daughter at the Six Dynasties Retreat one year ago. Yang seldom fretted about the past, but the satirical jabs at the Heavenly Kingdom hurt the old man's sensibilities and flew in the face of his respect for the new regime. Losing interest in the parade, Yang decided to follow them, pretending he had nothing else to do. But the two strangers, both about thirty, one fat and one thin, had already disappeared. The old man regretted not having a chance to scrutinize their faces more closely. As he blamed himself for his lack of vigilance, Yang spotted the pair as they emerged from a public lavatory. He then approached the two and purposefully hit the fat man's foot with his walking staff.

"You Old Devil! Are you blind? You act like a headless fly! Why did you hit me?" the fat man yelled.

Yang apologized profusely for his negligence. At the same time, he managed to get a good look at the two strangers. One, dark and fat, was heavily pock-marked, with a deep, dark scar on the left corner of his mouth. The other was pale and slim, with sunken eyes and hollow cheeks. The fat one spoke an impeccable Nanking dialect which convinced Yang that the man who had just insulted the new regime was the very same scoundrel he had encountered at the Six Dynasties Retreat.

His curiosity aroused, Yang could no longer stay calm, and he retreated into the lavatory for a moment before coming out to resume his vigil.

In the meantime, Hou Ch'ien-fang was also in the crowd observing the behavior of the multitude and eavesdropping on people's private conversations. Hou had always been in the service of the Eastern King. Before the taking of Nanking, he had been assigned there to gather military intelligence from the Ch'ing demons. He had achieved a great deal in this assignment and won the confidence of the Eastern King. After the establishment of the Heavenly Capital, he was awarded the title of honorary state minister, with the duty of transmitting court decrees. In actuality, he had always been a member of the secret service under the Eastern King and had spent much of his time visiting the court, the establishments of the various kings, military headquarters, and civilian quarters in order to ferret out covert illegal activities or the sources of rumors circulating among the people. Ever since the capture of Yung-an-chou the Eastern King had organized a huge network of secret agents, among whom Hou Ch'ien-fang was an outstanding one.

That afternoon, Hou had also heard the muffled dialogue between the two men to which he did not pay much attention at first. Then hearing the offensive phrase, "three hundred and sixty different trade guilds," Hou felt that the speaker's voice sounded quite familiar, but when he stole a glance at the fat, swarthy, pock-marked brute, the man seemed to be a perfect stranger. About to leave, Hou noticed the fat man whispering something in the ear of the thin man and that the two had left together immediately afterwards, followed by a third person, a white-haired old man carrying a walking staff. His suspicion aroused, Hou tailed them at a distance observing their activities. This scenario could perhaps be best described by the old saying, "The mantis tries to catch a cicada, unaware that a yellow bird is right behind him."

Hou followed them to the entrance of a long and narrow lane which in his vague recollection had been called Wuyi Lane in the old days. The two strangers walked together, talking and laughing casually. However, they turned their heads back frequently as if to see whether they were being followed. The old man with the staff walked closely behind them. Hou was familiar with the layout of the streets of Nanking. Taking short cuts, he quickly reached the opposite end of Wuyi Lane. By then the pair had hastened their pace and had almost reached the end of the lane also. The old man was nowhere to be seen. Lowering his head and pretending to be in a hurry, Hou bumped right into the fat man who was about to explode in anger when the intruder apologized and saluted him politely.

"Brother Ping-huan, how have you been?"

This caught the man off guard. Changing color, his face froze.

"You must have made a mistake," the fat man said lamely. "My family name is Yeh, not Chang!"

"I never said your name was Chang. You've made a confession without even being tortured. It's been almost a year since we saw each other at the Six Dynasties Retreat," Hou responded with a smile.

"What's the matter with you?" cried the fat man. "I've never heard of the Six Dynasties Retreat, or the Seven Dynasties Retreat for that matter!"

Hou closely scrutinized the man's face. His pockmarks were deep and close together; a deep scar was evident to one side of his mouth. Puzzled, Hou wondered to himself, "Could I be mistaken?" As he hesitated, the thin man hit him hard with his fist; the blow landed squarely on his right eye. As he tried to defend himself, an equally hard blow landed on his left eye. Hou saw stars and felt as if the whole world had turned upside down.

Later, when he came to, he straightened his clothing and wiped away the blood on his face. By then, the two strangers had disappeared without a trace. Even the old man was no where to be found. With no weapons on him, Hou was afraid that he might fall into the trap of the conspirators. He returned to the main thoroughfare where music was playing and crowds were gathering. The parade had just reached that part of the city.

Both Hou Ch'ien-fang and the old man had met Chang Ping-huan only once, but their recollections were quite clear—the swarthy, pock-marked fat man was none other than the scoundrel Chang Ping-huan.

Chang was a stipend student from Shang-yüan county. He had always taken advantage of his status as a *hsiu-ts'ai* to hoodwink his neighbors and oppress the common folk. A libertine by nature, he had squandered away his family fortune by feasting and whoring by the time he was thirty. Since then he earned his keep by instigating litigations among contending parties. At times he would sponge on relatives and friends who found him repulsive. The incident at the Six Dynasties Retreat a year ago was rather unremarkable and commonplace to him. Prior to the T'ai-p'ing army's entry into Nanking, Chang begged his father's friend, Ch'i Su-tsao, the provincial judge, to appoint him the "Auxiliary City Defense Officer," giving him a salary of a few taels of silver per month. When the T'ai-p'ing army approached the city, Ch'i ordered him to lead a force of over a thousand "volunteers," made up supposedly of residents of the south gate area, to fight the invaders on the outskirts of the city. These volunteers were actually mostly rice-shop apprentices from the south gate area who had been signed up by their employers—young men who had neither the motivation nor the training to fight the invaders. As soon as they left the city, they halted near the city gate and refused to go any further. At the time, Imperial Commissioner Lu Chien-ying and his army, having been defeated by the enemy, were returning from Wu-hsüeh. From a distance, Lu noticed a large concentration of armed men outside the city gate. Erroneously taking them for the attacking T'ai-p'ing army, he ordered heavy artillery fire on the group. Seeing the imperial army attacking soldiers outside the gate, the city defense forces too fired their guns at the congregation. As a result, several hundred of the motley force were exterminated. The Imperial Commissioner had succeeded in eliminating more than half of the "volunteers." Chang Ping-huan, however, narrowly escaped the massacre and hid himself in the basement of his benefactor's residence. After the T'ai-p'ings entered the city, Chang devised an ingenious plan to disguise his identity. He boiled a large pot of bubbling oil and added a few drops of water in it. Clenching his teeth, he put his face over the boiling pot, allowing the splashing hot boiling oil to blister his skin, thus the origin of his numerous "pockmarks." Afraid that people might still recognize him by the black mole on the left corner of his mouth, he pressed a red hot branding iron hard on the mole, creating a new scar. After a month of hiding in the basement of his benefactor's residence, he discovered by accident that the owner had buried large amounts of gold and silver bullion under the basement. After he reemerged from hiding, he learned of the death of his benefactor who had been killed on the day of the fall of Nanking. His residence was later turned into a men's quarters. One day, a heavily pock-marked man with a big scar on the corner of his mouth, calling himself Yeh Chih-fa, presented himself at the men's quarters, begging to be admitted as a member. Having become one, he worked hard on every assignment—sweeping streets, picking up wastepaper, and attending religious ceremonies—and gained the trust of the chief of the men's quarters. Whenever he was assigned to pick up rice or oil from the sacred commissary, he would stealthily transport portions of the treasure from the basement and hide them elsewhere. After all the hidden treasures had been thus removed, Yeh reported to the chief of the men's quarters that, through the recommendation of a fellow from his native town, he had accepted the job of "transport worker" in the Northern King's establishment, and that he would report to the new job the next day.

Although he had become a millionaire by now, Chang Ping-huan, now alias Yeh Chih-fa, could not squander his ill-gotten wealth on whoring and gambling as he had in the past, since all the gambling houses and brothels had been closed after the T'ai-p'ings entered the city. Whether he worked as a member of the men's quarters or as a "transport worker" for the Northern King, his rations of rice, oil, salt, and clothing were all the same. Everyone got the same amount of necessities, down to the quantity of pork rationed each month. This regulated, thrifty working life did wonders for Chang. Within one year, he was completely transformed from a pale and emaciated drug addict to a dark, fat man in vibrant health.

Yeh Chih-fa was different from ordinary folk. He had studied classics and was familiar with the didactical stories of Chinese history, such as the tale of the King of Yüeh who took his revenge after suffering untold hardships. His experience in dealing with officials made him aware of the fact that only by assuming an official position could one enjoy a life of luxury, and that in order to assume such an official position one must take political risks and become involved in high-stake gambles. Yeh realized to his dismay that his large hoard of gold and silver had no value whatsoever in a regime ruled by such uncouth men. Hence, it was imperative for him to play political games. By making use of his position as a transport worker, in fact, a sedan-chair bearer, in the Northern King's establishment, he made contacts in the imperial court, various king's establishments, frontier passes, naval camps, and men's quarters, which he utilized to ferret out those who held secret grudges against the new regime. Among the top army men, there were both old and new brothers who, suffering poverty and hardship, had done menial jobs earlier in life. Despite their great ambition to change the world, they remained illiterate and unsophisticated. Hence there arose the need in the army and government offices for the literate men, the so-called "teachers" who could work as scribes. Most of them were former *chü-jen*, *hsiu-ts'ai*, or private secretaries of the Ch'ing *yamen*. In addition, after the T'ai-p'ings took Wuchang and entered the Heavenly Capital, many former minor Ch'ing officials, businessmen, and members of the gentry had found employment in the various establishments and offices, especially in the men's quarters. Within a year, Yeh Chih-fa, well-versed in political chicanery and maneuvering, had made contacts with many dissidents who held deep grudges against the T'ai-p'ing regime. His plan was to take advantage of their political ambition and dissatisfaction with the T'ai-p'ing regime to induce them to become agents of the Ch'ing South Camp. When the opportunity presented itself, they would collaborate to help restore the city of Nanking to its rightful owners. His loyalty to the Ch'ing court would be vouched for by the former officials and members of the gentry now hiding in various institutions. When the Ch'ing army retook the city, Yeh wondered, wouldn't he be entitled to wear a red button on top of his hat?

However, his main difficulty at the moment was his inability to establish contact with the South Camp. He had tried once to deliver a secret message to Imperial Commissioner Hsiang Jung by heavily bribing a ruffian who had smuggled himself out of the city, but the would-be messenger disappeared without a trace. Yeh planned to go out of the city himself to make contacts, but having no contribution to the war effort, he was afraid his advice might not be taken seriously by the Imperial Commissioner. Again, since he had been a transport worker in the Northern King's establishment for sometime now, his face was familiar to many people. Therefore, it would be difficult for him to leave the city unnoticed.

On the Heavenly King's birthday, Yeh, like all the others, joined the crowd to watch the parade. Through a chance conversation, he met an old acquaintance and distant relation—the thin fellow with sunken eyes and hollow cheeks.

This man, whose name was Wu Wei-t'ang, had been a student of the imperial academy, and was now in his thirties. After the T'ai-p'ings entered the city, an official manufactory of silk and satin was established to produce silk and satin materials for clothes and shoes. Later, when the demand increased, the manufactory was expanded into a weavers' camp. Through the recommendation of a fellow from his native town, Wu obtained a job as a weaver in the camp. Silk and satin weaving was a celebrated tradition of Nanking. Most of the satin weavers came from Mo-ling Pass. There were also velvet looms for manufacturing such products as smooth velvet and swan velvet. The operators of these looms came mostly from Hsiao-ling-wei. In addition, there were gauze and silk looms as well. The number of workers totaled no less than seven or eight thousand. When Wu Wei-t'ang was in Hankow, he came to know the Ch'ing magistrate of Han-yang, Chao Teh-ch'e, who by this time had been promoted to the position of prefect of Nanking. Since Nanking had been taken by the T'ai-p'ings, Chao had established his temporary *yamen* in Mo-ling Pass. Through the intermediary of Chao, Wu Wei-t'ang sent a petition to the Imperial Commissioner Hsiang Jung. But the latter had doubts about the petitioner's claims and ability and only ordered his secretary to write a letter of commendation without taking any further action. However, Wu Wei-t'ang was delighted with the Imperial Commissioner's letter of commendation. He figured that in order to organize an effective collaborationist group, he would have to have sufficient members; and in order to have sufficient members, he had to have special pennants promising pardon from the South Camp in the event that the Ch'ing army would retake Nanking. As a weaver, he had no chance to go out of the city, so through the connection of a fellow from his native town, he made contact with a few workers in the Bureau of Fuel and Firewood.

The city of Nanking was cushioned by mountains in the rear and surrounded by water in the front. Several islands in the river were overgrown with reeds and rushes. Since the city dwellers depended upon the rushes and firewood for fuel, a Bureau of Fuel and Firewood was established to supervise workers in the collecting of cooking fuel from the mountains and islands. Every morning fuel collectors, each wearing a "waist tally," departed from the Peace Gate, Treasure Gate, or the West Water Gate to collect fuel and returned at night. Those who left by way of Peace Gate and Treasure Gate could easily reach Hsiao-ling-wei where the Ch'ing South Camp was located. But the number of dissidents Wu had organized so far totaled no more than a dozen which was not sufficient to carry out a real adventure. Although he had made contact with Hsiang Jung several times through the workers of the Bureau of Fuel and Firewood, Hsiang did not take him seriously.

On the day of the parade, Wu met Chang at the Heavenly Front Gate. Both men were happy to have found each other, having the same aspirations and purposes. They soon became fast friends as well as coconspirators. Little did they anticipate that there had emerged two intruders, one old, the other young, to foul up their plans. When the old man had hit Chang with his staff in front of the lavatory, the latter sensed that something had gone wrong. When they reached Wuyi Lane with the old man still following closely behind, Chang signaled Wu with a purposeful wink. The two conspirators turned around abruptly and struck the old man with their fists, rendering him unconscious. They then hurriedly carried him to a deserted house in the lane. It was when they were about to leave the lane that they were confronted face-to-face by Hou Ch'ien-fang who had recognized Chang and had called out his real name. Fortunately, Wu was swift and agile; he quickly landed two heavy blows on Hou's eyes, incapacitating him. The two men left the lane quickly and melted in the crowd.

The incident heightened the pair's hatred for the new regime. For over three decades, they had lived under the authority of the Ch'ing dynasty which had given them special privileges and status. The regime had bestowed upon them a sense of superiority and a license to oppress their neighbors and the common people. It had also imposed on them the obligation of wearing the horse-hoof sleeved official garment and of braiding their hair into long pigtails. Therefore, when the Ch'ing regime crumbled, they felt insecure, alone, and threatened like homeless stray dogs. Without special privileges and status, they became part of the common folk and had to perform menial jobs such as sweeping streets, picking up rags, whittling bamboo spikes, and carrying rice. How could they suppress their inner resentment that irritated them day and night? As they witnessed all those country bumpkins wearing golden hats and embroidered shoes, hailed as the "Lord of Ten Thousand Years" or the "Lord of Nine Thousand Years" and watched monks, Taoist priests, *yamen* runners, quacks, fortunetellers, astrologers, physiognamists, and whatnots wearing hats decorated with golden paper flowers, proudly parading in the streets, how could they contain the anger seething in their breasts? Imagine, even an itinerant singing beggar and a long-haired bandit spy dared to pursue them on the street as if they were criminals. How could they coexist under the same heaven with such a ragtag regime?

In Wu Wei-t'ang's imagination the rhythmic clacking of the weaving loom meshed with his own grinding teeth, while the swaying motion of the felt-covered sedan chair on his shoulders created a swelling tide of hatred and resentment in Chang Ping-huan's chest.

Now that their secret had been exposed, the plan of offering the city to the Ch'ing army had to be hastened. The pair finally presented a letter to the South Camp with a list of would-be defectors in the city, over a hundred names, through a worker in the Bureau of Fuel and Firewood. The individuals listed were distributed among various kings' establishments, craft bureaus, artisans' camps, frontier passes, and men's quarters, including a few retainers, waiters, and personal guards of the Eastern and Northern King's establishments. The letter indicated that on new year's day of the year of *Chia-yin* of the T'ai-p'ing calendar (February 4, 1854), they would manage to open Cheng-yang Gate and let the imperial army in during the holiday celebrations. The letter further indicated that when the Eastern King left his residence to direct the defense against the entering Ch'ing army, several guards mentioned in the list would kill him in the commotion. Hsiang Jung was delighted upon reading this letter. He appointed a trusted lieutenant to sneak into the city with the spy from the Brueau of Fuel and Firewood, bringing with them five thousand pennants with the character "Pardon" printed on each and a large amount of gunpowder and munitions.

Prior to this, Chang Ping-huan, alias Yeh Chih-fa, had a buddy named Hsiao who served as a "teacher" in the camp of Commander Ch'en Kuei-t'ang, the general in charge of the Cheng-yang Gate. The latter was an old Kwangsi "brother" and an opium addict. Chang used his illgotten wealth to buy a few cases of smuggled opium and presented the contraband to Ch'en. Ch'en agreed to look the other way when the scheme was implemented on two conditions: first, after the coup was successfully carried out, Ch'en would be given a military appointment equivalent to the rank of army controller of the T'ai-p'ing regime; secondly, he would receive an outright gift of ten cases of opium of the best quality. Otherwise, he would report the plot to the authorities. Chang readily agreed to these conditions. He wrote a secret letter to Hsiang Jung immediately and delivered the opium to Ch'en through the intermediary of Hsiao.

Time passed quickly. On new year's eve of the third year, *Kuei-hao*, of the T'ai-p'ing calendar, Chang and Wu assembled

The two dragged the unconscious old man to a deserted house.

the leaders of the conspiracy, about fifty in all, to participate in an oath-taking ceremony, symbolized by the drinking of wine mixed with blood. One of the participants was a brigade leader named Chang Tse-p'ei, a subordinate of Commander Ch'en Keui-t'ang, who would be the keeper of the gate the following night.

On that eventful night a new moon hung in the sky showing the silhouette of the flying eaves of the gate tower. All the official residences and government offices were brightly lit in celebration of the holiday. In the meantime, a newly promoted division commander from the Ch'ing South Camp by the name of Chang Kuo-liang, with an elite force of five hundred cavalry men, moved stealthily, bypassing the T'ai-p'ing camps in the city's outskirts. By two o'clock in the morning they reached the gate. The gate tower was enveloped in darkness. Uncertain as to what action to take, Chang Kuo-liang hesitated until he heard the sound of a signal gun, as indicated in the secret agreement, and the gate was thrown wide open with a clang.

Delighted, Chang's men gave out a loud cry and more than a hundred mounted soldiers crossed the drawbridge, led by Chang in front. As soon as they entered the city, the sound of bugles and the cry "kill!" came from all sides. Simultaneously, the T'ai-p'ing camps inside and outside the city gate were lit up with bright torches and gunfire focused on the intruders—the T'ai-p'ing army had lain waiting for them. Soon the five hundred cavalry men and horses were surrounded by the enemy and decimated mercilessly. Chang Kuo-liang, mounted on a swift horse, was able to flee with a few bodyguards. None of the hundred men who entered the city escaped.

When Chang Kuo-liang, red-eyed and dishevelled, came back to face his commander, he could not utter a word in his defense. Gnashing his teeth, Hsiang Jung banged his fist on the table, breaking his green jade thumb ring into pieces. The two arch ring leaders, Chang and Wu, however, were not aware of what had happened.

Prior to this, the Eastern King, in addition to his reputation of being a strategist and disciplinarian, had had the foresight to place a large number of agents in different branches of the army. The incident involving the defector Chou Hsi-neng in Yung-an-chou had proved the efficacy of this arrangement. The secret service system was employed to prevent the infiltration of Ch'ing spies as well as to detect potential defections of their own brethren. The agents had direct access in times of peace as well as of war to the Eastern King. After the taking of Nanking, agents were planted in the imperial court, various kings' establishments, craft bureaus, artisans' camps, and men's and women's quarters. Reports of serious incidents were dealt with by the device of "the Heavenly Father's descent to earth," while minor incidents were disposed of summarily by the Eastern King himself. Since his busy schedule prevented him from making detailed investigations of all reports, it was unavoidable that some agents would make false reports to frame their personal enemies.

The keeper of the gate on new year's night, Chang Tse-p'ei, was one of the agents planted in Commander Ch'en Kuei-t'ang's army. This incident, identical to the historical drama of the "Ruse to Defend an Empty City," was directed and enacted by Chang, with the approval of the Eastern King. Commander Ch'en was transferred to the Ch'i-li-chou Naval Station on new year's day, pending further investigation to determine whether he had been involved in the sedition.

In making emergency arrangements for the ambush, Chang Tse-p'ei did not have the complete list of the scheme's participants. On the next day, the Eastern King ordered a thorough search for defectors based on the evidence of the "pardon" pennants issued by the Ch'ing camp. A total of eight hundred-odd people were arrested, but the ring leaders, Chang and Wu, were not among them. Actually, about half of those arrested were innocent, and had been erroneously implicated or falsely accused by personal enemies.

Indeed, when Ch'en Kuei-t'ang was transferred to the naval station on new year's day, the "teacher" Hsiao knew something was amiss. He informed Chang and Wu of his apprehension. Wu knew some workers in the Bureau of Fuel and Firewood, from whom he borrowed two waist tallies. The next day, Wu and Hsiao left the city and were never seen again. By the time the secret service discovered the identity of the ring leaders Yeh Chih-fa and Wu Wei-t'ang, the latter had already disappeared.

What had happened to Yeh Ch'ih-fa then?

The search was carried out for several more days and a few more suspects were arrested, yet Yeh Ch'ih-fa was still at large. Inexplicably, among the one hundred or so personal guards of the Eastern King's own establishment who had participated in the conspiracy, few were caught.

The Eastern King issued an order to have all the suspects, more than eight hundred, put to death immediately.

FIVE

After the passing of the solar term "insects dehibernated," the weather gradually turned warm.

A man carrying two baskets full of vegetables on a shoulder pole travelled briskly on a path leading from a former prince's residence to the naval camp at Phoenix Gate. Although the load was not very heavy, he was breathing hard through his open mouth, and his brow was drenched with sweat. To cool down, he took his tattered cotton jacket off and fastened it on the shoulder pole. Noticing that the sun was still high in the sky, he dampened his straw sandals, shifted the pole to the other shoulder, and proceeded more slowly forward, wiping the perspiration from his forehead all the while.

As he approached the door of the kitchen of the Ninth Naval Corps Headquarters, the chief cook came out and greeted him cordially.

"You're early today, Chang 'the Seventh.' What have you brought us today?"

"I thought you would be waiting for the vegetables, Master!" replied Chang. "I've brought some chives and lettuce. They were just harvested this morning, still green and fresh. But if you wait any longer, their leaves will wither."

"You can take a vacation, Chang 'the Seventh,'" the cook said smilingly. "There will be no need for vegetables for a while."

"What's happened, Master?" the vegetable carrier asked, his voice trembling with surprise.

"I've heard from the secretary, Mr. Ma, that the Northern King's establishment has dispatched someone here to commandeer boats to transport troops to the front," said the cook.

"How many boats?" inquired Chang.

"I heard that they need at least two hundred. If so, you won't have to come for at least two weeks," answered the chief cook.

Still talking, the chief cook helped unload the vegetables. Chang thanked him and collected his pole and baskets. Then he walked toward the room where the secretary worked.

Secretary Ma shouted, "Good morning!" as soon as he saw Chang. Looking around, he saw no one else was there. Then, lowering his voice, he said, "Brother Ping-huan, you don't have to come here for the next ten or fifteen days. In fact, from now on you'd better not come here at all. You've been the Northern King's sedan-chair carrier, and you may not recognize other people, but other people may recognize you."

Hearing this, Chang Ping-huan's pock-marked face turned ominously dark. "Now that you've got your silver securely in hand, you want to destroy the bridge as soon as you've crossed it!" he said with a snicker. "Fine! When worst comes to worst, I'll confess and be drawn and quartered by horses, but someone else will have his 'heavenly lamp' lit!"

Alarmed, Secretary Ma interrupted his friend, his face turning ashen. "Brother Ping-huan, you've misunderstood me," he entreated. "We're in the same boat. Not to mention having shared the grace of the Ch'ing emperor, we have been brothers under trying circumstances for some time now. If I had intended to betray you, would I have recommended you to work in the vegetable garden?"

Secretary Ma had been a *bona fide* secretary of impeccable record. Only his real name was not Ma, but Niu. The year before the fall of Nanking, he had served as a secretary of criminal justice in the *yamen* of Shang-yüan county. On one occasion, he colluded with Chang Ping-huan in instigating a litigation case involving a widow accused of committing adultery. The two men had obtained a bribe of one hundred and eighty taels of silver each from the litigants. When their iniquitous involvement was exposed, Secretary Niu resigned under pressure, on the pretext of ill health. After the establishment of the T'ai-p'ing regime in Nanking, Niu, now alias Ma, came to work in the Ninth Naval Corps Headquarters through the recommendation of a fellow from his native town. Members of the corps, following tradition, called him "teacher." Sometimes he was even addressed with the honorific appellation "Your Excellency." Well versed in legalistic philosophy and skilled in sophistic eloquence, he quickly gained the confidence of his employer. Chang Ping-huan recruited him as a member of his group of conspirators. However, Ma had not been asked to participate in the city-gate plot, because he was known to be physically and morally weak. When the plot failed, Chang Ping-huan found refuge in the vegetable garden through Ma. As a rule, all military establishments in the city were supplied with vegetables cultivated by the soldiers or sailors themselves, aided by a few idlers who belonged neither to the military nor civilian quarters. These people, therefore, enjoyed a certain amount of freedom of movement. Hence, Chang Ping-huan, once alias Yeh Chih-fa, was now known as Chang "the Seventh," a vegetable gardener. There were several hundred gardeners who worked in the vacant lots that had once been part of a former prince's residence in the south city. Chang's presence, therefore, was not noticed. He worked diligently and with enthusiasm at his irrigation, fertilizing, sowing, and harvesting chores. In addition, he volunterred to bring the vegetables from the south city to Phoenix Gate where the naval corps was located. Fortunately, since he had been a sedan-chair carrier, his shoulders were accustomed to the heavy weight. On the pretext of transporting vegetables, Chang had found time to contact Secretary Ma and other members of his group who had not yet been exposed. By careful cultivation of contacts and bribery, he continued to solicit support for his seditious activities in the hope that he would succeed in the end and be restored to his former glory. Fortunately, after a lapse of three months, the memory of the tragic fiasco that had involved the execution of some eight hundred innocent souls had gradually faded in the public mind.

"We received an order from the Northern King yesterday," said Secretary Ma, knitting his brow. "Within a day or two, a large number of boats will be commandeered to transport troops to Hsiang-t'an, Hunan. I may have to go too. You wouldn't know this if I hadn't told you. If I have to be dragged along everywhere, I'll either be killed by gunfire from the government soldiers, or just be run into the ground by these stupid people. I'm so worried about my future that I can't do anything to help your project."

"How is your prestige around here, by the way?" asked Chang Ping-huan, hoping to draw him out.

"As you know, the corps commander is a fellow from my native town and he is well disposed toward me. Most of the brethren of the corps come from Hunan, Hupeh, Kiangsi, or Chekiang and are all on friendly terms with me."

"How many people of the Ninth Corps come from Hunan or Hupeh?"

"About fifty to sixty percent!"

Chang clapped his hands in jubilation. "You're supposed to be an expert in the legalistic school of philosophy, and you don't even know any strategies of sowing discord among people," he said joyfully.

By now Ma's forehead was covered with sweat. He implored Chang to explain further. With fingers flying and tongue wagging, Chang Ping-huan outlined his plan with great enthusiasm. Secretary Ma listened attentively, his eyes fixed on the narrator. Banging his fist on the table, he expressed his admiration and gratitude, saying: "I must salute you on your exceptional wisdom and farsightedness. I'm completely sold on your ideas. You truly are an empire builder as well as a savior of the afflicted. No wonder Imperial Commissioner Hsiang thinks so highly of you!"

Their conversation was interrupted by what sounded like an altercation between two parties, emanating from the waterfront. However, the two conspirators could not discern the content of the argument, because the wind was blowing the other way. But through the window they could see a mounted officer, followed by a small contingent of foot soldiers on the shore, yelling and gesturing at the sailors aboard a ship in the river. A flag identified him as a logistics officer of the Northern King's establishment. The sailors, led by an officer whose attire was that of a battalion commander, argued heatedly with the men on the beach. Soon the army officer ordered several of his soldiers to board the ship and drag the battalion commander by the hair to the shore. The latter, now surrounded by soldiers, was kicked about like a football. The agitated sailors began to shout and curse, creating a scene of absolute chaos.

"Let me go down and have a look," Secretary Ma said to Chang. "You stay here."

As he stepped out the door, Secretary Ma noticed his superior, the commander of the Ninth Naval Corps, hurrying towards headquarters, followed by a few of his top aides, all swearing and yelling. Secretary Ma signaled Chang with his eyes and the latter slipped out to the kitchen through the back door. Pretending to be thirsty, he begged for some water which he drank slowly in the courtyard. By then, the commander and his aides had sat themselves down in the office. Secretary Ma found a seat near the door.

"It's an outrage! It's an outrage! How are we brethren from Hunan and Hupeh going to function from now on?" the Corps Commander yelled at the top of his voice.

"Who do they think they are?" added one of his subordinates. "They can't bully others just because they are from Kwangtung and Kwangsi!"

"If they're so great, let them handle the boats and fight the enemy on water!" echoed another.

"Your excellencies," Secretary Ma waited a long while before putting in a word. "What's this all about?"

"The Northern King ordered his logistics officer, Chang Tzu-ming, to commandeer boats to transport troops to Hsiang-t'an," explained the Corps Commander. "I gave an order for two hundred boats to be readied for him, but that scoundrel rejected them saying they were too old and that he wanted only new ones. One of the battalion commanders made the comment that the new boats were still in the dock. That remark made Chang very angry and he complained that he, the logistics officer under the Northern King, had been slighted. How can a logistics officer be so powerful and arrogant? I would like to see what our Chief Commander of the Naval Forces, T'ang Cheng-ts'ai, has to say about the incident. Mr. Ma, will you please draft a report for me to our chief? I'm going to smash that turtle egg!"

Secretary Ma was waiting for a chance to exploit the grudges held by the naval officers against their army counterparts. It was the belief of the naval personnel that their contribution to the war effort had not been properly recognized.

"How high in rank is a logistics officer in the Northern King's establishment?" sneered Secretary Ma. "He thinks he's a big shot, but he's not even qualified to serve as an orderly to our corps commander, not to mention our commander-in-chief. As a matter of fact, your excellencies, all of you here in this room are experts in naval warfare. So far as your abilities and expertise are concerned, you are far superior than your counterparts in the Ch'ing imperial navy."

While they were talking, a naval officer ran over, bellowing at the top of his lungs.

"Corps Commander! Bad news! Chang Tzu-ming has so severely beaten several battalion commanders that 'blood came out from all their seven apertures.' They've been tied up and carried away on horseback."

"His mother's!" roared the corps commander. "I'll quit. I'll go back home to row my own boat!" He left the room in a huff, followed by his top aides and Secretary Ma.

The naval camp was in a turmoil. The sailors, several thousand of them, had created a pandemonium. Some rushed to the anchored boats ready to set sail; others dashed back to the barracks to pick up their belongings; still more were ready to descent on the Northern King's residence to rescue the kidnapped commanders.

"We all quit!" yelled several agitators among the incensed sailors.

"Before we quit," said one sailor loudly, "we must catch that turtle egg Chang Tzu-ming!"

While the sailors were milling around, totally flustered, they heard a commanding voice from a man standing on the shore.

"Brothers! You can't quit. If you do, you'll suffer the penalty of 'lighting the heavenly lamp' when you're caught. You might as well sail off your boats and join the imperial navy!"

Turning around, the corp commander discovered that the speaker was none other than Secretary Ma.

"Secretary Ma is right!" said the corps commander. "We'll go join the imperial navy and then come back and take our revenge! Brothers, go to your barracks to collect your belongings. Come back in one hour and we'll assemble on board ship!"

Secretary Ma was thrilled to the point of intoxication. Turning back his head, he saw Chang Ping-huan following him closely, making a thumbs-up sign.

"Brother Ma," Chang said, "I must pay homage to you this time. You have just brought a whole corps to the imperial navy by a simple remark. This is much more significant than the plot to open the city gate."

"Brother Ping-huan," Secretary Ma said urgently, sensing the volatility of the situation, "go back to the barracks quickly and put on a navy uniform. Be sure to get on a boat without being detected!"

When they returned to the river bank, several hundred flagships, cruisers, gunboats, transport ships, and bamboo rafts had their sails set and were ready to weight anchor instantly.

Just then, six mounted men galloped from Phoenix Gate to the river bank. In front, riding on a white horse was a man with a sallow complexion and a sparse beard, dressed in a yellow robe and a golden embroidered hat. Reining in his steed, the rider took in the situation in one glance.

"Brothers of the naval corps," he addressed them in a loud voice. "I, Yang Hsiu-ch'ing, have come to apologize to you. The Northern King has also come to beg your pardon. I've brought here with me Chang Tzu-ming, bound as a criminal. I salute all of you here on the bank. If you choose to leave, you may do so, but not until you've witnessed the punishment to be meted out to the culprits!"

By this time, the other five mounted figures had also reached the scene. In the lead was Hou Ch'ien-fang. The third mount carried the Northern King, Wei Ch'ang-hui, who was bound hand and foot. The fourth carried Chang Tzu-ming, similarly trussed up. The other two horses carried two lictors, each clutching a tiger-headed whipping stave.

"Beat them!" Hou Ch'ien-fang commanded. The two lictors immediately pulled the two culprits off their horses and administered the punishment.

Astounded, Chang Ping-huan felt as if a bucket of icy

water had been doused on his head. Secretary Ma was also dumbfounded by the turn of events. As the whipping proceeded, the several hundred vessels of the Ninth Naval Corps moved back to the shore.

In a flash a mount approached Chang Ping-huan from the rear. Before he had time to turn his head, Chang heard a familiar voice calling his name. "Brother Ping-huan! Don't tell me you've failed to recognize your old acquaintance this time!"

Chang Ping-huan did not know how to react; his pockmarked face trembled violently. Secretary Ma instantly fell on his knees before the speaker, banging his head on the ground repeatedly.

"Your Excellency, Your Excellency! I confess. May the Heavenly Father and Heavenly Brother have mercy on me. I've an old mother at home, over eighty. . . ." Ma wailed. Then, pointing a finger at Chang, he accused, "He is the chief conspirator. As Heaven and Earth are my witnesses, that's the truth!"

It was beyond Hou Ch'ien-fang's wildest dreams that he would be able to catch two major consipirators without exerting any effort. The two traitors had been the ringleaders of two recent serious seditious conspiracies which, if successful, would have shaken the very foundation of the Heavenly Kingdom. A month prior to this, Hou had been transferred from the post of Chief Transmitter of Decrees of the Heavenly Court to that of Vice President of the Board of Personnel of the Eastern King's establishment. He had become a personal confidant to his lord. When the Eastern King received the intelligence that one of the Northern King's subordinates had incited the defection of a whole naval crops, he had to take immediate, drastic steps to quell the imminent rebellion, including subjecting the Northern King to punishment. But Hou Ch'ien-fang received additional satisfaction from the fact that one of the ringleaders was a personal enemy who had struck him in an alley several months before.

Immediately after the whipping of the Northern King and his subordinate Chang Tzu-ming in front of the sailors on the river bank, the Commander-in-Chief of the naval forces, T'ang Cheng-ts'ai, arrived and led his men in hailing the Eastern King. "Long Live the Lord of Nine Thousand Years!" they shouted three times.

The Eastern King was overwhelmed by mixed feelings of anger, elation, and happiness. He was angry because a handful of Ch'ing spies had dared to attempt seditious plots such as opening the city gates to the enemy and inciting naval defection right under his nose. He was elated because he had been able to uncover the two major plots and had nipped them in the bud, thus enhancing his prestige and power in the court and military. Having commanded tens of thousands of troops in combat, the Eastern King understood the mass psychology of the common soldier and the importance of prestige among generals. He was happy because he had just publicly humiliated the Northern King against whom he had long held grudges, however insignificant. The punishment was open, fair, and just, commensurate to the crime of negligence which had almost caused the defection of an entire naval corps. Furthermore, the incident had given him a chance to send Hou Ch'ien-fang to search the Northern King's establishment on the pretext of looking for the naval commanders kidnapped by Chang Tzu-ming. And lo and behold, among those rescued was the famous courtesan, Red Phoenix.

Red Phoenix had been a concubine of the Northern King since being taken away from the women's quarters. After spending an amorous night with Hou, her lover from whom she had been separated for a year, she was promptly installed as the concubine of the Eastern King. In a way, it represented a promotion in status. She was all that a beautiful courtesan should be—charming, seductive, and seemingly docile. She was neither resentful nor cheerful about the turn of events, because she had long learned that her fate was beyond her control and that it was best to accept it resignedly.

The morning after the eventful victory, the Eastern King ascended Rarity Depository Tower in the Purple Cloud Enclosure in a state of intoxication, still relishing the extraordinary tenderness offered by his lovely partner of the night.

Awhile back, at the audience for new graduates, the Heavenly King was impressed by the supplicant yet straightforward speech delivered by the female *chuang-yüan*, Fu Shan-hsiang, but it was not exactly to his liking. Hence, he appointed the male *chuang-yüan*, Wu Yüan-hsün, to work in the Office of Book Revision with the title of honorary marshall to revise the Six Classics. The female *chuang-yüan* was assigned to work in the establishment of the Eastern King without an official title, as a partial *quid pro quo* for the gift of the four girls, Hou Hui-fang among them. After Fu Shan-hsiang entered the service of the Eastern King, she received praise and approval from both her master and colleagues for her profound knowledge of the classics and literary talent as well as for her sunny disposition. Two months later, she was appointed a board president with the title of honorary state minister and assigned to work in Rarity Depository Tower. Her duties included perusing documents and drafting decrees. Fu was addressed as the "female *chuang-yüan*" by all in the establishment, a title she relished. Instead of using the demeaning term "your humble servant" as required by normal court etiquette when addressing the Eastern King or other superiors, she always called herself "your younger sister" even in public. Proud of her achievements, she stuck to the religious appellation as if she was the equal of the leaders of the government.

The Eastern King recounted briefly the story of the seditious plot to Fu Shan-hsiang and ordered her to draft a decree commanding all civilian and military officials to tighten up their security measures. In another decree the Marquis of Hsiang-kuo, Ch'en Ch'eng-yung, and the Marquis of Wei-kuo, Huang Yü-k'un, in charge of criminal justice of the Heavenly Kingdom, were ordered to oversee the investigation and select a capable official to preside over the trial of the two spies.

Huang Yü-k'un recommended that the Custodian of Court Documents, Hu Yüan-wei, serve as chief judge. But the Heavenly King felt that Hu's position was too low and that since he had originally been a defected Ch'ing official, he would be an inappropriate choice, so, instead, the King appointed State Minister Meng Teh-en, relegating Hu to the post of court clerk. Hu Yüan-wei had originally been the prefect of Lu-chou, in Kiangsi. When State Minister Hu I-kuang led his army to lay siege to Lu-chou, Hu Yüan-wei opened the city gate and went to the invading general's camp offering to capitulate on behalf of both the defense forces and civilians of the city. The two commanders had a hearty talk and the victor accepted the surrender. In return for the easy victory, Hu I-kuang recommended the defector to the Heavenly King who made him the Custodian of Court Documents. Hu I-kuang himself was also awarded the title of the Marquis of Hu-kuo, making him a member of the hereditary nobility.

Having been confined in the prison of the Eastern King's establishment for three days, Chang Ping-huan knew that he was doomed and decided to implicate as many people as possible. Secretary Ma, for fear of torture, hanged himself using his own sash.

On the day of the trial, Chang Ping-yuan kowtowed repeatedly, admitting his guilt. He named in one breath thirty-odd defectors who had allegedly joined the demons. Among the names he singled out were: Associate Court Historian Cheng Fu-t'ing; Board President in the Northern King's establishment Chou Pei-shun; Court Physician Liu Ch'un-shan; Han-lin Academician Yen Ting-pang; Brigade Leader Chang Tse-p'ei, one-time keeper of the Cheng-yang Gate; Chief of Ch'in-huai men's quarters Yang Wen-fu, and many others. Of course, he had not forgotten his escaped companion Wu Wei-t'ang and Secretary Ma.

It was beyond Meng Teh-en's expectations that the case could be solved so easily. Meng had joined the T'ai-p'ings in Chin-t'ien and had been a personal guard of the Heavenly King.

F

For a time, he had been deprived of all duties on account of an accusation of adultery and after the taking of Nanking his appointment was suspended due to illness. Therefore, he was now anxious to prove himself by solving the case as expeditiously as possible. He quickly arrested all the suspects on the list and put them through the grill.

When they were brought before the court, all the suspects denied unequivocally that they were guilty. Some of them complained loudly; others sneered contemptuously, while a few merely ground their teeth in anger; still others refused to talk altogether. Meng Teh-en ordered them subject to severe torture. Prior to the trial, he had ordered the preparation of a variety of implements of torture in addition to what had been in use in Ch'ing demon's *yamen*. After putting the thirty-odd suspects to the usual tortures of ankle crushing, kneeling on chains, sitting on "tiger stools," and standing in wooden cages without achieving the desired result, Meng Teh-en resorted to an ingenious new invention which had proved to be most effective. He ordered the lictors to stick pig bristles into the suspect's nipples. Few could resist that without making false confessions.

However, two of the suspects refused to confess even after being subjected to the cruelest torture. One was Brigade Leader Chang Tse-p'ei and the other was old man Yang Wen-fu. Chang Tse-p'ei, red eyed, bit his tongue so hard that blood spurted from his mouth. "You can't distinuish white from black," he bellowed at the judge in a voice not quite human, "or a loyal man from a traitor. You've fallen into the trap of the demon's spy. The Heavenly Kingdom is going to fall!" Yang Wen-fu who had just regained his eyesight and human dignity, groaned pitifully. "Heavenly Father! Open your eyes, Heavenly Father! Open your eyes!" he implored. He had not expected that after he had met the two traitors in Wuyi Lane, his name would be revealed to Chang Ping-huan by a member of the men's quarters who had joined the conspirator's group. During the trial, their meeting in Wuyi Lane was advanced by his accuser as evidence of their secret rendezvous.

Court Clerk Hu Yüan-wei requested the Chief Judge Meng Teh-en to call for a recess in the court antichamber. There he suggested that the suspects should be interrogated individually without torture so as to avoid miscarriage of justice. Meng responded with a scornful look and ordered the scribes to report immediately to the Eastern King the confessions he had thus obtained.

After Meng's report reached the Eastern King's desk, the latter picked up a brush and without even a cursory perusal of its content, scrawled these words on the back of the document, thus sealing the fate of all the suspects: "Decapitation! Heads to be exhibited in public! No one is to be spared!"

The thirty-odd convicted "traitors" were marched to the execution grounds outside the Heavenly Front Gate. Most maintained calm expressions on their faces and met their death almost serenely. Knowing that there were only two modes of punishment according to the law of the Heavenly Kingdom— whipping and decapitation—the prisoners all preferred decapitation rather than to suffer a lingering torture more cruel than death.

The trial proceeded. Chang Ping-huan racked his brains recalling the names of all the civilian and military officials whom he could implicate. More than a dozen additional names were thus mentioned. But among them a few were natives of Meng's home county. Chang became aware of a new skeptical look that had come over the face of his shrewd judge, apparently doubting the veracity of his statements.

The news of the conviction of Yang Wen-fu had reached his two daughters the same day it had been pronounced. Tearfully, the two sisters went to solicit help from the "female *chuang-yüan*" Fu Shan-hsiang. "If the sentence had been pronounced by someone other than the Eastern King," said Fu after careful consideration, "your father's life could have been spared by appealing to him. But the order to decapitate has been written by the Eastern King himself; no amount of imploring would be of any use, and might bring calamity onto yourselves instead. My dear sisters, you'd better just provide some incense and fruits to offer to the soul of your father, and hope that he will ascend to heaven to be with the Heavenly Father and Heavenly Brother. There, at least he won't have to suffer any more false accusations and injustice as he had on earth!"

Chang Ping-huan discovered that his second list of conspirators had not produced the same result as the first; he knew now that his days on earth were numbered. Chang noticed that the court clerk was a man of few words and that the chief judge always addressed him sarcastically as "Your Excellency." From the jail-keepers he learned that the court clerk was Hu Yüan-wei, the fromer Ch'ing prefect of Lu-chou. During the next court session, Chang cunningly requested that he be tried by the court clerk personally. At the same time, he informed Meng Teh-en privately the following fabricated story: When he had been in secret communication with the Ch'ing South Camp, the demon commander Hsiang Jung had told him that the former Ch'ing prefect's surrender was a stratagem and that Hu had contacted the South Camp offering to act as an inside informant in order to redeem his crime of defection. The demon commander had instructed him to approach Hu for guidance and assistance in future operations. But since he did not know Hu personally, he had failed to establish contact. In order to prove the veracity of his story, Chang requested to be tried by the court clerk alone, with the chief judge witnessing the proceedings in secret; thus the truth would be revealed.

The trial progressed according to Chang's plan. From a hole in the wall the chief judge watched the proceedings from an adjacent room. Little did he realize that someone else was also watching from another room, through a similar hole in the wall.

The chief judge noticed that when the accused referred to the instructions of the demon commander with a meaningful smile, the court clerk's face turned ashen with terror, his brow covered with sweat. When the trial came to an end, the interrogator was rendered speechless.

The Eastern King received two identical reports, one from Meng Teh-en and the other from Hou Ch'ien-fang. The contents were the same except for one paragraph at the end of Meng's report which read as follows:

> On the occasion of the first interrogation of the demon spy Chang Ping-huan who divulged the names of thirty-odd traitors, Hu Yüan-wei appeared ill at ease and implored your servant to go easy on the suspects. Your servant, aware then that Hu had something to hide, observed him covertly. This secret has now been revealed, thanks to the manifestation of power of the Heavenly Father and Heavenly Brother as well as the wisdom and guidance of the Eastern King.

Two days later, in the afternoon, residents of the Heavenly Capital congregated again at the square outside the Heavenly Front Gate. This time, however, they came to witness the execution of traitors, not a parade of new graduates.

The square outside the Heavenly Front Gate was the site where the Heavenly King paid homage to the Heavenly Father and Heavenly Brother and where proclamations of the Court were read. It was also where the whipping and execution of high officials took place. The two modes of punishment—whipping and execution—had been performed frequently, but the most extreme forms of execution—"drawing and quartering by five horses" and "lighting the heavenly lamp"—were to be witnessed for the first time by the citizens of the Heavenly Capital.

In the late afternoon, over a hundred guards of the Eastern King's establishment escorted two prison carts toward a temporary platform constructed for the occasion. A battalion of executioners, wearing red jackets and tasseled shoes, marched to the square, each with a dagger dangling by his side. Their awesome appearance gave people a sense of uneasiness.

The Eastern King, the president of the Board of Punishments, and several retainers arrived on horseback. As soon as he dismounted, the Eastern King went straight to the platform, his face livid and devoid of any expression. A transmitter of orders read aloud the short decree of the Eastern King:

> The Ch'ing demon spy Chang Ping-huan and the Ch'ing demon informant Hu Yüan-wei have been proven guilty after due process of the law. The said individuals, having been examined and correctly identified, are to be bound and carried to the execution grounds, where they are to be put to death by being drawn and quartered by five horses and by lighting the heavenly lamp respectively. It is so decreed!

The executioners opened the wooden cages and brought out the two bound criminals. A "death pennant" was stuck on the back of each criminal. Chang Ping-huan, unable to walk, was dragged by two executioners to the ground like a sack of potatoes. His swarthy face turned even darker and his eyes were half-closed. By now, his dreams—the hidden treasure of glittering gold and silver and the beckoning red hat button of officialdom—had receded well beyond his reach. The spring sun seemed to have faded to a deadly pallor. All that remained was the trembling carcass from which his soul had already departed.

Hu Yüan-wei, on the other hand, waved away the executioners and walked forward without fear, his back erect. His gown had been taken away and exchanged for a prisoner's garb. His long hair spread over his well-muscled shoulders, and a rueful smile hung on his otherwise expressionless face.

By the time they reached the vicinity of the platform, the execution ground had already been surrounded by thousands of spectators who were waiting to see the tragic spectacle unfold before their eyes.

Five mounted executioners arrived behind the assembled masses. The horses, all stout stallions, were decorated with red-tasseled halters and sported golden bells on their necks.

The executioners wore red turbans, red uniforms, and red cotton shoes and were equipped with red riding whips, not unlike performers in a circus. They cantered in a circle around the square as if to show how sturdy and strong their steeds were.

Chang Ping-huan was dragged to the center of the square. Several executioners descended on him, loosened his bonds, and tied five heavy ropes to his four limbs and neck.

For a moment, he seemed to come to from his state of numbed shock. Unable to struggle in any way physically, he used his last ounce of strength to give out a piercing cry, like that of a wounded animal. But his cry was cut short as the loop of the heavy rope had tightened around his neck. The ends of the five ropes were fastened to brass rings dangling from the saddles of the proud stallions.

As a uniformed officer standing on the platform waved a small white signal flag, the mounted executioners brought down their raised whips onto the flanks of their horses; all five animals dashed furiously in five different directions. The gathered crowd pulled back like receding waves to make room for the galloping horses. After running a short distance, the riders halted their mounts. Clouds of dust remained suspended in the air. At the end of each rope trailed a limb covered with a paste of blood and dirt.

A muffled sound of excitement and anger came from the crowd. Some spectators expressed their regrets, while others sighed for relief. Still others felt disgusted with the sight and left quietly.

The sun was half hidden behind the distant mountains. Its crimson reflection engulfed the entire square. Gradually, the red gave way to purple as a night mist invaded the execution grounds.

Another group of executioners started to prepare the other criminal. They bound his torso with layers of white cloth heavily saturated with cooking oil. He was then tied upside down to a tall pine pole. By then it was already dark. Traditionally this mode of execution called "lighting the heavenly lamp" was always carried out at dusk when the proceedings could be witnessed at a distance.

Another executioner put a tall bamboo torch to the prisoner's cloth-wrapped feet at the top of the pole. In no time, hundreds of golden flames spurted like dancing, snarling snakes before the eyes of thousands of horrified spectators. Some of them had to turn their heads to avoid witnessing the horrible scene.

The cloth-bound torso began to writhe slightly, but the movement was quickly halted by the numerous golden snakes that thrust at it relentlessly. Soon the flames had consumed his whole body and an obnoxious smell of burning human flesh began to assault the nostrils of the spectators.

On the road leading from Phoenix Gate to the palace marched a contingent of over a hundred mounted soldiers. At its head rode a general whose horse cantered slowly. Of solid build and swarthy complexion with high cheekbones, the general cut a figure of youth and vigor. Noticing the flames dancing at a distance in the vicinity of the palace, he pulled back his reins to watch the unusual sight. The hundred or so mounted soldiers also came to a halt behind him.

The general was the Assistant King, Shih Ta-k'ai, who, having carried out the pacification work in Anhwei assigned him by the Eastern King a year before, had just returned to the capital. The job of pacification, completed in six months, had been a success. During this time, he had frequently travelled between the capital and Anhwei. Three days prior he had been ordered to return by the Eastern King to prepare for a new assignment, this time a western campaign. He brought with him a fifteen-year-old adopted daughter Pao-ying and several close aides, one of them named Tseng Chin-ch'ien.

"Chin-ch'ien," the general turned to tell his aide, "go to the Heavenly Front Gate and see what the fire is all about." Then turning to his adopted daughter, he said, "Pao-ying, go home quickly and tell your mother I'll be back as soon as I've seen the Heavenly and Eastern kings."

The two turned around their mounts with a tug of the

reins and vanished in the darkness. The contingent marched on. Shortly, Tseng Chin-ch'ien returned and reported to his lord breathlessly.

"The Eastern King has just executed two Ch'ing demon spies in front of the Heavenly Front Gate; one was put to death by being drawn and quartered and the other by lighting the heavenly lamp. The fire is from the 'heavenly lamp' which has just been lit."

"Who was the culprit?"

"The Custodian of Court Documents, Hu Yüan-wei."

"What was the crime?"

"Supplying information to the Ch'ing demons."

The Assistant King whipped his silky black mount with a whack and galloped toward the Heavenly Front Gate. The hundred-odd other riders followed. When the Assistant King reached the square, most of the criminal's dangling upside-down body had been consumed by fire. The Eastern King had returned to his residence and most of the spectators had dispersed. The Assistant King was still unaware of the fact that his own father-in-law, Huang Yü-k'un, who had recommended Hu as chief judge in the case, had been given three hundred lashes as an additional result of Chang Ping-huan's false accusations and Meng Teh-en's perfidy. Huang had further been deprived of his title of nobility as the Marquis of Wei-kuo and imprisoned pending further investigation. There he had attempted suicide by jumping into a pond, but was saved by the Marquis of Hsing-kuo, Ch'en Ch'eng-jung. The incident was kept a secret, for according to the law of the Heavenly Kingdom, a would-be suicide must suffer decapitation just for the attempt. Ch'en Ch'eng-jung was incensed by the whole affair and tendered his resignation to the Eastern King who responded by giving him two hundred lashes.

As the Eastern King left the execution grounds for his residence, his heart was heavy-laden with apprehension as foreboding as the gloomy atmosphere at the execution grounds. The Eastern King was an intelligent and sensitive man. He

"Lighting the Heavenly Lamp"

would often realize it when he had made an error in judgment but, being arrogant and obstinate, he would try to cover up his mistakes instead of rectifying the wrong. Since he was a pillar of the state and commander-in-chief of all the armed forces, enjoying the honorific titles of "Chief Pacifier," "Sacred Wind," "Teacher Hsiu," and "Redeemer of the Afflicted," he was above all persons except one. Furthermore, he was the bodily representative of the Heavenly Father on earth; therefore he embodied also the father of the Heavenly King. Owing to all these factors, he could afford to repeat the mistakes he had made, even though he himself had discovered that they were mistakes. It had never occurred to him to doubt the sincerity of the adulation expressed toward him, or that his position and power would always easily win genuine absolute admiration from others.

When he received Meng Teh-en's report accusing Hu Yüan-wei as a Ch'ing demon informant, the Eastern King had entertained some doubts. Then, witnessing the calmness in which Hu walked toward the execution grounds, he was almost certain that Hu's sentence had been the result of a miscarriage of justice. With his position and power, the Eastern King could have easily rectified the situation then and there. But he had made no such effort, not because Meng was a favorite and confidant of the Heavenly King, but because Meng's report had been approved by himself. Should Meng's dishonest conduct of the trial be made public it would have been tantamount to an admission of his own error, which would be detrimental to his absolute power and prestige.

The Eastern King's experience on the battlefield had taught him that one step taken backward could lead to a retreat of a hundred *li*, and that before beating a retreat, it was necessary to launch an all-out attack. It was for this reason that he had punished Huang Yü-k'un and Ch'en Ch'eng-jung.

Having deprived the two high officials of their titles of nobility and subjected them to lashes, the Eastern King felt even more perturbed. For, before he had inflicted punishment on Huang Yü-k'un, he had not realized that Huang was the father-in-law of the Assistant King. Since the death of the Southern King, Feng Yün-shan, the only man among his peers that the Eastern King held in dread was the twenty-four-year old "Lord of Five Thousand Years," who was due in the capital in a day or two. As for "shorty" Ch'en Ch'eng-jung, he was a strategist and leader of civilian officials, who not only enjoyed high prestige, but also had a hero for a nephew, the seventeen-year-old Ch'en Yü-ch'eng. The younger Ch'en had not so long ago led five hundred do-or-die devils in scaling the city wall of Wuchang resulting in the capture of that city. How would the Eastern King deal with the problems that might materialize as a result of his harsh treatment of these two high officials? These were the major concerns that preoccupied him on the way back from the execution grounds. He hoped fervently to be able to devise adequate and appropriate means to counter all possible repercussions.

Upon returning to his residence, the Eastern King went directly to Purple Cloud Enclosure. A new moon appeared to be hanging above the trees and the fragrance of lotus blossoms wafted in the air with each gentle breeze. Thus refreshed, the King's mind became less troubled. Instead of going to his study, he walked toward a newly built pavilion beside the lily pond.

As he approached the pavilion, he heard a hushed conversation between a man and a woman. In semidarkness he saw two figures, one seated and the other standing, embracing passionately. The King could discern in the feeble moonlight that the seated lover was none other than Red Phoenix. His heart skipped a beat in surprise and anger. Drawing his dagger, he threw it toward the shadow in the pavilion, where it struck a pillar with a twang. Red Phoenix uttered a cry of surprise and the other shadow fled onto the path around the pond. Red Phoenix just sat there without making the slightest movement. The Eastern King pulled out the dagger from the pillar, ready for the kill. Stretching out her neck, Red Phoenix seemed ready to receive the ultimate blow. But the shining weapon remained suspended in mid air and failed to descend on its target.

"Lord of Nine Thousand Years! Kill me if you want. It was I who invited him here tonight. I belonged to him before the heavenly soldiers reached Nanking."

This was the first time that Red Phoenix had spoken to the Eastern King since she became a member of his household. Speaking in her native Soochow dialect, her voice was enchantingly clear and melodious. Hearing her speak, Hou Ch'ien-fang came back to the pavilion and knelt before his lord.

"Lord of Nine Thousand Years!" he implored. "Let the two of us die together."

The King's dagger dropped to the ground with a loud clang. A burst of bone-chilling laughter ensued.

"My younger brother!" cried the Eastern King, "I was just kidding. You are my close aide. How could I kill you?"

Both Hou and Red Phoenix were flabergasted by this surprise move. The awkward scene was followed by a serious and frigid warning.

"Red Phoneix!" said the Eastern King in a voice exuding authority and self-confidence, "I'll give you two just one hour together. After that you will return to your room. Don't forget that you are my concubine now. If I ever catch you two together again. I'll have him drawn and quartered by five horses."

Without a lingering look, the king returned the dagger to its sheath and headed toward Cloud Gazing Tower.

Fu Shan-hsiang was waiting for him at the door. Without ascertaining what mood he was in, the female *chuang-yüan* spoke up straight-forwardly.

"Lord of Nine Thousand Years! The case of Hu Yüan-wei was a miscarriage of justice. Many of the eight-hundred-odd brothers you put to death were also wrongly accused!"

He threw the dagger together with its sheath on the table with obvious displeasure.

"Who told you so? Who?"

"Your final decision was based on State Minister Meng's report and his report was based on the demon spy's confession. You don't have to be a genius to detect his chicanery. Hu had surrendered to the Heavenly Kingdom over half-a-year ago and everyone knew that he was loyal and sincere. His position as former prefect as well as his switch of allegiance were well-known facts. If the Ch'ing demons used him as an informant, it would have been a very stupid act on their part."

Fu Shan-hsiang's remark was logical and to the point, her tone neither self-effacing nor arrogant. This was the first time she had expressed her opinion to the Eastern King, and had acted well beyond her duty as a secretary.

The Eastern King let out a sardonic laugh.

"The man has already returned to Heaven and you give me your opinion now. Are you looking for promotion or seeking death?"

Fu remained calm and unaffected. "When the eight-hundred-odd brothers were arrested, your younger sister, trusting that the Lord of Nine Thousand Years would make a wise decision, refrained from speaking. After the executions, your younger sister believed that Your Lordship would have learned a lesson and would be more prudent. It was rather unexpected that Your Lordship would entrench the mistake by implicating the two marquises. Your Lordship acted indiscriminately at first and then tried to cover up your mistakes. Your younger sister's death is insignificant; what really matters is the law of the Heavenly Kingdom and Your Lordship's reputation!"

Relaxing a bit, the Eastern King inquired benignly, "Have you heard any criticisms?"

"There's an old saying that tells us that it is more difficult to prevent public criticism than to dam a river. Such repercussions could be easily imagined." Fu's attitude was as serious as her tone was sincere.

In the bright candle light, the Eastern King stared at the pale face and downcast eyes of the proud yet modest girl with mixed feelings of disdain and admiration. Trying his best to suppress his temper, he said in an agreeable tone: "You may go. I understand."

As a man who had been a peasant, a charcoal kiln laborer, and a fighter in fierce, bloody battles who felt equally at home in both political and military arenas, the Eastern King was well versed in political manipulations. But aside from that he really knew very little.

What perplexed him most was that despite their totally different backgrounds, upbringing, and personalities, the two girls—Red Phoenix and Fu Shan-hsiang—shared one vital thing in common—their courage.

Where had these two seemingly helpless girls acquired such bravery and character, wondered the Eastern King.

SIX

A contingent of fully armed cavalrymen, with weapons gleaming under the bright summer sun, rode down the main thoroughfare leading from Hsiao-ling-wei to Ch'ao-yang Gate. The horses' hooves clattered rhythmically on the stone pavement.

It was the fourteenth day of the fifth month of the sixth year, *Ping-ch'en* (June 17, 1856), three days after the victory over the Ch'ing Imperial Commissioner Hsiang Jung and the complete rout of the South Camp that eliminated the main threat to the Heavenly Capital. The Eastern King, followed by a host of other generals, set out on a triumphal march. Accompanying the Eastern King on the march were the Assistant King Shih Ta-k'ai and the newly invested King of Yen, Ch'in Jih-kang.

The news of the victory spread like wildfire among the

residents of the Heavenly Capital. Everyone, regardless of individual status, was jubilant. A festival mood filled the air.

Since the establishment of the Heavenly Capital in Nanking in early 1853, a Northern Expedition had been launched, followed by a Western campaign. The forces of the Northern Expedition, however, had been completely wiped out in the spring of the fifth year, *I-yung* (1855), due to the strategic mistake of penetrating too deeply into enemy territory without adequate logistical support. The two generals commanding that expedition met their death bravely. Reinforcements, sent nine months after the launching of the expedition, and only at the insistence of Shih Ta-k'ai and Hu I-kuang, were too late and never reached the front. The Western Campaign started in the fourth month of the third year, *Kuei-hao*, (May 1853). In ensuing years the T'ai-p'ing record of victory and defeat was a mixed one; the situation had developed into a deadlock, a long-term seesaw battle between the two great armies.

During the three years subsequent to the establishment of the Heavenly Capital, a series of events had finally led the Heavenly King and the Eastern King to the realization that the two Ch'ing military camps—the North Camp at Yangchow and the South Camp at Hsiao-ling-wei—were not entirely harmless; that they could act like a pair of pincers and crack the Heavenly Capital like a walnut should opportunity present itself. In addition to daily skirmishes against small contingents of the imperial army, seditious activities such as those instigated by Chang Ping-huan and Wu Wei-t'ang also occurred from time to time. The two Ch'ing commanders, Hsiang Jung and Ch'i Shan, though incompetent and cowardly, remained small but persistent thorns in the side of the T'ai-p'ing empire.

It was State Minister Lo Ta-kang who had once advanced the strategies of "attacking the north and stabilizing the south." Since his death from battle injuries in the fifth year, *I-yung* (1855), no one in the court had seen fit to repeat his suggestion. After the transfer of the Assistant King from his pacification command in Anhwei to the Western front, the precarious situation there had gradually been stabilized. But Shih had no time to devote his energy to the overall planning. Aware of the obstinate character of the Heavenly and Eastern kings, he believed it would be futile to make further suggestions. Judging from the immediate situation of the Heavenly Capital, the elimination of the two Ch'ing military camps was a matter of first priority in terms of offense as well as defense. On this matter, at least, the opinions of the Heavenly, Eastern and Assistant kings were unanimous. An all-out war against the two Ch'ing military camps ensued as a result.

On the twenty-sixth day of the second month of the sixth year, *Ping-ch'en* (April 2, 1856), the T'ai-p'ing army under the leadership of the King of Yen, Ch'in Jih-kang, routed the North Camp at Yangchow; more than one hundred twenty batallions fell like dominoes. Ch'in's victorious army marched westward without encountering serious resistance. He then returned to Nanking to rest his men briefly at Swallow's Jetty, a town northeast of the capital. Then began the attack on the South Camp. By order of the Eastern King, Ch'in's army approached the objective from the northeast. Shih Ta-k'ai was ordered to march his forces in three columns to attack the enemy from the southwest. His troops hurried back from Kiangsi, travelling day and night on forced march, and cut Hsiang Jung's army in two in the outskirts of Nanking. Meanwhile, the Eastern King led the remaining forces in the city to attack the enemy's rear in the suburbs near Ch'ao-yang and T'ung-chi gates, destroying over twenty batallions of the South Camp. Under the combined lightning attacks of the three kings, Hsiang Jung did not have a chance to resist. He fled to the city of Tan-yang where he took ill as a result of his defeat. The two Ch'ing camps, once poised to pounce on the Heavenly Capital at the first opportunity for the past three years, had now been completely destroyed and the greatest threat to the T'ai-p'ing Kingdom removed.

By the order of the Eastern King, all the loot, weapons, and ammunition captured from the South Camp was removed to the city. A small contingent of soldiers was stationed at

Hsiao-ling-wei, and the three victorious armies were given rewards and feted for three days.

Before the triumphal march, news of the victory had been transmitted to the capital through a document marked "Extra Urgent." Upon its receipt, the Northern King Wei Ch'ang-hui immediately reported the news to the Heavenly King who ordered all officials and citizens to welcome the victorious army on the streets upon their return to the city.

The citizens of the capital were awakened from their dreams in the early morning of the seventeenth day of the fifth month (June 20, 1856), as mounted men from the Northern King's establishment passed through main roads and alleys, beating on brass gongs, proclaiming the joyful news of victory to the masses:

> By order of the Northern King, all civilian and military officials of the court, the army, and government offices, and brothers and sisters from the civilian quarters should present themselves on the sidewalks of the city's thoroughfares to welcome the triumphal return of the three kings.

Within the hour, Wei Ch'ang-hui, preceded by a full contingent of his insignia bearers, marched toward Ch'ao-yang Gate. At the parade's head was a black-bordered yellow silk flag with the words "Vice-Commander-General of the Army, the Northern King Wei." Stationing himself by the main road just outside Ch'ao-yang Gate, Wei respectfully awaited the heroes' arrival. Shortly afterwards a thousand cavalrymen led by the three kings arrived; their numerous flags obscured the sunlight as their horses' hooves kicked up a cloud of dust. One of the orderlies of the Northern King waved a signal flag, and three ceremonial gun salutes were fired, accompanied by the sound of gongs and drums.

At the head of the procession was the Eastern King, dressed in a yellow tunic with a golden hat on his head. Mounted on a tall stallion, he was followed closely by the Assistant King and the King of Yen. At the sight of the procession, the

Northern King dismounted and stood beside the road. As the Eastern King's mount approached, all insignia bearers cried out in unison:

Long live the Lord of Nine Thousand Years! Long live! Long live!

The Northern King knelt on the ground, saying, "The campaign has made so much demand on you, Fourth Brother! Second Brother has ordered me to greet you. I've been here quite a while!"

Without dismounting, the Eastern King reined his mount to a halt. Whinnying loudly, the white steed reared up on its hind legs. A faint smile appeared on the Eastern King's face.

"The campaign has made demand on you all, Brothers!"

The Northern King rose. The other two kings had already dismounted and rushed forward to greet the Northern King.

As ceremonial salutes were fired a second time, the four kings entered Ch'ao-yang Gate together on horseback. Each king's contingent of insignia bearers were already waiting at the gate and fell into the procession according to the status of their masters in the T'ai-p'ing hierarchy.

Summer days in the vicinity of the Yangtze could be very hot. The golden sunshine, the joy of victory, and the sound of gongs and drums had all combined to create an atmosphere of high spirits and enthusiasm. People abandoned themselves and fell into a paroxysm of exultation. Old men with white hair and beards and pretty girls in the first bloom of youth, all holding bouquets of fresh flowers, stood attentively behind incense tables set up on the roadside for the occasion. According to the custom of the Heavenly Kingdom, the incense tables were covered with red embroidered cloths and spread with delicacies and bowls of rice and tea. As the procession approached, the spectators craned their necks to catch a glimpse of the colorful flags and gleaming weapons. Their hearts, filled with pride, were beating to the rhythmic martial music of gongs and drums.

The citizens of the Heavenly Capital had waited for two hours on the street before the procession appeared. Although eager to see the silk-clad insignia and lantern bearers, the red-charactered official title placards, and the silk embroidered flags, the people were even more anxious to have a close look at the four kings about whom they had heard so much. Now they had been given the chance. Under a yellow state umbrella embroidered with dragons, rode on a white horse a middle-aged general, attired in a yellow tunic and a golden hat. He was blind in one eye which he kept shut. It was the Eastern King who bore the numerous self-bequested sobriquets of "Chief Pacifier," "Sacred Wind," "Teacher Hsiu," and "Redeemer of the Afflicted." Old men discussed the meaning of his titles and nodded their heads in agreement. One of them explained the mysterious old belief that a green dragon dwelled in the east and asserted that the Eastern King must have been the personification of that dragon. Immediately behind the Eastern King rode a light-complexioned, beardless general; all his personal insignia were bordered in black. The old man explained to his friend that the color black had always been identified with the north and with martial spirit. Thus he was almost sure that the general was the Northern King. Next in the procession, mounted on a gleaming black horse was the Assistant King Shih Ta-k'ai, a young general with a sombre face, high cheekbones, and sparkling eyes. His loose, long hair framed his face. Close behind him was a smart looking young girl on a tall, gray horse. She was identified as Pao-ying, the adopted daughter of the Assistant King. She was dressed in red from head to foot, with a short dagger dangling at her side. Her hair was coiled into a bun which stuck out from the central opening of a round gauze hat. Her headpiece was decorated with a few gems, but she wore no earrings. All in all she presented a charming and valiant appearance. The last figure in the parade was a middle-aged general. A pair of sunken eyes glittered in his long, broad-mouthed face. He was the King of Yen, Ch'in Jih-kang.

The generals were followed by a thousand-odd cavalry-men, all wearing red headgear and yellow jackets. They rode on horses of different colors which appeared before the spectators' eyes like a passing amber-colored cloud. The soldiers eyed groups of young girls as they rode past, faintly smiling and making postures to show off their valor. The sound of horses' hooves pounding the stone pavement was as impetuous and sharp as a summer shower, but like an evanescent summer shower, it soon faded away.

T he imperial garden was filled with the sound of gaiety and laughter. The Heavenly King had decided to celebrate the victory by entertaining the three kings and other high officials with a feast in the garden that had been completed only a year ago.

Table after table laden with abundant foods was set up under the tall cypresses and pines, in painted pavilions and pleasure boats. The lotus blossoms in the artificial pond had just bloomed and their faint fragrance wafted in the air. In an open pavilion in the center of the pond, connected to the shore by little zigzag bridges were set five banquet tables reserved for the three victorious kings and other selected high officials. All other guests were entertained elsewhere.

The tables were laden with rare and varied delicacies. Female officials in embroidered silk waited on the guests. The Heavenly King sat at the head table, while the Eastern, Northern, Assistant Kings and the King of Yen each sat at a separate table, each attended by two female officials of his own. Several high officials, including the King of Yü, Hu I-kuang, the Marquis of Tso-t'ien, Ch'en Ch'eng-jung, the Heavenly King's brother-in-law Lai Han-ying, and State Minister Meng Teh-en had been honored by special invitation to sit in the water pavilion.

The old T'ai-p'ing customs were still observed at this time. Smoking and drinking were strictly forbidden to the military men as well as civilians. Offenders were either whipped or decapitated. These prohibitions were followed even at the feast given by the Heavenly King. The head of the Imperial Kitchen was an old Kwangsi brother who knew the gastronomic preferences of the old comrades. Most dishes had been prepared by deep-frying or sautéing with liberal amounts of pepper and other condiments. Despite his lofty position as the sovereign of a kingdom, the Heavenly King still preferred the simple food to which he had grown accustomed in the past. Today the menu for his table consisted of seaslugs with cabbage, shark's fin with beansprouts, bird's nest with beancurd, and lichee nuts with pork. With the magic touch of expert chefs, these relatively common fare, by adding some exotic ingredients, had been transformed into extremely tasty gourmet dishes.

The atmosphere of the victory celebration feast was one of jubilation. Since the gathering was not held in an official hall, it had the informal casualness of a family gathering enlivened by the feeling of joy gained after a decisive victory. The several kings and high dignitaries present abandoned for once their recently acquired semimandarin language used exclusively in the court, and reverted to their old ways of speech when they were brothers in the early days in the military camp. They also conducted themselves with much less restraint than would have been required of them in the Dragon Hall.

The Eastern King recounted the details of how he had directed the attack on the Ch'ing North and South camps. He spoke in the unrefined language of a charcoal kiln laborer, a jargon that had seldom been used in public for the past three or four years. He described with enthusiasm how a demon general committed suicide with his own pistol after surrendering and how a homosexual friend of the head demon Hsiang Jung had been stabbed in his left leg because he had not fled fast enough.

The Eastern King jokingly compared the head demon who had confined himself in the city of Tan-yang to a turtle in an urn that could be caught anytime. Now, he triumphantly declared, not a single demon soldier could be found in the vicinity of the Heavenly Capital.

Pausing briefly, he signaled with a glance to the two

female officials who stood behind him. The two girls, Yang Ch'ang-mei and Shih Ting-lan, were among the four girls transferred from the palace to the Eastern King's residence since the time of the "Heavenly Father's descent to earth" two years before. Heavily painted and dressed in fineries, they looked even more attractive than before. But the Heavenly King did not recognize them, perhaps due to his absentmindedness. At the signal, Shih Ting-lan stepped forward with a scroll in her hands while Yang Ch'ang-mei moved to help unroll it, revealing a map. The two girls held the scroll in front of the Heavenly King for his perusal.

"In the fifth year *I-yung* (1855)," the Eastern King continued, "the Heavenly Kingdom had under its control eleven cities and districts, including Nanking, An-ch'ing, Chinkiang, Lukiang, and Wuchang. At the end of last year, four more districts, including Yüan-chou and Jui-chou in Kiangsi were added. In the spring of this year, two more districts, Kunchow and Ning-tu came under our control. Today, the Heavenly Kingdom's territory covers twenty-three districts and cities. Second Brother, so long as this younger brother of yours remains by your side, the territory of the Heavenly Kingdom will expand and become increasingly safer!"

At the end of the presentation, Yang Ch'ang-mei rolled up the scroll and handed it to a female official standing behind the Heavenly King for safekeeping.

"Not long ago, some people were worried that the two demon camps would swallow us up in a few gulps," the Eastern King said, gesticulating grandly. "In fact, the opposite has happened—in just two gulps, we have swallowed both camps, bones and all!"

The Eastern King's speech had been delivered in a manner bordering on impudence. He concluded with a resounding burst of laughter that sent the tableware reverberating. But with the exception of the Northern King, no one among the guests present responded with laughter. Even the Northern King's laughter was not spontaneous, and melted into thin air in face of the stony reaction of all the others present.

"Brother Ch'ing!" began the Heavenly King, deliberately and solemnly. The old brethren immediately realized that the Heavenly King had reverted to the tone customarily used in addressing his subordinates in the Dragon Hall. "This is the result of your careful planning as well as the grace accorded us by the Heavenly Father and Heavenly Brother!"

"The grace of the Heavenly Father and Heavenly Brother is omnipresent," interceded the Northern King. "Again, the grace and virtue of our Second Brother have spread over the four seas so that all people have submitted to us gladly. The prestige of the Heavenly Kingdom has been greatly enhanced!"

"Without the bloody sacrifice and valor of our old and new brethren, the three-year siege of the Heavenly Capital could not have been lifted," commented the Assistant King, his voice deliberately even. But his friend Hu I-kuang who understood him best detected that despite the calm voice he was greatly disturbed.

The atmosphere at the feast became awkward. No one ventured to utter a word. The female officials waiting on tables discontinued their hushed conversation and silence prevailed in the water pavilion. Only the accidental clinking of eating utensils could be heard.

As if to mollify the guests during this uneasy moment, a few female officials brought in several dishes of dogmeat and seafood.

It was the usual practice at all feasts given by the Heavenly King that he would frequently offer his favorite dishes to his trusted generals and officials as a sign of special affection and esteem. Today, he had ordered his female officials to bring dishes of braised dogmeat first to the two conquering heroes back from the front, the Assistant King and the King of Yen, and then to the Northern King and the King of Yü. Finally, a middle-aged female official was ordered to bring a dish of seaslugs and beancurd to the Eastern King. Perhaps by accident, the Eastern King suddenly raised his right hand. His sleeve caught the dish from the server's hand, dashing it to the ground, where it broke into countless pieces, splashing the food all over the place. The female server stood there dumbfounded, expecting harsh punishment. Unexpectedly, the Heavenly King was not at all angry. Instead, he gave the Eastern King a cold stare and ordered the server to clean up the mess and retire from the pavilion.

"Second Brother!" said the Eastern King quite nonchalantly. "Important people are apt to forget things. This younger brother likes nothing better than dogmeat." Then turning to Yang Ch'ang-mei, he said, "Go ask the Lord of Ten Thousand Years for a dish of dogmeat for me!"

Yang Ch'ang-mei went over and knelt before the Heavnly King. "Your servant begs for a dish of dogmeat for the Lord of Nine Thousand Years," she said calmly.

The guests all stopped eating and a deadly silence prevailed in the water pavilion.

The Heavenly King glanced at the kneeling female official. Now it dawned on him that this girl was none other than the supervisor of the female lake-diggers who had been taken away from him supposedly on the order of the "Heavenly Father" two-and-a-half years ago. The girl was now even more attractive than ever. The unpleasant incident vividly flashed back to his mind. Was it merely an accident that the Eastern King had chosen this girl to ask for favors, or had it been part of a deliberate design to humiliate him?

The Heavenly King was overwhelmed by mixed feelings of anger, shame, bitterness, and impotence. The girl's request did not register in his mind. Again, rather unexpectedly, the Heavenly King did not lose his temper.

"You've been waiting on us for hours today," he told the kneeling girl. "All of you must be tired." Then he turned his head and ordered to have a special table prepared for all the girls that attended the four kings. They left the pavilion together to enjoy their meal.

Meanwhile, the Eastern King stood up, went over to the Heavenly King's table and grabbed a dish of dogmeat.

"Thanks, Second Brother, for the favor," he said brazenly, carrying the dish to his own table.

Such unceremonial behavior took everyone aback. The Assistant King was about to rise to his feet, but the King of Yü tugged at his coat in the back. The Northern King who sat opposite the Assistant King, shook his head slightly, signaling him to stop. Ch'in Jih-kang, Ch'en Ch'eng-jung, and others looked at each other in consternation. Only State Minister Meng Teh-en continued to eat as if nothing had happened. His pale, round cheeks puffed with food, and his thick, fat lips were smeared with grease.

The Northern King had fully expected that an explosion would be imminent, knowing how obstinate and bullheaded the Heavenly King was. But what ensued was entirely beyond everyone's expectations.

"Brother Ch'ing!" the Heavenly King gave out a resonant laugh, throwing back his head. "You're narrow-minded indeed! I'm the sovereign of a state and I possess everything in the realm. Why should I be stingy about a dish of dogmeat!"

Turning around, he gave an order to one of his female officials. "Go tell the people at the Imperial Kitchen to prepare ten dishes of dogmeat for the Lord of Nine Thousand Years!"

The Eastern King busily devoured the dogmeat that he had grabbed from the Heavenly King's table, while observing the latter's reaction.

"Second Brother!" he rejoined, smirking. "When you were a poor school teacher in Kuan-lu-pu village, did you ever dream that you would live to see a day like this? In those days, you were lucky if you had a bowl of congee plus some potatoes!"

"How do you know?" asked the Heavenly King, his face flushed crimson.

"One of my grooms came from your village," the Eastern King continued, as if he were relating an interesting story. "He told me a ditty ridiculing the poor peasants of your village that runs:

"Kuan-lu-pu, Kuan-lu-pu,
the usual fare is congee with potato.
Whoever wants to eat rice that's firm
has to go to Hsin-kai-tu."

The guests at the feast, all of them old breathren from Kwangsi, laughed at the Eastern King's anecdote of the "good old days." Female officials waiting on the tables, though mostly from Kiangsu and Chekiang, also could make out the sarcastic tone of the Eastern King, for they had served in the palace for a number of years by now. They covered their mouths with their hands, lest their giggling might violate the court etiquette. Some younger girls, however, laughed so uninhibitedly that their shoulders shook and tears came into their eyes. This comic scene was a welcome stimulus to their otherwise drab existence.

"From time immemorial," the Heavenly King began in a didactic tone which again surprised the listeners, "many rulers of states have come from noble families, but not a few were of humble origin. Therefore, men of perception and knowledge never evaluate a man's worth by looking into his background, lineage, or social origin. Hsiang Yü was a descendant of the ruler of the state of Ch'u and Liu Pang was only a station master of the Ssu district. Able men like Han Hsin and Wang Ling deserted Hsiang Yü and went to support Liu Pang, because they knew Hsiang Yü was doomed to failure and that Liu Pang was a man of destiny. Liu Pang did not treat Fan Kuei, another great general, with contempt because the latter had originally been a dogcatcher; why should Fan Kuei treat his sovereign with disrespect because he had started out as a lowly station master?"

The Eastern King, his solitary eye blinking, listened to the words of the Heavenly King attentively. For the past seven or eight years, he had advanced himself from a member of the God Worshippers Society to Commander-in-Chief of the T'ai-p'ing Army and had learned to understand the main gist of imperial documents thanks to his native intelligence, although all his decrees and reports were written by his subordinates. He had heard the names of historical figures like Hsiang Yü and Liu Pang, but was unaware of the stories the Heavenly King had just told. What upset him most was the latter's use of literary expressions, which were beyond his comprehension, in narrating the tales. He also suspected that the King's references were analogies, designed to ridicule and humiliate him.

Fortunately, the King of Yü, Hu I-kuang, always alert and clever, intervened to ease the tense situation.

"Second Brother just told us the story of Liu Pang, the founder of the Han dynasty and his right-hand man, Fan Kuei," Hu said. "Fan Kuei had been a dogcatcher in his youth, but Liu Pang treated him as a hero and made him the commander of an army. The sovereign and the general worked together hand in glove. As a result of their combined efforts, they founded the Han dynasty."

"If Fan Kuei was originally a dogcatcher, I'll bet he was a dogmeat lover too," joined in the Assistant King with a resounding laughter.

The Northern King also tried to turn the conversation in another direction. "In ancient times there were many famous men who could drink and eat in large quantities. For example, a well-known general of the State of Chao, Lien P'o, at the age of eighty, could eat one peck of rice and ten catties of meat at one sitting."

"Fourth Brother!" he continued, sending the Eastern King a fawning smile, "You're still young. The burden of conquering the enemy and unifying the entire realm rests squarely on your shoulders. You should eat more for the sake of our sovereign and all the brothers and sisters of the Heavenly Kingdom. Come! Come! Let me present you with another dish of dogmeat!"

So saying, he delivered a dish of dogmeat to the Eastern King's table.

Five days later, the Eastern King summoned the Northern King, the Assistant King, and the King of Yen to his official residence to receive their new assignments.

"At present, although the two demon generals, Hsiang Jung and Ch'i Shan, have been defeated and the two camps destroyed, the demon chief Hsien-feng is planning to stage a comeback," declared the Eastern King gravely. "You three are the pillars of the state. Instead of staying idle in the Capital, you'll have to take up new, difficult assignments."

The Northern King was assigned to Kiangsi to manage military affairs there; the Assistant King was ordered to Hupeh to plan for the recovery of Wuchang, and the King of Yen, Ch'in Jih-kang, was sent to Tan-yang to eliminate the remnants of the Ch'ing forces there.

After all the preparations were made, the three kings started on their journeys. On such occasions civilian and military leaders in the court would go outside the city gate to bid farewell to the departing generals. When the Assistant King's turn came, he noticed that among the officials who came to send them off, the King of Yü, Hu I-kuang, was absent. His pretext was that he was ill. But the Assistant King remembered that only a few days before at the feast given by the Heavenly King, Hu had been full of vigor, the very personification of health and well-being. The fact was that Hu I-kuang had suffered a military reversal at Liu-an-chou the year before. His title of nobility, the King of Yü, had been taken away from him, although it was later restored. For a long time, he had isolated himself from friends, refusing to attend any social function. Being a close friend of the Assistant King, his absence from the farewell party appeared odd.

The Assistant King, accompanied by his adopted daughter Pao-ying, as well as several civilian and military assistants and a few hundred bodyguards, reached the riverbank by way of Phoenix Gate and were ready to board ships that would transport them upriver. On both sides of the Yangtze, the first crop of rice had ripened, turning the landscape a sea of yellow as far as his eyes could see. The Assistant King watched his soldiers leading their horses on board ship. This would be the harvest time in his native Kwangsi, he thought. Nostalgia totally engulfed him, and did not lift until his troops had all boarded and were ready to leave. He then dismounted and gave the reins and his crop to an orderly. Just at the moment, the commander of the naval forces, T'ang Cheng-ts'ai, arrived and knelt before him.

"Your servant T'ang Cheng-ts'ai awaits the word of Your Excellency, Lord of Five Thousand Years!"

The Assistant King stepped forward and helped him to his feet, murmuring, "Your Excellency, you're too kind!"

As he extended his hand, the Assistant King felt something being thrust into it. A quick glance proved that it was a piece of paper. Acting as if nothing had happened, the Assistant King boarded his flagship with his adopted daughter. T'ang Cheng-ts'ai waved the signal pennant, and the fleet of several hundred transport ships raised sail and departed.

As soon as he was alone on board, the Assistant King read the message which had been written in small characters. It read:

> The feast at the imperial garden showed that a coup is imminent. Now that the three generals have been sent away, a seditious takeover can happen any minute. As a pillar of the state, it is your duty to fight on the battlefield, but it is also your responsibility to rectify wrongs in the court.

The message was not signed, but the handwriting was clearly that of Hu I-kuang. The Assistant King was thoroughly disturbed; he felt the blood boiling inside him. A few seagulls followed behind the ships, gliding above the warm breeze that caressed the water's surface. Willows on both sides of the riverbank swayed gently in the wind. All the transports were now in full sail, struggling against the obstinate waves. The Assistant King stood on the prow of the ship, and laying one hand on the hilt of his sword, recited an ancient poem in a low voice:

Standards and pennants fly
　　high in the upper reaches;
The fate of the sovereign and his ministers hangs in
　　the balance.
Messages asking for assistance arrive like
　　snowflakes in a storm;
Should I turn the sails to reach the city under siege?
Distressed dragons and water sprites revive
　　when the tide turns,
Eagles and hawks soar to the heavens
　　when bright autumn arrives.
The sound of wailing and imploring disturbs
　　the quietness of the night;
Be patient, soon there will be delivery,
　　Count the days.

The Heavenly King's temper had become increasingly raw
and harsh. Female officials were breathless with anxiety
and kept their eyes downcast in his presence. Consorts and
concubines, too, behaved carefully and moved in trepidation.
The beautiful views and blooming flowers in the imperial
garden failed to unknit his brows; nor could the charming
songs and alluring damsels of the musical troupes relieve his
disturbed mind.

One hot summer night, the King's feet unconsciously
carried him to the apartment of Consort Hsieh. He suddenly
remembered that Consort Hsieh had been in ill-health ever
since he had kicked her and caused an abortion two-and-a-half
years before, leaving her pale and thin. In the past, he had
spent much time in her apartment. But since the incident,
he often halted at her door, restrained by his remorse from
entering. Consort Hsieh understood the Heavenly King's
state of mind and tried to avoid him whenever possible. He
turned and walked toward Consort Fang's apartment instead.

Consort Fang was finishing her evening make-up when the

King entered her boudoir. She helped him remove his coat and invited him to sit in his favorite chair—an imported swivel chair inlaid with mother of pearl. Before she started a conversation with him, she ordered her maid to bring in a candelabra of her own design to take the place of the red and golden threaded palace lamp which was in the center of the room. This candelabra had a stand made of green jade in the shape of a lotus leaf. From the base branched out three stems, each topped with a half blooming lotus blossom carved from either red or white jade. The light from the candles placed in the center of each flower was thus softened by the thin petals of the jade flowers. A few stalks of bamboo swayed in the wind outside the green gauze-covered casement window. "Denser than patters on the phoenix tail, the stirred leaves murmured with a pent dragon's moan."* A multileveled bookcase lined the wall, with packets of old books, antique ceremonial bronze vessels, and precious ceramic and procelain vases filling all available spaces. On a Soochow-style dresser, fitted with an imported mirror which was now covered with a piece of lavender cloth, only a few toilet articles were displayed. A western "eight-note" music box rested on a sacrificial table in a corner of the room. Facing the window was a lacquer-surfaced writing desk on which only two pen holders, an ink slab, and an open book with a paper weight placed on it were visible.

The Heavenly King rose from his chair and walked toward the writing desk. He removed the paper weight and found the book to be a Sung edition of the *Historical Memoirs*. In the early days of the revolt, he had labelled all Confucian classics as "heretical books." After the establishment of the Heavenly Capital, however, he had occasionally read some of these books at his leisure and had discovered that not all of them contained

---

*These two descriptive phrases *Lung-yin hsi-hsi, feng-wei sen-sen* were borrowed by the author from the famous novel, *Dreams of the Red Chamber*, depicting the sound of the swaying bamboo. The translation in quotation is by David Hawkes. *See The Story of the Stone*, Vol. I, p. 516.

heretical sayings, especially the *Historical Memoirs*. Consort Fang was certainly aware that this work was one of his favorite "heretical books." The Heavenly King took up the book, looked at the opened page, and found it to be the beginning of the chapter entitled "Biography of Hsiang Yü." He felt his heart leap. Automatically he walked to the window, sat down, and started reading. After some time, he became aware that he was surrounded in silence. The autumn breeze had reduced the humidity in the air. Turning his head, he saw Consort Fang who had already changed into evening attire, standing silently behind him. She responded with a faint smile to his glance. The candlelight filtering through the jade lotus petals reflected on the delicate and soft features of the consort, making the two beauties—her smiling face and the carved lotus blossoms—indistinguishable from each other. Consort Fang, imitating the casual style of the English barbarian women, had put on a white laced blouse and a long, dark red pleated skirt. Her long hair was braided into an "as you wish" knot, and a pair of delicate apple green jade earrings dangled from her ears. Dressed in this new fashion, she looked quite different from her daytime self. The King and consort stared at each other for a few moments. The English clock standing sentry in a corner sounded its musical chimes, indicating that it was almost midnight.

The Heavenly King had by now spent several nights in a row at Consort Fang's apartment. Queen Lai and Consort Hsieh, sensing that their lord was not as tense as before, felt much relieved. Aside from sending him his favorite food and pastries to Consort Fang's apartment, they tried not to do anything to disturb him.

Another evening, Consort Fang ordered her maid to move the swivel chair to the veranda and placed some fruits and a cup of "black dragon" tea on a side table. She deemed it her duty to help her lord enjoy a cool evening after a hot summer day. She sat on a small stool beside him. The maid lighted a stick of rare incense and a thin curl of smoke drifted in the air. To entertain her lord, Fang volunteered to play the *p'i-p'a*, a musical instrument which she played expertly. She held the *p'i-p'a* close to her breasts. Making a semicircle gesture with one hand, she plucked the strings effortlessly, producing sounds that touched a variety of human emotions. At times the music sounded like the pounding of impatient raindrops; at other times the charge of an ironclad cavalry unit. It was a wonder that so simple an instrument could produce such a variety of sounds. When played in a sentimental vein, the music could make the listener cry; when stroked angrily, it could make a coward fight. At the end of the recital, the mood was like that felt at the conclusion of a fierce bloody battle—the sound of warriors and horses gradually faded away, the field deserted, and the bugles silenced. Only a cool moon hung over the empty fortress and its silver light flooded the ground. All that remained was a sense of emptiness to mourn the fallen heroes.

After a long silence, the Heavenly King inquired: "What you played sounded like a depiction of war, although I don't know anything about music. Am I right?"

"It's an old melody," answered Consort Fang with a smile, "called 'An Amush from Ten Directions,' based on the story of the decisive battle fought in Kai-hsia between Hsiang Yü and Liu Pang. Although Hsiang Yü had the strength to move mountains and talent overshadowing his age, he was a man of obstinancy and poor judgment. He also lacked the power to make quick decisions and only paid lip service to the concept of benevolence and righteousness. His army was completely routed in the battle of Kai-hsia. He died at his own hand, cutting his throat at the Wu River Ferry."

The Heavenly King nodded and heaved a sigh of understanding. He suspected that Consort Fang had deliberately left the book *Historical Memoirs* open at the "Biography of Hsiang Yü" to warn him of impending disaster. His suspicion was further strengthened by the music she had performed tonight depicting the tragic ending of Hsiang Yü. Hot tears gushed from his eyes. He realized that this delicate and sensitive young woman understood him better than all the civilian

She played "The Ambush" on the *p'i-p'a* for him.

and military officials in the court put together.

Although the Heavenly King had always been a man of obstinate and strong character, in the past three years, after leaving behind scenes of bloody battle, he had begun to enjoy a decadent and soft life in the palace in the company of young women. His lofty desire for the salvation of mankind and his determination to achieve it had left him without a trace. Since he had long deserted the battleground, he had to find new things in life for stimulation and to heighten his spirits. He had isolated himself from his old brethren who had fought with him side by side in the early years, and was plagued by a sense of solitude and impotence. His large harem corrupted him not only morally but physically as well. He lived within the palace walls in a daze, going through nonsensical routine without purpose year after year. He witnessed the proud summer sunshine on the green tiles and flying eaves of the palace walls, where it cast dark shadows. He observed the winter snow assault the tall pine and cypress trees in the garden, then engulfing them in a sheet of white, followed by the singing orioles and blooming flowers of spring. The sound of battle used to make his blood boil; the soldier's life used to make him feel young and vigorous. But now with hundreds of attendants catering to his every whim as he enjoyed a life of honor and comfort, he felt he had deteriorated, both mentally and physically. He was sure that only one person, Consort Fang, would understand the humiliating blow he had experienced at the feast a few days prior. Not even his old companion Queen Lai or his favorite concubine Consort Hsieh could probe into the deep recesses of his subconscious mind.

But what was he supposed to do?

"My dear Consort," the Heavenly King said with a smile. "Suppose one of these days someone drives me to the bank of Wu River. What would you do?"

The smile on the Consort's face vanished instantly. Her answer came instantaneously, yet it sounded like a considered reply delivered after much careful thought.

"I'll never be Consort Yü who committed suicide before her lord. I'll cut the enemy's throat before I die."

Silence ensued for a few moments, only to be broken by the charming yet determined voice of Consort Fang.

"However," she continued, "I don't think your Lordship will let anyone drive you to the bank of Wu River. An old saying, 'You should't allow anyone the indulgence to take you for granted,' explains it all. When one is driven to the bank of Wu River, it would be too late then for him to regret the feast at Hung-men!"

Touched by what the young consort had just said, the Heavenly King nodded his approval.

A month had elapsed after the feast at the imperial garden. One hot and humid evening, a blue felt-covered sedan chair, escorted by two female guards, short swords on their backs and mounted on chestnut-colored horses, crossed the drawbridge of the palace, through the Sun Gate and stopped at the side door of the imperial living quarters. A swarthy complexioned, stubby "lion-nosed" young female guard dismounted agilely. Holding the reins in her hand, she knocked on the door lightly. The door soon opened and a gray-haired old man appeared. Obviously he was happy to greet the visitor—she was his daughter.

"Ah-li, I haven't seen you for a long time!"

"Dad, your hair is much whiter than before!" The girl stepped forward and whispered into the old man's ear. Then she introduced the other guard, a tall, fair girl, to her father. She handed over the reins of the two horses to the old man, trusting them to his care.

"Dad, would you please feed the horses?" she asked. "We'll accompany the lady for a brief visit at the palace, and be back real soon."

Courtseying briefly, the other girl politely addressed the old man as "Uncle Chung."

"Ah-hsiao, you two are inseparable, aren't you!" the old man said. "Is the lady coming?"

As they spoke, the sedan chair arrived. Hung Hsüan-chiao, Consort of the late Western King and the sister of the Heavenly King, alighted, wearing a military tunic and carrying a short sword. As the old man began to kneel before her, she stopped him quickly.

"Uncle Chung, you look fine."

"Thanks to the grace of the Heavenly Father, the Heavenly Brother, and the Heavenly King, I don't think I'll return to Heaven yet for another two or three years," he laughed heartily as he answered.

Hung Hsüan-chiao told the sedan-chair bearers to return and not wait for her. Then she turned to Ah-li, addressing her kindly.

"Ah-li, you haven't seen your father for a long time. Why don't you stay here and visit him? Ah-hsiao will accompany me to the palace."

Hung Hsüan-chiao had been the commander of the women's forces since the establishment of the Heavenly Capital. She was not very close to all of her three brothers, due to the fact that she had spent much of her time in the camp. Two of her brothers, who were much older than her, had never shown much affection for her when she was young. Now that they led a life of comfort and luxury, she had even less contact with them. Only the third brother, Hsiu-ch'üan, and her sister-in-law, Queen Lai, had maintained a normal relationship with her. Although she was younger than Hsiu-ch'üan by fifteen years, she often tagged along after this third brother of hers tending animals in the fields. As a teenager, she had joined the God Worshippers Society and later followed her brother to Thistle Mountain. For over twenty years, her life had been inseparable from that of her brother. Her sister-in-law had come from a neighboring village and they had grown up together. After Lai married her brother, the two women had become friends. Now, in addition to attending the business of the women's camp, Hung Hsüan-chiao spent her spare time either in practicing martial arts in her garden or in supervising her son's study. She came to visit her brother and sister-in-law in the palace only once in four or five months. Whenever she paid a visit, she would ride on horseback, followed by one or two dozen female guards. Ordinarily, the Imperial Front Gate remained closed after dark till dawn. Being a sister of the Heavenly King she was permitted to pass through the Sun Gate which led to the side door of the imperial garden. There was an inner gate, guarded by female officials, that separated the garden from the inner palace. Hung Hsüan-chiao's two most intimate followers—Ah-li and Ah-hsiao—were only eleven or twelve years old when their parents joined the army. As adolescents they had joined the women's army and had become personal guards of the commander. Ah-li's father, Chung "the Fourth," had been promoted to the position of brigade leader in the army, but had become tired of army life, so the Heavenly King appointed him doorkeeper at the side door of the imperial garden, because he was a fellow villager of the sovereign and, therefore, could be trusted. When Hung Hsüan-chiao came to visit her brother and sister-in-law, she always went through the side door. Since the old man had seen Hsüan-chiao grow up, there was no need to stand on ceremony. However, today the old man was puzzled by the fact that she had come in a sedan chair with only two attendants, arriving hurriedly after dark.

The old man's confusion was not without reason.

Although Hung Hsüan-chiao had little interest in court politics, through her own network among the female officials of the various kings' establishments she had learned about the humiliating incident at the victory celebration feast a month earlier. Ever since she joined her brother's revolt at Thistle Mountain, she had known the soldier of fortune, Yang Hsiu-ch'ing, who was then destitute but adventurous. Soon, she worked together with two young men, Yang and her future husband Hsiao Ch'ao-kuei, in training recruits. Yang had expressed his admiration for her more than once.

But in the opinion of the young girl, this young man was too cunning and crafty, which offset his intelligence and ability to put his experiences to use. She felt he had none of the innate goodness of a peasant. Instead, she fell in love with Hsiao Ch'ao-kuei, a practical and kind man of few words. They were married, with Feng Yün-shan acting as matchmaker. Feng, an early comrade, later invested as the Southern King, was aware then that Yang would not be a good match for Hsüan-chiao. Later, by virtue of his talent and manipulation, Yang had become commander-in-chief and the sole arbiter of political and military affairs. He had the trust of the Heavenly King, but was feared by all other officials. Before his untimely death, her husband had expressed several times his concern about Yang's trickery and arrogance. Therefore, in recent years she had paid special attention to Yang's every move for the sake of the future of the Heavenly Kingdom as well as for her brother's sake. Three days before, the wife of the King of Yü, Hu I-kuang, had visited her in the evening and told her some alarming news. Thus she felt the premonition that something terrible would happen soon.

Ten days prior to this, the Eastern King had sent a messenger to summon the King of Yü, Hu I-kuang, to his official residence for consultation. The latter had hurriedly put on his official gown and went over. But when he arrived in the main hall, he found it deserted. A retainer told him that the Eastern King was conducting a meeting in the conference hall in the garden and was waiting for him there. Although he was one of the old brethren who had participated in the revolt in Kwangsi, he knew that he and Yang had never been on intimate terms. This invitation was thus suspicious, to say the least. As he entered the Purple Cloud Enclosure, he saw light emanating from the conference hall and heard the sound of people talking and laughing. As he approached Cloud Gazing Tower, he became aware of several hundred armed guards hidden in complete darkness behind the trees and pavilions. Originally a military *hsiu-ts'ai*, Hu I-kuang had fought in many battles in recent years and knew what all this meant.

Adjusting his court gown, Hu entered the conference hall with disciplined composure. The first thing that met his eye was a sacrificial table in the middle of the hall upon which rested an altar of incense and other paraphernalia. A velvet curtain had been raised high and dozens of candles were burning brightly. A religious ceremony was in progress evidently. Several hundred officials were present. The military officials were headed by the Board President Fu Hsüeh-hsien, the civilian officials by Vice Board President Hou Ch'ien-fang, and the female officials by the Yang sisters. After the ceremony, they all hailed the Eastern King as the "Lord of Ten Thousand Years!"

Hu I-kuang hurriedly went forward and saluted the Eastern King, kneeling.

"Fourth Brother," he said, "Please pardon me. I'm late in offering my congratulations."

Reluctantly, he joined the others in hailing Yang as the "Lord of Ten Thousand Years." The meeting adjourned without incident.

Hu's predictions were proven by the events that ensued. As part of the Eastern King's conspiracy, the three kings had been sent away. Aside from the three kings, Hu I-kuang was the highest in prestige among the military officers. Therefore, he had been tricked into attending the ceremony, and by acquiescence had become a participant of the Eastern King's grand plan.

However, Hu was aware of the fact that despite his outward capitulation, the Eastern King would never trust him. To avoid detection by Yang's surveillance network, he sent his wife away in a sedan chair, on the pretext of visiting relatives. The sedan chair made a few rounds on the main streets and wound up entering the residence of Hung Hsüan-chiao through a back door. Thus informed of the incident, Hsüan-chiao went directly to the palace to inform her brother.

Chung "the Fourth" led the two horses to the stable. Figuring that Hsüan-chiao might need another horse since the sedan chair had left, he went to fetch one from the stable and fed the three animals together. He asked Ah-li about the reason for her lady's visit, but the girl just glossed it over as a social call. It was almost midnight when Hsüan-chiao emerged with Ah-hsiao at the side door. Stars sparkled in the sky over the dewdrop-damp ground. There were no female officials carrying lanterns to light her way. Hsüan-chiao, appearing to be much preoccupied, made a simple gesture to the old man and rode away with her two attendants into complete darkness.

An hour later, at the side door of the imperial garden arrived three sedan chairs, each followed by two retainers. A young retainer handed Chung "the Fourth" a pass. After carefully examining it, Chung opened the door and let them in. In his three years as doorkeeper, such an unusual experience happened rarely—only once or twice a year at most. What had happened that night was strange indeed. This retainer, he observed, told the sedan-chair bearers to set down the chairs at a secluded spot in a wooded area. Under the dim moonlight, Chung could barely make out three officials emerging from the chairs. Two of them appeared familiar to him; one of them was Queen Lai's brother, Lai Han-ying, and the other State Minister Meng Teh-en. Chung could not positively identify the third—a tall and thin figure. It occurred to the old man that the retainer who had handed him the pass was the one whom he had met at the King of Yü's official residence and that the King of Yü was a close friend of Lai Han-ying. It dawned on him that the three men must have been summoned by the Heavenly King and that their visit must have been related to Hung Hsüan-chiao's visit an hour earlier.

Chung invited the retainers and the sedan-chair bearers to his room and served them tea. He then went back to the side door to see if anyone else was arriving. By then, complete silence reigned both inside and outside the imperial garden. Only the chirping insects in the bushes were making noise—a sort of discordant symphony. It was in the third phase of the month; a half moon hung in the cloudless sky. The sound of the nightwatchman's rattle became nearer and nearer. Counting the number of strikes, Chung knew it was the third watch.

After the nightwatchmen passed the side door in their rounds, Chung, driven by his curiosity, climbed to a pavilion on the tallest artificial hill in the garden to get a glimpse of the imperial study. The study was situated in a green tiled tower with flying eaves, separated from the pavilion by two courtyards and several bamboo groves. From a distance, Chung could only see that the study was brightly lit with palace lanterns and that shadows of several people were moving about. Chung figured that something important must have happened in the court or that some urgent military intelligence from the front demanded their attention. It was rare that the Heavenly King met with his ministers at midnight. But what puzzled Chung most was that if the matter being discussed was so important, why were the Eastern King and other high officials not invited?

When the three officials left the palace, it was already the fourth watch, very close to dawn.

At the same moment when Hung Chüan-chiao was visiting the palace, the Eastern King was approaching Rarity Depository Tower, escorted by two lantern carriers and followed by four female officials, the two Yang sisters among them. The Eastern King signaled the female officials to wait downstairs as he mounted the stairs alone to the study of the female *chuang-yüan*, Fu Shan-hsiang.

The waiting female officials could hear the rising voice of the Eastern King, and knew that his anger was mounting. The female *chuang-yüan* kept her voice calm and her tone entreating. The dialogue was interrupted by a loud crash— some porcelain ware had been dashed to pieces. The Eastern King stamped out of the study, fuming. In no uncertain terms, he ordered Shih Ting-lan, one of the four female officials, to have the female *chuang-yüan* confined in the study, without permission to leave under any circumstances. He further ordered that anyone making inquiries should be informed that the female *chuang-yüan* was being punished for violating the smoking prohibition.

A similar incident took place at the imperial palace. About an hour after the departure of the King of Yü and the two officials, a palace official told Chung to open the side door to let three mounted couriers out. As Chung opened the door, three husky men with document pouches on their backs galloped through the gate and vanished into semidarkness.

Shortly thereafter, a female official in charge of plants and flowers sauntered into Chung's room. As if making casual conversation, she inquired with a smile:

"Uncle Chung, you must have worked hard catering to all the people coming in and out of the garden last night."

"I haven't seen anybody," Chung replied with professional alertness. Having been a military officer for a number of years, he knew how to handle a situation like this.

The young female official looked at the fresh horse-hoof prints on the sandy ground, smiled and left without saying another word.

The female official, named Hou Hui-fang, was the sister of Hou Ch'ien-fang. After her brother had presented her to the Eastern King as a gift, the latter had presented her to the Heavenly King as a replacement for one of the four girls that had been taken away from the palace as a result of the "Heavenly Father's descent to earth." Planted by the Eastern King in the palace as a spy, she was required from time to time to report whatever happened there. In return she was promised to be made a consort in the future. However, after entering the service of the Heavenly King, she had been assigned to work in the garden and thus had no chance to come into close contact with the Heavenly King. A few days before, the Eastern King sent her a message asking her to pay special attention to the Heavenly King's movements. When she came into the garden earlier this morning, she had seen the three mounted couriers rushing out with document pouches on their backs. Instantly her eyes caught the words "Extra Urgent" stamped on a document that partially stuck out from one of the pouches, also revealing the word "Assistant" as part of the name of the address on its cover. She was curious about the whole affair and tried to pry some information from Chung. The old man's denial made her all the more suspicious. She went back to her room and wrote a secret report, intending to have it delivered by a secret agent—a guard who had also been planted in the palace by the Eastern King.

As Hou Hui-fang was bringing the letter to the agent, she met a maid of Consort Hsieh. A flower lover, the maid went to the garden every morning to pluck a few sprigs of fresh flowers for her mistress and Consort Fang. Being a very observant person, the maid noticed Hou Hui-fang's nervousness and reported it to her mistress. Consort Hsieh had spent some time in the camp and was well-versed in military intelligence activities. She immediately sent two female servants to tail Hou Hui-fang and caught her right at the moment when she was handing over the secret report to the agent.

Without first reporting to the Heavenly King who was asleep, Consorts Hsieh and Fang decided to confine Hou Hui-fang in the grotto of an artificial rockery.

The residents of the Heavenly Capital spent that tumultous and eventful night in blissful ignorance. Unaware of the chain of events that had taken place in the night, they were awakened from their sleep by the roaring thunder that preceded an impending summer storm over the Yangtze River.

A few hours later Consort Fang, with the approval of the Heavenly King, imitating Hou Hui-fang's handwriting, wrote a secret report to the Eastern King, supplying him with false information.

But so far as the Eastern King was concerned, he had crossed the Rubicon and there was no turning back. He again staged a "descent to earth" by the Heavenly Father and ordered "Hsiu-ch'üan, the ungrateful one, to abdicate in favor of the respected and meritorious Eastern King." There was nothing the Heavenly King could do except bang his head on the ground and promise that the "sacred order" would be obeyed. The abdication ceremony was to take place on the seventeenth day of the eighth month, which happened to be the birthday of the Eastern King.

That his grand plan could have been so successfully carried out was beyond the Eastern King's wildest dreams.

SEVEN

The Northern King Wei Ch'ang-hui had been in a state of depression since the fifth month of the year when he had been assigned by the Eastern King to manage military affairs in the Kiangsi front. For the past three years, he had been infuriated time and again by the Eastern King's arrogance and arbitrary behavior.

Wei Ch'ang-hui had been a *yamen* clerk before he joined the rebellion and had purchased the title of student of the imperial academy which had made him an official of the regular ninth rank in the Ch'ing civil service. Naturally, he had nothing but contempt for Yang Hsiu-ch'ing, the lowly charcoal kiln attendant. After Wei joned the God Worshippers Society, he had made a list of his family's properties which were considerable and turned them over to the Sacred Treasury. All his family members, including his father, sons, nephews, maids, and menservants, joined the T'ai-p'ing army as soldiers. Hence he commanded much respect from his peers. He considered himself one of the founders of the movement. It was beyond his expectation that when Hung Hsiu-ch'üan assumed the title of the Heavenly King two months after the rebellion started that this charcoal kiln attendant would be named commander of the main army, while Wei himself was only appointed commander of the right army, making him number four in rank of the T'ai-p'ing hierachy. Among the five commanders, Wei only held Feng Yün-shan and Shih Ta-k'ai in esteem. Yet, curiously, the two men were not jealous of Yang at all. Therefore, Wei had to keep his peace and wait to see what would happen. Soon he found that the charcoal kiln attendant was a man to be reckoned with. Under Yang's command, the T'ai-p'ing army took Yung-an-chou, surrounded Kueilin, occupied Yüeh-chou, captured Wuchang, and finally marched victoriously to Nanking in one fell swoop. Reevaluating this "Lord of Nine Thousand Years," Wei changed his attitude toward him from disrespect to one of obsequiousness.

After the taking of Nanking, the Heavenly King had decreed that all civilian and military officials had to first report to the Northern or Assistant king who would, in turn, report to the Eastern King. The Eastern King would report to the Heavenly King when he deemed it fit. Wei had hoped that after the establishment of the Heavenly Capital the Eastern King would take exclusive care of military affairs and that Wei himself would be responsible for all civilian matters. But his expectation did not materialize. Hence, in addition to his jealousy toward the Eastern King, Wei began to nurture a secret hatred toward the Heavenly King as well.

But what angered him most was the incident in which Chang Tzu-ming had roused the naval forces almost to the point of mutiny. The punishment of several hundred lashes he suffered by order of the Eastern King in front of thousands of naval commanders and soldiers humiliated him. After he was carried back home on a stretcher, he found that his beloved Red Phoenix had been taken away from him as well. This was tantamount to adding fuel to fire. But this was one of those many things against which he could not openly protest.

With the exception of the two rivals and some of the female officials and concubines in their establishments, very few people outside were aware of this incident. Although Wei had no intention of antagonizing the Eastern King for the sake of a woman, he felt it was an insult that he could not swallow. Hadn't the ancients said that "fornication with the wife of a friend is strictly forbidden"? How could an elder brother appropriate his younger brother's woman? The beguiling smile and ringing voice of Red Phoenix were not something he could easily forget. Wei was tormented alternately by nostalgia, indignation, and fury.

During the victory celebration feast in the imperial garden, his frame of mind was entirely different from that of the Assistant King and the King of Yü. He was neither concerned with the Heavenly King's embarassment, nor with the Eastern King's recalcitrance. In fact, he had rather hoped that the Eastern King could have been even bolder in his defiance, making the Heavenly King's humiliation even more unbearable. He had learned from an ancient classic on legal strategy and trends in human relations that among the stratagems there was one called the "flying pincers." The general idea was that in order to gain the upper hand over one's political enemy one had to first use assiduous flattery and studied deference toward the opponent, rendering him blind to reality, inflating his ego, and making him feel as if he was "flying" in the clouds, and then, like a pair of "pincers" to crack down on him. Wei Ch'ang-hui was aware of the personalities of both the Heavenly and Eastern kings: one was obdurate and self-important and the other scheming and treacherous. Now that the political and military power was exclusively in his hands, the Eastern King was not one who would be content to be under the domination of another person. Once he became full-fledged, he would no longer miss an opportunity to take the place of his sovereign. On the other hand, the Heavenly King, unlike the last scion of a decaying dynasty, would not feel too impotent to take decisive steps when his ministers became unruly and seditious. So far as Wei's own position is concerned, the best policy would be to follow the teaching of an old fable about the struggle between a snipe and a clam that could only benefit the fisherman. Therefore, at that crucial feast, although he was aware of the veiled struggle between the Heavenly and Eastern kings, Wei feigned ignorance and tried not to offend either party.

The situation was rendered transparent when Wei and the other two generals were ordered to leave the Heavenly Capital five days after the feast. Wei was sure that the climax had arrived, and that a seditious drama would unfold itself soon, since the only army remaining in the Heavenly Capital belonged to the Eastern King. Yet he could not request to stay in the capital. Even if he had remained, it would not have been beneficial to him. He would become "a turtle confined in an urn" or, even worse, "a piece of meat on the butcher's chopping board." Therefore, he accepted the assignment without hesitation. But covertly he placed his retainers in the capital to monitor the situation and report to him in Kiangsi whenever needed.

After Wei reached Kiangsi, he had no intention to advance. He stationed his troops in Jui-chou, going to and fro within a confined locality. The Ch'ing general, Tseng Kuo-fan, was now in the city of Nanchang, unable to make any move since his defeat at the hands of the Assistant King a year and half before at Hu-k'ou where his naval forces were completely destroyed. Detecting no sign that Wei Ch'ang-hui's troops would advance, Tseng sent small contingents to disturb Wei's rear camps, robbing him of nonessential items, such as utensils and supplies. His real purpose was to probe the intention of the T'ai-p'ing army. But Wei only ordered his soldiers to stay put and not to be tempted by the enemy's aggressive overtures.

One of his retainers arrived one day in the middle of the seventh month of the sixth year, *Ping-ch'en* (August 1856), and reported that the Eastern King had been hailed by his subordinates as the "Lord of Ten Thousand Years" in his official residence and that a seditious coup appeared imminent. Upon hearing this, Wei merely smiled, stroking his luxuriant beard, and asked about the response of the Heavenly King. The retainer replied that the Heavenly King appeared to be unaware of the plot. Wei ordered the man to return to the Heavenly Capital and report any further developments.

That evening the Northern King ordered his troops to prepare breakfast at the third watch, march forward at the fourth, and rout the enemy at the fifth watch the following morning. But after engaging the enemy in a brief encounter, he ordered the sounding of gongs as a signal for retreat. The same routine was repeated for three consecutive mornings. One of his trusted generals, Hsü Tsung-yang, appeared in the headquarters and inquired bluntly:

"Lord of Six Thousand Years! When do you plan to retreat?"

"Hsü 'the Eighteenth,'" Wei addressed Hsü Tsung-yang by his familiar name, "I've only begun to engage our enemy. Where does this idle talk of retreat come from?"

"Lord of Six Thousand years, you can't conceal the truth from me. I'll wager that the retreat will be tomorrow morning, if not tonight."

Wei pat Hsü on the back and said with a smile, "'Eighteenth,' you are really my trusted man."

Hsü was one of the old brethren from Kwangsi and was an army marshall with the title of vice state minister. Hsü had been ordered by the Eastern King in the first month of the fourth year to lead reinforcements to assist the Northern Expedition Army. But before he could reach the front, his army was decimated. He escaped with his life and returned to the Heavenly Capital where he was deprived of his commission and title and thrown into prison, pending investigation. However, owing to the fact that he was an old acquaintance of the Northern King who valued his valor and honesty, the latter begged the Eastern King to give Hsü a second chance. Thus he was assigned to Wei's army to redeem himself, though his title had not yet been restored. Hsü had started as an ordinary private and was a well-seasoned soldier, but he had no interest in familiarizing himself with court politics. He only knew by experience that the tactics of the T'ai-p'ing army often involved the mixed employment of retreat and attack. After an attack was launched, the army would advance a few *li* one day and several tens of *li* the next day until it approached the enemy's camps; it would then retreat suddenly in the night, sometimes covering a distance of over a hundred *li* in a stretch. Hsü noticed that the Northern King had ordered attacks for several days in a row, yet he had not ordered a general advance after a few small victories had been proclaimed. Hsü was by then certain that the Northern King had decided to withdraw his army soon.

Knowing that Hsü was a simple soldier, the Northern King did not want to reveal everything to him, so he said smilingly:

"In my opinion, there will be a bloody battle in the vicinity of the Heavenly Capital. Being in distant Kiangsi as we are now, we can only take a defensive stance, not an offensive one. Otherwise if a crisis should arise in the Heavenly Capital, our route of retreat could be easily cut off."

Hsü was indeed a simpleton. He did not understand what his superior meant. The North and South camps of the Ch'ing demons had been completely eliminated, he reasoned to himself. The head demon of the South Camp had committed suicide in the besieged city of Tan-yang. The other head demon Tseng Kuo-fan was a sitting duck in Nanchang. There was not a single demon soldier inside or outside the Heavenly Capital. How could there be an inevitable "bloody battle"?

Wei Ch'ang-hui did not reveal his true intentions to his close subordinate; he also concealed them from all the other generals under him. Ten days prior to this, he had already ordered his retainers, bringing with them "boat tallies," to prepare two hundred fast frigates ready for use, ostensibly for the transport of gunpowder and ammunition. The order specified that this was to be a military secret and was not to be revealed under any circumstances.

A few days later in the early afternoon a mounted horseman galloped swiftly into the Northern King's headquarters. The rider's head was covered with perspiration that trickled down his dust-covered face in streams. He dismounted quickly and rushed into the main tent.

The messenger was another retainer the Northern King had placed in the capital to gather information. He had left the capital that very morning when he learned the news that the Heavenly Father had again descended to earth in the official residence of the Eastern King, ordering the Heavenly King to abdicate in favor of the Eastern King. The former had acquiesced in front of all civilian and military officials. The abdication ceremony was to be held on the forthcoming birthday of the Eastern King. Hearing this, Wei Ch'ang-hui drew his sword from its scabbard, and, laughing mirthlessly, slashed at his document-strewn desk with a savage whoosh.

"Where do they intend to allocate me, Wei Ch'ang-hui?" he roared.

Immediately he ordered a general attack on the Ch'ing demons at dusk. The soldiers, having barely marched twenty *li*, were ordered to beat a sudden retreat. By dawn the army had withdrawn about one hundred *li*. At Jui-chou, Wei ordered them to set up camp, build fortifications, and dig trenches as if preparing for an assault on Nanchang. But during the night, the Northern King, aided by Hsü Tsung-yang, led his three thousand elite troops in a rush on the estuary of Lake Po-yang where the two hundred fast frigates had been assembled. The soldiers were ordered to hide themselves in the holds of the frigates which sailed immediately from the estuary to the Yangtze River, embarking on a downstream race to the Heavenly Capital.

It was on the twenty-third day of the seventh month of the sixth year, *Ping-ch'en* (August 29, 1856), that the frigates reached Hu-k'ou for supplies. A secret edict of the Heavenly King arrived at Wei's camp. The latter received the imperial messenger in private, ordering all attendants away.

The imperial messenger was dressed in a brigade commander's uniform, but the observant Wei Ch'ang-hui immediately recognized him as a palace guard. The messenger, previously seen galloping out of the imperial garden several nights before with a document marked "extra urgent" in a knapsack, had reached the Northern King's headquarters in Jui-chou. Having been informed there that Wei had left for the Heavenly Capital, the messenger travelled night and day until finally catching up to him at Hu-k'ou. Dressed in the uniform of a brigade commander, the messenger had ostensibly been assigned to procure gunpowder and ammunition in order to avoid search at various passes manned by the Eastern King's soldiers. This camouflage had been planned by the King of Yü, Hu I-kuang, at the conference held at the imperial study that eventful night.

Instantly, the imperial messenger removed a package wrapped in yellow silk from his sack, pulled out the document marked "Extra Urgent" and presented it to the Northern King. The latter received it with both hands and opened the envelope, revealing a piece of yellow silk on the top of which were printed the words, "Imperial Edict of the Heavenly King" in the Sung style script. Beneath the heading was the body of the edict written by the Heavenly King himself in his usual cursive style. The language of the edict was half-literary and half-colloquial.

> The Heavenly King issues the following edict:
> Hear ye, Brother Ch'ang! You are our chief aide and
> the pillar of the state. In the universe, the only
> supreme authority is the Heavenly Father. Within
> the four seas exclusive power belongs to your
> Second Brother. Now, there is an evil one who has
> usurped the appellation of the "Lord of Ten Thou-
> sand Years" in his official residence. According to

Heavenly Law he should be put to death. When this edict reaches you, please return to the capital immediately to quench the revolt and inflict heavenly punishment on the culprit. It has been said:

> Like a straight cloud-piercing arrow
>   everything is certain;
> The eyes of the Heavenly Father
>   remain eternally open;
> Retribution for good or evil never
>   fails;
> The crimes of usurpation and arrogance can
>   never be forgiven.
> So it is decreed!

After reading the edict, the Northern King smirked and said sarcastically:

> The Lord of Ten Thousand Years orders me to go to the capital to quench the revolt and kill the culprit. Yet His Majesty has promised to abdicate in favor of him, following the examples of Yao and Shun in ancient times. Could it be that His Majesty wants to smear the golden seal of the new dynasty with my blood?

Sweat covering his forehead, the imperial messenger expressed great alarm. "When your servant left the Heavenly Capital," he exclaimed, "he had not heard anything about the abdication. When did the Lord of Six Thousand Years hear that?"

"Although the Heavenly Father does not descend to earth via my body," Wei said with a smile, "I too know a thing or two about what happened in the court a thousand *li* away!"

"The Lord of Six Thousand Years has such foresight," the messenger said, falling on his knees. "It proves the Heavenly Father is omnipresent and the Heavenly King will be blessed.

In your humble servant's estimation, this must be the Heavenly King's strategem to postpone the crisis. Pray, my lord, you need not entertain such a suspicion. Will Your Lordship go back to the capital as soon as possible?"

"Fine," said Wei. "Please go back and report to the Lord of Ten Thousand Years that during the victory celebration feast in the imperial garden, I had already sensed that the evil one would carry out his seditious design sooner or later. Therefore, although I've deployed my troops facing the enemy, I've been constantly preoccupied with the safety of the capital. Since the Second Brother has sent me a secret edict, I will travel night and day until I reach the capital."

After the messenger left, the Northern King called in Hsü Tsung-yang, and ordered him to transmit an oral message to his three thousand elite soldiers that there would soon be a bloody battle in the vicinity of the Heavenly Capital and that they were to reach the capital within three days by sailing downstream that very night.

"My brother!" he turned to Hsü. "This time, we'll accomplish something really great. You needn't worry about the restoration of such an insignificant title as vice state minister!"

Hsü was still unconvinced. How could there be a fierce battle in the vicinity of the Heavenly Capital, he wondered.

More than two hundred fast frigates raced downstream under full sail in the moonlight. A gentle breeze blew over the soft grass on both shores. In the river thousands of silvery wavelets silently greeted the armada. Within the frigates' cabins were hidden three thousand elite soldiers, while the prows and sterns were piled up with boxes labelled "gunpowder" and "ammunition." Showing their transportation certificates at all customs and passes, they encountered no obstacles on the way.

Wei Ch'ang-hui, dressed in a division commander's uniform, stood on the prow of the leading frigate, with one hand on the handle of his sword and a faint smile on his lips. No matter how the future unfolded, he thought, he would be treading on safe ground. In case the Eastern King succeeded in taking over the throne from the Heavenly King and the latter submitted without a struggle, Wei would follow the Mandate of Heaven and put down all who dared to oppose. Then he would be a pillar of the new dynasty. On the other hand, if the Eastern King had faked the will of the Heavenly Father and forced the Heavenly King to abdicate, public protest among all officials would be aroused to indict the Eastern King for usurping the crown, a crime not to be tolerated by the Heavenly Father and Heavenly Brother. Wei would then be in a position to clean up the usurpers in the court with his military might and become an eminent figure for having quenched the revolt. The extra urgent document would be a testament of his authority empowered by the sovereign. A third and final hypothesis would be a situation involving a death struggle between the two sides with both suffering irreparable harm. In this case Wei's return with his men would occur at an opportune moment and his future would be assured beyond anyone's imagination. If he were to admit the truth, the third alternative was what he fervently wished for.

Three days later, it was the twenty-sixth day of the seventh month of the sixth year, *Ping-ch'en,* of the T'ai-p'ing calendar (September 1, 1856). A new moon had just risen over the eastern horizon. The two hundred fast frigates, with their precious cargo of three thousand elite troops, arrived at Mid-river Inlet, just outside the capital. The Northern King told Hsü Tsung-yang to wait for orders, while the frigates were anchored at the east side of the inlet. The Northern King, still attired in the uniform of a division commander, headed quietly for Phoenix Gate, followed by only twenty-odd personal guards. He presented his certificate as procurer of gunpowder and ammunition to the gatekeepers who found it to be in order. Thus the party slipped into the city.

It was the time of the year just after the solar term "Height of Heat." The scorching summer heat had gradually subsided toward the evening. From the military camps outside the city gates came the intermittent sound of conch blowing, which gave the listeners feelings of desolation and sadness. The residents of the city had retired to dreamland. The faint moonlight reflected on the stone-paved streets made them look as if they had been newly washed. With the exception of the swishing of gentle breezes and the chirping of insects, the whole city was enveloped in silence.

The Northern King and his personal guards sneaked into his official residence through the back door. A trusted lieutenant who had been assigned to remain in the capital came to report to him:

> About half-a-month ago, the King of Yen, Ch'in Jih-kang, returned to the Heavenly Capital by order of the Heavenly King. He was commanded to stay in his residence and not to show himself in public, pending the arrival of Your Lordship, at which time everything will be discussed.

The Northern King was elated, believing that the King of Yen had shown deference to him and that the Heavenly King had deemed him indispensable. He told the lieutenant to invite the King of Yen to his residence for an important consultation.

From Ch'in Jih-kang, the Northern King learned of the recent developments in the court. He was told that the abdication ceremony to be held on the Eastern King's birthday as promised by the Heavenly King was only a stratagem to buy time. In order to allay the suspicions of the Eastern King, the Heavenly King had ordered an inventory made of the gold and silver bullion in the imperial treasury. He had further ordered the Bureau of Imperial Garments to make a robe embroidered with nine dragons and a golden crown decorated with two pairs of dragons and phoenixes; the Bureau of Decorations had been commanded to paint the Dragon Hall, while the Bureau of Lanterns was instructed to make multicolored lanterns to be hung on the Heavenly Front Gate. Preparations for the sacrificial ceremony to the Heavenly Father as part of the rite of abdication of the throne in favor of the Eastern King were drawn up. The Eastern King had also notified all civilian and military officials as well as his own subordinates to participate in the ceremony, in which he would receive the imperial seal and ascend the throne.

The King of Yen further told the Northern King that a similar secret edict had been sent to the Assistant King. But for reasons he was unaware of the Assistant King had not yet arrived.

After hearing this report, the Northern King paced back and forth in his study for a long time; obviously he was greatly agitated.

"Brother Jih-kang," he said, "The moment of truth has arrived. The fate of the Heavenly Kingdom is to be determined at this very instant. To repay the blessings that the Heavenly Father and Brother have bestowed on me as well as the special favors that the Heavenly King has constantly shown me, I, Wei Ch'ang-hui, shall not shirk from my responsibilities even if it means losing my head and splashing my blood. What we need to do is to attack before the enemy is prepared and deal him a preemptive strike."

The Northern King and the King of Yen, each accompanied by a few personal guards, arrived stealthily at the side door of the imperial garden in the middle of the night. Both were exuberant—almost as if they were intoxicated for the first time in many years.

In the imperial study, Wei Ch'ang-hui fell on his knees immediately as he confronted the Heavenly King.

"Second Brother," he said, sobbing. "I am late in arriving to serve my sovereign in his time of need."

The Heavenly King, also in tears, helped Wei rise with both hands and invited both men to meet the King of Yü who had been recuperating at home for some time; the widow of the Western King, Hung Hsüan-chiao; the Queen's brother Lai Han-ying; and State Minister Meng Teh-en, all of whom were either relatives or trusted subordinates of the Heavenly King.

The Heavenly King had lost weight since the victory

celebration feast two months earlier. But his spirit remained high and he was still full of self-confidence. His voice trembled with excitement as he spoke.

"Brother Ch'ang! It is good of you to assist us in time of stress and chaos. Your army has travelled quickly. You are the only one inside and outside the court that the state can rely upon. On your shoulders rests the responsibility of slaying the evil one. Brothers and sisters! You must help each other and obey Brother Ch'ang's orders from now on. Anyone who refuses will not be forgiven by the Heavenly Father and Brother or me!"

Having completed his emotional speech, the Heavenly King drew his "demon-slaying sword" and cut off a corner of the table in front of him with one stroke. He then handed the sword which had never left his side to the Northern King.

The Northern King was moved to tears. Since the time when he knew Hung Hsiu-ch'üan as a teacher and later as the Heavenly King, never once had he heard him make a more emotional speech. Looking directly at the face of the Heavenly King, he found the sunken eyes below the heavy brows also brimming with tears.

Wei Ch'ang-hui accepted the sword with both hands and went to stand at the center of the room.

"Second Brother," said Wei in a trembling voice, "and brothers and sisters. Incompetent though I am, can I do nothing when the fate of the state is hung in a balance? According to the classics on military strategy, all actions should be taken swiftly. The evil one has plenty of spies all over the place. To save the state, we must take immediate action. Whether we'll succeed or fail will be determined tonight!"

In the presence of the Heavenly King, Wei ordered forthwith the King of Yü and State Minister Meng Teh-en to assemble all their trusted subordinates and private guards to occupy strategic points and to block all thoroughfares leading to the Eastern King's residence. The widow of the Western King, Hung Hsüan-chiao, and the Queen's brother, Lai Han-ying, were to lead the palace guards in guarding the inner city and the Dragon Hall. Wei Ch'ang-hui himself and the King of Yen would lead their men to enter the Eastern King's residence at the fourth watch that very night to deal with the culprit. If everything went well, a signal fire would be set in Rarity Depository Tower. All men participating in the coup would wear white armbands to distinguish themselves.

Having completed their plans, participants went about to fulfill their assigned jobs. Twenty-four palace guards, in full military attire, remained to protect the Heavenly King who waited in the imperial garden for the good news.

The Northern King then sent a trusted guard to bring a message to Hsü Tsung-yang who was waiting for orders at Mid-river Inlet. Hsü was commanded to lead his three thousand elite soldiers in a dash to the capital. The Northern King had made it clear that all guns and heavy equipment were to be left on board ships. The soldiers were to bring only light arms and enter the city through the West Gate. The Northern King had found that Mid-river Inlet was close to the West Gate which was only a short distance from the Eastern King's residence. The soldiers could enter the West Gate and charge directly into the residence in no time.

The King of Yen's one thousand soldiers just returned from the Tan-yang front were stationed outside T'ung-chi Gate. The Northern King summoned them into the city immediately to take up position behind the rear door of the Eastern King's residence. They were to conceal themselves in civilian dwellings and prevent the Eastern King's armed guards from putting up resistance.

All preliminary preparations had been completed by the third watch of the eventful night.

In the past two months, the Eastern King, flushed with success, had been in an elated mood. The three years since the establishment of the Heavenly Capital had been extremely favorable ones for him.

Preparations for his ascension to the throne were completed in two months' time. His main energies had been concentrated on the deployment of soldiers inside and outside the Heavenly Capital. After the taking of Nanking, the army of the central court stationed in the city and its suburban areas had been placed under his direct control. The armies outside the capital, commanded by several generals who were his trusted lieutenants of the lower rank, could not pose any threat to him. The only individuals who caused him some concern were the four kings—the Northern and the Assistant kings and the Kings of Yen and Yü. Yang Hsiu-ch'ing had made careful individual evaluations of each one of them. Although the Northern King, Wei Ch'ang-hui, was second to him in command, the rich man from Kwangsi was no peer of his, so far as talents and prestige were concerned. For the past three years since the establishment of the Heavenly Capital, Wei had shown nothing but deference to Yang. Furthermore, the Heavenly King had never bestowed any special favors on Wei. The King of Yen, Ch'in Jih-kang, was a man of extraordinary valor, and a hero on the battlefield, but nothing more. Of the four he was the least calculating, and thus the easiest to handle. The King of Yü, Hu I-kuang, however, had originally been a military *hsiu-ts'ai*, and was a man of considerable literary and military talent. Yet, he had never been given any important assignment by the Heavenly King. Due to the loss of Liu-an-chou, he had been deprived of his title of nobility which had been restored only recently. By nature, he seemed to be not overly ambitious or competitive. Not long ago, the Eastern King had entrapped him in participating in the private ceremony in his residence where he had joined the other sycophants in hailing Yang as "the Lord of Ten Thousand Years," thereby placing himself in a compromising position.

The only individual who caused Yang Hsiu-ch'ing real concern was the Assistant King Shih Ta-k'ai, nicknamed "Dare-to-Resist Stone." A man of lofty ambitions and strategic knowledge, Shih had proven himself in battle and was known to all as the "invincible one." He was one of the brethren who had joined the rebellion at the inital stage, yet he had never maintained special intimacy with any one of the leaders. In addition, he always had a penchant for the unpredictable. Yang had treated him judiciously and with due respect, but Shih had always asserted his independence and maintained an attitude of indifference. He and his three brothers, also commanders in the army, were called the "Four Tigers of the Shih Family." Yang was aware of the fact that the three brothers were simple military men and that one of them had been executed for the loss of Wuchang. The real tiger in Yang's eyes was the youngest and most ambitious one nicknamed the "Dare-to-Resist Stone."

It was based on these calculations that the Eastern King had dispatched the three kings to the front two months earlier. Shih Ta-k'ai was sent to the farthermost Hupeh front where the fighting was more frequent and responsibilities heavy. After his ascent to the throne, Yang figured, as an old saying went, "the rice has been cooked," the three kings would not be able to do anything. When the time came, he would bribe them with high positions and rich enumerations or threaten them with military annihilation; either way they would be unable to resist. If worst came to the worst, and Yang was threatened with attack, he would close the gates and sit out the siege. Faced with an inpenetrable city, with the Ch'ing demons pressing on in the rear, the attacker would be concerned only with his own preservation and not with what happened within the walls of the Heavenly Capital.

H aving been hailed by his subordinates as the "Lord of Ten Thousand Years," and with his plan set in motion to force the Heavenly King to abdicate in his favor, the Eastern King returned to his private quarters in an expansive mood. The first person to greet him was the female official Yang Shui-chiao, who reported to him nervously that the female *chuang-*

yüan, Fu Shan-hsiang, and her jailor, Shih Ting-lan, had both escaped, apparently in an act of defection.

Hearing the news, the Eastern King only raised his eyebrows slightly and made a contemptuous gesture of dismissal with his hand. Seeing that he had neither exploded nor ordered a search, Yang Shui-chiao kept her silence and stood to one side. The Eastern King had an inkling why the female *chuang-yüan* had escaped. When he told her his plan and asked her to participate in it, promising her the future status as a pillar of the new dynasty, she had replied that she was content with her present position and had no ambition to rise to such heights. The Eastern King was sure that after he became the sovereign, in a month's time, Fu would come back to the fold, begging for pardon on all fours.

As a demonstration of the generosity of a forthcoming monarch, he told Yang Shui-chiao not to reveal this event to anyone, nor to order a search for the escapees.

His expansive mood not disrupted by the news of the defection, the Eastern King recalled many historical episodes the female *chuang-yüan* had told him, such as the "Massacre of the City of Chia-ting," and the "Ten Horrible Days of Yangchow," all depicting the atrocities the Manchus had committed when they first came to China. She had intimated that he should consider the future of the Chinese nation as his primary object and imitate the loyal deeds of Chu-ke Liang of the Han dynasty. She recited a poem of Tu Fu about Chu-ke Liang which included the following stanza:

> To discuss the affairs of the state, the Lord
> visited his humble hut thrice;
> To serve the two sovereigns of the dynasty,
> the minister offered his loyal heart.

Imagine the female *chuang-yüan* advising him to emulate Chu-ke Liang, to serve his sovereign loyally until his last breath! "Bah!" he said to himself. "I, Yang Hsiu-ch'ing, should

loyally serve that spineless, debased, and incompetent non-
entity?" Among all the stories that the female *chuang-yüan*
had told him, the one he appreciated most was the story of
the tenth-century general who executed a military coup at
Ch'en Bridge and thereby established the glorious Sung dynasty
with himself as its first emperor.

As he walked in his private quarters, engrossed in deep
thought, he approached unwittingly the apartment of his
favorite concubine, Red Phoenix. He heard a charming voice,
saying:

"The Lord of Ten Thousand Years is here. Come and
wait on His Lordship."

It was the voice of the white parrot, jumping up and
down in his golden cage. The Eastern King tapped lightly
on the cage. "After I move into the imperial palace," he
promised, "I'll make you the transmitter of orders."

As he turned the corner, twelve female attendants on
night duty came forward to greet him. The young girls. dressed
in swirling silk uniforms, moved toward him like a whirlwind,
curtseyed and chanted in unison: "Hail the Eastern King, may
he live ten thousand years!" The Eastern King nodded with a
smile; their voices were much more natural and pleasing than
that of the parrot. He dismissed them with a wave of his hand
and entered the apartment.

Red Phoenix was in the midst of her evening toilet,
sitting in front of a multimirrored dressing table, attended by
a Soochow maid, her hair dresser. She caught a glimpse of
the Eastern King in the mirror, but pretended to be unaware
of his presence. She let the old maid remove her kingfisher
jade and pearl jewelry, piece by piece, from her coiffure.
Upon the entrance of the Eastern King to the inner chamber,
the maid quickly curtseyed with a smile and retreated.

Without disturbing Red Phoenix, the Eastern King went
to sit on the crystal bed, watching her finishing her toilet in
the mirror. He noticed that her hair was combed in a chignon,
adorned with a single green jade hairpin. Under her heavily
penciled eyebrows, her bright eyes sparkled, conveying an
expression of neither adoration nor scorn. Not until she

spotted the Eastern King sitting on the bed did she give him a vague smile, revealing two rows of even, white teeth. Such a smile from her was quite rare in the Eastern King's recollection.

Parting the beaded curtain, a palace maid of fifteen or sixteen entered, carrying a red-laquered tray and fell on her knees before the Eastern King.

"Lord of Ten Thousand Years," she said. "Here's the ginseng and musk brew prescribed by the imperial physician Li, just fetched from the kitchen."

Without extending his hand, the Eastern King ordered the maid to bring the brew to him. She brought the small cup to his lips and with one hand supporting the back of his head, helped him drink the contents in one gulp. After the maid took her leave, Red Phoenix stood up and went over to sit beside her lord on the bed.

The bed had been a birthday present from Meng Teh-en to the Eastern King a year after the establishment of the Heavenly Capital. It was made by clever craftsmen from Soochow. A little over five feet in width, it had been constructed from hollow glass bricks on its three sides. The hollow bricks were filled with water in which gold fish of various colors swam amidst aquatic plants. It gave the sleeper the illusion that he was in the legendary crystal palace. Even in hot summer nights the sleeper would not feel the oppression of the heat. In front of it hung a curtain made of strings of pearls interspersed with precious stones. In the reflection of the palace lanterns, the curtain was a rarity that dazzled the beholder. Red Phoenix helped her master undress when the nightwatchman's rattle sounded twice. It was the second watch.

The Eastern King's sleep was beset with a series of strange dreams—dreams that were inconsequential and fragmented. As his dreams began, he found himself in a yellow robe embroidered with nine dragons, with a golden crown engraved in a double dragon and phoenix design on his head. Even his felt boots were decorated with dragons. As he was ascending the throne, he heard the assembly of military and civilian officials, the Heavenly King, Hung Hsiu-ch'üan, among them, hail him as the "Lord of Ten Thousand Years." In the multitude he noticed the Northern King smiling fawningly, and the Assistant King keeping a stony silence, while the King of Yü lowered his head in deep thought. He also spotted Red Phonenix in a white gown, smiling at him at as she joined the crowd in performing the ceremonies of obeisance. But when he tried to converse with her, the answer he received came from the parrot, "The Lord of Ten Thousand Years is back. Come and wait on him!"

In his dreams, he returned to the palace in a sedan chair, amidst the cheers of the multitude, followed closely by Red Phoenix in her white gown. She repeated endlessly in parrot style:

"Lord of Ten Thousand years is back! Lord of Ten Thousand Years is back!"

But he saw no lanterns, no pennants, no title placards, and no musicians in front of his sedan chair then. He did not seem to be riding in the customary sedan chair, but on horseback. He was reeling and rocking beyond his control. "Where am I?" he wondered.

He seemed to be on the battlefield, leading tens of thousands of soldiers engaged in a fierce fighting. Sword clanked against sword, people dashed to and fro, gunpowder exploded all about, as arrows whisked by like raindrops.

His horse was galloping at high speed and the dust its hooves kicked up mixed with gunpowder could be seen as well as smelled.

His horse seemed to carry him over fields, forests, lakes, and streams. He could see his own shadow on horseback reflected in a clear stream. Oh, how clear and cool the water in the stream seemed to be! In it the plants appeared so green and the goldfish so colorful.

The steed now seemed to fly over lofty mountains, broad rivers, and deep ravines directly into the white clouds.

From the clouds, he seemed to see millions of Ch'ing demons below on earth. No, they must have been the sacred soldiers of the Heavenly Kingdom, the children of the Heavenly Father, his own brethren and sisters. They all had on them bamboo helmets and tunic uniforms, their flags waving in the wind.

"Kill . . ." they shouted.

"Kill . . ." he wanted to shout, drawing his bejeweled dagger, but something in his throat muffled his voice.

"Kill . . . Kill . . ." he struggled and found his voice at last.

Suddenly he woke up. He could hear the thumping of his heart and feel his whole body drenched in cold sweat. Under the faint light of the palace lanterns, he saw with his solitary eye, only half open, Red Phoenix beside him, also awake, her eyes wide open and filled with terror.

"Kill! . . . Kill!" an intermittent shout came from a distance, sometimes loud, sometimes faint, drifting with the wind through the window.

"Kill," he repeated to himself in a state of stupor. "Kill whom? Who is shouting? Where am I?"

"Kill, Kill, Kill!" the shouts became louder and more distinct. The sound of metal striking metal, the cries of the desperate and the moans of the wounded now all came clearly to his ears.

A female official was running, followed by several serving maids. As they ran, they yelled, "Heavenly Father, have mercy on us!"

This was followed by the sound of heavy disordered footsteps, the shrieks of terror-stricken women, and the clang of swords. Red Phoenix, still in his arms, was trembling like an autumn leaf.

As Yang pushed her away, ready to jump out of bed, several flaming torches were thrust into the bedchamber, reflecting the dancing shadow of the intruders on the wall.

Lit by the flaming torchlight, two red figures approached the bed. Yang was not sure whether the redness was a reflection of the flames, or if it was the figures themselves who were smeared with blood.

Red Phoenix uttered a piercing cry and fell out of the bed by the pearly curtain. She knelt before the intruder, completely naked.

"Lord of Six Thousand Years," she implored, "Spare me! ..."

You slut!" the Northern King hissed, thrusting a gleaming sword into her full bosom.

Instantly, a figure behind the Northern King jumped forward. "Wei Ch'ang-hui!" the man yelled in a hoarse voice. "How dare you kill my Red Phoenix?"

The speaker was Hou Ch'ien-fang. He tried to help Red Phoenix up with one hand while wielding a short sword with the other to ward off Wei's second thrust.

"My dear, my love," Red Phoenix begged, fresh blood oozing from her mouth. "Please kill me! I wish to die at your hand!" A sad, distorted smile came to her pale face.

Another intruder, Hsü Tsung-yang, was right behind Hou. Without uttering a word, he stabbed Hou in the back.

"My dear, my love!" Red Phoenix kept moaning incoherently in Hou's arms. "Let both of us die together!"

Hou swayed a little. His unstable hand thrusted his dagger into Red Phoenix's bare bosom, then using both hands he clumsily cut his own throat.

In his stupor, Yang saw what had happened in that instant. With a shudder, he came completely to his senses. Pulling out the bejewelled dagger hidden under his pillow, he rolled off to the other side of the bed.

Hsü Tsung-yang, who was behind Wei Ch'ang-hui, jumped onto the bed with sword in hand. But he was cut down by Yang who was hiding behind the pearly curtain. The dagger struck him in the stomach and he fell down from the bed on his back.

Wielding his "demon-slaying sword" given him by the

Heavenly King, Wei slashed at the pearly curtain, scattering the pearls like a sudden shower. The tip of the sword also slashed the cover of the palace lantern, sending it swinging violently in front of the bed.

Yang Hsiu-ch'ing jumped down from the head of the bed, trying to attack Wei from the side. But Wei wielded his sword obliquely and with a slash relieved the dagger from Yang's hand.

Wei, aiming the tip of his sword at his opponent, forced Yang into a corner of the room. Now, all Yang could see clearly was the vicious grin on Wei's distorted face.

"Lord of Nine Thousand Years!" Wei said menacingly, "The Heavenly Father will not descend to earth through your body today."

The tip of the sword was an inch or so from Yang's chest. Completely naked and disarmed, Yang had absolutely no means to evade the onslaught.

The "demon-slaying sword" had been bestowed by the Heavenly Father upon his son, who, in turn, had given it to another son. It now pierced through the breast of yet another son until its tip struck the wall behind him.

With his powerful hands tempered by years of hard labor in the charcoal kiln, Yang grabbed the blade of the "demon-slaying sword" in a last desperate struggle. His hands were covered with blood—one could not tell whether it was blood from his hands, the blood on the sword, or the blood from his chest.

Now his gradually dimming eye stared at the face of Wei Ch'ang-hui—the brother with whom he had shared life-and-death struggles on the battleground, the brother with whom he had suffered so many hardships and miseries.

Pinning Yang onto the wall with all his strength, Wei bellowed at him with such vehemence that he sounded like a howling, hungry wolf:

"Lord of Nine Thousand Years, go with your red devil to face the Heavenly Father together!"

He quickly withdrew the sword from Yang's body and

The "demon-slaying sword" pierced through his chest.

watched with satisfaction the blood ooze from the wound. Turning around, he saw that the naked body of Red Phoenix still writhing in pain, and administered a *coup-de-grace.*

The call for death could again be heard. Ch'in Jih-kang, naked from the waist up and brandishing a long spear, rushed toward Wei Ch'ang-hui.

"Lord of Six Thousand Years," Ch'in cried. "I've sent all the rebel guards outside the residence to Heaven!"

"Quick, tell the brothers to light the signal from Rarity Depository Tower," Wei ordered.

A few soldiers rushed to the tower, stepping over the corpses of slain female officials and maids lying haphazardly on the ground all over the place. Soon a fire started in the tower. Against the light of the fiercely burning tongues of fire, one could see small pieces of blackened paper flying to the sky like butterflies. They were the remains of the tower's treasured collection of rare books and scrolls of painting and calligraphy!

As dawn approached, mutilated bodies and abandoned weapons littered the ground everywhere—on the streets, in front of various official establishments and on the shores of the great Yangtze River. Under the blue autumn sky, dried dark red blood could be seen splashed on walls, on doors, and on the stone-slabs of the streets, while yet uncongealed blood flowed in little rivulets along the stone pavement, trickling down toward the river.

Numerous corpses in yellow or red tunics floated downstream in the Yangtze. Groups of dark brown vultures hovered over them, squawking happily. The one-time children of the Heavenly Father had provided these scavengers a feast with their bodies.

Those who had cried were now silent; those who had moaned were now still; and those who had writhed in pain had become stiff, immobile objects. All those who were still alive closed their eyes in disgust.

The fire had razed Rarity Depository Tower to the ground. The blue glazed tiles of the main hall and other buildings, now covered with a sheet of black ashes, no longer gleamed. In the morning sun, the flames had lost their brilliance and fury and turned into puffs of black and grey smoke, not unlike an attractive and vivacious young girl suddenly transformed into an old, toothless hag. The odor of scorched buildings and human flesh stung the eyes and nostrils of the citizens of the Heavenly Capital, driving them behind closed doors.

The Heavenly Capital, as silent as death, was still basking under the bright and beautiful sun whose light was as invigorating and buoyant as ever. Outside the capital, the powerful Yangtze kept rolling along, although perhaps a bit less boisterously. Carrying so many bodies of the Heavenly Father's children silently with motherly care, she washed their wounds with gentle waves; she caressed them softly with infinite love; and she whispered into their ears words of solace and repentance. The great river had seen so many tragedies in history. This was only one of them. She neither understood nor attempted to understand the reasons behind such tragedies. For the past several millenniums she had nourished her children with her own milk. Like a kind, doting mother, she had time and time again witnessed her own children fight and kill each other in her arms. But she never punished or scolded them for their ignorance and recklessness. She only wept silently. Her tears converged into streams, into billows, and into torrents that surged in the river. Children of the Han race, have you seen the undulating currents of the great river? They are the accumulation of Mother Nature's tears! Have you heard the endless whispering of waves all year round? That is the sound of Mother Nature's wailing.

The sun had risen high in the sky. It viewed the aftermath of what happened the night before with an air of relentlessness and solemnity.

The Northern King and the King of Yen arrived at the

Heavenly Front Gate and dismounted in front of the stone tablet marked "Dismount." They walked toward the Dragon Hall, followed by a dozen armed guards. The Front Gate was wide open. There was no master of ceremonies to give commands and no hailing of "Long Live!" to be heard. Their quick footsteps reverberated in the marble corridors of the palace halls. Several doorkeepers watched with alarm the approach of a dozen or so blood-stained individuals hurrying toward the Dragon Hall.

The Heavenly King was waiting for them. Hu I-kuang, Hung Hsüan-chiao, and Lai Han-ying had left to lead groups of guards to partrol the streets and pacify the people. Only the Heavenly King and Meng Teh-en, attended by several female officials, remained.

The Northern King did not follow the prescribed rule of court etiquette requiring that he kneel before the Heavenly King, but stood erect just as the Eastern King used to before.

"Second Brother," he reported, "I've procured the head of rebel Yang!"

Taking Wei's backward glance as a cue, Ch'in Jih-kang, holding a red laquered platter, stepped forward and knelt before the Heavenly King. On the platter was Yang's blood-stained severed head. His hair was tied into a knot.

The Heavenly King turned his eyes away, murmuring something that sounded like a groan or a prayer. . . .

"Second Brother," the Northern King said in a solemn voice, "There are still plenty of the rebel's followers left. What are we going to do with them? You'll have to decide immediately."

"How many of them are there?" the Heavenly King asked, as if awakening from a dream.

"The followers of the rebel Yang inside and outside the capital plus the guards of the eight gates totalled no less than thirty thousand. I've dispatched twenty thousand of them to heaven last night and early this morning. Although all those in the city have been exterminated, those stationed outside amount to ten thousand."

"Why don't you order your men to go out and exterminate them?"

"Lord of Ten Thousand Years," the Northern King said in a sarcastic tone, "I've brought to the capital only three thousand elite soldiers. Jih-kang has one thousand, making a total of four thousand. During the fighting last night and this morning, half of them have returned to heaven."

"We have eight hundred youth vanguards for the defense of the palace," said the Heavenly King.

"Adding the eight hundred to the remaining soldiers would increase the total to twenty-eight hundred. How can they fight against ten thousand rebels?"

Sweat covered the Heavenly King's forehead. Hesitatingly, he said: "I'll draft an edict to summon the troops in the fields back to meet the crisis."

"It's too late!" interrupted the Northern King abrupty. "For the troops to come back from the nearest station, it will take at least two or three days. The ten thousand or so followers of Rebel Yang are apt to take action in the meantime. Should they come into the city, my own life notwithstanding, the reign of Second Brother will be at stake. If success is snatched away from us at the last minute, how can we face the Heavenly Father on high?"

"We don't have sufficient soldiers within the city for its defense and those outside will take too long to arrive," asked the Heavenly King, "what is there for us to do?"

The Northern King stepped forward. From his pocket he took out a memorial and handed it to the Heavenly King with both hands. "This is my suggestion," he added.

The Heavenly King took a cursory look at the hastily written memorial, his heavy eyebrows contracting violently. After a long while, he heaved a deep sigh and reclined on the imperial throne.

"Brother Ch'ang," he said. "If I follow your plan, how can I face the Heavenly Father and Heavenly Brother? How can I retain my credibility among the people? I'll be condemned in history forever!"

To this the Northern King replied: "In ancient times Ch'in Shih-huang, by burying alive the capitulated soldiers of Chao—four hundred thousand strong—was able to unify the country, whereas Duke Hsiang of Sung, too concerned with humanity and righteousness to arrest two enemies, proved to be the cause of his own undoing. The fish and the bear's paw are both delicacies, as the saying goes, but you must choose only one. When faced with a life and death struggle, you must risk a decisive action!"

EIGHT

T wo days later, on the twenty-ninth day of the seventh
month of the sixth year, *Ping-ch'en* (September 4, 1856),
the sound of disorderly footsteps could be heard early in the
morning in the streets of the Heavenly Capital. A group of
officers and men formerly under the command of the Eastern
King had returned to the capital, in response to the Heavenly
King's edict.

The sky had been overcast since early morning; murky
clouds gathered, separated, scudded around, and assembled
again in formations, as unpredictable as human affairs. Like
gunsmoke in the battlefield, they blocked the sunlight and
rendered the sky eerily dark.

The group of men was only a portion of some ten thousand soldiers formerly under the Eastern King's direct command, who had survived the bloodbath and had assembled

on O-Mei Peak, outside the capital, where dense forest and luxuriant underbush flourished. Prior to their arrival, there had been only a few barracks here with a garrison unit of no more than a thousand men. On the day of the Eastern King's death, the President of the Board of Rites, Fu Hsüeh-hsien, was on an official mission outside the city. When he started to go back the next morning, he was greeted on the way by hundreds of blood-smeared, wounded officers and men. From them he learned of the tragic events that had taken place the night before. Fu then turned his mount around and led the refugees who had not eaten for a whole day to O-Mei Peak. Fu ordered his men to the suburban areas to gather all the stragglers. Within two days, ten thousand men, mauled both mentally and physically, assembled in this little hilly area. Most of them were dressed in tatters and carried broken weapons. All were full of wrath. Fu Hsüeh-hsien gave an order that the remains of the rations were to be shared by the newcomers. A few remaining horses were also slaughtered for food. The heterogeneous assembly, consisting of officers without soldiers and soldiers without officers, was totally disorganized. Many men displayed open wounds, while others had been broken spiritually. They slept under the trees, lying about haphazardly, watching the murky sky with listless eyes. The lightly wounded cursed everything and everybody incessantly, while the severely wounded cried and groaned to themselves. Even after past defeats on the battlefield against the Ch'ing army, they had never looked so pathetic and desperate.

Fu Hsüeh-hsien assembled several divisional and regional commanders to discuss what possible measures they were to take. Some of the radicals wanted to fight until they had retaken the capital and settled accounts with Wei and Ch'in. Others declared that they would rather go back to Kwangsi and forget about the whole thing. Still others pleaded that the first priority should be to find food for the hungry and medicine for the wounded.

But where could they find substance to fill the stomachs

of these wounded and hungry brethren? All available game, such as rabbit and deer in the forest and bushes of the O-mei Peak area had been hunted down and all edible vegetation exhausted. As time went on, starvation of the remaining soldiers was a certainty.

On the morning of the twenty-eighth day of the seventh month (September 3, 1856), Fu Hsüeh-hsien ordered a division commander who was a fellow villager of the Northern King to disguise himself as a subordinate of the latter, and go to the city to gather information. A few hours later, he galloped back, yelling breathlessly:

"The Heavenly King has issued an edict, granting amnesty to all of us!"

The edict of amnesty ran as follows:

Traitor Yang has committed the crime of usurping the title "Lord of Ten Thousand Years." On the night of the twenty-sixth day of the seventh month of the sixth year, *Ping-ch'en* (September 1, 1856), he attempted a military coup, thus incurring the wrath of the Heavenly Father who informed us of the events by a secret edict. Accordingly, we ordered the Northern King and the King of Yen to have Yang executed. This is ample proof that the will of the Heavenly Father shall always be respected!

However, the Northern King and the King of Yen, not knowing the true intentions of the Heavenly Father, have wantonly massacred many brethren formerly under traitor Yang's control. This was not in accordance with the Heavenly Father's humanitarian principles. Another secret edict of the Heavenly Father has instructed us to arrest and punish the two erring kings. The punishment of whipping is to be carried out publicly outside the Heavenly Front Gate on the twenty-ninth day of the seventh month. All brethren formerly belonging to traitor Yang's units are children of the Heavenly Father, and are invited to witness the punishment which we shall impose on these two wrong-doers on behalf of the Heavenly Father. All are welcome to attend the meeting provided that they do not bring their weapons. From now on, all are to be reinstated as officials and sacred soldiers of the Heavenly Kingdom and shall be treated equally regardless of past affiliations. A poem goes:

> Heavenly Father and Brother sanction my
>   authority on earth;
> Like a beacon His eyes search back and forth.
> Those who sin cannot escape everlasting
>   punishment;
> Blessed are those who firmly believe in the truth.

It is so decreed!

Great agitation overcame the remnants of the Eastern King's men. Some were prepared to accept the Heavenly King's amnesty and to attend the meeting in the capital the next day, while others entertained doubts about the sincerity of the imperial edict and took a wavering attitude. The majority pressed with hunger and illness expressed only frustration and disappointment. "Who is interested in witnessing punishment with empty stomachs and open wounds?" they asked.

Fu Hsüeh-hsien advised inaction and waiting to see how the edict was actually implemented. But most of the ten thousand or so soldiers were sick or wounded. Nor were there any rations or medicine. How could they resist if an army were dispatched from the capital to exterminate them?

As the debate went on, a messenger from the Heavenly King, State Minister Meng Teh-en, arrived with large quantities of food and medicine. His arrival created another flurry. Some men cheered with joy while others wept in sorrow. They cheered the magnanimity of the Heavenly King and wept for the heinous death of the Eastern King. . . .

Meng Teh-en reiterated before he departed for the capital the invitation to witness the punishment the next day.

About two thousand soldiers and officers opted to go to the capital. The remaining eight thousand chose to stay at O-mei Peak, either because they still entertained doubts about the Heavenly King's sincerity, or because of their severe wounds which rendered them immobile. Fu Hsüeh-hsien, however, decided to wait for further development in the capital.

It was a long and silent trek from O-mei Peak to the capital. The two-thousand-odd soldiers, deep in thought, had not been aware of the Eastern King's attempt to usurp the throne. They had only been informed that in a recent descent of the Heavenly Father to earth, the Heavenly King had promised to abdicate in favor of the Eastern King on the latter's birthday. These soldiers had no preference as to who would be the sovereign so long as it was the will of the Heavenly Father. What really concerned them was the quick defeat of the Ch'ing demons so that they could be reunited with their families and enjoy a peaceful life as the citizens of the Heavenly Kingdom. Rural life in the Yangtze Valley was rich, attractive, and tranquil. They recalled how they worked hard on seeding, planting, weeding, and harvesting at different times of the year, and how young peasants, dark and well-muscled, would work together with charming country maidens, singing folk songs all the time. They saw in their mind's eye rice stalks with golden panicles standing proudly in the paddies under the sun; they relived the satisfaction of threshing grain, hitting the stalks against the slotted frames. Their hands, now calloused by constant wielding of swords and spears, were itching to hold sickles again. They longed for the days when they could carry food on their backs instead of guns and ammunition. Oh, when could they start their homeward bound journeys? Their little pieces of land and their small vegetable gardens must have been laid waste for lack of cultivation; their small straw huts surely needed rethatching. What possible reason was there for them to remain here?

When they heard the news of the execution of their commanding general on charges of treason two days before, the men could not believe their ears. They felt sorrow as well as indignation as they vividly recalled how Yang had trained new recruits in the virgin forests of Thistle Mountain, instigated the revolt at Chin-t'ien, planned military strategies at Yung-an-chou and led the armada down the broad Yangtze to Nanking. However, they realized that a drastic change had transformed their respected commander, in the three years that had elapsed since the establishment of the Heavenly Capital, from a person who was accustomed to simple fare to one who enjoyed only great delicacies; from a man dressed in tattered clothes to a dandy attired in theatrical costumes. He had deserted the fraternal camp life for the luxurious life of a Chiangnan metropolis. His ambition to avenge the wrongs brought about by a foreign race had made this lowly laborer feel, for the first time, the dignity of man, entitled to happiness and self-respect. All this, it was said, had been bestowed upon him by the omnipotent and omnipresent Heavenly Father. But who had ever seen personally this Sacred Lord on high? They had had frequent contact with the Heavenly and Eastern kings during the fighting days—they were all of different surnames but had been as closely knit as brothers should. Back then they all wore the same soldier's uniform, ate the same rations from the sacred commissary, and slept in the same camp. But after the establishment of the Heavenly Capital, none of the soldiers had the opportunity to meet with their top leaders. Only on special occasions could they catch a glimpse of the imperial palace or the official residence of the Eastern King, their roofs adorned with green tiles and gates with yellow satin, where they could hear from a distance the master of ceremony's command to hail the "Lord of Ten Thousand Years" or the "Lord of Nine Thousand Years." All these sights and sounds had a special appeal to the common soldiers. They did not question their legality or propriety. They were convinced that their future and welfare had been guaranteed by the Heavenly King and a handful of his brothers of different surnames who also bore the title of kings. In the eyes of the soldiers, their leaders were nothing less than the personification of living gods. How could they ever imagine that the gods would kill each other or that one of them would pierce the heart of an intimate and loving brother with the sword given by the Heavenly Father?

The edict of the Heavenly King clearly stated that although the Eastern King was the chief culprit, the Northern King and the King of Yen had also committed crimes by murdering innocent people; and that their wanton killings had incurred the wrath of the Heavenly Father who had ordered the Heavenly King to have these two arrested and punished in the presence of the officers and men formerly under the Eastern King's command. This pronouncement had touched the hearts of the soldiers. "Oh! Most sacred Heavenly Father and beloved Heavenly King," they cried aloud, "only you appreciate our innocence; only you understand our sorrow and misery!"

As the men trudged along the streets of the Heavenly Capital, their eyes were assaulted by the sight of bloodstains on the walls and paving stones everywhere. Their hearts were as gloomy as the grey clouds in the sky. With heavy steps and ponderous hearts, they marched toward a destiny as uncertain as if they had just been defeated on the battleground.

As last they reached the Heavenly Front Gate. In front of the huge wall, a platform had been constructed for the sacrificial ceremony to the Heavenly Father. Over the platform was hung a yellow silk awning, and red curtains decorated both sides. Several glass palace lanterns were hung high in the front. A huge square table covered with a golden embroidered cloth was placed in the center of the platform. On the table were placed bowls of rice and tea and dishes of delicacies; two lit oil lamps stood on both sides of the table.

The soldiers were familiar with the religious ceremony—it was performed in the camps as a compulsory routine every seventh day. Participating in the ceremony gave them a deeper sense of solemnity and divinity, especially after the tragic massacre. According to the prearranged orders of the day, the invited soldiers sat in neat formation facing the platform, while the two thousand soldiers of the Northern King and the King of Yen sat in rows way behind.

First, a musician struck a brass gong in measured slow intervals sixty-four times. Its sound reverberated in the open square as if it would penetrate the deep recesses of the listeners' hearts. Then the musicians played three pieces of ceremonial music, one after another. When the music stopped, silence ensued in the square.

A palace deacon came forward to lead the assembly in responsive prayer:

"Praise the Lord on High. . . ."

"Praise the Lord on High. . . ."

The deep baritone voices of the soldiers were sincere, resounding with deep religious conviction.

Next, a female palace decree transmitter, wearing a plain yellow gown and a round embroidered gauze hat, took the place of the deacon. She read the edict of the Heavenly King which condemned the excesses of the Northern King and the King of Yen and spelled out their punishments before the assembled soldiers.

The voice of the female official was solemn and sorrowful. The four thousand soldiers in the square listened in absolute silence. As soon as the female decree transmitter finished her reading, the Northern King and the King of Yen, trussed up in heavy ropes, were brought out to the platform.

Each was relieved of his official gown and hat, wearing only undergarments with their hair dishevelled. They were led by four imperial guards carrying beating staves at the ready.

Amidst the shouting of the imperial guards, the two kings were made to lie down flat on their stomachs on two boards. When the third beating of the ceremonial drum ceased, two professional lictors brought the whipping staves down upon the buttocks of the kings with vehemence. Another two lictors cried out the number of strokes. Everyone present heard clearly the peculiar sound of bamboo hitting human flesh.

The Northern King began to cry. But as the bamboo stave continued to rhythmically rain down on his back, his cries turned into a howl.

The King of Yen's groans became transformed into pathetic pleading.

"Heavenly Father, please have mercy! Heavenly Father, please have mercy!"

Many of the soldiers assembled in the square were moved; some even to the point of tears. Whether they had been under the command of the Eastern King, the Northern King, or the King of Yen, they all expressed sympathy, understanding, and forgiveness.

The melodramatic event finally concluded with eight soldiers carrying the two badly beaten kings on the two boards away from the platform. They were supposed to be taken into the imperial prison.

A suffocating silence prevailed in the square. Some of the soldiers and officers, in their extreme naïvety, still wept in sympathy with the punished culprits. They were convinced that the Eastern King was probably guilty. But the Heavenly Father was compassionate and the Heavenly King was fair and just—even the Northern King and the King of Yen with their meritorious record had been punished for their excesses. Justice had been done and those who had suffered or died could rest in peace. What had happened was nothing more than a bad dream, and like any bad dream, it would pass away and lead to a new beginning.

As the two kings were carried away, a loud thunder-clap was heard overhead. The soldiers had not noticed that the sky had been laden with layers and layers of black clouds throughout the day. Although it was an early autumn afternoon, the sky was as dark as a late autumn day after sunset.

Black clouds chased one another and the roar of thunder sounded like iron wheels rumbling in the sky. A bolt of lightning pierced through the cloud formations and dazzled the eyes of the assembled multitude for a brief instant. Raindrops began to fall sporadically at first, then intensified gradually, finally changed to a heavy downpour. The cool autumn rain, pregnant with flashes of lightning, was awesome and threatening. It was followed by a blast of wind of immense intensity that swept the open, shelterless square.

The palace deacon, appearing on the platform again, announced to the assembled soldiers:

"The Heavenly King has decreed that all officers and men formerly under the command of the Eastern King may retire to the palace waiting rooms on the left and right of the front gate. They will be served a meal by the grace of the Heavenly Father and the Heavenly King. All officers and men under the command of the Northern King and the King of Yen may return to their barracks immediately!"

The two thousand odd officers and men formerly under the Eastern King's command were overwhelmed. With hunger-pangs in their stomachs, they gratefully rushed to the palace waiting rooms, expecting to enjoy a declicious meal. The rain had turned into a torrential downpour which sounded like the charge of a calvary brigade trampling across a roof.

The huge doors of the Heavenly Front Gate were thrown wide open. From the windows of the palace waiting rooms where they now gathered, the officers and men saw numerous youth vanguards in short jackets and red headbands, armed with gleaming swords and daggers, rush in like a whirlwind. Before the guests knew what was happening, these youthful vanguards had stopped traffic to all doors and windows of the east and west palace waiting rooms. Meanwhile, an imperial guard shouted loudly.

"The remnants of the Yang rebels have entered the palace grounds without permission. The crime is punishable by death!"

The eight hundred youth vanguards who had rushed into the palace directed their swords straight at the unarmed, defenseless, hungry, and weary men who were waiting for their promised meal from the Heavenly King. In a moment, the glittering weapons of the vanguards cut left and right; blood flowed freely and the ground was littered with human flesh. Shrieks of agony, anguished curses, and pathetic groans arose to the very heavens, diminished only by the howling wind and battering raindrops. Blood and brains spattered as the arms of the executioners danced ecstatically. One man's breast was pierced through; the head of another was lopped off; yet another lost his arms or legs. Some of the haphazardly strewn corpses on the floor had frightened looks on their faces and had died with their eyes wide open. Others murmured incomprehensibly before they breathed their last, imploring mercy from the Heavenly Father. A couple hundred young and agile men tried to escape, but were quickly cut down by the vanguards stationed at the doors. A few struggled until they reached the drawbridge, but were confronted by the soldiers of the Northern King and the King of Yen who had not returned to their barracks, brandishing their weapons at them in the storm. The remnants of the Yang rebels had no place to go and no chance to escape.

"Compassionate Heavenly Father," they seemed to plead, "open your eyes and witness this unheard-of premeditated massacre. Please make your voice heard and answer your sons, 'Is this heaven or is this hell?'"

The east and west palace waiting rooms became the graveyard of the two thousand men. Not a single one escaped with his life.

It was a complete victory for the Northern King and the King of Yen who had planned the massacre. The two thousand corpses were dumped into the Yangtze River the next day. The eight gates of the capital were now guarded by the soldiers of the King of Yen who had been ordered back from the Tan-yang front. Other contingents made rounds of the capital to flush out any remnants of the rebels. The official residence of the Eastern King had been razed to the ground. The Northern King also sent word to bring back his troops from the Kiangsi front posthaste.

The deluge lasted for two days and two nights. Although the bloodstains on the streets were washed away by the rain, the odor of death and the smell of the decomposed corpses permeated the atmosphere. The sad news reached the remaining eight thousand other officers and men formerly under the Eastern King's direct command. Everyone was full of indignation and hatred. Under the leadership of Fu Hsüeh-hsien, they vowed to avenge the tragic deaths of their brethren.

On the third day, the Northern King and the King of Yen, limping as a result of newly sustained wounds, were summoned to the palace. As they passed through the Heavenly Front Gate, they did not observe the usual etiquette of waiting for permission to proceed and hailing for the chief by the assembled officials. There was no feeling of liveliness usually accompanying an imperial audience; the atmosphere was more like a wake or a funeral.

In the Dragon Hall, the King of Yü, Hu I-kuang, the Consort of the Western King, Hung Hsüan-chiao, State Minister Meng Teh-en, and other officials who had not perished in the massacre stood gravely in two rows. As the Northern King and the King of Yen entered the Dragon Hall, a dead silence prevailed.

"May I report to Second Brother," the Northern King stepped forward and announced, "the remnants of the Yang rebels, thirty thousand in all, have been punished by the Heavenly Father. I've ordered my soldiers to return immediately from Kiangsi to provide adequate defense for the capital."

"Thirty thousand in all!" the Heavenly King was obviously ill at ease; his voice and lips were trembling. "Twice you have massacred innocent brethren in violation of the will of the Heavenly Father. You have ignored my repeated advice. The public opinion of the court is greatly incensed. Is there anyway you can explain for yourselves?"

"Lord of Ten Thousand Years!" the Northern King snapped, apparently taken aback. "What is this? What I did was done by the order of Your Majesty. Everyone in the court heard or knew about it."

The face of the Heavenly King turned pale. "I've already told you," he retorted, "that ruse of yours—using self-abuse to gain advantage—is too malicious. Now, just as I've predicted, all civilian and military officials in the court have put the blame on me, and I have no way to vindicate myself. It was you who put me in this untenable position!"

It was to be expected that after the crisis was over the Heavenly King would be more concerned about his reputation for being a benevolent and fair ruler than anything else. In short, he wanted to have his cake and eat it too, realized the Northern King.

"Lord of Six Thousand Years!" the Consort of the Western King stepped forward, speaking with passion. "The Eastern King had planned sedition and the Heavenly King had ordered you to quell the plot. But Yang's officers and men had not participated in the treason. Why should they suffer such a cruel massacre?"

"Consort of Western King!" the Northern King replied sarcastically, "How many heads do I have? Without the decree of the Heavenly King, would I have dared to do such a thing?"

"May I put this question to the Northern King?" asked the King of Yü, also stepping forward. "On the pretext of inviting the hungry soldiers to partake of a meal given by the Heavenly Father, a cruel massacre was carried out! Whose idea was that?"

"Whose idea was that?" the King of Yen, unable to hold his temper any longer, snarled, "You may address this question to His Majesty!"

The Heavenly King banged his fist on the table, expressing his mounting anger. "What impudence!" he roared, "The King can do no wrong! I can address a question to you, but you may not address a question to me!"

Ch'in Jih-kang fell on his knees, still fuming.

An uncontrollable rage plagued the Northern King. Without considering the possible grave consequences, he roared:

"Lord of Ten Thousand Years! I would never have expected that after eliminating the serious threat to your throne you would turn around and conspire to put all the blame on me in order to earn yourself a good name!"

Turning around abruptly, Wei stomped out of the hall, his head erect and chest thrown out. Ch'in Jih-kang scrambled to his feet and followed suit.

The sound of their heavy, impatient footsteps echoed throughout Dragon Hall, creating an unsettling feeling in the minds of the assembled military and civilian officials.

For more than ten days now, the Heavenly Capital had been in a state of complete anarchy. The soldiers of the Northern King and the King of Yen, in the name of the Heavenly Father, Brother, and King, searched for the remnant rebels in the city day and night. They plundered, raped, and murdered mercilessly and their victims included military officers and men, male and female civilian officials, as well as the common people, young and old. Naked corpses floated from the West Water Gate to Hsia-kuan and from there to the Great River. The air was saturated with the odor of putrid corpses and bloody carnage which persisted relentlessly.

The soldier's appetite for murder and wanton destruction increased as time went on. Not only those against whom they had held minor grudges were summarily killed, even total strangers were labelled "Yang rebels" and ruthlessly slaughtered. But killing is energy consuming. The murderers began to feel exhausted as the orgy continued.

Human blood used for irrigation can produce a strange fruit called "hatred," and "hatred" is always the cause of further bloodshed. The former Eastern King's men who had escaped massacre were now exploding with hatred. They realized that the slogan "All are God's children" was nothing but a bare-faced lie. If the Eastern King and the Northern King who had shared danger and hardship on the battlefield could kill each other so wantonly, it was no surprise that their followers could mete out to each other such cruelties without blinking an eye.

All their beliefs evaporated. The "Heavenly Regulations" were trampled under foot. The "paradise" built in the hearts of the followers of the God Worshippers Society over the past ten years collapsed. All religion, morality, and humanity had vanished; what remained were madness, fury, and hatred.

The remaining men of the Eastern King left their temporary camp in O-mei Peak and entered the city fully armed. They killed, plundered, raped, and set fire to everything within reach to vent their pent-up hatred. Engaging the soldiers of the Northern King and the King of Yen in desperate battle, their swords lost their sharp edges and their spears' long handles were broken in the struggle. When their arms were maimed, they bit their enemies with their teeth and tore their enemies' throats out with their fingernails even when their own abdomens had been cut open. The fierce onslaught continued day and night and in every conceivable place. On the riverbank they used their last ounce of strength to push their opponents into the water. Stones were hurled from rooftops and the wounded groaned in the shadows of walls. The entire city was thrown into madness and paralysis by the hatred and bloodshed.

Wei Ch'ang-hui and Ch'in Jih-kang could not enjoy a moment of rest; there were enemies hiding in every corner of the city. They could only close their eyes for a few minutes in the night, surrounded by many blazing candles and rings of sentries guarding their safety. Their eyes were bloodshot from lack of sleep.

Finally, twenty thousand soldiers under the command of the Northern King arrived from the Kiangsi front where they had been lingering. As soon as they entered the Heavenly Capital, they created another sea of blood by butchering all the "Yang rebels" now under the leadership of Fu Hsüeh-hsien. Only then the city, where infants were forbidden to cry, at last regained some semblance of peace.

The secret edict of the Heavenly King reached the Assistant King Shih Ta-k'ai while he was still fighting the Ch'ing demons in the vicinity of Wuchang. That was on the thirtieth day of the seventh month of the sixth year, *Ping-ch'en* (September 5, 1856). It was also the day after the massacre by ruse of the Eastern King's officers and men. Shih Ta-k'ai deducted that since Yang had usurped the appellation of "Lord of Ten Thousand Years" in the presence of the members of the court, a coup would be as inevitable as "an arrow fitted to a drawn bowstring." Yang's birthday, the seventeenth day of the eighth month, on which date the ceremony of abdication was supposed to take place, was less than a month away. Shih was confronted with a staunch enemy at the same time that a crisis was brewing in the capital. What was he supposed to do?

Shih summoned his trusted officers for a conference in the camp. Most of them suggested that they should return to the capital to exterminate the usurper. A minority thought that despite the urgency of the situation, there would be no real fighting in the capital. This group believed that the Assistant King was capable of solving any thorny problem when the need arose. It would be better for him to return with a few followers to assess the situation first and then proceed accordingly.

The Assistant King chose the latter option. He reasoned to himself: In the secret edict, the Heavenly King did not describe the situation in detail, nor did he suggest what next step the Eastern King might take. The capital and its vicinity were entirely under the control of the Eastern King's men. If he brought with him a small contingent of troops, it could be easily wiped out, should there be a confrontation. If he marshalled a large army to march on the capital, it would take much time and cause alarm which might upset the delicate situation. His first priority would be to assess the true situation in the capital and then decide what step should be taken next.

Having entrusted the responsibility of commanding the

troops to one of his top generals, Shih brought with him only two trusted subordinates, State Minister Chang Sui-mou and Vice State Minister Tseng Chin-ch'ien. He was also accompanied by his adopted daughter, Pao-ying, and a dozen guards. They proceeded westward by the water route in haste.

While travelling, the Assistant King kept his silence and remained incommunicative. Familiar with his habits, his adopted daughter and close associates knew that he was contemplating the situation in the capital and planning his next step. He had always fallen into such a mood before each important battle.

But that was only part of his considerations. The Assistant King's mood was not only contemplative, but also remorseful. He was thoroughly aware of the arrogance of the Eastern King as manifested by the latter's actions at the imperial feast and the true motive behind his dispatching of the three kings to distant fronts. His suspicion was further strengthened by the note he had received from the King of Yü. How stupid he had been to concentrate on the fighting at the front! As an old saying went, he had only been blocking the tiger from the front door, but forgetting about the wolf sneaking in through the back door.

His vexation was not caused by his lack of foresight alone. He had studied the classics when he was young and was well-versed in history and human affairs. But he had none of the preconceptions of historical events that usually restrained a pedant. He regarded the great figures in history, both heroes and villains, such as Huang Ch'ao, Li Ch'uang, or the first emperors of the Han and Ming, as birds of a feather. In his opinion, a man should not be judged by his success or failure. But since the establishment of the Heavenly Kingdom, however, there had occurred a series of inauspicious events in the short span of a few years. This recent turn of events was entirely beyond his expectations and a cause of his deep concern and vexation.

What was his private assessment of the personalities of the Heavenly King and the Eastern King? The Heavenly King had founded the God Worshippers Society and laid down its principles. These included many ridiculous and specious dogmas which Shih could not swallow, yet he had never openly challenged their validity. The Heavenly King had established a religious sect and appropriated for himself the position of leader. But at least he was deeply religious and sincerely believed in the dogmas of his own creation. On the other hand, the Eastern King had never considered the creed of the God Worshippers Society as a religion but as a strategy to be used for the advancement of his own political ambitions. In this respect he was much more clever than the Heavenly King. In Shih's unbiased evaluation, the Heavenly King was obstinate and full of himself, as well as incompetent and ignorant. The Eastern King, on the other hand, was cunning and clever, and could be dangerous and treacherous to his friends. Since joining the rebellion six years ago when he was twenty years old, Shih had shared moments of life and death with these two. A certain feeling of comradeship had developed among them; however, there had been a drastic change in the relationships among the top leaders since the establishment of the Heavenly Capital. Shih admitted to himself that he had begun to harbor resentment against the Heavenly King and distrust toward the Eastern King. Wasn't it true, he wondered, that "sharing troubled times was easier than sharing prosperity," as an old saying went? Since he had joined the rebellion, the one person he really respected was the deceased Southern King Feng Yün-shan, whom he considered to be both a teacher and an elder brother. In the management of public affairs, Feng was straightforward yet prudent; he always took care of priorities and discharged his duties with flexibility. In treatment of his brothers, he was extremely sincere and willing to make personal sacrifices. Ah! If only Feng were alive, Shih would have helped him to take the throne no matter what the cost.

"Sui-mou," he suddenly called out for his intimate subordinate. "You have read the *History of the Three Kingdoms.* What is your opinion concerning the story of Ts'ao Ts'ao and

Emperor Hsien of Han as compared to that of Chu-ke Liang and his incompetent sovereign?"

Chang Sui-mou was not surprised by the question put to him by his commanding general. The Assistant King had frequently posed such questions in his discussions with his intimate subordinates, first listening to their opinions then advancing his own. Their deep friendship was enhanced not on the battlefield where their common fate was determined, but in such friendly discussions carried on in camp where personal opinions could be freely expressed. This young general, who was only twenty-eight years old, and had received only a rudimentary education, was particularly intimate with his commanding officer.

"Your Lordship," Chang replied, "I am of the opinion that at the end of the Han dynasty the country was in a turmoil, and the people suffered greatly. Ts'ao Ts'ao took up the affairs of the state as his own responsibility. He took the throne from the enfeebled Emperor Hsien of Han, and thereby eliminated all his competitors and saved the people from further suffering. From this point of view, I consider Ts'ao Ts'ao to be nobler than Chu-ke Liang."

"But historians of subsequent generations," rejoined the Assistant King, smiling, "have unanimously considered Ts'ao Ts'ao a usurper and a rebel, and Chu-ke Liang a model loyal minister who served his sovereign wholeheartedly until his last breath."

"That is the opinion of pedants," Chang replied, "What the true story was I have no way of ascertaining, owing to my limited knowledge. But from the novel the *Romance of the Three Kingdoms,* I understand that Chu-ke Liang tried to help his incompetent sovereign, knowing that his effort would be wasted, just because the young emperor's father had visited him in his hut three times. He had put personal loyalty above the well-being of the common people. He stuck to the ancient principle, 'A true man should die for the person who really appreciates him!' while Ts'ao Ts'ao, on the other hand, took a more pragmatic view. Ts'ao once said,

'If not for me, who could tell how many people would call themselves emperors and how many people would call themselves kings?' This to me is truly a sincere and noble attitude."

The Assistant King smiled. He turned to Tseng Chin-ch'ien and asked, "what do you think of Sui-mou's ideas?"

Tseng Chin-ch'ien, a little over thirty and older than Chang Sui-mou, was barely literate. He was reserved and conservative in nature. After contemplating for a while, he replied, "I think there is validity in Brother Sui-mou's idea. The aim of warfare is the control of the state. The purpose of gaining control of the state is to save the people from suffering, not to repay personal obligations. I came from the countryside and have never been in school, but I feel that the old saying 'A true man should die for the person who really appreciates him' is not noble enough."

The Assistant King nodded, his look sobering. Turning to his adopted daughter, he asked, "Pao-ying, what is your opinion?"

"In the presence of my father and two elders," Pao-ying said with a modest smile, "how dare I express my opinion?"

"You may," commanded the Assistant King. "Don't be bashful. I know you have read widely. You are a child of ambition and profound knowledge."

"Living in a topsy-turvy world as ours," Pao-ying began gravely, "if one is lucky enough to survive, he should consider the suffering and anxiety of others as his own suffering and anxiety. He should not offer his life just for the sake of individual friendship and should not be concerned with his personal profit or loss, glory or ignominy. Many historical figures, such as Ching K'o and Nieh Cheng, who were chivalrous and selfless, are lauded by historians. But they were not as noble as such national heroes as Wen T'ien-hsiang and Yüeh Fei whose concern was on the whole of humanity. There is a difference between a brave man and a noble man."

The Assistant King and his two subordinates nodded in agreement. Pao-ying then continued, "When a person takes up the affairs of state as his own responsibility, he ought to acquire courage and humanity of a higher order and banish all concerns about life and death, glory or ignominy, praise or vilification, and ups and downs in life!"

Just then the commander's boat passed through a whirlpool. Splashes of water chased the waves behind. The Assistant King engrossed himself in deep thought and the rest of the group kept silent.

S hih and his party arrived at the Heavenly Capital in a dark night in the first week of the eighth month. As was his habit, he ordered his adopted daughter to go home while he went to visit the Heavenly King in the middle of the night. From the Heavenly King, he learned of the cruel massacre that had happened over the past two weeks. But the Heavenly King concealed the truth about the deceitful murder of the two thousand men and, by hint, attributed all the blame to the Northern King.

An hour later, the Assistant King and Chang Sui-mou appeared in the study of the Northern King. As always, the movements of the Assistant King were unpredictable and swift, whether on the battlefield or in court. The Northern King had anticipated his return, but not his sudden unannounced appearance in the middle of the night. Furthermore, he seemed not to have brought troops with him. This made the Northern King feel rather uneasy.

In the past, the Northern King had always maintained a condescending attitude toward this "younger brother" who ranked next to him in the T'ai-p'ing hierarchy. After all, his courtesy title claimed one thousand years less than his own. But the young commander was respected inside and outside the court and dreaded by the Ch'ing demons; hence, the Northern King was obliged to pay a certain amount of respect to this "younger brother," especially after the great massacre. He had a premonition that something inauspicious was going to happen.

The Northern King received the uninvited guests in his heavily guarded study. Chang Sui-mou, due to his inferior status, stood behind the Assistant King.

"My younger brother," the Northern King began with a sigh, "if you had returned a little sooner, my situation would not have been as bad as it is now. The Heavenly King wanted to eliminate the threat to his throne, yet he also wanted the people to regard him as a humane and benevolent ruler. I am not a sophisticated person and don't know how to satisfy him on both accounts. Now that the crisis is over, the Heavenly King has put all the blame on me in front of everyone in the court, and vilified me in public. That's what has made me disheartened."

"Rebel Yang deserved death," the Assistant King's answer was sharp and solemn. "But what crime can you attribute to his subordinates?"

"When you are engaged in a life and death struggle in the middle of the night, indiscriminate killing cannot be avoided."

"Granted," the voice of the Assistant King took an even more serious turn. "But I understand that it was your idea to lure Yang's men into the city and have them—two thousand unarmed brethren—murdered. Did that happen in the day-time or at night? Was it by accident or was it premeditation?"

"My younger brother," the Northern King now sounded incensed, "when enemies fight, it's either kill or be killed. Furthermore, I was only carrying out the Heavenly King's secret order. Could I refuse to obey his order?"

"If the ruse was the Heavenly King's idea, you should have advised him against it. If it was your idea, then your crime is unpardonable indeed. You have murdered several thousand brethren in the vicinity of the court and dispatched over a hundred thousand innocent people of the capital to Heaven. Imagine the grievances you've caused. Do you have any regard for the Heavenly Father, the Heavenly King, and the Heavenly Kingdom?"

"I've shouldered heavy responsibilities and endured

unjust criticism solely for the sake of the Heavenly Father, the Heavenly King, and the Heavenly Kingdom!" the Northern King shot back, his forehead drenched with perspiration.

"The people are the foundation of the state. You have murdered countless brothers and sisters and destroyed the people's confidence in us. You have incurred the people's indignation, as well as the wrath of the Heavenly Father, the Heavenly Brother, and members of the court. In other words, you've destroyed the future of the Heavenly Kingdom." His voice trembled with rage.

"Lord of Five Thousand Years," the King of Yen, Ch'in Jih-kang, silent heretofore, tried to put in a word. "It's too late now. In your opinion, what's the best thing to do?"

"The best thing? You two should admit your guilt and make a public apology. You should have yourselves trussed up and taken to the imperial prison, where you should wait for punishment to be meted out by the Heavenly Father and Heavenly Brother. The Heavenly King should also issue a public proclamation, admitting his own mistakes. Then by eliminating all the dishonest and evil individuals and appointing upright and capable ministers, it will be possible to put the court back in order. If we fail to take these steps, the fate of the Kingdom will be doomed and the situation will be unsalvageable!"

"Oh! Is that what you think?" exploded the Northern King, no longer able to suppress his anger. "You must be one of the Yang rebels yourself, Shih Ta-k'ai!" The Northern King stood up but before he could utter the words, "Come! Someone!" Chang Sui-mou leaped forward and brandishing a dagger in his hand, grabbed his adversary's arm.

"What do you want?" the Northern King shouted at him.

"I want you to see the Lord of Five Thousand Years out of your residence!" Chang replied calmly, still grasping the arm of the Northern King.

"Lord of Five Thousand Years and younger brother Sui-mou," Ch'in Jih-kang intervened, a forced smile on his twitching face. "We are brothers. Everything can be discussed. No need to resort to force!"

The Assistant King remained unperturbed. Turning to the King of Yen, he said calmly, "You are a member of the nobility of the Heavenly Kingdom and a commander of an army in the front, yet you can't differentiate good from evil, and let yourself drift with any current. Don't you realize that you are burying your future and bringing calamity to the state? One of these days, I am afraid, you'll die without a grave."

Having finished his tirade, the Assistant King turned around and commanded Wei Ch'ang-hui, "See me out immediately!"

An hour later, two captains of the guard from the Northern King and the King of Yen's establishments led nine hundred soldiers to surround the residence of the Assistant King on three sides while Wei Ch'ang-hui himself led five hundred men to break into the front gate.

The harvest moon festival was fast approaching. But that night the sky was covered with dark clouds and a cool breeze blew continuously. The people of the Heavenly Capital whose lives had been spared in the bloodbath were already in dreamland. Darkness reigned in the city. With the exception of the rustling gentle breeze, the chirping insects, and the rambling waves in the Great River, no other sound could be heard in the stillness of the night.

Without torches or battlecries, the fourteen hundred soldiers led by the Northern King had tightly surrounded the Assistant King's residence.

Having arrived at the residence a short while ago, Pao-ying and Tseng Chih-ch'ien had just finished their dinner, and were conversing with the Assistant King's wife, his six concubines, and his daughter about life in the camp in Hupeh. The six-year-old son of the Assistant King, sitting on Pao-

Chang grabbed the arm of the Northern King.

ying's lap, played with her sheathed dagger. Suddenly the sound of heavy footsteps, mixed with the noise of muffled conversation and a clang of metal began to be heard.

Pao-ying's trained ears were sensitive to changes in her surroundings. Putting the child down, she stood up. "What's that noise?" she inquired.

"Let me go and have a look," Tseng said.

As he stepped out of the door of the room, a group of soldiers wearing white armbands rushed in, cutting the curtain with their gleaming swords. One of them shouted, "Here they are! Don't let a single one escape!"

"Pao-ying, you help the ladies get out through the window," urged Tseng, "I'll take care of the intruders."

Instantly Pao-ying grabbed her little brother. Carrying him on her back, she jumped on top of a table. Kicking off the window frame with one foot, she beckoned to the ladies, exclaiming, "Follow me! Quick!"

The ten guards the Assistant King had brought back were having dinner in the back room. By the time the other retainers of the Assistant King's establishment were alerted by the commotion, the intruding soldiers had already invaded every corner of the premise. A fierce battle ensued and savage battlecries reverberated in the halls.

Tseng Chin-ch'ien, having received two cuts on his shoulders, sprawled obliquely by the door of the study, where he supported himself with his own dagger. He murmured incoherently, "Pao-ying, go quickly. I'll take care of the intruders."

While the Assistant King's guards and the invading soldiers fought in the courtyards, all the women of the establishment perished in pools of blood, except Pao-ying, who escaped to the rear garden with the child on her back. She climbed a tall tree and from there jumped over the wall.

The Northern King and the King of Yen had won another decisive battle. A total of three hundred victims lost their lives, including the Assistant King's seven consorts and a daughter, his guards, retainers, and officials, Tseng Chin-ch'ien among them.

Before they had taken action against the Assistant King's establishment, the Northern King had ordered mounted men to deliver a message to the guards of the city gates that without a pass issued by his establishment no one was permitted to leave the city. When the Northern King found that his enemy was not among the three hundred victims, he was sure that the Assistant King was hiding in the palace.

To him, the Assistant King had become a more formidable enemy than the Eastern King. The man must be destroyed immediately, vowed the Northern King, lest he would pose a real threat to his existence. Therefore, he led over one thousand men and marched toward the palace of the Heavenly King.

B y the light of the red palace lanterns, the widow of the Western King, Hung Hsüan-chiao, dressed in red military attire and accompanied by two aides, Ah-hsiao and Ah-li, engaged in a conversation with the Northern King and the King of Yen from the top of the palace gate tower. The female officials and women fighters, several hundred strong, also appeared on the gate tower with their gleaming weapons in hand. They appeared not only smart, but also dignified and efficient under the lantern light.

"Consort of the Western King," Wei Ch'ang-hui demanded, his voice solemn. "Are you aware that the Assistant King had left his military post and sneaked into the capital without permission?"

"I only know that he came to the capital to quell the rebellion by a secret order of the Heavenly King," Hung Hsüan-chiao replied in an equally solemn voice.

"The Assistant King is in collusion with the remnants of the Yang rebels in their attempt to overthrow the court."

"Do you have any proof?"

"Sneaking into the city at night and making covert

movements are proof enough."

"Is that so?" Hung Hsüan-chiao said with a grin. "What is the meaning of the fact that you, the Northern King and the King of Yen, have brought armed troops to the palace at night then?"

"We come to seek an imperial audience to advise His Majesty to take precautions."

"Only one person at a time can be admitted for an audience inside the Heavenly Front Gate."

"The remnants of the Rebel Yang are still rampant in the capital. We can't afford to venture out without proper protection."

"There are no remnants of the Rebel Yang in the palace," Hsung Hsüan-chiao shot back, her anger mounting.

"Please don't be angry. I have an important message to convey to His Majesty in person."

"Lord of Six Thousand Years, you are a pillar of the state. Don't you know there's no precedent for ministers to seek audience in the middle of the night?"

"The military situation demands immediate attention."

"If so, hand in your memorial. I'll report to His Majesty on your behalf."

"In the event that the military situation suffers on account of the delay, neither you nor I can bear the responsibility!"

Hung Hsüan-chiao turned to Ah-hsiao and commanded, "The Northern King is probably unaware of the Heavenly King's edict that has been posted on the wall of the Heavenly Front Gate. Read it out to him."

Ah-hsiao read the edict in a clear voice: "Officials, high and low! Proceed no further; whosoever violates this rule, away his head shall go!"

Gnashing his teeth, Wei Ch'ang-hui sweared indignantly, "Consort of the Western King! If the military situation suffers and the rebel escapes, it may not be Wei Ch'ang-hui who loses his head!"

Hung Hsüan-chiao, her hearty laugh ringing in the air,

answered calmly, "Don't worry, Lord of Six Thousand Years! Whatever punishment there is, I'll accept it gladly. You have forced entrance into the palace in the middle of the night with armed soldiers, in defiance of the concerted opinion of court officials and the common people. I advise you to be more careful from now on!"

In a blinding rage, the Northern King and the King of Yen withdrew their troops, realizing that they were impotent at this point.

NINE

"The crisis in the Heavenly Capital has reached a critical stage," the Assistant King said to his adjutant as they came out from the Northern King's residence. "We've probably arrived a little too late. I'm afraid that Wei Ch'ang-hui will now follow in Yang Hsiu-ch'ing's footsteps and invade the palace. Such a move will allow the Ch'ing demons to take advantage of the situation and attack the capital. If that happens, the Heavenly Kingdom will come to an end. Sui-mou, let's hurry back and crush Wei's plot!"

"If the Northern King intends to harm Your Lordship, will he leave your wives and children alone?" pleaded Chang Sui-mou earnestly. "May I humbly suggest that Your Lordship go to the palace to wait for further developments, while I go back to the residence to lead the guards in escorting your family members safely out of the city? This would seem to be the only way we can play safe."

"What time do you think this is?" Shih Ta-k'ai snapped impatiently. "If Wei Ch'ang-hui wants to harm my family, he probably has started already. If we go back right now, it would be tantamount to walking into a tiger's den."

Chang did not dare to argue further. The two men rode hurriedly down the streets of the capital in the windy, dark night.

A group of mounted soldiers on patrol approached from the opposite direction, their horses kicking up sparks from the stone pavement. Chang quickly pulled the Assistant King by the arm and the two veered immediately into a side alley.

"Lord of Five Thousand Years!" Chang whispered. "We can't go through the city gate. This alley leads to the Minor South Gate where the city wall is low. We can let ourselves down over it."

The two men lowered themselves over the city wall. From a former subordinate who was manning the pass, they obtained two mounts and left the troubled city in great haste.

While galloping on horseback, Shih Ta-k'ai was engrossed in deep thought. He was remorsefully critical of himself. As a commanding general, he felt he was lacking in overall planning. He was proficient in dealing with enemies, but did not have the necessary foresight to meet the internal cirsis. Just now, he had blundered into the tiger's den, narrowly escaping with his life. The safety of his entire family was still hanging in the balance. Couldn't he see it was futile to talk to such grossly insensitive individuals such as Wei Ch'ang-hui and Ch'in Jih-kang about loyalty and righteousness? It appeared that there was no other option except to marshall his troops back to the capital to meet the crisis. What a pity! The situation in Anhwei had just been stabilized and the fighting in Hupeh had just begun. The crisis in the Heavenly Capital *had* to occur at this inopportune moment! Was this the will of Heaven, or a man-made calamity?

The Assistant King had been ordered to the Hupeh front

only two months earlier. His main force was still stationed in the Ning-kuo camp. The rest of his troops were scattered at Wuhu and An-ch'ing in Anhwei as well as in other cities in Hupeh and Kiangsi provinces. He decided to go to the Wuhu camp first, and to assemble his forces in the Ning-kuo camp to be ready for action.

By daybreak, the two riders had covered a distance of sixty *li*. They reached the Wuhu camp at dusk when all the barracks were already brightly lit.

In the same night right after their arrival, the Assistant King called an emergency meeting of the military council. He reported on the situation in the Heavenly Capital and explained the necessity of meeting the crisis. After the brief conference, the officers left in an atmosphere of indignation and anxiety.

Few of the officers slept that night. After six years of bloody fighting, the newly-laid foundation of the Heavenly Kingdom was now threatened with total collapse. They were horrified by the turn of events. Despite the fact that the camp was quiet as usual—the soldiers were fast asleep while the horses were safe in their stables—the officers were overwhelmed by a sense of helplessness and depression. They remembered the mood of joyous, high-spirited exhilaration they had always known before battles in the past. But now they only felt despair and apprehension, like members of an isolated army that had penetrated too deep into the enemy's territory without reinforcement troops in sight, bracing for a last desperate fight. They stared from a distance at the main tent of the Assistant King where candles burned throughout the night, revealing the restless shadow of the tall, young general.

Early next morning, the Assistant King dispatched six subordinates, each accompanied by ten guards, to the various camps in Kiangsi, Hupeh, and Anhwei provinces, with his orders to immediately decamp and reassemble to be ready to march on the capital. The Assistant King, Chang Sui-mou, and a few others travelled back and forth between Wuhu, Ning-kuo, and An-ch'ing to make preparations for the expedition. At the same time, agents were sent to the capital to obtain intelligence concerning the movements of the Northern King and the King of Yen as well as developments in the court.

In ten days, the six subordinates returned one after another to the Wuhu camp and reported that all regional commanders had decamped immediately and that some were already on their way. Delighted, the Assistant King personally drafted a proclamation in the name of the Heavenly King launching an attack on the Northern King and the King of Yen.

That night, the Assistant King took a walk outside his tent. Before his eyes stretched rows of tents for dozens of *li* and countless campfires. From far and near he heard the sound of the nightwatchmen's rattles.

He recalled the conversation between himself and his adopted daughter on the way back from Wuchang not long ago. The Eastern King had been killed for his ambition and arrogance, but his place had been taken by the treacherous Northern King who took pleasure in indiscriminate killing. Everyone in the court felt that his own position was precarious and that the affairs of the state were in disarray. Should he follow the example of Ts'ao Ts'ao and take the throne for himself from the obstinate, dawdling Heavenly King? Or should he emulate the loyal and selfless Chu-ke Liang who did his best despite the fact that he was fighting for a losing cause? Having studied classics in his youth, Shih believed that humanity and righteousness were the fundamentals in conducting oneself and treating others, as well as in governing a state and ruling the people. He could not convince himself to follow the famous maxim attributed to Ts'ao Ts'ao: "Let me turn my back on others rather than let others turn their backs on me." Yet he could not see what there was to justify his undivided devotion and loyalty toward this self-important and muddle-headed Heavenly King, or his decision to attempt the impossible and sacrifice himself. But no matter what course he would choose, he had to first get rid of the Northern King, or else he would never achieve anything at all. However, recent events—Yang Hsiu-ch'ing's attempt to usurp the throne and the premeditated murder of Yang by Wei Ch'ang-hui—had turned the blood of old and new brothers cold. If he tried to make history repeat itself once again, wouldn't it also make him a villain in the eyes of posterity?

The Assistant King was faced with a dilemma. Scattered in the various camps in three provinces were a hundred thousand men under his direct control. With his talent and prestige, he was sure that he could save the situation without difficulty. But what should be his next step once the crisis was over? Turning his head upward, he saw a sky that was as clean as a newly washed bowl. A multitude of stars vied with each other for brightness, and a round pale yellow moon rose in the eastern horizon. He calculated that the mid-autumn festival time was fast approaching. A horse neighed in the distance, enhancing his feeling of desolation.

As Shih mulled over his future plans, he heard a sentry loudly demand the password from a visitor and the sound of horse hooves clattering just outside his tent. He recognized the visitor's voice as that of his adopted daughter, Pao-ying. Hastening his footsteps, he rushed from the tent to greet her.

A guard held the reins as Pao-ying dismounted and ran toward the tent. As soon as she saw the Assistant King, she fell on her knees, wailing uncontrollably.

"Father, I am back at last!"

The Assistant King helped his adopted daughter up. Under the candlelight, she looked pale and exhausted; her hair was disheveled; her clothes were tattered; and her crystal clear eyes were brimming with tears.

Pao-ying related what had happened since that fatal evening. While Tseng Chin-ch'ien and the guards fought desperately with the invading soldiers, she had climbed up a tall tree and jumped over the wall. As the soldiers were concentrating on catching the Assistant King, they hadn't paid much attention to the back of the residence. Carrying her younger brother on her back through back alleys under the dim moonlight, she had suddenly been confronted with two mounted patrols. Swiftly she thrust her dagger deep into one patrolman's chest before he could draw his sword. Pao-ying quickly mounted his horse and galloped away. The other patrolman yelled, "Catch that spy!" but did not dare to give chase. Pao-ying then went to the private residence of the King of Yü, Hu I-kuang, who received her warmly. As she untied the child from her back, she found that the little boy had died, apparently from injuries he had received. The next day Hu I-kuang's men received the news that all members of the Assistant King's household, more than three hundred in all, had been killed. Hearing the news, Pao-ying wept so hard that she fainted.

After recuperating for a few days, Pao-ying was invited by Hu to a private meeting to discuss future plans.

"The two murderers, Wei and Ch'in, have committed such hideous crimes that they have become outlaws in the eyes of everyone in the Heavenly Kingdom," declared Hu I-kuang. "I'm sure an act of usurpation will be attempted soon. Since your father didn't go back to the residence that night, he is probably in the camp at Wuhu or Ning-kuo, preparing to fight back. The best plan for you now is to go to the camp, find your father, and persuade him to march on the capital to save the court and avenge the wrongs done to his family and the country."

Pao-ying dressed herself in a male serviceman's uniform. Accompanied by four guards of the King of Yü, she was able to leave the city without being detected.

As Pao-ying related her story, Chang Sui-mou and several ranking officers entered the tent and listened intently. They realized that since the Assistant King's family members had all been mercilessly murdered, their own families could have fared no better. Everyone was greatly alarmed and hoped that the Assistant King would give the order to march on the capital right away.

The Assistant King did not want to display his emotions before his subordinates, and tried his best to suppress his tears. His face livid, he ordered his adopted daughter and the assembled officers to return to their barracks. Just then a horse could be heard neighing at the outer gate of the main tent, followed by the sounds of brief conversation and commands. In an instant, T'ung Jung-hai, commander of the Wuhu camp, entered the tent, bringing an officer from West Liang-shan with him.

"Lord of Five Thousand Years!" T'ung began, kneeling before his commander, "the thug Ch'in Jih-kang and fifteen thousand of his men have attacked us in the rear. They are now at West Liang-shan."

The officer from West Liang-shan fell on his knees, weeping. "Most of our brethren stationed at West Liang-shan have ascended to Heaven under the attack of Ch'in's troops. I was ordered by the division commander to report to the camp commander and Your Lordship. At the time of my departure, the division commander had sustained five wounds, and only three hundred men survived!"

"Ch'in Jih-kang!" cried Shih Ta-k'ai with a sneer. "He even dared to attack my troops. Jung-hai, let's take a trip now!"

Two guards rushed to the stable to prepare their mounts. "Lord of Five Thousand Years!" T'ung Jung-hai said hesitatingly. "Precautionary measures must be taken first. Let me gather three thousand men before we go."

"Ch'in Jih-kang's fifteen thousand men are nothing but useless garbage," roared Shih Ta-k'ai. "If you are afraid you may remain here." Then, turning to the adjacent tent, he called, "Pao-ying, you come with me."

Having had her dinner and washed, Pao-ying had just retired, but had not yet fallen asleep. Hearing her father's command, she replied, "I'm coming, Father!" Quickly donning her military uniform and grabbing her short sword, she appeared in front of the big tent in no time.

T'ung Jung-hai did not dare say anything more. He gave orders to an officer to immediately gather about one hundred mounted guards, armed with weapons and torches to wait for the signal in front of the tent.

The Assistant King entrusted Chang Sui-mou with camp affairs during his absence. He rushed out of the tent like a whirlwind, gave the assembled guards a quick glance, and mounted his black horse. Raising his whip high, he galloped out of the camp without the traditional sounding of the conch and the beating of drums, closely followed by T'ung Jung-hai, Pao-ying, and the hundred-odd mounted guards. The full moon was now in the center of the sky, shining over the contingent that raced down the main road toward West Liang-shan.

While the Assistant King was redeploying his troops, news of his military preparations reached the Heavenly Capital. In response the Northern King ordered the King of Yen, Ch'in Jih-kang, to lead his men, fifteen thousand in all, to oppose Shih Ta-k'ai. The Northern King was fully aware that Ch'in's ability and military strength were no match for those of Shih, but he could not spare any of his own forces to fight his adversary. Other than the staunch and obedient Ch'in Jih-kang, there was no other general he could dispatch.

Ch'in Jih-kang was keenly aware of the situation too. Originally a farmhand, Ch'in was trained on the battlefield and became a seasoned and brave fighter. But he was not endowed with the ability to understand the complexity of court politics and intrigues. Owing to his loyalty to the Heavenly King and abhorrence of the Eastern King's arrogance, he came to the capital in response to the Heavenly King's secret edict. Under the direction of the Northern King, he helped eliminate the Eastern King. Later on, however, he was disheartened by the Heavenly King's shifting of all the blame on the Northern King and himself. On the other hand, he felt insecure when he was threatened by the Northern King's highhandedness. He was not as ambitious as the Eastern King or the Northern King. But his instinct of self-preservation told him that he must maintain good relations with the Northern King. He now found himself in a quagmire from which it would be difficult for him to extricate himself.

Before Ch'in left the capital, he knew that the Assistant King had sent out proclmations calling for the gathering of troops to march on the capital. He realized that for him to oppose the Assistant King was no different from "hitting a stone with an egg." But if he should refuse to obey the order, it would ruin his relationship with the Northern King. He accepted the assignment most reluctantly.

The fifteen thousand men started their journey westward by land and water. They were told that the Assistant King had defected and was starting a revolt and that the Heavenly King had ordered the King of Yen to put up a defense against the rebellion. As the troops slowly proceeded on their journey they felt less and less convinced of the veracity of what they had been told. Since the Assistant King had been fighting under the Eastern King for the past several years, they figured, it was plausible that he would raise an army to avenge the latter's tragic death. But they were puzzled about the senseless killing among the leaders. The recent events deprived them of the capacity to differentiate the leader who was loyal to the Heavenly King from the one who had allegedly defected to the enemy. In the mind of the T'aip'ing soldiers, the Assistant King had always represented their ideal of bravery and leadership. If the Assistant King were defecting, who else could they put their trust in?

As Ch'in Jih-kang's troops were dilly-dallying, uncertain of what to do next, a transmitter of orders from the Northern King's establishment reached the camp of Ch'in Jih-kang and ordered the latter to advance immediately and to eradicate the two thousand troops of Shih Ta-k'ai stationed at West Liang-shan, halfway between Wuhu and the capital.

Ch'in Jih-kang was aware that the elimination of a small

contingent at West Liang-shan was not vital to the defense of the Heavenly Capital. The Northern King just wanted him to "yank the tiger's whiskers," so that there could be no compromise between the Assistant King and himself.

Ch'in Jih-kang was thus placed in a back-to-the-wall position. He was obliged to annihilate Shih's two thousand troops in a surprise night attack during which the defending division commander died. A few hours before the brigade commander reached the Assistant King's camp, Ch'in Jih-kang had already taken over the camp at West Liang-shan on the north bank of the Yangtze River. His mission accomplished, the Northern King's messenger then went back to report the good news to his lord.

At about four o'clock in the morning of the following day, as Ch'in Jih-kang was still fast asleep in his tent, a sentry reported lights approaching in the front. Ch'in ordered that the soldiers in the barracks should not be disturbed. Then he quickly dressed and left his tent, sword in hand. The moon was hanging over the western horizon and a few stars twinkled in the sky. A string of bright moving torches could be seen approaching from a distance. Before he could order the blowing of conches and beating of drums, the Assistant King and one hundred odd mounted men had already reached the main tent of the camp, blocking its entrance and exit.

Ch'in Jih-kang, as if suddenly- awakened from a stupor, broke out into a cold sweat that trickled down his back. Quickly he fell on his knees and paid obeisance to the intruder.

The Assistant King ordered his men to surround the tent. Then he, Pao-ying, and T'ung Jung-hai dismounted and walked straight in. Sitting himself down behind the table, he threw his dagger on it. With a scathing sneer, he said:

"Ch'in Jih-kang! I heard that you've just scored a big victory. Please accept my congratulations!"

Ch'in Jih-kang banged his head on the ground and stammered nervously, "Lord of Five Thousand Years! I, Ch'in Jih-kang, am bound by an imperial edict. I can't help myself."

The Assistant King pounded the table with his fist. "Are you bound by the edict of the Heavenly King or the order of a vicious thug?" he roared. "Brothers killing brothers! Strife within the household! Thousands of innocent people of the capital have been dispatched to Heaven. Not one single member of my family of three hundred was spared, and you still are not satisfied. Now, you've set *me* up as your target. My head is right here. If you've got the guts, come and get it."

Ch'in Jih-kang kowtowed nonstop, his face covered with perspiration. "I, Ch'in Jih-kang, would never dare!" he pleaded.

Drawing her sword from its scabbard, Pao-ying jumped forward, pulling Ch'in Jih-kang's hair by her other hand. "Father!" she cried, "Let me kill this rat, this vermin, an enemy of the state and people!"

"Halt!" the Assistant King ordered his daughter to stop. Then turning to Ch'in Jih-kang, he roared, "Yang Hsiu-ch'ing's behavior was outrageous and Wei Chang-hui's even worse. The fratricide has made all of us a laughing stock. You have killed all my family members; our past sentiments of sworn brotherhood have been completely scrapped. You don't have an ounce of human feelings, but I can't be a man lacking in righteousness, to be condemned by posterity. Since the thug Wei Ch'ang-hui and you have committed crimes together, neither will escape punishment so easily. Pao-ying, cut off his hair and let him keep his head for the time being!"

Pao-ying cut Ch'in's long hair with one slash of her sword and threw it on the ground.

"Thank you, Lord of Five Thousand Years, for sparing my life," Ch'in said, kowtowing, "I'm aware of my grave crimes."

"If you are aware of your crimes, you should go back to the capital and arrest the thug Wei and hand him to the Heavenly King to be punished for the sake of the Heavenly Kingdom!"

"I've made enemies with the brethren in the court. The

Heavenly King may not trust me anymore. Furthermore, I have only a few generals and a small number of soldiers. I am no match for the Northern King."

"Bah!" the Assistant King retorted angrily. "You are afraid to offend Wei Ch'ang-hui, yet you are not afraid to offend the people and the sacred soldiers of the Heavenly Kingdom. If you are not afraid of the Heavenly King, naturally you are not afraid of me!"

Still kneeling, Ch'in Jih-kang did not dare to raise his head; sweat trickled down from his forehead.

"If you regret what you have done," the severity in Shih's voice did not lessen. "You should follow me back to the capital and together with me attack the vicious thug in order to save the Kingdom."

"Lord of Five Thousand Years," Ch'in Jih-kang pleaded desperately. "On the day I left the capital, the Northern King put my residence under surveillance. In the name of protection, my family members are actually being held as hostages. If I should follow you to the capital, all my family members, several hundred in all, will suffer death at the hands of the Northern King."

This infuriated Shih Ta-k'ai even more. Grinding his teeth audibly, he glowered at Ch'in's swarthy, narrow, stupid face. "You are still thinking of protecting your family even if you'll have no way to protect your own head tomorrow."

Shih Ta-k'ai returned his sword into its scabbard in disgust as he spoke to his adopted daughter and T'ung Jung-hai. "I've wasted time in talking to this man. He knows nothing of loyalty and righteousness. Let him suffer what is his due."

He strode out of the tent. Pao-ying and T'ung Jung-hai followed, their swords still drawn. In the meantime a hundred of Shih's guards had been deployed in a circle surrounding the main tent. On horseback, each of them, with a torch in one hand and a sword in the other, was patiently waiting for orders. Together with the scores of generals and hundreds of guards of Ch'in's camp who had also come, they could overhear the conversation between the two commanders.

As the Assistant King mounted his satiny black horse, the mounted guards parted to form a human passageway for him. The generals and guards of Ch'in Jih-kang's camp who had been silent throughout the proceedings, did the same. The distraught Ch'in Jeh-kang rushed out from the tent, his remaining hair flying.

"Lord of Five Thousand Years," Ch'in cried. "When you march your troops to the capital, I'll be your rear guard. Please put in a word for me before the Heavenly King to commute my death sentence. I'll fight hard against the Ch'ing demons, and when everything returns to normal in the capital, I'll come to you to ask your pardon."

The Assistant King did not reply. Cracking his whip down hard on his mount, he galloped between the human walls, closely followed by his adopted daughter and T'ung Jung-hai. The hundred mounted guards, holding their torches high, trailed behind. Viewed from a distance, the procession looked like a fiery dancing dragon.

After a distance of ten *li* from Ch'in's camp, the guards put out the torches. The Assistant King's black mount slowed its pace. The wind ceased to whistle into the men's ears and the constellations overhead seemed to have stopped turning and spinning.

Only then did the Assistant King relinquish his self control. Hot tears silently trickled down his cheeks. But they went undetected; not even his adopted daughter, usually observant, had noticed them.

On the first day of the tenth month, one hundred thousand troops of the Assistant King formerly stationed in An-hwei, Kiangsi, and Hupeh provinces had regrouped and assembled in a triangular area, encompassing the Wuhu, Ning-kuo, and An-ch'ing camps, waiting to march on the capital. During that night, the Assistant King called his subordinate generals to take part in an oath-taking ceremony in the main tent of the Ning-kuo camp.

The generals, about three dozens in all, sat in a circle. Candles burned brightly. The Assistant King positioned himself in front of a table in the center of the tent. Behind him stood his adopted daughter. His expression was solemn and his voice trembled slightly.

"Since we established our capital in Nanking, five years have elapsed. It has always been vital that we must carry out our task in a harmonious way in order to eradicate the Ch'ing demons. Unfortunately, Traitor Yang attempted to usurp the throne, in violation of the original intent of the revolution. After the death of Traitor Yang, his subordinates and troops, who were innocent, should not have been implicated. But the vicious thug Wei Ch'ang-hui took the opportunity to carry out a massacre which made everyone in the capital fear for his life. At this moment, with the Ch'ing demons menacing us on all sides and our brethren killing each other in the capital, the very survival of the state is hanging in the balance. Since the fate of the Heavenly Kingdom is at stake and the people are anxiously waiting for delivery, how can I, despite my limited abilities, neglect my duty by not offering my services at this critical moment? All of you are my brethren on the battlefield and have shared with me both danger and adversity. I hope that no one will have second thoughts concerning our campaign to clean up the evildoers in the capital. If we are successful, we will restore law and order in our society, drive away the barbarian intruders, preserve the heritage of the Chinese nation, and save the people from sufferings. If we should fail, my brothers, happiness awaits us in the nether world for having ended our lives on the battlefield. Anyone among you who does not agree with me please feel free to leave. I'm not going to put pressure on any of you!"

Chang Sui-mou stood up from a seat in the back and solemnly announced, "Anyone who does not wish to go to the capital to exterminate the hoodlums may say so and leave the tent."

The thirty-odd generals remained quiet, intently staring at the face of the Assistant King. A dead silence prevailed in the tent. Chang Sui-mou raised his arm and declared resolutely to his commander, "Lord of Five Thousand Years! None of our brothers have any second thoughts. We'll follow you to the capital!"

Early next morning, under a bright blue autumn sky, the Assistant King's one hundred thousand troops started to move toward the capital amidst the red foliage along the River, flags fluttering and weapons gleaming in the sunlight. One could see a forest of moving masts in the river and clouds of dust along the roads on its banks.

Even as the Assistant King was assembling his troops for the campaign, there was a drastic change of the political scene in the Heavenly Capital.

The two-month-long massacre had turned the Heavenly Capital into a desolate, terror-stricken place. Bandits, fraudulently carrying the flags of the Northern King's establishment, plundered and murdered innocent people in sparsely populated areas. In the evening, dogs ran amuck through the streets and alleys carrying limbs of the dead. Those still alive tried to sneak out of the city gates by all conceivable means to escape the worst possible fate.

The Heavenly Capital was now a city under the sole control of the Northern King. His words determined the life and death of all citizens. The massacre increased his power to do evil and his power to do evil fanned his wild ambitions. He was no longer satisfied with the title of "Lord of Six Thousand Years," and would not rest until he would be addressed as the "Lord of Ten Thousand Years." In his eyes, the Heavenly King was nothing more than a useless appendix. He did not need to follow the footsteps of the Eastern King to force the Heavenly King to abdicate. He would simply remove the latter from the throne and take his place.

But so far he had not yet taken the final step, because he was still inhibited by certain apprehensions. In order to remove the Heavenly King, he would have to first publicly denounce the sovereign by enumerating his crimes to convince the public. Secondly, he would have to install ample defense facilities to repel possible attackers. On both accounts, he felt that he was not yet fully prepared.

However, Wei also felt that it was equally uncertain whether or not he should wait for the opportunity to present itself. Uppermost on his mind was the Assistant King who had an army of one hundred thousand stationed in the upper reaches of the Yangtze. He could visualize Shih's scorching eyes watching over him day and night. Other military leaders, such as Yang Fu-ch'ing, the brother of the Eastern King, and Li Hsiu-ch'eng, all had control over large number of troops in the vicinity of the capital. They had not taken any action yet, only because they were preoccupied with the Ch'ing demons. If they should raise their flags and join forces with Shih Ta-k'ai to attack the capital, Wei would be in a rather untenable position.

The Northern King was also facing insurmountable difficulties in the capital. The King of Yü, Hu I-kuang, had confined himself in his home again after the assassination of the Eastern King, professing that he was ill. In the eyes of the Northern King, Hu I-kuang was a dangerous figure. Outwardly he seemed to be easy-going, humble, and polite, but in reality he was rather calculating and full of tricks—not someone to be taken for granted. The Northern King had sent a court physician to visit Hu at home. The physician had reported that the King of Yü was afflicted with some kind of cardiovascular disease. Since the assassination of the Eastern King, his condition had been further complicated by a neurological disorder of unknown etiology. In the opinion of the physician, Hu was demented most of the time. He would not utter a word for long periods of time, and only on rare occasions spoke a few incomprehensible sentences as saliva dribbled from the corners of his mouth. His was declared to

be a terminal case, with little hope for recovery. Being informed of this, the Northern King felt somewhat relieved.

The palace was now guarded by women soldiers and
youth vanguards under the command of Hung Hsüan-chiao
and Meng Teh-en respectively. From the inner city to the
Heavenly Front Gate and the bridge over the imperial moat,
heavy guards were posted at every entrance. Torches burned
brightly throughout the night indicating that the Heavenly
King was serious in his intention to guard the palace while
waiting for the arrival of the Assistant King.

The Northern King had now become constantly touchy,
almost to the point of belligerence.

One evening, the patrol at Treasure Gate caught a traitor
among a group of people who were fleeing the city. An important document had been allegedly found on him.

The Northern King ordered the traitor sent to his official
residence to be interrogated by himself. Before his arrival, a
trusted retainer presented to the Northern King the document
which he had obtained. Wei was greatey shocked. The document turned out to be an imperial edict written in the usual
casual style of the Heavenly King, addressed to the Assistant
King. It contained, *inter alia,* one sentence which particularly
angered him:

> I hope you'll bring your troops back to the
> capital to eliminate the hoodlum Wei so as to save
> the court and people.

Who could the traitor be? The Northern King wondered.
Something made him suspect that it was the King of Yü, Hu
I-kuang.

His suspicion was not unfounded. Soon Hu I-kuang,
heavily bound, was brought into the study of the Northern
King by two guards.

The Northern King sat himself behind a table.

"Your Excellency, King of Yü!" he greeted Hu with a
grin, venom dripping from his words. "We haven't seen each
other for quite a while." Then he shouted to the guards,

"Loosen the ropes! Bring a chair! Serve tea!"

"Two months ago, Your Excellency and I devised together-er, in the presence of His Majesty, ways to eradicate Rebel Yang and his followers," he continued, sighing gravely. "Yet soon afterwards, Your Excellency spoke ill of me before the Heavenly King and conspired with the Assistant King to kill me. How unpredictable human nature is! This was entirely beyond my expectations!"

"Six years ago," Hu I-kuang began, with a calm smile on his face, "when the Heavenly King started the revolution with a handful of brothers, I was lucky to be allowed to join the ranks and to fight on the battlefields. Our original plan was to work together harmoniously to defeat the Ch'ing demons for the sake of the country. But Rebel Yang attempt-ed to usurp the throne and you, Wei Ch'ang-hui, now follow in his footsteps. This was also beyond my expectations!"

Infuriated, Wei banged his fist on the table, making the tea cups dance up and down, clinking jarringly.

"Shut up!" he snapped, "If I, Wei Ch'ang-hui, could kill someone like Yang Hsiu-ch'ing, I can kill ten like you, Hu I-kuang!"

"Indeed! I'm delighted to hear that!" Hu said noncha-lantly, apparently unimpressed by the threat.

"Shih Ta-k'ai is deploying one hundred thousand troops outside the city gate," Wei Ch'ang-hui changed the subject, his agitation lessening, "with the obvious purpose of appropri-ating the throne for himself. And you are assisting him in his evil design. This is detrimental not only to the interests of our sovereign, but also to yourself. Has this ever occurred to you?"

"That may be the case," Hu I-kuang replied calmly, "You've murdered so many of your brothers and now you're holding the Heavenly King as your hostage. People are indig-nant and the capital is threatened. Did you do all this in the interests of the Heavenly Kingdom or for your own sake?"

"I'm not going to argue with you," Wei said with a forced smile. "However, there is something for which I need your consent. If you agree to it, you need not die!"

"Thank you for being so considerate," Hu said smilingly,

"I'd like to hear it."

"I'm planning to send out a proclamation to solicit all military personnel, inside and outside the capital, to attack Shih Ta-k'ai. The proclamation would be more effective if it were under the joint signature of the three of us—you, me, and Ch'in Jih-kang."

"May I ask what would be the reason for issuing such a joint proclamation?"

"When Rebel Yang was carrying out his schemes, Shih Ta-k'ai failed in his duty to come back immediately. After Rebel Yang was killed, Shih deployed a hundred thousand men to threaten the capital. His intentions are crystal clear. Do we need further proof?"

"Ha! Ha! Ha!" Hu responded with a hearty laugh. "I know you had once been a legal secretary in the *yamen* of Kuei-p'ing county. You are now using that expertise in twisting facts and making false claims."

"You refuse to sign your name then?" Wei's smile quickly vanished from his face.

"Even if I'm willing to put down my signature, would I be able to hoodwink all the people under Heaven?"

"If that's what you think, don't blame me for not saving your life."

"Why should I blame you? A man of principle living in the present world cannot escape death if he refuses to play sycophant to his superior, refrains from intimidating his sovereign for self-interest, fails to enhance his power by murdering others, or hesitates to sell his friends down the river without batting an eye. I, Hu I-kuang, have every reason to forfeit my life today."

"Your own life may not amount to much to you. But don't forget that you have an old mother, several children, and a few hundred household members who will also suffer death on account of your stubbornness."

"I, Hu I-kuang, won't beg for life by debasing myself. My mother and children wouldn't either!"

"I have respect for your literary talent as well as your

military expertise."

"My talent cannot save the state or pacify the people; my ability in military strategy cannot eradicate the enemy or unify the country. My only option now is to face a brave death and not to become a laughing stock in the eyes of posterity."

"There are only a few left now of the sworn brothers of yesteryear. We are all human beings full of emotions. You and I have been sworn brothers despite our different opinions. I beg you to reconsider my proposal."

"I've considered it thoroughly. Of the sworn brothers who have failed to live a useful life and to die a proper death, I'll not be the first, nor the last!"

"What do you mean?"

"I've failed to put the affairs of the court in order and have not died a glorious death on the battlefield. This is what I meant by not living a useful life and not having a proper death. But I'm afraid that, after my death, someone's head will be hung on the city gate as punishment for being a depraved son of the Heavenly Father and a traitor to the Heavenly Kingdom. His life and death will be worse than mine."

"Are you alluding to me?" Wei roared with obvious anger.

"Who else could it be?" Hu kept his composure.

Wei yelled loudly at the guards on duty at the door. "Bring me that barbarian pistol of mine!"

A guard handed him the pistol he had bought from a foreigner sometime ago.

"I'll send you to Heaven with your body intact in deference to our past relations as one-time sworn brothers." Grinding his teeth, Wei said with apparent pain. "If you are afraid, you my turn your face around."

"Wei Ch'ang-hui," Hu laughed heartily, "wait until you go to the execution ground, you may have to turn *your* head around then."

Three successive shots were heard and the smell of gunpowder filled the study. All three bullets had penetrated

Hu's chest.

Hu's body sat erect in the chair, his eyes wide open, staring at Wei menacingly. Wei felt as if every hair on his body were standing on end. He let out a loud cry and fled the study.

In his moment of tension, Wei failed to notice the tears streaming down the face of the bearer of his pistol.

There could be no excuse for further delay. The Northern King engaged himself in assembling his trusted generals and men throughout the night to prepare an attack on the palace.

The soldiers under Wei's control, aside from those who were on duty guarding the city gates, numbered less than ten thousand. With the Assistant King's troops deployed in the vicinity of the capital, Wei could not withdraw any of the soldiers guarding the city gates. Although the women soldiers and youth vanguards defending the palace were brave and seasoned fighters, many of them fell ill, having exerted themselves day and night. The able bodied now numbered less than eight hundred. Wei decided to follow the strategy used in his attack on the Eastern King's residence—he would capture the enemy's stronghold by surprise.

At the third watch that night, he led a thousand men and marched quietly toward the palace. They approached first the Sun Gate at the rear. When he heard the shouting of women soldiers, he realized that the defenders were prepared. He ordered his soldiers to turn around and head toward the Heavenly Front Gate instead. The gate tower was wrapped in total darkness and silence enveloped the vicinity of the drawbridge over the imperial moat. Wei, brandishing his sword to signal his followers, commanded, "Attack!"

Instantly, a dozen palace lanterns were hoisted onto the city wall. With the sound of drums quickening, women soldiers in full uniform appeared on the tower, their battlecries loud and piercing.

Precisely at this moment, something nobody had ever anticipated happened: Wei's trusted guard who had always carried the barbarian pistol for him fired it point blank at him from the back. The bullet went through his chest.

His pistol carrier fired at him point-blank from the back.

Before he could make a backward glance, Wei fell backwards to the ground. An hour later, his head was severed by his followers and brought to the Dragon Hall. For some inexplicable reason, one of his eyes was shut while the other remained open. The Heavenly King ordered to have the head preserved in a saline solution and delivered to the Assistant King for his examination. Even then Wei's eyes remained the same—one shut and one open.

An imperial edict was then issued to the effect that all the remaining followers of Yang and Wei were to be granted amnesty. Meng Teh-en was dispatched to Ch'in Jih-kang's camp with the job of persuading him to return to the capital to receive punishment.

Ch'in Jih-kang had since fought a few battles with the Ch'ing demons along the Yangtze. When he heard the news that the Northern King had been murdered by his own bodyguard, he was greatly relieved. But at the same time, he was terribly worried about his own future.

Meng Teh-en approached Ch'in Jih-kang with deliberate kindness. He said, "Your Excellency performed a great service in helping eliminate the Yang rebels. But unfortunately you abetted Wei in his wanton massacre. The Heavenly King is granting you a chance to redeem yourself. You are ordered to return to the capital. The Assistant King, being a gentleman of generous nature, will not punish you for past offences. If you refuse to come with me, however, how are you to explain the fact that you are deploying on your own an army in the vicinity of the capital?"

Drenched in cold sweat, Ch'in Jih-kang implored pathetically, "I've been guilty! I swear I won't commit any crime a second time. I wish Your Excellency would beg the Heavenly King and the Assistant King to grant me a chance to prove myself."

Thus the two of them went back to the capital together, with Ch'in's troops following. As soon as they reached the city, Meng ordered the troops to remain in the suburban areas while he accompanied Ch'in to the palace for an audience with the Heavenly King. When they stepped inside the Heavenly Front Gate, Ch'in had a feeling that something was drastically wrong. Suddenly Meng cried out loudly, "Arrest him!" Out of nowhere two dozen imperial guards jumped on Ch'in unceremoniously. Without further ado, they cut off his head.

Soon it was that time of the year again when red leaves fell from the trees and the northern wind began to sweep over the metropolis. On the twenty-second day of the tenth month of the sixth year, *Ping-ch'en* (November 30, 1856), the Assistant King and his troops entered the Heavenly Capital after a long and arduous trip down the Great River.

P rior to his return to the capital, the Assistant King had dispatched a delegation headed by Chang Sui-mou with a memorial to seek an audience with the Heavenly King. In the memorial, Shih requested that grain from the heavenly granary be distributed to famine victims, that the wounded, sick, and destitute be taken care of, and that a proclamation be issued to pacify all. Chang Sui-mou and the other officials visited the various civilian quarters to comfort the residents and to help refugees return home.

As soon as his troops were settled on both banks of the Yangtze River near the capital, Shih entered the devastated city accompanied by only a thousand men and officers, without the customary insignia carriers and musicians heralding his presence. As a gesture of respect for the people, he walked bareheaded in the streets, leading his horse behind him. His soldiers all did the same.

The Heavenly Capital looked like an old man suffering a terminal disease. Although in the city proper the blood stains on the walls had been washed away and the stench of decomposed corpses had vanished, in suburban areas, human bones were scattered everywhere and nearby villages remained silent without even a barking dog or a crowing cock. Tall weeds grew in the fields. It was a pathetic sight.

On the streets, the residents again followed the custom of putting up red scrolls on their doors. In front of each door stood a table covered with a red cloth, with an incense burner and bowls of rice and tea on it. Old men and young girls, pale, emaciated survivors of the holocaust, stood behind the tables to welcome the return of the Assistant King.

It was an impressive scene as the Assistant King walked past the tables, leading his horse as he greeted each and everyone with sincere and kind words:

"Incompetent and unrefined, I'm unworthy of your elaborate and sincere welcome. Now that our government has suffered reversals, administrative policy needs to be changed. I'll do my best to assist our sovereign to achieve a complete reform so as not to disappoint you."

A white-haired man stepped forward and addressed him in a trembling voice:

"Lord of Five Thousand Years, the leaders of the Heavenly Kingdom have slaughtered each other in wanton bloodbaths, while we, the common people, suffer the consequences. Your reputation as an upright and capable leader is known to all. You are the only one we can pin our hope on. We, therefore, sincerely welcome your return and pray you to deliver us from evil."

A pale, slim girl offered a cup of tea to the Assistant King, saying, "The people of the Heavenly Capital have long referred to you as the Virtuous King!"

The Assistant King accepted the cup of tea and drank it in one gulp. "What did I do to deserve such a compliment!" he responded.

Several youths said in chorus, "Indeed, Assistant King, you are the only one who deserves this title."

Tears rolling down his cheeks, Shih was deeply moved by the sincere reception given him by the residents of the capital. He proceeded slowly on foot toward the Heavenly Front Gate amidst the cheers of the people.

The Heavenly King rose from his throne to receive the Assistant King in the Dragon Hall which was packed with military and civilian officials, some of whom were so excited that they could not restrain their tears.

Shih Ta-k'ai hurried forward and fell on his knees, "Second Brother, please pardon me for arriving late!"

In the presence of the assembled officials, the Heavenly King formally invested Shih Ta-k'ai as the Virtuous King and Commander-in-Chief of the Army. A female official brought in a golden seal wrapped in silk and handed it to Shih.

"Second Brother, please hear what I have to say," Shih said gravely, still kneeling. When we gathered at Thistle Mountain and became sworn brothers, our aims were to eradicate the Ch'ing demons, to take their capital, to save the people from their unbearable sufferings, and to restore the heritage of our ancestors. Unfortunately, Yang and Wei, the two archrebels, thirsty for power, have made the Heavenly Kingdom a hell on earth, and caused the people to suffer a worse fate as a consequence." His voice became thick with emotion. After a pause, he continued, "The underlying cause of these upheavals can be traced to Yang and Wei's unbridled ambitions and nothing else. Not satisfied with their lofty titles, they wanted to convert the whole country into their private domains.

Transfixed by Shih's speech, the assembled officials listened attentively with respect and admiration.

Although brought up in the countryside, I studied the classics as well as martial arts. For surging in my breast was warm, ardent blood which I was always ready to spill at the appropriate time and for a worthy cause. At the very beginning of our campaign, Second Brother instilled in me a sense of responsibility to save the people. I've never shirked from that responsibility. In the past six years, I've gone through numerous hardships and dangers in order to achieve that purpose. I've promised myself that when our aims are achieved, I shall retire without a second thought, so that I can be spared of the criticism for holding a sinecure and the shame for outliving my usefulness. As the ancients say, "Bows and arrows are stored away when all the birds are bagged." Furthermore, being a simple person with limited knowledge and inadequate experience, I feel it has always been beyond my capacity to participate in court affairs. What would the people say if I were bestowed with new titles and high honors which I did not properly deserve? I hope Second Brother will understand and accept my sincere plea.

The Heavenly King hesitated for a moment before asking reluctantly, "If Brother Ta doesn't want to accept the title and the seal, how is he going to control his subordinates?"

"I started out as a simple soldier and now I command over a hundred thousand men and have had vast experience on the battlefield. It was my sincerity that enabled me to control my subordinates, not my titles."

Blushing, the Heavenly King stammered, "If so, what would our brethren inside and outside the court think of *me*?"

Shih Ta-k'ai knocked his head on the ground and replied, "Incompetent as I am, I feel lucky to be able to participate in court affairs. In the future when I make suggestions concerning state affairs, I'll be happy if Second Brother would consider some of them and put them into practice. This wish of mine comes from the bottom of my heart. I beg you to grant me this!"

Shih Ta-k'ai had refused the title of power which the Heavenly King chose to bestow on him, because he was aware of the many stories in history which call for "storing away bows and arrows when all the birds are bagged." He also knew well from these legends that "hunting dogs are cooked and eaten when no more rabbits can be found."

TEN

During the months following his return to the capital, the Assistant King occupied himself with state affairs totally, snatching only a few hours' sleep every night. The Heavenly Capital, as well as its suburbs, was in a state of paralysis following the holocaust. Political and military reforms had to be devised and implemented. Realizing that the Heavenly King relied a great deal on him, the Assistant King endeavored his utmost to make relevant plans, request their approvals, and supervise their implementation. The first of his suggestions to the Heavenly King was that the verdict reached concerning the crimes committed by each of the late kings—East, North, and Yen—be publicly announced, so as to uphold the law and dignity of the Heavenly Kingdom. Accordinly, the court declared the following: First, since the Eastern King had rendered meritorious service before his attempted usurpation, his descendants should inherit his title of nobility now that he had returned to Heaven. Next, the Northern King and the King of Yen had massacred many innocent people and attacked the palace with intention to usurp the throne; hence their crimes were unpardonable. Now that they had been executed, their descendants would not be implicated, but their titles of nobility were to be forfeited. Finally, since the King of Yü, Hu I-kuang, had served his sovereign loyally and had died in service, his descendants should be given ample compensation and his son should inherit his title.

The Assistant King had not married again after the tragic deaths of his wife and six consorts, for his mind was preoccupied with the political and military affairs at hand. Each time one of his trusted generals ventured to advise him to remarry, he would dismiss him with some pretext. His generals did not insist, knowing that he always put state affairs before private affairs. For the past several months, the Assistant King had slept alone in his study. The inner quarters were under the supervision of his adopted daughter, Pao-ying. To alleviate the unremitting pace of work that her father had imposed on himself, Pao-ying tried to add a few amenities to his joyless life. She cleaned and adjusted the old guitar that had gathered dust for a long time in his study. She sharpened and polished his bejeweled sword until it shone brightly; she placed on his desk some of his favorite books such as *Tso's Commentaries, Songs of Ch'u,* and *Historical Memoirs.* To enliven the atmosphere in the study, she saw to it that the flower pots on the window sills were changed every so often. Each time he returned after a day's hard work at the court, he would either play a few familiar compositions on the guitar, practice swordplay in the corridor, read several chapters of one of the books, or compose a few poems. But none of the attendants in the residence ever saw a smile on his face. Clearly, the Assistant King kept a busy schedule partly to suppress the excruciating pain in his heart.

As the news of the fratricide among the leaders reached Peking, the Emperor Hsien-feng was exhilarated beyond description. One imperial edict after another was dispatched to the Ch'ing camps in the field, ordering the generals to accelerate their attacks on the T'ai-p'ings. Several satellite cities surrounding the Heavenly Capital, such as Ning-kuo and Jui-chou were under constant attack. The T'ai-p'ing commander of Yüan-chou opened the city gate and surrendered unconditionally to the enemy. The military situation became more critical each day.

What shocked the T'ai-p'ing court most was the fall of Wuchang on the thirteenth day of the eleventh month (December 20, 1856). The T'ai-p'ing naval forces in the upper reaches of the Yangtze had been completely routed. The two generals assigned to guard Wuchang, one a brother of the Northern King and the other a cousin of the Heavenly King, fled before the attackers reached the city. Having retaken one city after another in Hupeh, the Ch'ing commanders readied themselves for an assault on the capital itself.

The Assistant King appeared one day before the Heavenly King in the Dragon Hall and offered his services in leading his troops to recapture Wuchang.

"Occupying this strategic position in the central plain is of the utmost importance," declared the Assistant King. "Wuchang is a focal point of contention between the Ch'ing demons and us. With it in his grasp, our enemy would have control over the approaches to the Heavenly Capital and Hunan and Hupeh provinces. Furthermore, Wuchang is also the gateway to Szechwan and Kwangtung. Its loss, therefore, threatens the continued existence of the Heavenly Kingdom. If the occupation of many of our cities in Kiangsi and Anhwei by the Ch'ing demons could be compared to the binding of our hands and feet, the loss of Wuchang would be equivalent to placing a noose around our necks. I suggest that we first recover Wuchang and restore lines of communication in the upper reaches of the Yangtze. Then I'll coordinate with our generals in the field to attack the Ch'ing demons in Kiangsi, Hupeh, and Anhwei. After these steps are taken, we may attack Kiangsu and Chekiang in the south and send troops to the north. Second Brother, please consider my proposal and come to a decision!"

The Heavenly King, however, was hesitant and would not give a definite answer to Shih's suggestions. After repeated prodding from the Assistant King, he revealed that he needed him, the Assistant King, and his one hundred thousand men to defend the Heavenly Capital. The Assistant King was to remain in the capital and assist in court affairs, as well as direct the defense of the city. The military situations at Wuchang and on other fronts would be handled by the generals already in the field.

The Assistant King could tell that the Heavenly King did not reveal all that was on his mind. He was familiar with the Heavenly King's character: once his mind was made up, nothing in the world could change it. Under these circumstances, Shih was obliged to revise his plan. He suggested instead a "combined defensive and offensive strategy": In areas where the Ch'ing demons were strong, such as Chü-yung, Li-shui, and points below Chinkiang, the T'ai-p'ing generals would be ordered to take a defensive stance; in areas where the T'ai-p'ings were stronger than the Ch'ing demons, such as in the border areas of Anhwei and Hupeh, the T'ai-p'ing generals would be ordered to take offensive action.

After his "combined defensive and offensive strategy" had been accepted by the Heavenly King, Shih appointed Ch'en Yü-ch'eng, a young and valiant general, and Li Hsiu-ch'eng, a more mature and experienced commander, to attack the Ch'ing strongholds in Anhwei and Hupeh provinces early in the seventh year, *Ting-ssu.* Their forces reached the vicinity of Wuchang and were poised for a final assault.

That spring, there was a revival in T'ai-p'ing morale. On the outskirts of the capital, new growth on the willows and fresh blossoms on the peach trees made the countryside as pretty as a colorful picture. The rumbling of the river sounded more like people carrying on an animated conversation than someone registering complaints. Newly planted rice sprouts stood proudly in green paddies that stretched as far as one's eyes could see. The bones of the dead had long since been buried, and bloodstains had been washed away. There were even smiles on the faces of children and teenagers.

But the aftermath of the slaughter remained in the hearts of the people like marks chiseled on an old tree. The buoyancy which characterized the kingdom's early years had disappeared, as had the brotherly love among comrades. When the officials conducted religious ceremonies in the capital, few people bothered to attend. People reacted to the teaching that "within the four seas all men are brothers" with cynical suspicion and outright ridicule. When old and new brothers met on the streets, they still dismounted with the usual salutations, but these rituals were devoid of the enthusiasm and sincerity of old times. The Heavenly King resumed his old habit of abstention from court meetings except in emergencies. A new silk poster was hung on the Heavenly Front Gate with the imperial injunction, "Officials high and low! Proceed no further. . . ." Again, it was inscribed in the sovereign's cursive-style handwriting.

Never before had the Assistant King felt so depressed and lonely. The pressure of work and mourning for his family members had taken their toll. But what he felt most acutely was the loss of his warm relationship with the Heavenly King and other leaders of the Kingdom. Being a sensitive person, the Assistant King realized that he had been ordered to remain in the capital not merely for the purpose of defending it, but because of the fact that for him to have a large army in the field may not have been in the best interests of the Heavenly King.

The attitude of indifference and suspicion was clearly manifested in the Heavenly King's posture of silence.

Thus the Assistant King was obliged to remain in the capital to carry out the defense plan. In civilian matters, his first concern was the problem of procuring food and medicine for the surviving residents of the city. He sent many officials to Anhwei and Kiangsi to buy large quantities of grain to be transported immediately to the capital. However, even in this simple and humanitarian endeavor, he was confronted with numerous obstacles.

A part of his troops had been ordered to return to the Kiangsi fronts, but the main portion of his soldiers was assigned defense duties at city gates and in the outlying areas of the capital. After the massacre, death, pestilence, and a wholesale exodus had reduced the productive capacity of the people by half. Aside from the large amount of food needed for the hungry civilian population, military rations also depended largely on the purchased grain from outlying territories. But control over the supply and transportation of grain in the Heavenly Capital was now in the hands of the Heavenly King's two elder brothers who were making a sizable profit in the process. All officials dispatched from the capital for food acquisition were required to obtain passes from their offices. All violators were punished as smugglers. In a few months, the two brothers of the Heavenly King became the biggest hoarders of grain as well as of gold and silver in the capital. Even the commissary officials of the Assistant King were subject to the regulations issued by the pair. Both civilian and soldiers began to voice their complaints as food supply dwindled and the situation became desperate.

The Assistant King was very much incensed by what he heard. Several times he went to the palace to seek an audience with the Heavenly King. But the Heavenly Front Gate remained closed to him, because the yellow silk poster prohibited entrance into the palace without permission. Thus discouraged, he found solace in reading old books, such as *Tso's Commentaries* and *Historical Memoirs.* In the past, he could not appreciate fully the thinking of the ancient writers—their patriotism and their helplessness seemed to him somehow exaggerated, but now their words touched a sympathetic chord in his heart.

One evening, Chang Sui-mou came to Shih's study and related to him some unconfirmed rumors which were supposed to have originated from the palace. This made his unsettled mind even more uneasy.

Since the internal struggle started, the Heavenly King spent his days in anguish and trepidation. Among the eight kings, himself included, who had started the rebellion, the Southern and Western kings had died early in action; the Eastern and Northern kings and the King of Yen had been killed as a result of their plots to overthrow him; the King of Yü had died heroically as a martyr. Of the eight, only the Assistant King and himself remained.

The Heavenly King was fully aware that at the beginning of the rebellion, relationships between the leaders were harmonious and congenial. But after the establishment of the Heavenly Capital, things had turned sour. With the exception of those who had died early, almost every one of the kings had coveted his throne. Within half-a-year, three ambitious leaders had died one after another in internecine struggles. The young and proud Assistant King who had come to the capital to render assistance was warmly received by the officials and common people even before he took over the reins of the government. When he attended court, his words seemed to carry an overtone of arrogance and contempt. What did he mean when he said he was "unwilling to accept a sinecure position" and that "bows and arrows are stored away when all the birds are bagged"? When he was about to be invested the "Virtuous King," he had resolutely refused to accept the title. When his request to fight in the front was rejected, he expressed disappointment. What was the real purpose behind his plan to leave the capital with his huge army?

After the massacre and the attempted entry by force into the palace, the Heavenly King had slept in the study and had seldom gone to the inner palace. Hung Hsüan-chiao had since withdrawn her women soldiers from the palace, and visited her brother and sister-in-law only once a month. The Heavenly King spent most of his time in the company of his two brothers and with Meng Teh-en and Lai Han-ying, his brother-in-law.

One evening, while discussing court affairs, brother Hung Jen-fa said:

In the final analysis, nobody outside the Hung clan can be trusted. All the leaders who had followed you in the rebellion had slept on straw mats with you in the camps and shared bowls of congee with you when hungry. They fought for you to gain control of the kingdom, but all of them had entertained selfish motives. So far as this one nicknamed "Dare-to-Resist Stone" is concerned, I wonder why he had dillydallied when he was ordered to return. Now that he has returned, he wants to leave the capital with his troops again. When you wanted to bestow on him the title of "Virtuous King," he resolutely declined the offer. Yet when he was hailed as "Virtuous King" by the common people, he accepted it readily with great joy. My younger brother, can't you see what kind of a person he really is? If you don't plan ahead, you'll suffer the consequences. You are a straightforward man, while he is a scheming crook. Take the matter of famine relief as an example. It was clearly an opportunity for him to use the silver of the sacred treasury to buy the good will of the people for himself. When the people are convinced that he is a benevolent administrator, then you yourself will have to invite him to sit on the throne. By then, he will not have to use force like the other two did. Where shall we, the members of the Hung clan, go then? With his one hundred thousand men stationed in the vicinity of the capital, we won't even have a burial place when we die. In my opinion, it would be better for us to surrender to the Ch'ing demons. Maybe we'll be awarded official titles, and, if not red hat buttons, perhaps peacock feathers to decorate our headgears. Anyway, it would be better than dying at the hands of our own comrades!

The Heavenly King was thoroughly disturbed by his elder brother's words. He shouted at him for everyone to hear:

"What are you talking about? I didn't ask you for advice. I've issued an edict a long time ago that no relatives of leaders without official title be allowed to participate in political discussions. Do you think that since you are my brother, I won't put you to death if you violate this rule? The next time you come here, you're only allowed to talk about family business. If you still keep on meddling in state affairs, I'll have you thrown out!"

"So long as you know that what I've said is for your own good," Hung Jen-ta replied with a sneer, "I'm satisfied. Don't forget that blood is thicker than water and that no arm ever bends outward." Having finished speaking, he stomped out, very much chagrined.

A few days later, the Heavenly King summoned Meng Teh-en to his study. He had maintained a close relationship with Meng who had served as his bodyguard. Having no compunction to bare his heart to his friend, the Heavenly King related to him what his brother had said and asked for his opinion.

"Your Majesty and the several kings are all loving sons of the Heavenly Father," Meng said, after having performed the usual kowtow ceremony. "You are sworn brothers and even though there are times when differences of opinion may occur, there is no room for outsiders to intervene. One of the demons' heretic books has said, 'Brothers may fight among themselves at home, but they will unite to repel intruders from outside.' The Assistant King has come to the capital to help quench the rebellion, and his merit cannot be slighted. Being young and impatient, he may have said something improper. But Your Majesty is magnanimous and should overlook his occasional transgressions as an elder brother would treat his younger brother."

The Heavenly King kept his silence for a long time. Meng sensed that something was amiss, and quickly changed his tone.

"However, what Your Majesty's brother said was based on well-calculated and seasoned reasoning which should be taken seriously."

The Heavenly King kept his silence, indicating neither approval nor disapproval. Feeling caught in an awkward situation, Meng added:

"Your Majesty is noble and wise and well-versed in military and civilian affairs. Your decisions on all matters have always been proven correct and appropriate. Yet you still maintain a modest attitude and seek advice from your servants. This proves that your magnanimity excels that of the Emperors T'ai-tsung of T'ang and T'ai-tsu of Sung. What your servant has just said consisted of nothing but worthless remarks!"

Greatly nonplussed by the lack of response from his listener, Meng felt himself sweating all over. He kowtowed several times before retreating from the imperial study.

With a heavy heart, the Heavenly King strode toward the inner palace and entered Consort Fang's apartment. She was playing chess with Consort Hsieh. At the sight of their master, both kneeled down to receive him. He waved his hand and ordered them to stand up. Looking at the unfinished game, the Heavenly King sighed lightly.

"This game portrays the contest between Ch'u and Han, two states which were locked in endless struggle. If I had known what would have happened, I would not have started the rebellion in the first place!"

Consort Hsieh stood silently. Consort Fang, being more daring and articulate, spoke up with a smile.

"If Your Majesty had not started the righteous rebellion, would he be able to sit on the throne of the Heavenly Kingdom today?"

"I would rather be an unsuccessful candidate for the *hsiu-ts'ai* degree and a school teacher in Kuan-lu-pu for the rest of my life!" the Heavenly King said with a rueful smile.

"Lord of Ten Thousand Years," Consort Hsieh intervened with obvious concern, "You are overburdened by state affairs. You have lost weight!"

"Exactly," the Heavenly King replied. "If there is a truly worthy person, I'll be glad to give him my throne without hesitation. I myself would emulate Hsü Yu in leading a hermit's life from now on."

"Lord of Ten Thousand Years," said Consort Fang, her tone turning serious. "Although it is said that brothers are like one's limbs and wives are like one's clothes, we, being your consorts, will do anything within our power to help you solve your problems."

"I've been bothered by these sworn brothers of mine," the Heavenly King confessed. "We worked together harmoniously in the early days of the rebellion. But as soon as we reached the Heavenly Capital, each one began to nurture his private designs and degenerated into a murderer. Now we are confronted with the Ch'ing demons outside and dangerous plotters within. I'm caught in the middle."

Consort Hsieh ventured innocently. "Now that rebels Yang and Wei have been executed and that the Assistant King has come back to take charge of state affairs, what else does my lord worry about?"

"I'm scared of my sworn brothers," said the Heavenly King. "Do you know the story of the first emperor of Sung at Ch'en Bridge? When his subordinates enrobed him in yellow and proclaimed him emperor, he accepted it as the Mandate of Heaven. Who would refuse when such opportunity presents itself?"

"There are plenty of examples of fratricides in history," Consort Hsieh insisted on displaying her pedantic knowledge. "Instances of usurpation happen mostly either among blood relations or imperial relatives . . ."

She stopped abruptly when she noticed a meaningful side glance from Consort Fang. The Heavenly King walked impatiently back and forth. He began to recite a poem of the first emperor of Han in a low voice:

A great wind rises and clouds scatter.
My authority extends from sea to sea.
Now that I am going home,
Oh, where can I find gallant men to guard the four
    frontiers?

Silence prevailed for a long while until Consort Fang broke it with these astonishing words:

> The first emperor of Han started out as a lowly station master, but he succeeded in assembling many capable men around him and united the country under extremely trying circumstances. He was a true leader of great capability and wide experience. But after he had firmly established himself on the throne, he ruthlessly killed many generals who had helped him in his bid for power. Hence the historians referred to his actions with such metaphors as "bows and arrows are stored away when all the birds are bagged" and "the hunting dogs are cooked and eaten when no more rabbits are around." His tactics caused tremendous unrest among his followers. It was quite fitting that he should be criticized for his excesses.

When he heard the metaphor about the birds and rabbits, the Heavenly King instantly became angry, recalling that this was exactly what the Assistant King had alluded to in the court meeting the other day. However, his anger subsided after a second thought and he admitted to himself that there was a certain amount of truth to the remarks.

Having heard different opinions advanced by his brother, a trusted minister, and two favorite consorts, the Heavenly King still vacillated about which path he should take. At first what his elder brother had said sounded repulsive to him, yet he found it harder and harder to dispute its plausibility.

"Oh, Heavenly Father," the Heavenly King prayed earnestly. "Please tell your bewildered son what to do!"

Every time Hung Jen-ta visited his brother the Heavenly King, he always went through the side door of the imperial garden. Being a peasant most of his adult life, he felt uncomfortable in following court etiquette. There were less restrictions when he went through the side door which was guarded by an old acquaintance, Chung "the Fourth." Since both had come from the same village, they always found something to talk about: When his advice was rejected by the Heavenly King, Hung felt rather chagrined, and bared his heart to Chung without reservation.

Having heard what Hung had to say, Chung responded jokingly, "Why should Your Excellency be bothered by such things? So long as the imperial kitchen will provide you with all the delicacies you can eat, you have nothing to worry about in this world."

But privately Chung was worried. He had once served under the Assistant King and still worshipped him as a hero. Out of respect for his erstwhile commander, he passed the information on to a close associate of the general, Chang Sui-mou.

A special court meeting was convened by command of the Heavenly King one day in the fourth month of the year *Ting-ssu* (May 1857). During the brief gathering, the Heavenly King did not say a single word. A female official read aloud an imperial edict proclaiming that Hung Jen-fa, one of the two brothers of the Heavenly King, was to be invested King of An and that the other, Hung Jen-ta, was to be named King of Fu. They would both participate in the management of political and military affairs. The pair were also to be responsible for defense preparations inside and outside the capital. Meng Teh-en was assigned to take care of court affairs. All officials were required to report to these three officials on all matters and they would, in turn, report to the Heavenly King.

When the female official finished reading the edict, the Heavenly King announced that the meeting was over. The Assistant King noticed the icy expression on the Heavenly King's face which contrasted so sharply with the warm welcome he was accorded when he had returned several months prior. He realized that during the six years following the establishment of the Heavenly Capital, his relationship with the Heavenly King had gradually changed from one of brotherly comradeship to one of rigid formalities between a sovereign and his minister.

This too obvious situation offended the sensibilities of the Assistant King. He began to feel that only three options were open for him. He could choose to placate the Heavenly King's brothers so as to satisfy their vanity, and bide his time until state affairs got so messed up that the very existence of the kingdom was threatened. By then he would be needed again to save the situation. But he realized that, not being an astute leader, the Heavenly King could never perceive danger until the last minute; nor could he make quick decisions. If he chose this option, he might unwittingly reenact the Yang and Wei crises and thus further weaken the foundation of the Heavenly Kingdom. The second option would be to sacrifice his own future by remaining in the capital and trying to accomplish the impossible. But again he knew that the Heavenly King was suspicious of him and would not entrust him with any real responsibility. Under the covert attack of his enemies, he might one day lose his life. His death would not amount to much, but it would not help the Kingdom. Therefore, both options were unsatisfactory and not in conformity with his cherished principles.

The only choice left to him was retirement from active service which was his long cherished desire. An ancient maxim, "Retire as soon as your job is done," seemed to be relevant in his present case. Success or failure, he reckoned, depended partly on human effort and partly on fortune. But only a wise person knew when to retire before he was forced to do so. However, at the present juncture, he further reasoned, the Ch'ing demons were active and fighting was intense. If he left without an army, he would not be able to protect himself. Besides, where could he find a safe place to retire to?

Would a general commanding a hundred thousand men

who had seen hundreds of battles, a man well-versed in history and classics and capable of devising military strategies, shed tears upon reaching the end of his road?

The Assistant King found himself in a dilemna. Reading a few poems from the Sung edition of the *Book of Songs* at random, he was moved to tears. He threw down the book and played on the ancient guitar. As luck would have it, two strings snapped, one after the other. Heaving a deep sigh, he sank into a depression.

A gentle breeze lifted the curtain. The door of the study had been left ajar. The flickering candlelight made the atmosphere all the more desolate. As he was about to walk to the garden for some exercise with his sword, he saw a young scholar walk univited into the study.

The Assistant King was surprised at the intruder. Before he could make inquiries, the scholar stepped forward and, with a smile, saluted him politely. The Assistant King found the intruder's face familiar, but could not recall where they had met. While he hesitated, the intruder spoke smilingly.

"Lord of Five Thousand Years! More than a year has elapsed since we met at Rarity Depository Tower. This younger sister of yours had failed to communicate with you since."

The strange address reminded the Assistant King that the intruder was none other than the female *chuang-yüan*, Fu Shan-hsiang. He had sent people to search for her in the previous winter, but was told that she had disappeared before the Eastern King carried out his usurpation plot and that she was nowhere to be found.

"Why, the honorable *chuang-yüan*, how have you been?" The Assistant King saluted her and ordered tea. "You must have learned of the internecine disasters that have plagued our court. It proved that you had the foresight to leave the locus of trouble. How wise you were to do so! I have been the commander of an army, but I had no inkling of what was to happen. I was stupid indeed!"

"I am an insignificant person who has a little knowledge of history and classics. Living in these troubled times, I was fortunate enough to have served in the Heavenly court. Even though I have deserted my post, I am still a citizen of the Heavenly Kingdom. I only regret that I have not been able to complete the job to which I was assigned and thus have become a laughing stock to my peers. Since Your Excellency's return to the capital, the people's confidence in the government has greatly increased. But I am afraid that Your Excellency's grand design has not been entirely free from obstruction."

"You are entirely correct!" the Assistant King could not suppress his amazement.

"If so, what does Your Excellency intend to do?" Fu asked in a friendly way.

"I have no viable plan so far," the Assistant King answered apologetically, forcing a smile.

"A noble person living in a troubled world is obliged to make difficult decisions. If he is lucky enough to have a brilliant and enlightened man as his sovereign, he would be able to assist him in planning state policies and engaging in life-and-death struggles. Even if he has to sacrifice his own life or suffer undue hardship as a result, it would be worthwhile for him to do so. On the other hand, if no enlightened sovereign is there for him to serve, then he should assume the responsibility of putting the affairs of state in order himself. With a large army at his command, he should be able to unify the country and assume the role of empire builder, and at the appropriate time, he should proclaim himself the founder of a new dynasty. A wise man would not confine himself in a besieged city and hesitate to make stupendous decisions when every card has been laid out on the table."

The Assistant King's face took on a solemn look. He declared: "When the Heavenly King and several of us sworn brothers started the rebellion, we vowed that we would treat each other as blood brothers in life as well as in death. Yang and Wei broke that vow and murdered each other. They have already suffered Heavenly punishments. Among the eight sworn brothers, only the Heavenly King and I now remain alive. Although the Heavenly King is weak and unable to differentiate good from evil, I, Shih Ta-k'ai, will not desert him or take his place, despite my present difficulties. Such action would earn me a bad reputation for posterity!"

"When I first became an official in the Heavenly court," Fu explained, "I read over and over again the 'Proclamation on Attacking the Barbarians in Conformity with the Will of Heaven' with great enthusiasm. The Eastern King told me that it had been drafted by Your Excellency."

"Indeed," replied the Assistant King. "I wrote it when I was young and inexperienced."

"I still remember a few lines that I can recite right now:

> The evil spirit of the barbarian demons fills the atmosphere we live in and pollutes the very air we breathe. Their atrocities surpass those of all other barbarians in history. . . . Following the will of Heaven, the Han nation will rejuvenate itself. Everyone hopes that freedom will be restored to all the people. . . . There are obvious reasons why the demise of the barbarian demons is imminent. . . . It is our intention to restore our lost territory and to strengthen the rule of the Lord on High!

From this proclamation, it is clear that Your Excellency was aiming at the restoration of the Han nation and the salvation of the oppressed people. That you are confined in the capital without a definite plan for the future does not seem to be compatible with your original ideals. What you should do now is regroup your troops, replenish your military equipment, and leave the city immediately to pursue other viable plans!"

"If I abandon the undertaking before its completion," said the Assistant King, "it would be an act not in conformity with the principles of loyalty, humanity, and righteousness. I cannot and shall not take such a step!"

"It is quite obvious that the Heavenly King is incapable

of completing this undertaking by himself. Among all the officials of the Heavenly Kingdom, only Your Excellency is able to discharge this responsibility. If Your Excellency is restrained by such minor considerations and lets this crucial opportunity slip away, he is practicing the loyalty of a moron, the humanity of a woman, and the righteousness of a provincial man."

"I shouldn't repeat the mistakes made by Yang and Wei," the Assistant King said lamely.

"The fact that Yang and Wei tried to take the throne from the Heavenly King shows that they were lacking in loyalty and righteousness. Your Excellency is pursuing other plans and endeavors to take territory from the Ch'ing demons. It has nothing to do with loyalty or righteousness."

"But I'm only fit to be a minister, not a sovereign!"

"I'm afraid that before long Your Excellency will not have a chance to be a minister, not to mention a sovereign."

"Wouldn't you say I should retire now in order to save my life?"

"Where do you think you might go?"

"I would like to have your opinion on this subject."

"It has occurred to me that Your Excellency might lead his army away and march to Szechwan, following the footsteps of Liu Pei of Shu Han."

"I should think that an excellent idea," the Assistant King nodded in agreement. "You see, by occupying Szechwan not only would the territory of the Heavenly Kingdom be vastly expanded, but the forces of the Ch'ing demons would be diverted as well. If I succeed in this, I'll be one of the three powers in the realm. If I should fail, I can at least preserve my strength there in that far-off corner."

"But an army penetrating deep into the enemy's territory without support is entering upon a dangerous undertaking. Don't forget the example set by the commanders of the Northern Expedition Forces."

"I believe I am more resourceful than those two generals. Szechwan is a rich country with abundant human and material resources, enough to support me for a lifetime."

Fu stood up and spoke in a grave voice: "I hope Your Excellency will consider the interests of the nation and people as his first priority. So long as Your Excellency is aiming at the restoration of the Han nation from the control of the barbarians and the salvation of our people from the suppression of foreigners, success or failure should not be the primary consideration. Your Excellency will have lived a useful life in this world and have earned the respect of coming generations. I wish to bid Your Excellency farewell now."

Having finished her speech, the female *chuang-yüan* left as quietly as she had come.

Pacing his study, the Assistant King pondered the questions Fu had put to him. She had forced him to reveal his secrets. He had great respect for Fu's analysis of the situation. In just a few words, she had pointed out the untenable position he was facing and the future options he had to consider. He was surprised that he had been indifferent to her presence in the past. The Eastern King, in employing her as a secretary to handle documents, had apparently abused her talents. Of all people, she had been the only one to have a premonition of the Eastern King's impending downfall as a result of his ambitions, and had escaped to avoid implication. This was proof of her wisdom and foresight. If he could have her as an advisor, she could contribute much to his future work.

The Assistant King rushed from his study, hoping to persuade her to stay. But she had disappeared without a trace. Upon inquiry, the gatekeeper reported that the visitor had professed to be a messenger from the palace bearing an important message and that he hadn't dared ask for details.

The Assistant King was disappointed at not being able to obtain Fu's services. He had missed her by a hair's breadth. He went back to his study, feeling all the more out of sorts. Although Fu's words had helped him arrive at his final decision, he was still undecided as to when he should leave the city.

It was during the first watch when a retainer came to the study to report that the consort of the Western King had come to pay him a visit.

This gave the Assistant King a jolt. Although he and Hung Hsüan-chiao had been close in the early days, training recruits in Thistle Mountain together, there had never been a close friendship between the two. After the establishment of the Heavenly Capital, he had little contact with her. This lady commander was known to him as a person of unusual honesty and bravery who was always straightforward in dealing with her colleagues. Her visit at this late hour signified business of compelling importance. He quickly adjusted his clothes to receive his nocturnal visitor.

Hung Hsüan-chiao was in full military uniform. With a piece of red silk she tied her hair in a bun, instead of wearing the customary gauze hat. A short sword hung from her waist and she wore a pair of red felt shoes on her feet. She was followed by two female attendants.

"Lord of Five Thousand Years. Do you know why I am paying you this visit?" The female commander spoke with unusual directness.

"A visit by the Consort of the Western King portends very urgent military or state business at hand."

"And is also related to the safety of Your Excellency."

The Assistant King thanked her profusely. "The Consort of the Western King needs not speak further. I understand what it's all about. You've taken a great risk to come here in the middle of the night. Permit me to express my gratitude for your selfless action on my behalf."

"The Lord of Five Thousand Years and I worked together at Thistle Mountain. The friendship that developed between us, I believe, is not of the ordinary kind. I would be remiss in my duties if I failed to inform you when I know that you are in trouble." Hung Hsüan-chiao continued, her voice trembling. "I've never been afraid of the consequences resulting from my own actions. If I become the target of a fratricidal plot, I would not submit to my fate meekly without a fight. Lord of Five Thousand Years! I don't know whether you are aware of the fact that you have become the target of some schemers. I suggest that you leave the city immediately. It will be in your best interests."

"I am aware of the fact that some people cannot tolerate my presence. But I cannot bear to leave the state and the institutions that I've helped build. Hence my hesitation and delay."

"I think you'd better go. In less than ten years, since the establishment of the Heavenly Kingdom, several incidents of fratricide have taken place. I don't wish to witness another such incident happen to the gratification of the Ch'ing demons. If Feng Yün-shan and my husband, Hsiao Ch'ao-kuei, were still alive, they would never have allowed the affairs of the Heavenly Kingdom to sink to such a low level." Hung Hsüan-chiao spoke with intense emotion, her eyes brimming with tears.

The Assistant King was moved by these remarks. They expressed exactly what he wanted to say but had suppressed for obvious reasons. He kept silent momentarily.

"Lord of Five Thousand Years! You should make a quick decision now. Even if my brother can't fulfill our mission, we must let the Ch'ing demons know that there are still capable men in the Heavenly Kingdom who can carry on the struggle. You must leave the capital within three to five days, or else it will be too late," Hung said sincerely.

Gratitude, surprise, exhilaration, and mortification were the mixed feelings that simultaneously assaulted the mind of the Assistant King. Without further reservation, he declared frankly to his visitor:

"I'll accept your sincere advice. But I want to assure you that even if I leave the capital, I'll not establish a kingdom of my own and will remain a part of the Heavenly Kingdom. In the event the Heavenly King should order his forces to attack me, I would avoid confrontation with the expeditionary army. If I should make any headway in my endeavors, it will only add to the glory of the Heavenly Kingdom. If I should suffer defeat, I will not drag down the good name of our brethren!"

Hung Hsüan-chiao and the Assistant King bid farewell

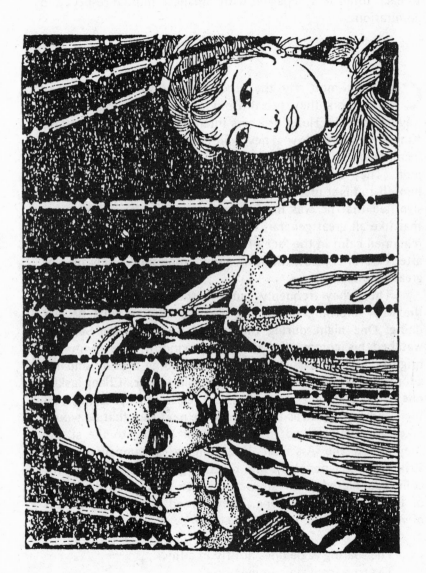

The Consort of the Western King persuades him to leave.

to each other and departed with enhanced mutual respect and admiration.

Chang Sui-mou and the other generals were disturbed by the rumors they heard from their friends and old colleagues that the Hung brothers intended to deal the Assistant King a merciless blow. They believed that the Assistant King, being sensitive and observant, would certainly be aware of the plot. They noticed that the Assistant King had confined himself to his study, reading and playing with his sword, which signified that he was making an important plan. They knew that like all great generals in history, their commander always remained calm in the face of grave crisis. They felt certain that after careful consideration, he would announce a new plan of great significance.

Thus, they frequenly came to the door of his study in the early morning or late at night to observe what he was doing. One night during the second watch, Chang Sui-mou watched his commander through a window. The room was brightly lit. The Assistant King was reading a book and his adopted daughter was tuning the old guitar. Chang asked one of his colleagues to join him in requesting a meeting with their commander so as to ascertain the next step that he would take. As they walked in the corridor leading to the study, they heard the Assistant King singing, accompanied by a strikingly melancholy tune on the guitar. Chang and his colleague halted their steps to try to make out the lyrics of their commander's song. They turned out to be excerpts of verses from Ch'ü Yüan's *Song of Ch'u:*

> The soaring eagle does not fly in a flock;
> T'is true from time immemorial.
> You can't fit a square into a circle,
> Neither can travellers of different destinations
> follow the same path!

I can suppress my ambition, humble my heart,
    suffer abuse, and accept humiliation,
But I'll hold fast to the path of righteousness till
    my death, to meet the expectations of ancient
    sages.
I'll ride in a phoenix carriage harnessed to jade
    steeds;
Travelling with the wind to an unknown destina-
    tion.
I'll set free the wheels at dawn and reach there by
    evening.
The road is long and the journey tedious;
I'll search for the path that controls my destiny.
I water my steeds in a celestial pool, and rest my
    mounts in the distant land.
I pluck a mulberry branch to shade my eyes from
    the sun, and roam about with a free mind!

Chang Sui-mou looked askance at his colleague. The latter, understanding his implication, nodded in agreement. The song told them clearly that their commander had finally decided to leave the capital.

Early next morning the Assistant King led his officers and generals in an exodus from the Heavenly Capital. He ordered his troops in the south of the Yangtze to move toward the Wuhu camp where they would regroup and prepare to embark on a westward expedition.

The Assistant King waited until most of his troops had crossed the river before he and his close associates boarded a boat. It was early summer, and the fields on both shores of the river were carpeted with a sheet of deep green. Junifers and dwarf pines covered undulating hills from where the call of the cuckoo underscored the agony of the departing travellers.

Watching the ever-disappearing waves and listening to the incessant call of the cuckoo, the Assistant King no longer made any attempt to hide the tears that rolled down his cheeks.

Soon a curtain of night mist fell on the river, rendering the sky and water indistinguishable. Waves rhythmically hit the sides of the boat and then vanished silently without a trace. The vicissitudes of his life during the past several years—the ups and downs, the twists and turns—flashed through his mind's eye. Who would have foreseen that he had to conclude this stage of his career with a planned abandonment?

He knew that he was heading for an unknown destination. The future could not be more precarious, and the long road was full of hidden dangers. But he had passed the point of no return and his die had been cast.

Six months earlier, after he had returned to the capital, he had ridden with his adopted daughter on an inspection tour of the city walls and other scenic spots. While enjoying the beautiful scenery under the slanting sun and recalling the history of the rise and fall of ancient dynasties, he had composed a poem on horseback. Pao-ying had recorded it in writing upon their return home.

"Pao-ying," the Assistant King suddenly broke the silence. "Do you still remember the poem I wrote with the title 'Comments on Scenes of the Heavenly Capital'?"

"Sure, I remember it in it's entirety," replied Pao-ying. Then she recited:

Sounds of drums and bugles cast a sombre mood;
The center of contention still lies in the land of Ch'u and Wu.
While swords and spears gleam under the shining sun,
Human suffering and meaningless destruction will not conclude.
Waiting for delivery are the mountains and rivers of the realm.
Alone in a tower I solemnly made my vow.
If the rise and fall of a kingdom could be a single man's responsibility,

Embarking on an arduous and uncertain journey.

How dare I throw away this opportunity of
destiny's rendezvous?

The Assistant King remembered that he had meant to
compose another peom then, but the pressure of state affairs
had been so great that he never found time to do so. Now,
listening to the splashing waves and watching the vast span of
water, he composed another poem to express his current
sentiments:

Like the short sword dangling from my side, words
from my pen also brought me fame.
"Chasing deer in the central plain" to me is a proud
and serious game.
The bright moon guides the lone fisherman lake
bent,
While the long sword—the black Phoenix—awaits
action in my tent.
All heroes in history true to their friends remained;
A real man never cares what's lost and what's
gained.
Homeward bound, I shall with the wind sail.
Only the Great Dipper in the sky follows my trail.

The sky was studded with bright stars. The boat raced
against the swift current. In no time he could hear the sounds
of horses neighing from the riverbank. The generals under his
command had been eagerly awaiting their chief's arrival on
the shore for quite a while.

— end —